It was as it had be... well. Maria was naked in the water, Alex stood on the shore. But this time there was no amusement in his smoke-clouded eyes. Only desire, raw and haunted—like the expression she glimpsed sometimes in her own lonely mirror.

She realized now what had compelled her to turn. She had felt him there. She had sensed the sheer power of his gaze on her naked flesh, the feverish longing that reached out to touch and inflame her own. She must have made a sound, a cry of joy or welcome, or perhaps she took a step forward, for he was in the water suddenly, his clothes drenched, plastered against his body, and he was taking her in his arms.

There was no conscious thought. There was only instinct, all the pent-up emotions they had fought so long. He was kissing her, burying his face in her hair, murmuring things she could not understand, as he lifted her onto the bank and gently set her down. She eagerly reached for him, and together they plunged into a sea of passion that claimed them both. . . .

Dawn Shadows

ANNOUNCING THE

TOPAZ FREQUENT READERS CLUB
COMMEMORATING TOPAZ'S
1 YEAR ANNIVERSARY!

THE MORE YOU BUY, THE MORE YOU GET

Redeem coupons found here and in the back of all new Topaz titles for FREE Topaz gifts:

Send in:

◆ 2 coupons for a free TOPAZ novel (choose from the list below);

☐ **THE KISSING BANDIT,** Margaret Brownley

☐ **BY LOVE UNVEILED,** Deborah Martin

☐ **TOUCH THE DAWN,** Chelley Kitzmiller

☐ **WILD EMBRACE,** Cassie Edwards

◆ 4 coupons for an "I Love the Topaz Man" on-board sign

◆ 6 coupons for a TOPAZ compact mirror

◆ 8 coupons for a Topaz Man T-shirt

Just fill out this certificate and send with original sales receipts to:

TOPAZ FREQUENT READERS CLUB-1ST ANNIVERSARY
Penguin USA • Mass Market Promotion; Dept. H.U.G.
375 Hudson St., NY, NY 10014

Name_____

Address_____

City_____ State_____ Zip_____

Offer expires 1/31 1995

Dawn Shadows

by

Susannah Leigh

A TOPAZ BOOK

TOPAZ
Published by the Penguin Group
Penguin Books USA Inc., 375 Hudson Street,
New York, New York 10014, U.S.A.
Penguin Books Ltd, 27 Wrights Lane,
London W8 5TZ, England
Penguin Books Australia Ltd, Ringwood,
Victoria, Australia
Penguin Books Canada Ltd, 10 Alcorn Avenue,
Toronto, Ontario, Canada M4V 3B2
Penguin Books (N.Z.) Ltd, 182–190 Wairau Road,
Auckland 10, New Zealand

Penguin Books Ltd, Registered Offices:
Harmondsworth, Middlesex, England

First published by Topaz, an imprint of Dutton Signet,
a division of Penguin Books USA Inc.

First Printing, August, 1994
10 9 8 7 6 5 4 3 2 1

Topaz is a trademark of Dutton Signet,
a division of Penguin Books USA Inc.

Printed in the United States of America

Yesterday in Misty Memory

The mists of memory
Rise out of the darkness,
Swirling,
Softening;
Bringing yesterday
Into the morning.

Chapter 1

Seven years ago now.... No, eight.

Maria stood in the hillside garden of the small stone house that had been her childhood home and tried not to remember. It was just past sunrise. A faint breeze stirred, welcome, for the night had been exceptionally warm. Eight years ... and it still tore her heart apart.

She glanced down the hillside, only half focusing on the silent port beneath. Dawn was just turning from pink to shimmering gold, and the small village of Lahaina was still asleep. Only one man could be seen, a solitary figure shuffling slowly toward the outskirts of town, and judging from the uncertainty in his step as he wavered from one side of the deserted dirt road to the other, he was out late rather than up with the sun.

Earlier in the spring, and again in the fall, ships would be massed in the harbor, as many as three or four hundred whalers, disgorging bawdy crews of seamen as they waited to pick up supplies or anchored for repairs in the relatively sheltered ocean roads between Maui and the lush green hills of Lanai. But now there were only a handful: tall-masted vessels, their proud, billowing sails furled, silent silhouettes against the horizon.

Maria's eyes rested reluctantly on one that lay some distance from the others. The *Shadow Dawn*, a part of the haughty Barron fleet that covered the seas from Boston around both capes to the whaling grounds of the northern Pacific and the vastly profitable China trade. You could always tell a Barron vessel, they said. The brass was gleaming, the decks so highly polished they almost seemed as mirror-bright as the water; and the *Shadow* had distinctive lines. She could pick it out even without being able to read the name on the hull.

Eight years . . . and the *Shadow Dawn* had been in port that morning, too, though she hadn't known it at the time, of course. It had been only a ship then, one of all the others, nothing special to make it stand out. A flowery scent wafted up with the breeze, reminding Maria why she had come, and she bent abruptly to cut a bouquet of carefully nourished roses, their color so deep they looked more purple than red. Her mother's one extravagance, the one thing the rigid father Maria could barely remember had allowed his frightened young wife to bring with her on the long voyage from New England.

Eight long years to forget and get on with her life. And yet . . .

She stood for a moment, absolutely still, the roses forgotten in her hands. And yet sometimes she could remember every detail. As if it were happening all over again. Not in the past, but the present . . . Sometimes she almost felt that *he* was there. That if she stretched out her hand, his would appear, strong and warm, to enclose it. She could see the faint smile just beginning on his lips . . . the laughter in soft, smoky eyes turning slowly, tantalizingly to passion . . .

"Maria McClintock, you are a fool!"

She spoke the words aloud, to stiffen her resolve. But it didn't work—it never did when the memories started, as now, called back by a word or an image or a smell. The pain was still there, but with it a familiar sweetness that even the passage of time

could not blunt or take away, and there was nothing
for it but to surrender.

The years were gone, and she was back again in
that other bright morning, so long ago and yet so
close. And he was with her, as he had been then
and always would be, in some inexplicable way, even
though she had lost him forever.

It had been dawn then, too. Maria could still see
the sky, a pale lavender blue, gently suffused with
pink along the horizon. Not a wisp of cloud showed
anywhere. The crystalline surface was broken only
by the graceful arc of a *moli* bird, the albatross omen
of seamen's legends, soaring in broad circles toward
Haleakala in the distance. A scent of flowers hung in
the air, not her mother's cherished roses but the
lighter, lemony fragrance of wild hibiscus, which dot-
ted the hillsides with clusters of white.

She could still feel the energy of the filly beneath
her, frisky and willful, shaking her head as if to
throw off the reins as she sensed the nearness of the
grassy glade just ahead. Spring then, too, but earlier,
March easing toward April, and the air had been still
and sultry. Too sultry. Maria had been awake most
of the night, and even here in the wooded hills above
Honuakula, the plantation that had been her home
for the better part of a year, there was no respite.

She heard the water before she saw it. So did the
filly, and she was pulling on the reins again, harder
this time, prancing impatiently. It was all Maria
could do to hold her back.

"Easy, Kanani," she urged. "Steady, girl. We'll be
there in a minute. You'll have all the sweet, juicy
grass you want then, you greedy thing!"

Her laughter blended with the splashing of the
water as they rounded the corner to the secret place
she had always thought of as hers alone. And perhaps it was—at least she had never seen anyone else
there. Water cascaded from a mountain stream, spar-

kling and frothing over a miniature cliff, perhaps seven or eight feet high, into a pool so clear she could see the moss on the rocks at the bottom. There was no hibiscus in that secluded dell, but the shrubs that surrounded it were dense and fragrant, and grass grew like thick velvet plush to the water's edge.

It was, Maria thought then—and would forever afterward—the most beautiful spot on earth.

Dismounting, she tossed the reins over the filly's head and took the bag she had flung across the saddle. No point wasting time with a hobble for her mount. Kanani never strayed far when they came to the glade. And even if she did, Honuakula was within walking distance, albeit quite a hike.

This is my special place, Maria thought with pleasure as she kicked off her thin-soled slippers—hardly appropriate for riding—and strolled over to dip her toe in the water. It was just icy enough to send a tingle through her.

But then, nothing about her attire was appropriate! Maria chuckled as she dropped her bag onto the ground and began to remove the gaily colored calico gown that passed for a dress on her morning rides. Those who thought they had a right to dictate her affairs would have been horrified! When she was alone, or with native friends, she had taken to wearing the long, loose Mother Hubbards that the shocked missionaries had pressed on the naked women they had discovered on their arrival twenty years before. The comfortable *muumuus* and graceful, long-trained *holokus*, all suitably modest, but done up in vivid colors that delighted the Hawaiian heart. Today, especially rebellious, she had chosen a *pau*, a divided petticoat that let her ride, quite unfemininely, astride.

Well, those who dictated her affairs could not see her now! And they wouldn't so long as she took care not to return too late. She didn't care if they liked it or not!

Her special place ... Maria stood at the water's edge and let the coolness drift up, enveloping her. Her refuge—the one place where she was safe and happy, where the ugliness of Honuakula and everything it stood for couldn't intrude. The one place where she could be young, carefree Maria McClintock again, and life was magic and full of dreams.

All too often now life seemed stifling and constrained, like the stays and corsets she was ordinarily required to wear. She sometimes felt as if someone had taken the laces and was pulling tighter and tighter, until she couldn't breathe. Until she was sure—

Maria tossed her head defiantly, shaking off the thought with the red hair that tumbled out of its pins and spilled onto her shoulders. What a ninny she was, fussing over things that couldn't be changed! Not every young woman's life turned out to be a romantic daydream. She would face the things she had to. She would deal with them—but not now. Not here. Not in the one place on earth where she still felt free.

Her clothing was off now, and she let the petticoat fall carelessly to the ground. Nudity had never embarrassed her. She had grown up almost on her own. Her mother had been too busy with what was euphemistically referred to as the "family business," the grog shop she ran with her second husband in town, to pay more than cursory attention, and Maria had spent most of her time with native servants and their families. She had seen them dress in the most outlandishly ostentatious finery for church on Sunday, then come home, strip off every last stitch, and loll stark naked around grass-thatched huts with dogs and chickens and pigs running through them!

And she had romped equally naked with their children, and thought nothing of it, until she had begun to develop, rather later than usual, and her mother had finally taken notice.

"I will not have it, Maria," she had said with surprising sternness. Ordinarily Mama was the vaguest of parents when it came to giving orders. "It is not seemly at all. You are behaving like a savage! It's quite all right for the *keokis*, the little Hawaiians, but you don't see missionaries' children showing their limbs and everything else! Besides, you'll ruin your complexion. Redheads cannot tolerate the sun. You are going to turn into a mass of ugly freckles, and what man will want you then?"

"But my complexion is fine, Mama," she had protested in all innocence. Being accustomed to the Hawaiians with their open and extremely free ways, she truly had not understood what her mother was getting at. "I don't have any freckles—at least not many. And it's much too hot to wear all those clothes."

"You didn't have breasts, either," her mother reminded her, "until this year. You mark my words. Keep on frolicking in the sun, and the freckles will come. Heat or no, from now on you are going to remain fully clothed or you will not play with the *keokis* anymore. Do I make myself clear?"

It was some time before Maria figured out what had really made her mother nervous. For all the bawdy activities that went on in little rooms above the grog shop, Lena Owen could be surprisingly prudish, and plain talk with her daughter was not one of her strong points. But by that time it had been too late for talk anyway.

Maria took a thick towel out of her bag, spread it out on the ground beside the pond, and found a bar of sandalwood-scented soap. At least, thank heavens, her mother had been wrong about one thing. She didn't have a redhead's complexion. Her skin was too bronzed for fashion, but even though she obediently powdered it down, her mirror told her that the color set off her hair and the piercing blue of her eyes. And the dreaded freckles had never come.

Maria took a deep breath, the soap still clutched

in her hand, and plunged waist-deep into the pond. The cold was jolting but wonderfully exhilarating, and she dipped deeper, all the way up to her neck, letting the water flow over and through her.

Later she would swim like a native, agilely and expertly, out to the deeper end of the pond, then back to wade in the shallows again. But now the waterfall beckoned, and Maria half walked, half glided into the bubbly white foam at its base. Tilting her face into the spray, she wet her hair thoroughly, rubbed it sudsy with the soap, and rinsed it out.

She was used to the chill of the water now. It felt clean and refreshing against her skin, and she tarried for a moment, savoring it. The cascading water was just loud enough to drown out the rustling of the breeze in the foliage, and the whistles and chirps of the pretty crimson *'apapanes* that would be whirring around the flowering *koa* trees. She was just rinsing her hair a second time when she became aware of a sound. A faint whinny—a snort perhaps—as if Kanani had been disturbed by something.

She pulled her head out of the water to hear better. The sound came again. Clearly a snort this time, echoed by an answering neigh.

Two horses? Maria spun around, startled to see a man standing on the bank watching her.

Her first reaction was one of indignation, not alarm. He had been spying on her, the cad! He had come across her bathing privately in a mountain pool, and instead of having the decency to retreat— or at least turn his back while she retrieved her garments—he was just standing there. Gaping at her!

And apparently he had been there for a while, for he had dismounted and his horse was some distance off!

Maria raised her eyes to meet his with a flash of righteous indignation. But the hot retort she had planned died on her lips as she focused on him. She could not have said, even later, looking back and

trying to understand, what it was about him that so
fascinated her and held her gaze. It was as if some
invisible force had taken hold and riveted her eyes
on him. She could not turn or look away.

He was tall, well over six feet, but it was not height
that gave him a sense of power. Nor was it his shoulders, which were indeed quite intriguingly broad, or
the muscles that seemed to ripple across his chest,
faintly visible through the thin shirt that clung to him
in the heat. The power came from somewhere within.
It was in his bearing, the way he held his head. As
if he had been born of a superior race, not a mere
mortal at all but something different. Something rare.

It was a fascinating illusion, and Maria let herself
linger on it, just a second longer than propriety and
common sense allowed. The sun caught his hair,
turning it a sandy color, though it might have been
almost any shade of brown, and his eyes were gray,
set so deep she could not read their expression,
though she felt a sudden, inexplicable longing to
know what it was.

Impossible to read his mouth, too . . . Strong, sensuous, turned up slightly at the corners, as if to laugh
or—what? And why on earth did it matter?

She was too caught up in the moment to analyze
her feelings or even think about them. Almost against
her will, her eyes drifted down again, as if to memo-
rize every detail of this unexpected stranger who had
evoked such an amazing response in her. The muscular shoulders were just as she had remembered . . .
his shirt was open halfway to his waist, showing
glimpses of tanned skin beneath . . . his hips were
narrow, trousers well cut and tight-fitting, molded to
his body . . .

Then she saw what she had missed before—or perhaps it had not been there yet. The very obvious,
unmistakable proof of his desire for her, which he
was making no attempt to conceal!

Her eyes snapped up abruptly, only to find that he was looking at her in a most disconcerting manner.

Definitely laughter in his mouth now! And in the hooded gray eyes that dropped slowly, insolently, taking in every part of her body with a frankness that ought to have been insulting.

Maria gasped with horror as she realized she had been standing in front of him absolutely naked! And gazing at him with a look more suited to a harlot who had business on her mind! Nudity might seem perfectly natural to her, but he was clearly off one of the ships in the harbor. And seamen tended to think in earthier terms when confronted by a naked lady.

Belatedly Maria crouched down until she could feel the water lapping safely up against her chin. What in heaven's name had possessed her?

"If you were a gentlemen," she protested indignantly, "you would throw me my towel instead of staring at me like that."

"I don't recall claiming to be a gentleman," he replied evenly. "And I thought the staring was mutual."

"Did you indeed?" Maria felt as if she were blushing all the way down to her toes. "Apparently you have an ego as well as caddish tendencies! I was only startled, *naturally*, when I turned from bathing to find a scoundrel rudely ogling me."

"Naturally ... and you were struck speechless. A condition which, fortunately, seems to have been remedied." He was still laughing. Maria noticed that he picked up the towel, though he made no move to toss it to her. "By the way, I should warn you—it doesn't work."

She watched him warily. "What doesn't work?"

"Ducking under the water that way. Remarkable, isn't it, how clear these mountain streams are? Quite enchanting."

Maria looked down with dismay. He was right! Every detail of her body had, if anything, been magnified by the gentle ripples. Her breasts, which she had thought were rather on the small side, looked absolutely huge, nipples jutting out, erect and impertinent.

From the cold, of course—not her involuntary reaction to him!

She willed herself to stand up and stride out of the water. He *was* a scoundrel, and there was only one way to deal with scoundrels! She had to be firm and direct. No showing any weakness.

"My towel, sir," she said in a voice she trusted was properly imperious.

"Your towel," he agreed, though not quite with the abashment she hoped as he held it toward her.

Maria reached out her hand, but never quite made it, for their eyes met again. This time she saw in those smoky depths not impudence, not mockery, but the expression she had yearned for without realizing it before.

He wanted her—as she needed to be wanted—but there was more to it than that. He felt the same intense, indefinable emotion that had swept over her when she looked up and saw him on the grassy bank. She could not have said how—there was no sense to it, no reason—but she knew that the connection between them ran both ways.

She also knew that he was going to kiss her. And she was not going to do a thing to stop him.

The towel dropped unnoticed on the ground as they came together, shamelessly, scandalously. Maria recognized the little thrill that ran through her body, though she had never felt it before, except in her dreams. His lips were as she had imagined, hard and gentle all at once, making no demands, simply claiming, as he must have sensed she longed to be claimed.

Her mouth was opening of its own volition, instinctively welcoming the intrusion of his tongue. She felt herself go limp. She was quivering so badly, her knees were so weak, she would have fallen if his arms had not been so strong around her.

Caressing hands—hard, impudent hands—pressed her taut against him. His erection was a throbbing challenge, taunting her belly, and Maria felt the passion course, a palpable current, as sensuous as the rush of the waterfall, from his potent male body into hers.

She tried to think what she was doing, but it had happened so suddenly. His mouth, his body, was so hot on hers. She tried to tell herself this was wrong, insane. He was going to pull her down on the ground and take her right there.

But all she could remember was the ugliness she had left behind. The terribly empty life with no promises ... no more dreams. Fate had given her one unexpected, incredible chance at happiness. The only chance she would ever have to know what it was to love ... and be loved. She could not give that up. Today, this morning—this one sweet, brief hour—would have to last her for the rest of her life.

Only he wasn't pulling her down; he was drawing back instead, and just for an instant Maria was alarmed. Had she proved inadequate in some way? Was he merely toying with her? Then she saw the way he was looking at her, and she understood.

Not a cad after all. Not a scoundrel but the gentleman he had disdained to claim before. Even after what had passed between them—after the brazen way she had behaved—he was giving her a moment to change her mind.

It was then she knew that she loved this man, and would love him the rest of her life.

"The answer to your question," she said softly, "is yes."

And then he *was* pulling her down, as sweet and compelling as the urgency of their kiss, and the ecstasy she barely dared to dream of was hers at last.

*   *   *

It was not until later that she even learned his name. They were lying together on the lush green grass, touching tenderly, familiarly, as if they had been lovers for a long time instead of strangers who had just come together minutes before.

"They call me Sandy," he said, offering no last name, but none was needed. They were comfortable enough with each other to require nothing more.

"Because your hair was the color of sand when you were younger?" Maria guessed. "But it's darker now. I think I like men with brown hair."

"You think?" He raised himself on one elbow to give her an amused look. "I would have expected, after what just went on between us, that you would be sure."

"I was sure," Maria replied. "Even before . . . *that*. I was sure the moment I saw you—only it had nothing to do with the color of your hair."

"The color of my eyes, then?"

"A bit, perhaps . . . but it was more the expression in them. I knew you, how you were going to make me feel when you touched me. I knew what your mouth would taste like. . . . I—I've never felt like this before. This is all so . . . new to me."

"I know," he said quietly. His lips brushed her hair where it spilled onto her forehead and cheek. "I know."

And he did. Maria sensed that, and it intensified the dazzling, utterly unexpected love she had found for him. It was like a special gift, life's compensation for all the anguish and loneliness, and her heart swelled with gratitude.

She looked up to study his face with the sunlight behind him. Strong bones, as if chiseled by a master sculptor, hard but not harsh. The softening effect of his eyes, muted and smoldering. The way his mouth turned up at the corners, ready to laugh gently, lovingly. She hungered to know more about him, to store every detail away in her memory.

"You're from one of the ships in the harbor?" she asked. "A whaler?"

He seemed to hesitate, but only for an instant. "The *Shadow Dawn*," he admitted. "And she's a trading vessel—bound for Canton."

"One of the Barron ships?" Maria was just young enough to forget everything else for the moment. "But that's exciting! Why, the Barrons have ships *everywhere*! I'll bet they're the richest family in the world. And probably the most important."

Sandy smiled indulgently. "They have their share of wealth, that's for sure. But even back in Boston there are a handful of men who are richer than Gareth Barron and his son and grandsons. And more important—though I daresay the old tyrant would throw himself into the sea before he'd acknowledge it."

"You sound like you know Boston well." Maria regarded him curiously. "That's where you're from?"

"I am," he conceded. "But I trust you won't hold it against me.... Here, girl, what's this? You're laughing at me? Because of my stern Yankee heritage?"

"No." Maria giggled. "I was just thinking—my mother always warned me never to have anything to do with common sailors. I imagine this was what she was afraid of."

"Ah ..." Sandy's eyes glittered with amusement. "And here I thought I was quite an uncommon sailor."

"I don't know about that, but you are a most uncommon man."

She was surprised to hear her voice drop low in her throat, an invitation she saw answered in the deliciously erotic look that came over his face. His lips were parting but slowly, almost languidly. No hurrying their sensuous delights, as if time were standing still and this morning could last and be savored forever.

Maria lowered her eyes shamelessly. A pulse of excitement shivered through her as she saw that he had grown hard for her again. So soon, she marveled, and imagined how it was going to feel to have that part of him enter and fill her again. Her body was already reacting, aching and throbbing with the bittersweet pain only he could assuage.

He seemed to be waiting. Maria reached out her hand tentatively, letting it run lightly across his chest, fingertips tingling with the man-feel of his skin, his muscles, crisp curls of masculine hair. He responded at once, drawing her into his arms, holding and fondling, gently at first, then with the aroused passion they both desired.

One hand was cupping her breast. Maria shivered with delight. A big hand, completely enveloping the soft mound of flesh, thrusting her nipple up so he could take it into his mouth. He was playing with her now, alternating sucking and flicking his tongue in swift darting motions over her feverish skin until Maria's whole body was writhing with pleasure and anticipation.

It was the most exquisite agony, waiting for him to possess her again. Little whimpers slipped out of her mouth, animal sounds, surprising but somehow not embarrassing her.

I love you, she longed to cry. I *love* you—but that would not be fair. There had been no commitment between them, nor could there ever be. How could she ask for promises when she wasn't prepared to give them herself?

He seemed to understand, for he drew briefly back from her breast. His eyes blazed with passion, compelling and barely controlled, as if it were all he could do to manage the moment it took to say:

"This is not dalliance, love. Not just an hour or a morning for me."

Love. How easily the endearment flowed from his lips. It was not much, but it would have to do.

"Nor for me," she said, her voice muffled with longing. "Nor for me . . . but we don't need to speak of it. Words aren't important between us."

"Not now anyway," he agreed, and his mouth took up where it had left off before. Her breast recognized and thrilled to the familiar sucking motions; her belly seemed to know even before his lips and tongue moved lower what he was going to do, and the little tremors of heat that flushed over her anticipated his touch.

There was the same urgency that had accompanied their previous lovemaking, but not the same haste, and Maria had the tantalizing luxury of exploring and enjoying each new sensation. Everything had happened too quickly before. It had not been the first time her body had been touched by a man, but it had been the first time she had responded so completely, and she had been carried along on currents too overwhelming to resist or understand.

Now she was excruciatingly conscious of every caress, every moist, darting flick of his tongue as he moved slowly down her belly, teasing and tormenting every inch of her skin.

His kisses were ravishing and agonizing both, and Maria tangled her hands in his hair, unconsciously drawing his head closer to that spot where all her need and hunger centered. He resisted a moment, increasing the anticipation, seeming to know just how long she could bear to wait, before he finally surrendered.

Jolts of pleasure and the most delicious pain burst through her as at last he touched her *there*. Kissing, sucking, as with her nipples—she cried out with longing, and he was thrusting his tongue inside, an intrusion that shocked but excited her.

Then, just as she was sure she would die of the torment, he ceased his assault. Suddenly his mouth was on hers. Maria was aware of the taste of herself on his lips, shocking again but intoxicating, as swiftly, surely he penetrated her.

She knew him now, this man who had been her lover only once before, and she sensed that he belonged to her as surely as she had belonged to him from the moment she first saw him. She was ready for the waves of rapture that swept over her, one after another, carrying her higher and higher to the peak she now recognized. Ready for the last sweet moment of resistance, for the little series of explosions that seemed to tear her body apart. Ready for the answering groan that came out of his mouth as he sank, spent and weakened for the moment, onto the receiving warmth of her body.

They lay beside each other for a long time afterward, kissing and talking. Not saying anything in particular. Just whispering the little endearments common to lovers throughout the ages, but seemed to each new pair magic and unique.

"You have the advantage, you know," he said after a while. "Most unfair, don't you think? You know my name, and I have nothing to call you but 'love'."

"That's all right." Maria nestled closer, enjoying the way their bodies fit, even when they were not connected. "I like it when you call me 'love'."

"So do I, but I wouldn't mind something else—for a little variety. Do you have a name?"

"Polly," she replied, surprised as she heard it come out of her mouth. She hadn't been Polly for years, since she was a little girl and the Todds had still lived on Maui with their four rollicking boys and perky little Rachel who had followed her around like an adoring spaniel puppy. She couldn't think what had prompted it now, except perhaps that that had been a happier, carefree time. "It's only a nickname—but I prefer it."

"It suits you," he said. "A pretty name."

And a safe one, Maria thought guiltily. No one would recognize it. Even if he made inquiries about her in town, which she doubted—he didn't seem the type to trumpet his romantic conquests—who would associate "Polly" with her? Everyone would assume some sea captain had brought his daughter and whisked her safely inland, or perhaps a visitor had arrived by private vessel at Honuakula. Her secret would be safe.

They frolicked for a while in the icy pool, splashing water over each other like children as they waded out and stood together under the silvery spray of the waterfall. The cascade felt wild and enticingly exhilarating, and they kissed again and tried to make love there, but the rocks were too slippery and they fell, laughing and thrashing about, passion abated for the moment.

Maria marveled as she watched her Sandy swim, at how strong and supple his body was. Bronzed skin and lean, hard muscles moved with fluid grace. He was almost as deft in the water, she thought, as he had been before—doing other things with her. She smiled to herself as she watched him skim underwater, like a fish, then burst to the surface again.

"I thought sailors weren't supposed to be able to swim," she teased. "Aren't they notorious for that?"

"Ah, but I told you, I'm a very uncommon sailor," he responded, and pulling her down with him beneath the water, managed in those few brief seconds quite thoroughly to make her forget everything else.

They made love one more time on the grassy bank before Maria got up reluctantly and put on her clothes. She was pressing her luck enough as it was. It would be approaching noon before she slipped back from the stables into the house.

"I have to go," she said, thankful as she pulled the loose garment over her head that she had not donned more fashionable garb. She didn't know how she could have borne the constraining pressure of stays digging into her ribs and breast. "I have a life, you know—outside of you. And people who will be expecting me."

He did not try to question her. "You'll be here again tomorrow?"

"At dawn," she promised. "When the first cool shadows stretch across the earth. I'll be here every day at that time. As long as you want me."

"Then you'll be here every day for the rest of your life. For I will want you forever."

Forever had lasted a week and a half. Maria and Sandy had met every morning for a few sweet hours and reaffirmed their love in the sunlight and water and private shady hollows beneath the shrubs and trees. Words had flowed as easily as passion, and they had spoken of everything and nothing. Not the details of their lives, which had truly seemed insignificant, but the essence, the feelings, the things that really mattered.

Maria had learned that he loved not the sea but the land, and it seemed a strange preference in a man who had chosen to go before the mast. But then he spoke of quiet nights, staring out across the moon-swept ocean, wind in his hair, the taste of salt spray on his mouth, the sting of it in his eyes, and she thought she understood.

And she spoke of her feeling for the island that had been her home for nearly as long as she could remember. Of its earthy, fun-loving, big-hearted people, of the legends and nature that were so intertwined sometimes it was hard to tell where one left off and the other began. She pointed out the pretty red *'apapanes*, and showed him how to distinguish between the raucous chirps and melodious whistles that made up their various calls. And the great gnarled *hala* or pandanus trees, with their massive, twisted roots rising out of the soil into the air. The early settlers had brought them all the way from Polynesia in their dugout canoes, and their narrow leaves were still dried and woven into mats. And the *a'ali'i*, sacred to the hula goddess Laka, whose bright red clusters were used in hair leis or boiled over hot stones for *kapa*-cloth dye, and whose foliage was crushed and rubbed on rashes and insect bites.

She told him of the demigod Maui, whose great love of fishing had created the islands, for when his fishhook had caught on the ocean floor one day, he had pulled it up, and lo—the volcanoes and water-falls and flowers had come with it! It was Maui who had captured the sun and forced it to slow its passage so the days would be longer and there would be more time for fishing and swimming and tending to taro and cane. She told him of the silversword, a brilliantly glittering plant on the slopes of Haleakala, whose life culminated after a few short years in a burst of purple-and-yellow-flowering glory a week before it died.

Their closeness grew in those precious days, and Maria found herself trusting this man more than she had ever dared to trust anyone before. She did not know when she started to believe that perhaps, after all, it did not have to end. She only knew that she found herself wondering more and more if there wasn't a way. If she could find the courage to tell him, they might—just might—be able to work things out together.

It would be selfish, she knew. It was fraught with peril. She was not the only one who stood to lose everything. But she was young and in love, and love was its own reason. And foolishly, irrationally she let herself hope.

It only made it all the more painful when the end came, abruptly and unexpectedly.

She had not been the least bit worried that night when her presence had been required at a dinner being given in a large room attached to the grog shop, where such events that passed as social functions in Lahaina were usually held. There was little risk that Sandy would hear of it. Sailors off ships in the port were hardly likely to be invited.

And even if the captain of the *Shadow Dawn* happened to be there—and if one of his men had happened to mention a bawdy water nymph named Polly—he would not be thinking of her when he was introduced to a properly corseted young woman in a deep blue velvet gown, her hair piled in the latest fashion on top of her head, and her neck glittering with sapphires and diamonds.

The light was dim, the room hazy with the gentlemen's pipes and cigars, and it took Maria's eyes a moment to adjust as she entered after spending a short time with her mother in the private chambers upstairs. Her heart stopped for an instant as she spotted a tall stranger across the room. His back was turned toward her, his shoulders straining the expensive fabric of a well-cut coat.

She caught herself with a faint half smile. There *was* more than one tall, broad-shouldered man on earth—even if there was only one for her.

Another man was standing beside him. Maria grimaced with distaste. She had never cared for Lucifer Darley, but it looked like there was no way to avoid speaking with him now.

"You've met Royall Perralt, haven't you?" Darley was saying as Maria approached. "Our largest 'landowner'—though that's a misnomer. The old reprobate somehow managed to convince Governor Hoapili to give him a ninety-nine-year lease on an extremely choice bit of acreage. Quite unheard of in the islands. What are the *alii*—the nobility—coming to? . . . And Maria," he added, glancing her way, "his beautiful wife. What a delight, dear lady. I had not realized you would be in attendance."

Maria barely heard his last words, for the stranger had turned and was looking at her. A flicker of pleasure showed for just a moment in smoke gray eyes before reality intruded and the light was gone.

Sandy! Maria longed fervently for the ground to open and swallow her up. Why had she been so smugly certain he wouldn't be invited? He had told her himself that he was an uncommon sailor. She knew perfectly well that young men of excellent families sometimes took to the sea. For their health perhaps ... or a thirst for adventure.

"*Mrs.* Perralt," that familiar voice was saying, the emphasis subtly but unmistakably on the first word. No one else would hear the disdain—his self-control was remarkable after that first brief second—but Maria did, and she burned with shame as she realized what he had to be thinking. "What a surprise, finding such a lovely young matron in this raucous port. I congratulate your husband, madam. He has won himself a prize."

Maria felt suddenly as if she couldn't breathe; her corset was laced so tight she was terrified she was going to faint. He was thinking that she was a married woman, bored and playing around—and how could she blame him? It was her own fault for being such a coward. She should have told him!

"Sir—" She acknowledged him with a cool nod, but that single word was filled with all the pleading she dared. If only they could be alone for a few minutes. If she could just explain ...

But it was past the time for explanations. There was a distance in those beloved gray eyes, as if a shade had been drawn, shutting her out forever. Maria could have wept with despair. He was an honorable man—much too honorable for a tawdry affair with a married woman—and she knew she had betrayed him in the one way he would never forgive.

You are a liar, those eyes were saying as clearly as if he had spoken aloud. And a cheat. I don't like liars. I don't like cheats. And I don't dally with women who belong to other men.... And you, madam, are another man's wife.

But I'm not! she longed to cry out. I'm *not*! I have never been Royall Perralt's wife, and I never will be! But, oh, heaven help her—who would believe her if she dared to blurt out the words?

And why should they?

Maria blinked back the tears that stung her eyes and threatened to humiliate her. Half the people in that room—no, more than half—had attended that farce of a wedding where she and the lean, distinguished-looking man beside her had joined their hands and lives at the altar.

Everyone believed he was her husband. They would think she was jesting if she tried to disclaim it! Not a one of them knew the terrible secret that had turned her life upside down—or the cruel, insidious pressures that forced her to continue that distasteful charade.

Only three people on earth knew the truth, and two, for their own selfish reasons, would never speak of it. The third had been afraid ... until now.

And now it was too late. Now he had already turned away, and Maria knew he would never look back again.

Chapter 2

Maria had only the faintest recollections of her early childhood. She had been barely three that spring dawn in 1820 when the first shipload of missionaries from New England had sailed into sight of what newcomers were still calling the Sandwich Islands. Although she did have some fleeting memories of the long sea voyage, she was inclined to believe that they came mostly from stories she had heard later. Of the cramped quarters, four and six couples squeezed into a cabin, the stench and the seasickness, the long, excruciating hours of kneeling on a swaying deck, praying for the success of their noble mission—and, Maria suspected, a bit more ignobly, for deliverance from their present ordeal.

The arrival was much more vivid in her mind. Having seen the excitement generated by a new vessel, even at the height of the season when there might be as many as a dozen a morning, Maria could well envision it. To this day, the scene had not changed much. The men would paddle out in their dugout canoes, especially the *alii*, who had their dignity to maintain, and some brought their women with them, but most of the girls, their exuberance undiminished even by years of missionary influence, leaped into the water and started to swim.

They made a colorful sight as they glided gracefully through the waves, their pretty patterned gowns tied on top of their heads. Once on deck, nudity was covered, but only briefly as, chattering and giggling, they looked over the new men and picked out old favorites. Then the dresses were off again, with equal enthusiasm on both sides, for no one had yet managed to convince these girls that lust was evil and sex without marriage wrong; and if trinkets and scissors and coveted iron nails changed hands, they looked on it not as prostitution but presents, in which their youthful hearts could delight.

Maria had heard her stepfather talking about it often enough, with great bawdy bursts of laughter. Some of the raunchier captains, it was rumored, disappeared into their cabins for days at a time with as many as three or four of the nubile beauties, while the men used the deck and public areas for similar purposes. It had gotten so out of hand on some of the vessels that a gun was fired at dawn to clear out the ship, another at dusk, when work was done, to let the girls know it was time to come back.

They had not had dresses on top of their heads, of course, that day the missionaries had arrived, for the stern men and women of God had not yet put the natives into clothing. But otherwise everything would have been much the same.

Maria could just imagine the shock in the eyes of those devout wives as hordes of naked dark-skinned girls ogled their husbands, pointing out potential attributes with gestures frank enough to transcend any barriers of language. Or the gasps from the good ladies' lips when one of the *alii* pulled up in a canoe with two or three of his wives, weighing the better part of a ton in total—decorated only with a few feathers and leaves and a scarlet damask umbrella to shield them from the sun!

She could also imagine how terrified her young mother must have been. Marlena McClintock had been barely more than a child herself that fateful morning, just nineteen, with a child of her own, and the long voyage had left her a widow. She did not grieve for her husband. Abner McClintock had been a hard, cold man, devoted only to the faith that dominated his life, and she had never been able to please him or meet his exacting standards. But he had been a good provider, and she was aware suddenly that she was utterly alone, in a place she had never so much as seen, with no one to offer protection or support.

The company of missionaries had been put in an extremely awkward position by her recent bereavement. Abner had been not a reverend but one of the lay members of that dedicated group, a carpenter whose services would have come in handy but were not essential. Nor had he been particularly popular with the others, and they were more than a little put out at having to make arrangements for his widow.

But they did owe her something, as they magnanimously agreed when they all gathered to discuss it. After all, she had given up a relatively comfortable home and come halfway around the world in the service of the Lord. They could hardly leave her stranded. Somehow the money would be found for her return passage.

To the astonishment of every one of them, Lena refused. She was a small woman, so frail it looked as if a wisp of breeze could carry her away, but she raised her chin and looked them square in the eye.

"Thank you," she said, "but that won't be necessary. I have no intention of going back."

All the arguing in the world could not persuade her to change her mind. Lena McClintock had no idea what faced her in Lahaina, but she knew perfectly well what would happen if she returned to her family, and just what sort of husband they would pick for her next time.

She had no illusions about being able to manage on her own. She had to have a man to take care of her, and a man in the strict standards by which she had been raised meant a husband, whether she liked the idea or not. But at least she could pick her own.

As it turned out, she had more than ample selection. In the white community—the *haoles*, as they were known to the Hawaiians—there were few women, none of them young and unattached. Lena, being exceptionally pretty, had no trouble attracting suitors, even with the encumbrance of a young child.

The men were marginally acceptable, of course. The noses of the other wives pinched ever so slightly as they reviewed the matter among themselves. One would not associate with such types at home, of course—much less consider them as potential marriage partners—but here, well, perhaps, considering the circumstances and the Widow McClintock's predicament, allowances might be made.

What they did not even consider was that the Widow McClintock would choose the one man for whom no allowances were possible!

Dudley Owen was twelve years Lena's senior and decades beyond her in worldly experience. He was the brash, boastful proprietor of the largest and most popular drinking establishment in Lahaina, with rooms upstairs for the usual purpose. The best that could be said about the place was that at least it was clean. The doctor came every week to examine the girls, and sailors and captains alike were checked with a thoroughness that could be either embarrassing or titillating, depending on who did the checking and where and how.

And as if that were not bad enough, the man kept not one but two native mistresses in adjacent rooms in his own quarters over the saloon!

It was utterly beyond the good servants of the Lord why a beautiful young widow, with all the men who wanted her, would select someone like that. He was only an inch or two taller than she, burly of body, with a face that looked as if it had been smashed in by the hand of a careless midwife at birth. Hardly the sort of handsome devil who usually tempted devout young ladies from the straight and narrow.

Lena could have told them if they had cared to listen, though they wouldn't much have liked the answer. She had found out, even before that hasty wedding, that passion could be a pleasure rather than a duty, and she had fallen totally, hopelessly, and forever in love with him. The mistresses were moved out, she proved to his satisfaction and her own that she could take their place, and she was happy enough not to give a fig what anyone else thought.

Life with Dud Owen was not easy. He built a stone house for his wife and her young daughter high on the hillside where it caught breezes from the ocean. A pretty place, but Lena quickly discovered that the mere removal of a couple of mistresses did not spell an end to temptation. After she came across her husband one time too often in the rooms upstairs—and doing more than supervising the girls—she promptly moved out of the new home into his considerably less comfortable bachelor quarters.

That did not end her lusty husband's infidelities. It would have taken more than one sharp-eyed woman to do that, but at least it forced him to make an effort not to get caught. Dud Owen did love his wife. Despite the very blatant weaknesses of his flesh, he truly wanted to please her; and Lena, because she adored him, came to uneasy terms with the behavior her vigilance could diminish but never quite stop.

Thus it was that Maria grew up unsupervised, or supervised only by Hawaiian servants, which amounted to much the same thing. Lena was not a bad mother. She still found time to check in on Maria every day. She made sure the house ran smoothly and her daughter wanted for nothing. But the actual child-rearing was left to natives, an arrangement which Maria did not find the least bit unpleasant. It had taken her no time at all to discover how easily a spirited little redhead could twist those good-hearted folk around her finger.

If there was anything incongruous about being the daughter of a missionary turned saloon- and brothel-keeper, Maria was not aware of it. There were three kinds of people in those early days on the Maui coast: the genial natives with their free and careless lifestyle; the raucous seamen and store owners, and the barkeeps who catered to them; and the missionaries, whose sole purpose in life was to reform them both.

It was an uneasy blend, but Maria, who had never known anything else, did not realize it. To her it was simply the way things were, and she coexisted comfortably in all three worlds.

The missionaries had the smallest part in her life. Maria's stepfather, who hated the "blasted sanctimonious sons of bitches" almost as much as the sanctimonious sons of bitches hated him, had forbidden her to have anything to do with them. Only Abby Todd, the one woman who had consistently supported Lena and refused to cut her dead on the street, was excepted, and Maria spent much of her time playing with the Todds' four sons and the baby, Rachel, who was nearly five years younger than she.

It was a happy time. The Todds looked on her as one of their own, teasing her as they teased each other and shortening the more formal Maria to "Polly." There were days when she almost felt like she was part of the family and little Rachel was her own small sister.

Happy . . . but brief, for it all came to an end when the Reverend Gideon Todd disappointed his colleagues almost as much as Maria's mother had, though in a very different manner. He was a big, handsome, silver-tongued man—born to preach the word of the Lord, it was said, and people flocked to his sermons. Converts were guaranteed. Clearly his calling lay in the pulpit. Why, then, he lost interest and turned instead to the study of medicine was as much a mystery as why Lena McClintock would waste her life on the likes of Dud Owen.

It was blamed at the time on old Doc Friedrichs. Not altogether fairly, for Gideon already had the rudiments of medical training, though no doubt he was influenced by the crusty German, who got along wonderfully well with the natives, tolerably with the townsmen, and was so disdained by the missionaries that they eventually brought in their own doctor. How, after all, could they call a man to minister to their wives when his hands had been occupied who-knows-when with who-knows-what parts of a prostitute?

Maria knew nothing about the dilemma that faced the good reverend in his honest desire to serve God. She knew only that after a few years he packed up his family and moved on to new challenges in faraway China, and the civilizing influence of a Christian home was abruptly removed.

The rest of her childhood was spent almost exclusively with native children, especially in a pleasant grass-thatched house where their housekeeper retired in the evening—and a good many afternoons, which would have annoyed Lena greatly. It was in a *kuleana*, a kind of compound where everyone lived together, sisters, brothers, cousins, aunts, grandparents, spouses—sometimes more than two to a family. It was a noisy place, with a small, neatly tended taro patch, sugarcane to suck on whenever she wanted, and pigs rooting in the dirt and feeling free to wander in and out with the children and chickens.

Her closest companion in those days was the housekeeper's daughter, Ilimi, who was the same age but considerably more developed, physically and socially. Ilimi had already gained intimate knowledge, which she was more than willing to share, about things that were still just a curiosity to her playmate. Maria's own figure did not fill out until she was nearly fifteen, but then it happened quickly, and she went in a few months from a scrawny child, all arms and legs and huge blue eyes, to a young woman whose body showed promise of being lushly feminine.

With the new curves came new stirrings, new emotions, and what had previously been curiosity turned into something much more compelling.

Ilimi's older cousin was well on his way to showing her what could be done with those stirrings. His name, Keahi, as he delighted in bragging to her, meant "fire," and Maria could well believe it, for there was a definite fire blazing somewhere low in her belly, spreading quite pleasurably all through her, as he drew her over to the shadow of a clump of shrubbery.

She went willingly, not even thinking it might be wrong. No one had discussed such things with her— the Hawaiians considered them perfectly natural and Lena had been much too prudish—and Maria was quite happy to follow her instincts without a qualm.

She was wearing the long, loose robe her mother had insisted on, but it was not much of a barrier. Keahi had it pulled up to her neck and was touching her all over and coaxing her to touch him, which she did with no reluctance. She did not know what had happened to his *malo*, or breechcloth. Somehow it seemed to be gone, and he was explaining that he was going to hurt her, but not much and not for long, and then she was going to like what he did to her.

Maria was more than ready for him. Her whole body was warm and tingling. She was alternately fascinated with the size of that organ he was going to push into her and wondering whether it would really hurt, when suddenly a hand grasped her shoulder and she felt herself being yanked roughly to her feet.

"Here, girl, what be the meanin' of this?" Dud

Owen's voice was hoarse, his face red with rage. "Do ye want to break yer mother's heart? Shame on ye, strumpet! Ye'll be showin' up in the family way next, and what will we do with ye then?"

Maria could only stare at him, stunned. It was hardly likely her mother would pay enough attention to get her heart broken! And why on earth was he so angry? She had walked in unexpectedly and discovered him in exactly the same position several times with her mother—and once with one of the girls.

"I—I'm sorry," she stammered. He was jerking her dress down with one hand, even as he started pulling her toward the road with the other. "I . . . I was just . . ."

"I know what ye were doin'," he said gruffly. "I'm no green lad. I've eyes in me head. And ye'll not be doin' it again. Ye hear me, girl?"

Maria heard, but she did not understand. She only knew that he was still furious with her, though he did not speak again as he dragged her down the road, veering off into the narrow lane that led up the hillside. Furious as he had never been before—and her mother was going to be furious, too—and she couldn't for the life of her figure out why.

She was to learn soon enough. And though neither she nor they could possibly anticipate it, it was to be a bitter lesson.

Five days later Maria found herself sitting in the sparsely furnished front parlor of the small stone house facing the man her parents had chosen for her to marry.

It had all happened so quickly she had barely had time to catch her breath. Clearly pleasure with a young man prior to wedlock was not acceptable for the daughter of brothel keepers—primarily, Maria supposed bitterly, because some sort of resulting scandal would make it impossible for them to find her a "suitable" mate. Heaven forbid they should get stuck with her on their hands forever!

It had been a shock, standing in the hallway the night she had been caught with Keahi and overhearing them discuss it. At least her mother had objected, taking her side for the first time Maria could remember.

"She's so young, Dud," Lena protested with surprising vehemence. "She's just fifteen years old. She needs more time—"

"Ye were fifteen when ye were wed," her stepfather broke in gruffly. "And as lusty a wench as that one, I'll warrant." He placed a lascivious hand on her generously rounded backside, and Maria, peeking through a crack in the door, saw her mother weakening. She never stood out long against Dud, especially when he started getting amorous.

"Yes," Lena admitted. "I *was* fifteen . . . and look how that turned out!"

"Not so bad in the end, eh?" His hand was roving, squeezing his wife's buttocks and making her squirm with pleasure. Maria was just embarrassed enough that she would have turned away if they hadn't been discussing her future. "Ye're happy enough here, aren't ye? I've heard no complaints. . . . Or do I not please ye, woman?"

"You do, and you know it. But I was lucky, Dud. I found a man I could love. Eventually. But what came first. . . ." She shuddered visibly. "Maria might not be so lucky."

"There'll be no need of luck for the girl. We'll find yer daughter a good man. Not rich, I grant ye, but good. A man who will be fair and treat her right. . . . Can we do as much if she comes home one fine day her belly swollen with child? A pretty inconvenience that'll be then."

A pretty *inconvenience*? Maria blinked back her tears, determined not to humiliate herself as she recalled the haste with which her mother had given in.

It was becoming clearer now what they were so upset about. Maria understood vaguely that there was some connection between the things men and women did together and the .subsequent birth of a child, though no one had ever discussed it with her. And an illegitimate baby would ruin her forever in the Christian community. At least among the *haole* Christians. But—an inconvenience?

Strangely, irrationally, it was her mother's betrayal that hurt the most. Lena had never been particularly affectionate. She had never had the warm, open arms of an Abby Todd, and Maria had learned not to count on her for emotional support. But she was still her mother, and there was somewhere deep inside a hunger for her love and acceptance. To be dismissed as merely *inconvenient* seemed more than she could bear.

"Are you feeling as awkward as I, Maria?" The voice that broke into her thoughts was well modulated with just a hint of humor. "You look like you are—and no wonder. I doubt society has ever invented anything quite so stilted as a middle-aged man meeting formally with a pretty girl to negotiate the possibility of marriage."

Maria glanced across the room at the man standing next to the fireplace, leaning with exaggerated casualness against the *koa*-wood mantle. There was nothing out of the ordinary about him. His hair was a neutral color, his eyes neutral, his features blandly shaped, but his face seemed kind.

"I don't feel awkward," she said. "At least I don't think I do. But then, I don't know how I'm supposed to feel."

He smiled. "You're honest. I like that. I hope we will always manage to be honest with each other."

Maria was surprised to find herself smiling back. The man her parents had chosen for her was the same man that old Doc Friedrichs, feeling his health fail—and not trusting the new missionary physician—had chosen as his assistant years ago. By purest coincidence his name was also Fredericks, spelled differently but confusing nonetheless, and they had soon become known as "Old Doc" and "Young Doc" to set them apart.

Old Doc was gone now, and sorely missed, but Young Doc had begun to take his place, and Maria, though she had never particularly thought about it, had always liked and trusted him.

"I hope we will," she agreed. "It doesn't sound so terribly difficult."

"It doesn't, does it? But you'd be surprised how often it is." He shifted his weight slightly but continued to lean against the mantel as he looked down at her on her chair across the room. "Let me start then by being perfectly honest with you. You are a beautiful young woman . . . and very desirable to my masculine eyes. I would like very much to have you for my wife. But I'm not sure you would be quite so pleased having me for a husband."

He paused, as if waiting for a reply.

"I—I don't know what to say to that," Maria stammered, feeling suddenly as awkward as he had said she looked before. "I don't know you . . . though I don't suppose that matters. Lots of women marry men they hardly know."

"It matters like hell." He made no effort to apologize for his language. "It's a barbaric custom, arranging marriages without any consideration for feelings. I won't have it! You're not going to marry me without knowing me. Inside and out. And knowing everything about me. . . . You have heard I've been married before. My wife was very beautiful, too. A young native woman."

"I know," Maria replied, wondering why he had brought it up. Most unattached men of his age had at least one wife somewhere in their past. "I remember seeing her sometimes, I think . . . I was very little.

They say she died in childbirth, and the baby, too. I'm very sorry."

"It was a long time ago, Maria. The hurt has healed. I mention it now only because I want everything to be clear between us. If we marry—if you agree to marry me—you will not be expected to take second place in my heart. You and you only, no memories intruding, will be my wife."

Maria caught her breath. There was a contained ardor in his voice that was genuine and very flattering.

"I think," she said softly, "my parents have already agreed."

"It is not their agreement I want. Your mother cares for you, very much. Your stepfather, too, in his gruff, bearlike way. They see you growing up, and they are afraid for you ... so they try to keep you safe. But it's not always possible to keep someone else safe. Or fair. What *they* want for you isn't relevant. It's what you want for yourself."

He had left his post by the fireplace and come to stand almost directly in front of her. Maria wanted to tell him that her mother wasn't the least bit afraid for her—she was just worried about being inconvenienced—but things were getting all muddled, and she couldn't put it into words. There was something confusing, and distinctly intriguing, about having an older man lay his heart out in front of her. Treating her for the first time like a sensible being with a mind and judgment of her own.

"And if I don't know yet what I want?" she asked.

"Then I will have to help you figure it out." He reached down, taking first one of her hands, then the other, in both of his own. "There is a considerable difference in our ages, Maria. You are used to younger men. You look at them, and your heart responds ... and your body, too, which is good. It's a healthy reaction. But when you look at a man like me, can you think the same things? *Feel* the same things?"

"I . . . I suppose so. I don't see why not. It never occurred to me before, but . . ."

"This is very important, Maria. When a woman marries a man, she lies beside him in his bed. It would be a perpetual nightmare for both of them if she cringed every time he touched her."

"I . . . don't think . . ." Maria said, feeling a little giddy and not knowing why, "I would cringe if you touched me."

"Shall we make sure?" He was pulling her up gently, almost before Maria knew it. Suddenly she was standing so close, her cheek almost brushed his shoulder.

"I'm going to kiss you, Maria . . . and then we will know. Once and for all."

And they did. It felt strange at first as his mouth approached hers. Premeditated somehow, not at all as it had with Keahi. But then he was kissing her, a long, hard, increasingly passionate kiss, and Maria quickly learned that experience could be more than a match for callow youth.

She was weak with the bewildering new sensations he seemed to know just how to rouse, and trembling almost violently, when she finally felt herself being released.

She would not have been the least surprised if he had taken her over to the couch and had her right there. But he only laughed, lightly and tenderly.

"I think," he said, "it's going to be all right."

It was more than all right. Maria was beside herself with excitement that night as she put on a smooth cotton gown, slipped into bed, and imagined the time when she would no longer be sleeping there alone.

We'll find a good man for her, Dud had said— and, oh, miraculously they had! Even her mother's betrayal did not seem so cruel anymore, and Maria fell asleep thinking that perhaps, after all, her parents just might have been wiser than she.

After that unrestrained kiss Maria had fully expected the wedding to take place with nearly as much haste as if she had indeed come home with a swollen belly. But to her amazement—and not inconsiderable annoyance—Young Doc Fredericks insisted on waiting until she was sixteen.

"But that's half a year away!" she wailed when he told her. She had been so sure he wanted her as much as his kiss had made her want him. "I'll die if I have to wait that long. Truly I will."

"You only *feel* like you will." He grinned mercilessly. "If anyone dies from the frustration, it will probably be me! . . . Fifteen is much too young. I'm a doctor—you'll have to take my word for it. Your body is still growing. You're just on the threshold between childhood and maturity. I can't take the chance of getting you pregnant so soon."

"Lots of girls have babies when they're fifteen," she persisted. "Besides, it takes months and months for that to happen. I'd be sixteen anyway by the time I had it."

A strange, closed look came just for a second over his face. "I've already lost one wife to childbirth. I'll not risk another that way. . . . But come your sixteenth birthday, I'm going to rush you from the altar to the bedroom so fast it will leave all those old biddies clicking their tongues in the churchyard!"

"What?" Maria said, giving in not because she wanted to, but because she knew she had no choice, "we're going to have to go all the way to the bedroom? What an unimaginative man!"

"And what a brazen hussy," he had replied. "I can hardly wait for your birthday."

Laughter had eased the slight moment of discomfort between them, but Maria was to remember afterward that look on his face, and she was aware of a nasty pang of something very akin to jealousy. Apparently his feelings for his late wife were not quite as much in the past as he had let on. But she also knew that he truly cared for her—he was not putting off their wedding to suit his own purposes—and she tried to content herself with that.

Their courtship turned out to be quite conventional. No more unchaperoned conversations in the parlor, but they took long walks together in the afternoon—when he could tear himself away from his work, which was not often—or at dusk along a deserted stretch of beach with waves crashing against the shore. Sometimes Maria found herself feeling unexpectedly shy with this man who was now her fiancé, and then he would laugh and tease her because she kept forgetting and calling him "Dr. Fredericks."

His name, as he told her, was Alonzo, but everyone called him Fred, which for some reason came hard to her lips, and she usually compromised by referring to him as "Doc Fred." He still laughed, but seemed to enjoy it, and after a while, even when she became comfortable enough to stroll hand in hand with him along the coral sand, it remained as a kind of endearment.

For the most part, Maria let him talk. He could go on and on for what seemed like hours about his practice in Lahaina, his patients, what he was trying to do there—what he longed to do—though with each passing year, it seemed, he had grown more and more disillusioned with the limits of his own knowledge and the inadequacy of medicine in general. It was not particularly interesting, but Maria sensed his need to share these things with her, and she tried to be patient and listen.

He would kiss her sometimes, on the veranda when he brought her home at night, or just as the sun set over the beach, but carefully, very gingerly, not at all as he had that first time.

Even then her body stirred. Maria knew he felt it, too—she sensed the strain in his arms as he fought the impulse to draw her closer—and she would lie awake nearly all night afterward, aching for him to be there with her. Wondering why he didn't understand that she was all grown up now and hungered for and needed his passion.

"I want you to make love to me," she whispered one night when the kiss had lasted a little longer than usual. It seemed so foolish, waiting when there was no point. They were betrothed, after all, and it was only a few months. "I want you to teach me what it is to be a woman. . . . I want you to teach me now."

"Ah, God, Maria," he groaned, and she thought for one dizzying instant that he was going to give in. But honor won, as it always would with a man like that, and she went inside—for the last time—alone.

She was often to wonder, in the years that followed, what life would have been like if Doc Fred had been just a little less decent. A little less concerned with her welfare and his principles.

But he had been decent—he hadn't compromised his principles—and when she finally stepped up to the altar, it was to meet a very different man.

Chapter 3

There were candles burning in the hallway. Later, whenever Maria looked back on that day, she always remembered the candles. Faintly sputtering, with an acrid odor of smoke that lingered in the nostrils.

It was still an hour from dusk, but there were no windows in the hall, and lights were kept burning around the clock. Not many, just one sconce at the base of the dingy stairway, another at the head, to provide a minimum of visibility. More than one of the men who climbed those narrow steps had no desire to be seen.

It had been some time since Maria had been in the small cubicles upstairs from the tavern, or even the quarters her mother shared with Dud Owen. She had run freely all over the place as a little girl—Lena had been much too preoccupied to more than shoo her occasionally away—but in recent months the rules had gotten tighter. And since she had become engaged to Doc Fred, they had been spelled out strictly and clearly. No more going upstairs. For any reason whatever.

She would not have been there now had her fiancé not been too busy to meet her that evening—and had she not run into Ilimi, arms full of fluffy white towels and hopelessly out of breath. She was late, as usual, and her young man was going to be furious.

Maria smiled. Having been promised in marriage to the son of one of the more important *alii*, who had recently been converted and was taking Christian values enthusiastically to heart, Ilimi did not actually work in the rooms upstairs. But neither she nor her intended saw any harm in picking up a little extra cash running errands and fetching and carrying, though Maria noticed he tended to get abusive when her other occupations made her keep him waiting too long.

"Here, let me take those," she said, grabbing the towels and a bar of scented soap from the flustered Ilimi. "I swear, you couldn't be on time if your life depended on it. Hurry now—I can take these upstairs. To the bath? It's not yet occupied, I trust?"

Ilimi nodded. "I think it's being prepared for someone important. Maybe one of the Barron captains ... but he shouldn't be there yet. Your mother is going to have us both whipped if she finds out about this. She meant what she said about your never going upstairs again."

"My mother is in the kitchen, having a set-to with the new cook, who naturally can't do *anything* right! And Dud is in the bar, standing drinks for some of his cronies—so you can imagine where he'll be for the next seven or eight hours. Get along with you now. You know you're dying to go."

For all her bravado, Maria nonetheless cast a nervous look over her shoulder before she started up the stairs. No one was in sight, and she breathed easier. It would take only a minute or two, then she'd be back down again, and neither her mother nor stepfather would be any the wiser.

The bath was at the near end of the hall. One of the larger rooms, though it held only a copper tub with a stool next to it and a high rectangular table some distance away for towels and toiletries. Maria took a quick peek through the door. It appeared to be empty, and she stepped hastily inside. There was a candle here, too, a single flame, set on the broad sill of a window that had been shuttered to exclude all but a few faint rays of sunlight.

She had almost reached the table and was about to place the towels on it when she heard a faint splashing behind her. Turning, she saw a head she had not noticed before sticking up from the high-sided tub. Dark hair, touched with gray at the temples, set off dark eyes that seemed to glow black in the shadows.

Attached to the head was a pair of shoulders, which, though she could only see a small portion of them, were very clearly naked.

Maria recognized the man instantly. James Royall Perralt was the most prominent citizen in that small community, where everyone knew at least a fair portion of everyone else's business. He came from an old French family in Charleston, it was said, supposedly of noble background, though he had actually been born in La Louisiane, which made him a citizen not of the United States but France.

Shielded from the lustier parts of his physique by the tub, Maria dared, just for a second, to let herself wonder about him. He was the only *haole* landholder on the island, having talked the Hawaiian governor into some property, where he was reputed to be experimenting with sugarcane. He had used his personal fortune—which must have been considerable—to turn the plantation, Honuakula, into a breathtaking showcase, though, Maria, of course had never seen it. She did recall his wife, an exotic but cheap-looking Frenchwoman who had run off years ago with someone else and been killed during a storm at sea.

In spite of herself, Maria was intrigued. Every instinct told her she ought to drop the towels and run. Even naive as she was, she knew it was wildly inappropriate to remain alone in a room with a man who had not a stitch on.

But he was French—even though he didn't have the appropriate accent—and she had heard that those wine-drinking, womanizing, papist devils were the most unashamedly debauched creatures on earth. The only "Frenchies" she had ever seen were sailors on some of the cruder vessels, which was hardly the same thing, and she couldn't help being curious.

It was that curiosity which proved her undoing. She must have taken a step forward, for he loomed halfway out of the tub. Maria could see nearly down to his waist. He was not young, but he kept himself fit, and quite startlingly tan, and she was not finding him altogether unpleasing to look at.

"I-I just brought the t-towels," she said clumsily. She tried to move back, but she stumbled and nearly fell. "Nice and soft ... our very best. And p-perfumed soap. All the way f-from Paris."

She felt a terrible fool, stammering and tripping all over her words, but he seemed more amused than annoyed. He started to laugh, a not altogether comforting sound.

"Am I such a monster, red? Here I thought my body was in good condition. Is it my face that dismays you? ... Or are you so besotted at the sight of my male virility you can barely speak? No, no—don't leave the towels all the way over there. Put them here. On the stool where we can reach them later. And the soap. I'm sure we can find some, uh, interesting uses for it."

When Maria did not reply but stood there, trying desperately to think of some way to get out of the room without offending him—her mother would surely hear then where she had been!—the rakish leer on his dark features turned to irritation.

"Have you lost your tongue? Or don't you understand simple English? I told you to bring those things over here!"

There was a sharp edge of command to his tone, and Maria's feet moved automatically. She realized her mistake only when she had nearly reached him.

One strong hand shot out, grabbing her arm and pulling her roughly almost against him.

"Please, sir . . ." she gasped, suddenly frightened as the towels fell from her grip to the floor. "Let me go."

"I said come *here*, and I meant it." His eyes were black with some suppressed emotion Maria could not identify. More anger, it seemed, than lust. "I don't like playing games. I like my women hot and ready. Didn't they tell you?"

"I'm not here for—*that*," she murmured. "I just came to bring the towels. I didn't know you—I didn't know anyone—would be here."

He was looking at her strangely, as if trying to figure something out. Then slowly a light began to dawn.

"*Maria. . . ?*"

She nodded, and he laughed again, darkly.

"By God, you've filled out nicely. I almost didn't know you. Who would have thought that scrawny little carrot-top would turn into such a beauty? . . . So your stepfather has you working for him, does he? And that's all right with Mama? Well, never mind. Their lack of parental niceties seems to be my gain."

He was dragging her down, using both hands now, even before Maria could take in his words. She tried to pull away, but she couldn't break his hold.

"You want to come in the water with me?" he suggested lewdly. "Have a nice bath first? . . . It's amazing what you can do with a bar of soap. . . . No? You just want to get on with it?" He was rising out of the tub, still grasping her tightly. Maria was horribly aware of the warmth and wetness of his body. "All right, honey, that's just fine with me."

"No . . ." Maria struggled, but her mouth was pressed against his shoulder, and the word came out muffled. His hands were groping under the loose Hawaiian gown she almost always wore, and she wished fervently she had put on a corset and every bit of underclothing she owned! Anything to slow him down, though she sensed he was so aroused even that would not have stopped him.

His fingers brushed against her breast—the gown was almost up to her shoulders now—and a fleeting memory of the way Keahi had touched her sent unexpected little shivers through her. This was what she had lain awake imagining all those long nights alone in her bed. This was what she had yearned for with the man who was so soon to be her husband.

It was only a moment, but Royall seemed to sense the change in her, and whatever little chance there had been that he might relent and let her go was lost. She had not been responding to him; she had been responding to the bewildering new ripening of her own body, but he had no way of knowing that, nor would he have cared if he had. He was inflamed with desire, and impatient at her continuing resistance.

"I told you," he said hoarsely, "I tolerate no games." One hand tangled in her hair roughly, forcing her face up to his even as they sank together on the soft towels on the floor. "You want this. I felt you trembling before. You want it as much as I do. You can hardly wait for it."

I *don't* want it, Maria longed to cry out. I don't! But in a terrible, humiliating way she knew that she did. She was young, eager, curious. She did want to learn about passion—but not like this! Not crudely, savagely, without a shred of tenderness. Surely he understood that!

She felt the towels beneath her now, the weight of him on top. She tried to protest, but he must have heard that first faint whimper, for his hand clamped tightly over her mouth. Maria had one brief glimpse of his erection, massive and terrifying—she thought she had never seen anything so huge—and then her body was being ripped apart, suddenly and excruciatingly.

"Oh!" she gasped, and was surprised that the sound came out. Apparently he had removed his hand in the consuming ardor of the brutal assault. Just for a second he seemed to hesitate, as if startled. "You hurt me," she protested. "Oh, please ... it hurts so much."

"Only for a minute." The words came in sharp, rhythmic pants with his breath as he drove into her again, seeming even more excited. "Just a minute, then you'll be begging for more. You're going to love it."

Keahi's words, or close enough, and in a strange, terrifying way they were partly true. Maria's mind rebelled at what this man was doing to her—her heart was sick with horror—but her body perversely, treacherously, was aching to respond. The pain had subsided; in its place was a new burning sensation that called up needs and feelings she could neither understand nor control.

If only he would whisper one word of love.... Maria longed to reach out of herself, to search for something beyond that pile of towels on the dirty floor, sodden with her own maiden blood. If he would be gentle, thoughtful, caring. If he would just stop for a moment and hold her in his arms, murmuring to her, caressing ...

Then, abruptly, she heard a hoarse grunt and he was pulling out of her. Maria felt something hot and sticky spilling onto her belly, and all the sweet illusory longing was gone. Only shame and disgust remained.

How could she have imagined, even for an instant, that the invasion of her body by such a man could approximate lovemaking? She turned away and curled into a little wounded ball, hating herself almost as much as him for the ugly violation she had been powerless to resist.

She had not even dreamed it could be like this! She began to sob uncontrollably, not caring who heard or what anyone thought. Intimacy between a man and a woman was supposed to be beautiful. Fulfilling. She was not supposed to feel used and humiliated. He had not even cared enough afterward to take a minute to comfort her!

She was too wrapped up in her own misery to hear the faint scrape of the door as it opened, but nothing could have blocked out the shriek that followed.

Startled, Maria looked up—and saw her mother staring into the room. Lena Owen's normally lustrous brown eyes were flashing black with fury.

She thinks I did this deliberately, Maria thought, and realized helplessly that she had brought it on herself. Her flirtation with Keahi, the way she had pressed Doc Fred to move up their wedding date— no wonder her mother thought her an incorrigible wanton. She lowered her eyes guiltily, waiting for the tongue-lashing that was sure to come.

But Lena did not waste more than a brief glance on her daughter. She was neither stupid nor ingenuous. Maria's tears, the dress bunched up over her breasts, the red marks not yet turning to bruises, the bloody towels, told her only too well what had happened. And she knew exactly who was to blame.

"You swine!" She hurled herself at Royall Perralt, beating ineffectually with her fists against his chest. "You animal. You—*bastard!* That's my daughter you have ruined. My own innocent little girl. I could kill you for this!"

"Here, here," Royall cried petulantly. He raised his arms to deflect her attack, which he managed quite easily, for anger had left her so blind she hardly knew what she was doing. "I had no way of knowing the girl was a virgin. How should I? In a place like this. . . . And I don't think she's really quite as innocent as you make out."

"Animal!" Lena hissed. She threw out her arm toward where Maria still cowered unhappily on the floor. "Pig! You can see she's never been with a man. And look at those marks. You had to use force. You are an *animal*!"

"And you are getting repetitious ... and rather boring." He turned and looked at Maria with an oddly speculative expression. Suddenly she felt naked, as she never had before in the surf and on the beaches of that uninhibited isle. Clutching her dress awkwardly, she pulled it down as best she could, but he had shifted his gaze back to her mother and was not looking at her anymore.

"I do acknowledge, however," he was saying, "that I have wronged the girl, albeit unknowingly. I am prepared to make it right."

"Make it *right*?" Rage and indignation quavered in Lena Owen's voice. "You think all you have to do is offer cash, and everything will be all right? Tell me, you son of a bitch, will cash make my daughter whole again? Will it give her back the opportunities she has lost today—and for what? Five minutes of gross amusement, if it even lasted that long! This is my *daughter*! Her life is never going to be the same again. You think you can offer me *cash*, and I will say, Oh, what the hell, it doesn't matter?"

There was more pain than anger in her voice—not for herself but for the daughter whose life would "never be the same again"—and Maria realized for the first time that her mother did love her. It seemed a cruel way to find out.

Royall's expression had turned cold at Lena's taunts, but he was not backing off. "You wrong me, madam, if you think I am such a fool. I do not for a moment believe that cash will atone for what has taken place here. I was offering, naturally, to make it right in the only way possible."

"You mean ..." Lena's expression wavered. Wariness came into her eyes, and her lips pursed unconsciously. Maria felt the first twinges of apprehension as she looked from one to other and back again.

"But certainly," Royall replied. "Make what arrangements you choose, and I will honor them. I ask only that there be no undue delay. I think under the circumstances, that, uh, would be wise."

"I think, under the circumstances," Lena agreed, "perhaps you are right," and Maria, seeing the relief that flooded over her face, understood at last what was going on. A bargain had been struck between her mother and this man—and she was the object of that bargain.

Her honor had not, after all, been bartered away for cash. The medium of exchange was love and genuine concern—but the result would be the same.

She was going to marry Royall Perralt.

The wedding was set for six weeks from that afternoon. Maria was not, after all, to be quite sixteen when she walked down the aisle.

Surprisingly, it was her stepfather who objected to this when the subject was broached. "Don't like the man," he said gruffly. "Never have. He be a bad drinker."

"You've been known to have a bit too much yourself," his wife reminded him. "On occasion." She was much too pleased with the way things had turned out to be annoyed at this unexpected obstinacy. "As I recall, more than one concerned soul tried to warn me off when I insisted on marrying *you*."

"Aye, but the bottle affects men in different ways. I be a good, cheerful drunk. I like to have fellows around me, and bawdy women who know how to laugh. He turns morose, that one, and locks himself in, they say, for days at a time. Get the doctor to take her anyway. He's a good man. He'll not hold what happened against her."

"They say, they say!" Lena sniffed contemptuously. "If rumors were gold pieces, this town would be the richest place on earth. The doctor may be a good man, but he's dull as last week's leftovers, God help him—and poor as a church mouse and always will be. Don't you see, Dud? My daughter has a chance to be mistress of Honuakula. Acres of sugarcane, a magnificent mansion, every luxury money can buy—how can a stone cottage compare with that?''

"Better a humble abode with a man who cares," he replied glumly. "What good will all that fancy frippery do the girl if he does not treat her well?''

"It's more than 'frippery'—and Maria will have no cause to complain about him, thank you! Royall Perralt is a gentleman. Doesn't he always treat the girls properly when he comes here ... well, except for some of the rougher ones, and then what do you expect? She'll have a grand life with him. I know she will. I couldn't have hoped for anything better!''

Her mother's enthusiasm had a way of being contagious, and there were times when even Maria almost found herself looking forward to the wedding, though she had distinctly mixed feelings about the man she was to marry.

Objectively observed, she had to admit Royall was not a bad catch. He was much too old for her, perhaps thirty years her senior, but he still looked lean and virile, and with his dark hair and eyes and swarthy, tanned complexion, he was more than passably handsome. His manners were flawless, his courtesy, after that first, abrupt encounter, unfailing. And he had agreed to do the honorable thing. What more could any woman reasonably expect?

The plans for the wedding proceeded in a flurry of last-minute activity. Dud had taken upon himself the unpleasant task of notifying Doc Fredericks, for which Maria would be eternally grateful. She didn't know how she could have faced him; indeed, it would be months before she could even look at him when they passed on the street.

He had taken the news with characteristic generosity. Sensing her embarrassment, he had not confronted her, but had penned a kind, tactful note. If she was pleased with the arrangement, he wrote, then he was happy for her. If not—if she had any qualms, any doubts at all—he would be there. She had only to come to him.

But how could she when she couldn't even admit her qualms to herself? Maria had no idea whether she really wanted to marry Royall Perralt, whether she could love or like or even tolerate him, but she was not to be given the opportunity to question her feelings. Lena, determined there would be no repeat of that previous outrage, made sure her daughter was not left alone for a moment, even ordering one of the servants to sleep in her room at night, and Maria barely managed to exchange a few perfunctory words with the man who would occupy the rest of her life.

She did not truly notice the lack. There was a whirlwind tour of Honuakula, which proved even larger and more opulent than she had imagined; there were dinners and luncheons and parties on the beach, and most of the time she was too caught up in the excitement to think or worry about what lay ahead.

Just sometimes she would catch Royall looking at her from across the room, very strangely, and a funny little shiver would run down her spine.

She couldn't help remembering the terrible humiliation she had felt after he had used her and left her lying alone on the brothel floor. But she remembered, too, that brief moment his touch had excited her, and she tried to cling to that. If he treated her differently now ... if he made her feel cherished ... if he took the time to be tender ...

And surely he would. He had possessed her casually before, like the whore he had every reason to believe she was. This time he would be coming to his wife.

The woman with whom he had chosen to spend the rest of his life ... the woman he loved, or hoped he would come to love as the days—and nights— brought them closer together.

Surely he would caress her first, whisper sweet words in her ear, prepare her with infinite patience for the tantalizing delights she had only begun to glimpse.

Those pretty illusions were shattered on her wedding night. It was nearly dawn before Royall finally came to her room. Maria had been lying in bed in the filmy silk gown Ilimi had helped her put on, her back propped against a pile of pillows, waiting nervously—and wondering as time went by if something was wrong. Had she displeased her new husband in some way and he had decided not to come?

Then the door opened, and he appeared, dressed only in a nightshirt, with a candle in his hand, which he set unsteadily on a table under the window.

A candle again, Maria thought helplessly. She could smell liquor on him, and even naive as she was, she sensed it was not a good sign. There had been brandy and fine champagne at the gala that followed the wedding, the only concession to Royall's French heritage, for, surprisingly, he had not even suggested a papist ceremony. But it was not wine she sniffed now, or brandy. It was the familiar aroma of *okolehao*. A crude, extremely potent native drink which gentlemen and even most of the sailors avoided unless nothing else was available. Or they wanted to get very drunk.

There were no caresses, no sweet, whispered words, no attempts to make a frightened young bride feel cherished. He simply climbed into bed, pulled up his nightshirt and her gown, ground himself against her in a hard, furious rhythm ... and failed utterly to accomplish anything more than their mutual embarrassment.

Maria did not know how long he tried. It must have been at least thirty minutes, perhaps an hour— still not a word had passed between them—when at last he got up, he took the candle again, and without looking back, went through the door and closed it behind him.

Maria lay on the rumpled sheets, trembling, and watched as the light came slowly through the window. She did not know what had just happened. She was too inexperienced to understand the complexities of a man's physical makeup. She knew only that this wasn't how she was supposed to spend her wedding night, and she didn't dare let herself think about what might be yet to come.

Royall was properly apologetic the next day. He did not appear until well after noon, and then he was pale and somewhat shaky. But instead of avoiding her, as Maria had half expected, he sought her out where she was sitting in the garden.

"Any man who drinks at his wedding is a damned fool," he said bluntly. "Alcohol may increase expectations, but it greatly diminishes performance."

Recalling the lusty behavior of some of the sailors who barely managed to crawl up the steps to the rooms over the tavern, Maria was not so sure. But as Dud had said, the bottle affected men in different ways, and she didn't want to make things any more uncomfortable than they already were.

"I expect you are right," she agreed. "I have heard it said often enough that some men should not drink."

A look of amusement came over his face. "And I am one of them," he replied dryly. "As I clearly proved last night. I shall do my utmost to redeem myself . . . later."

As it turned out, he did not. For all his good intentions, Maria noticed that the odor of drink accompanied him once again as he came to her room. He had not imbibed as much perhaps, but the result was the same. Try as he would, he could not manage an erection, though he spent several hours on the effort, forcing Maria to perform intimacies that were embarrassing and increasingly distasteful.

And completely useless.

No matter what she did—no matter what he insisted on—his male organ just lay there, soft and pink, curled up in its nest of dark hair. Maria thought about how massive it had looked before, rock hard and menacing . . . and how puny it seemed now. And wondered which disgusted her most.

He tried again for three more nights before finally giving up. When he left the room the last time, both of them knew he would not be coming back. Even his male pride had to admit that passion between them was not going to work.

This time he was drunk for a week. When he finally sobered up, he forced himself to face her again. It was not easy for him. Maria understood that, and she tried not to hate him too much as he came to her in the small morning room off the rear parlor.

It was a pretty room, with sunlight streaming in. She had always liked it there before.

"I'm sorry, Maria," he said quietly. "I honestly didn't believe this would happen again. I would never have married you if I had."

"Again . . . ?" Maria's knees felt weak and she had to sit down. What was he saying? *Again?* "You mean it's happened before?"

He was looking at her strangely. "What have they told you about my previous life? Not much, I'll wager . . . although I was relatively honest with your mother. I have been married twice, before Claudine—whom you probably remember. The first was a long time ago. In Charleston. I was not much older than you are now. You can probably guess what happened."

Maria was silent. She sensed what it was costing him, this brutal frankness about his own failings, and in a way she had to admire him for it. But she was not sure she wanted his confidences.

He seemed to understand what she was thinking. "The girl was my parents' choice, but I was not reluctant. She was a pretty little thing, from a family even more prominent than mine. I thought I was looking forward to the wedding night. I had had some experience ... in the usual places. But she just lay there, shivering—she was terrified of me—and I couldn't make myself do a blasted thing!"

He went over to the window and leaned against the sill with both hands, looking out. His back was straight beneath a broadcloth jacket, too warm for the day.

"She was sent back to her family in the morning. There was no blood on the wedding sheets, you see ... her purity had not been proved. The marriage was dissolved. Her people could not object. There was a legitimate question about her maidenhood— there had been an uncle, apparently, with perverted tendencies—but that was not the reason for the lack of blood. They knew it and we knew it. Nasty little truths like that have a way of being whispered about. I was sent to live with a branch of my father's family in Louisiana, where I had been born."

He turned to look back at her. His features were strained and harsh with the light behind him.

"It happened again there. I married a very beautiful second cousin. I thought I was besotted with her. I had erotic dreams about her every night. My bed linen was disgusting. But the time came, and I looked at her and I thought, 'This is my *wife*' ... and God help me, the idea left me emasculated."

Maria found her eyes drifting toward an ornately carved *koa* table on the far wall. This man was her husband—she was going to spend the rest of her life with him—and she couldn't even bear to look at him.

"You don't have to tell me these things, Royall—" she started to say, but he cut her off.

"You have a right to the truth. That's the least I can do. All my ugly little secrets bared for you. . . . That marriage was dissolved, too, though for the appropriate reason. It was, as you can imagine, impossible for me to remain in Louisiana after that."

"Or to return to Charleston . . ."

"Or return to Charleston," he agreed. "I was given a portion of my inheritance in advance so I could start again someplace else. And I'm sent generous sums at periodic intervals to make sure I'm never tempted to embarrass my relatives by trying to go back."

"And yet you married again?" Maria said, curious in spite of herself.

"Ah, yes—Claudine. She wasn't a lady like the others. She was a regular slut, just right for me. As you may have gathered, I have no trouble at all when it comes to whores. . . . A common little thing, Claudine Doral, she was . . . much too clever for her own good. She was afraid if she gave herself to me first, my lust would be slaked and I wouldn't marry her. . . . Unfortunately, it was *after* the wedding that the slaking occurred."

"So she left you?"

"Naturally. Claudine was a greedy creature, but her greed was more for sex than gold. I wasn't sorry when she left. It was a relief. And I won't pretend I was sorry when I heard she had died. . . . But I honestly thought things would be different with you, Maria. I was so sure. I had already had you once. My masculinity had responded. Swiftly. There had been no problem then. I thought . . . I hoped I was finally going to break that vicious circle."

Maria remembered the way she had caught him looking at her sometimes, and at last she understood. "But you didn't?" she said softly.

"No, I didn't. And I regret that deeply." He started to laugh, mirthlessly under his breath. "I've often thought how ironic it is. I'm as amply endowed as a

man can be—the chits in the whorehouse always
squeal and pretend to be alarmed at my size—and I
can't even manage the most rudimentary coupling
with my own wife. . . . Am I being too blunt? I'm
sorry, my dear. Bluntness is to be the only way I can
handle it. I have, it seems, one small quirk. I can't
make love to a good woman. And even a Protestant
service automatically makes her 'good.' "

He went over to the bell pull and tugged sharply.
"Some tea for you? I think you could use it. And I
can use a drink. Brandy this time—don't look so
alarmed. No *okolehao*, I promise you."

The servant came in, a young man Maria did not
know. Royall gave him the order and waited until
he was gone before turning back to his wife.

"I'm sorry this has happened, but it has. There'll
be no dissolution this time. The relationship *was* con-
summated, if somewhat before the ceremony." His
voice turned cool, impersonal, the soul-searching
over, as if he had dismissed it as unprofitable. "I'm
afraid you're stuck with me. A bad bargain, but that's
the way it is. I'll do my best to make it up to you."

A brisk breeze wafted up the hillside, whipping
Maria's hair around her face and calling her sharply
back to the present. The sun was well above the horizon now; the dawn shadows were crisply delineated,
and the sea was bright and glittering. Clouds had
begun to drift in from the east.

In his way, Royall had kept his word. Maria raised
a hand to brush the hair back from her cheek. If he
couldn't offer her a complete marriage, at least he
could lavish on her every extravagance money could
buy, and he did.

A party gown in the latest ladies' book from Paris
had caught her fancy? It was made up immediately,
in tissue bayadere or mousseline de soie. She longed
for glittering jewels? There were diamonds in her
ears, emeralds at her wrist, and a necklace fashioned

of perfect deep blue sapphires, set with stones of a slightly paler hue to match the color of her eyes. She had an exquisite house, exquisitely furnished, all the latest conveniences, servants at her beck and call any hour of the day or night, everything a woman could possibly want except passion and love. And companionship.

She had tried to talk to Royall at first, and to be fair, he had tried to talk to her. But except when he spoke of his feeling for the land—the crops he was planting and the natural world he cherished and took surprising care not to damage or destroy—they had little in common. As the weeks had passed, the silences between them had grown longer and longer, and Royall had begun spending most of his time in the plantation office in a separate building behind the main house. He had even taken to having his dinners brought in, and Maria had been so relieved she had barely realized how lonely she was.

He had only come to her as a man one more time. He had a deep hunger for a son—visible proof, Maria supposed, of the virility he longed for but did not possess. Or perhaps he simply had the natural male craving to pass on his name. At any rate, the subject had arisen with increasing frequency. He had even begun to hint darkly that he wouldn't mind if she had a brief affair, as long as she took care to be discreet—and the resulting issue was assumed to be his.

Maria was horrified. She already had bitter proof of how cruelly society treated sex outside of marriage. And that was when she had still been free! Now she had taken solemn vows before God and everyone who had been watching in the small mission church. She could not so easily forget that, nor could her honest spirit abide the tawdry cheapness and secrecy he suggested.

Royall had not been so easily thwarted. Maria shivered, just remembering, all these years later. When he had realized he was not going to get her into another man's bed, he had determined to try with her again. Thinking a bawdier location might help, he arranged with her parents to return to the brothel bath, saying he wanted to relive "precious memories." They must have had qualms—what reasonable people wouldn't?—but how could they refuse now that he was her husband?

It was even more brutal than she had imagined. He dosed her almost to the point of nausea with the purplish-red fruit of the *pu'aha-nui* shrub, said to aid in conception, dressed her in satin and black lace, and forced her to do things that turned her stomach even more. She was nearly overcome with despair by the time he finally convinced himself she was someone else and managed to get hard enough to drive his engorged member into her.

Maria felt all over again the disgust and humiliation. There were some things time didn't diminish. She had been his wife that day—he had rights to her body—but it seemed even more like rape than that first savage attack. She vowed then that, pregnant or not—no matter what happened—she would never, *never* let him touch her again. She would die before she could ever relive that horrible degradation!

It had been barely two weeks later when she had stood in the doorway of the plantation office, catching a faint whiff of exotic perfume which mingled cloyingly with the floral scent of the garden, and learned that Royall Perralt still had one last ugly secret he had been hiding from her.

A sharp pain jabbed through her hand. Maria looked down, surprised to find that she was still clutching the thorny-stemmed roses. With an effort she forced her fingers to relax.

She had been so excited when she had stumbled on to the truth. She had been so sure it would set her free. It seemed the answer to everything. How could Royall possibly expect her to remain with him after what she had just discovered?

There will be no dissolution this time, he had said. But that had been mere bravado. He couldn't keep her from having this marriage set aside, for it had been based on the one lie that was absolutely guaranteed to invalidate it. Neither God nor the laws of man could hold her to it.

Maria let her gaze drift back to the garden. The roses, still moist with dew, looked so pretty in the morning light. She had been so sure . . . and she had been wrong. The one thing she had not counted on was Royall's iron will. Appearances had to be maintained at all costs. He was not going to be run out of town by shameful gossip again.

She had learned his last—and most vulnerable— secret, but she couldn't prove it. Without proof it would be her word against his. Maria could well imagine what people would think if she came out with such a wildly groundless accusation. She would look like a hysterical young woman. And he would look the aggrieved husband, patiently trying to deal with her fancies, seeking help from the missionary doctor perhaps when she got too far out of hand.

Even her mother and stepfather wouldn't believe her. How could they, especially since Royall had seen to it that their business affairs were tied intrinsically with his own benevolent interest? He had been extremely generous with his cash, winning over even her reluctant stepfather by financing lavish expansion and several new buildings. But he now owned part of everything that had been theirs, and Maria was bitterly aware that he could call in the debt at will.

"Try to expose me," he had warned her, "and I'll ruin you. And everyone you care about. Keep your mouth shut . . . and I'll continue to buy all the diamonds you want."

As if diamonds mattered! Maria had loathed him at that moment—as she had ever since—more than she had thought she could ever loathe any human being. It was not the jewels and the gowns that held her back. It was not even her parents' welfare. It was simply the commonsense realization that no one would believe her anyway.

Royall would keep his threat. She knew that. He would inflict all the pain he could. And it would have been for nothing.

At least *she* knew the truth.

Maria set the roses down on a low wall beside the house and tried to think if she needed to do anything else before she left. There was some small comfort in having the truth for herself. In the eyes of the world she might be the wife of James Royall Perralt. But in her own eyes, in her own heart, she knew she was free.

There had been no commitments—she had belonged to no one, she had owed no one anything—that morning she had looked up from a cool mountain pond and seen a tall, sandy-haired man with a devilish glint in his eye . . .

"Mama!"

Maria looked down the hillside at a small boy cutting impatiently through guinea grass and *pua-kala* poppies because the curves on the path took too long. Royall had gotten the son he wanted. A spirited seven-year-old with unruly copper-bright hair that flew in every direction in the breeze.

"Mama!" he called again. "Where *are* you? I've been looking everywhere for you!"

"Up here, Mack. In Grandmother's rose garden. What on earth has you in such a dither?"

Maria smiled as the boy reached the fence and, instead of going ten steps around to the gate, scrambled over the pickets. It was amazing, the energy of a child. He must have run all the way from the town house, on the other side of Lahaina, and he barely seemed out of breath.

"I saw the carriage below, so I knew you were

somewhere around. Ilimi sent me to find you. The boys are going surfing. She said I could go with them—they promised to teach me!—if you said it was all right. Can I go, Mama? Can I?"

His excitement brimmed over, making it impossible for him to stand still. "Well, what do you think I'm going to say to that?" she teased. Ilimi's marriage had not worked out, and she had come back with her four sons to work in Maria's household. A good arrangement for both of them, for they both needed a friend, and the boys were good playmates for Mack.

"I think *yes!*" Big blue-gray eyes glowed with the confidence of a child who knows he is loved. Royall liked to say his mother had eyes that color, Maria thought irrelevantly. Perhaps he was right.

"You're very sure of yourself." She laughed. "Oh, all right, all right, you can go. Just hold on until I wrap these stems in some wet newspaper. Ilimi will see that the boys wait for you . . . and we wouldn't want the roses to dry out. Go inside and see if you can find something to hold them so I won't get black smudges all over my hands and skirt."

Maria suppressed a grin as he raced into the house. He had been dying to protest—she had seen it in that bright little face—but he had realized, wisely for his seven and a half years, that it would only take longer if he did. Royall, to give him his due, had been a good father, at least when he was sober. He was strict and had no gift for warmth, but he spent time with young Mack, teaching him about nature and farming, and the boy looked up to him.

She had barely finished wrapping the roses when Mack reappeared with an old pewter pitcher. Hardly what she would have chosen, but it would serve as a makeshift vase. A small whirlwind of vitality and red hair was already tumbling down the hillside toward the carriage before she even got a firm hold on the handle.

Tucking the roses into the pitcher, Maria threw one

last quick look at the house to make sure Mack had closed the door behind him. The clouds were getting heavier now; she could smell the promise of rain in the air. As she turned back, her eye fell on the ship in the harbor again.

The *Shadow Dawn.* . . . Of course. That was why the memories had been plaguing her all morning. The *Shadow* and its captain, Jared Barron, whom she had glimpsed occasionally in town. She had only seen him from a distance, but he had made her heart stop more than once. Something in his looks, his bearing . . . What was there about these tall, arrogant, granite-hard Yankee men that made them seem so much alike?

She had thought once that she had met one who was different. Gentler, softer, more able to love and give. But she had been mistaken.

For a moment Maria stood absolutely still, everything else forgotten, even the flowers in the pewter vase. She had swallowed her pride the morning after that terrible dinner party and gone to tell Sandy everything and beg for his help.

Only when she had gotten to the harbor, she had looked out at the ocean . . . and the *Shadow* was gone.

They had sailed with the sunrise. Remembered tears stung Maria's eyes again. Or were they tears anew? He had left without so much as a word. Not because he was angry, but because that was the way he had always intended it. He had never planned on saying good-bye.

Maria knew little about ships, but she knew they did not move about capriciously. They kept to charts and schedules. Common sailors could hardly get their vessels to weigh anchor at a moment's notice because they felt thwarted by ladies who had played them false.

Sandy had known all along that the *Shadow Dawn* would be leaving in the morning! He had known the last time they had been together, and he had not even had the kindness to warn her.

She had stood on the beach, as she stood now in her mother's garden, feeling utterly betrayed once again by a man. He had told her that their lovemaking was not a mere dalliance for him. He had implied he wanted much, much more . . .

But he had only been playing man-games with her. Saying what he thought she wanted to hear. Because he knew very well what he wanted from her!

She had been a fool to love him. She realized that now, from the vantage point of time and bitterly earned maturity. She had been a fool to listen to his treacherous, honeyed words. A fool to trust him, just because she had wanted to so desperately. She would never let herself love or trust a man again.

"Mama!" The impatient protest came from halfway down the slope. "Do stop pokeying around! I swear, you're the *pokiest* creature on earth!"

Maria's expression softened as she looked at her son. It had not been for nothing, after all. The pain and humiliation. She had a child she loved—beyond the love she could ever have felt for any man—and that was enough.

It was not the past that was foolish, but continuing to dwell on what was over. Her life was here and now, and its core was this precious treasure that was more than a compensation for everything else. She would nourish him and protect him, and make a better job of it than her mother had with her. No one would ever hurt or frighten him as long as there was a breath left in her body.

"I'm coming, Mack," she called down.

Chapter 4

Alex Barron stood at the helm of the mighty *Jade Dawn*, the flagship of the Barron line, and squinted into the morning sun. The Hawaiian Islands had barely been dots against the billowing gray clouds on the horizon only an hour before. Now he could make them out clearly. Lanai to starboard, and Kahoolawe—Molokai just port of the narrow channel, and beyond, Maui with its harbor at Lahaina.

No one watching would have taken him for anything but a seaman and a Barron. He was a tall man, straight-backed and strong, with an unmistakable air of command. His features were rugged, like the rocky New England soil that had nurtured that iron-willed, arrogant clan; his skin had a mariner's deep tan, and little lines were beginning to form in the flesh around his eyes. The collar of a lightweight jacket was turned up, and an erratic wind caught sun-streaked brown hair and blew it back from his face.

Lanai loomed larger, just ahead. They were making good time despite an occasional lull. Alex frowned faintly as he picked out the shoreline that fronted Lahaina in the distance. Visions of cheap taverns came into his mind, raucous saloons with brawling sailors spilling out onto the street, and the tinny sound of music punctuated by wheedling cries as women, not always young anymore, leaned enticingly out of second-story windows.

The men were excited at their approach. Alex

could feel it in the way they sprang jauntily into the rigging, setting to their tasks with more of a will than usual. The island had long been a favorite spot for making repairs to the ship and taking on provisions—to the crew it was the nearest thing to paradise on earth—but Alex had learned to see it with different eyes.

The thought was oppressive, and he shrugged it off with the jacket which had gotten too warm in the sultry sea air. He was feeling tired and jaded suddenly. Almost old enough to be what he was. A senior captain of one of the most prominent shipping lines in the world.

The sleek-hulled clipper listed slightly, and Alex called out to the helmsmen, making an adjustment to their course. He was not officially in command of this particular vessel. That honor went to his younger cousin, Matthew, though in reality the duties had been divided between the two men on the voyage from Hong Kong. Or more accurately, since Matthew was traveling with his very lovely bride, Rachel, Alex had taken most of the duties on his own broad shoulders.

"Here, cousin—what do you think you're doing?" a voice shouted over the wind and the groaning of the sails and shrouds. "What's this madcap speed? And with land so near? You'll be running us aground on the rocks if you're not careful."

Alex grinned as he turned to see Matthew Barron coming up beside him. It was a longstanding joke between them. It was he, in fact, who was cautious, and Matthew the one whose impetuosity had more than once brought them to the brink of disaster.

"Point well taken," he replied with mock solemnity. "Shall I furl the sails now, Captain? We can sit and wait patiently for the tide to drift us in."

"Does the tide come out this far?" the younger man asked ingenuously.

"There's one way to find out."

Matthew laughed easily. He was the runt of the tall Barron clan, barely reaching six feet, and the one to whom laughter came the most naturally. With his blonde hair and blue eyes, he was also the most conventionally handsome, particularly since he had covered the stubborn Barron jaw with a neatly trimmed beard to please his young wife.

"It's been a long journey," he said. "For both of us. I was just thinking what it must have been like when you and Jared set out from Boston in the *Shadow Dawn*—what is it, ten months ago now?"

"It wasn't pretty," Alex replied with a slight grimace that held more humor than annoyance. Old Gareth Barron, the patriarch of the clan, had been furious when he had heard that Matthew had had the impertinence to take a cargo of opium into the hold of his ship. Not because he had had any qualms about the morality of it, but because he had been afraid mounting public opinion would diminish his proud clipper. And his profits! "To say that Grandfather was angry would be like saying a hurricane is a bit of a breeze. You were to be straightened out immediately! And Jared, being Jared, naturally felt he was the one to do it."

"My big brother does tend to react that way." Matthew threw him a curious sidelong look. "You must have been angry yourself. You were supposed to be in command of the *Shadow*, and Jared didn't think twice about taking it away from you. Even though you were the elder and had more experience."

"I don't expect I was very gracious about it." Alex glanced automatically at the man he had stationed on the mainmast topgallant yard. Getting a signal that the harbor approach was going smoothly, he turned back to his cousin. "But Grandfather's mind was made up, and there had been enough divisiveness in the family as it was. Besides, Jared reminded me what it would be like if I had to carry him as a *passenger* on my ship."

Matthew laughed again, prompting Alex to laugh with him. "I can imagine. Jared is not very good at sitting back and letting other people give orders. There would have been mutiny or murder—or both! ... And it did come out all right in the end."

"It did indeed," Alex had to agree. Though partly due to luck. Jared had been sidetracked just long enough by a young Frenchwoman, Dominie d'Arielle, to give Matthew time to straighten himself out, and they had arrived in the new city of Hong Kong to find family honor already restored. "And not just 'all right'. You won your lovely Rachel ... and Jared and Dominie, I trust, are together now and disgustingly happy."

Matthew cast a thoughtful glance at the shore, still some distance away. He couldn't help remembering that Jared had last been seen sailing out of Hong Kong harbor like a madman in pursuit of Dominie, who had been abducted by a former suitor. "You do think she's safe, don't you? Jared did rescue her in time?"

"The man who took her wasn't a monster, Matt. Only an old fool infatuated with a beautiful young woman. He probably thought she'd been pirated by a bawdy blackguard with sin on his mind. Jared can look like a pirate, you know. And sin is never far from his thoughts."

"Or mine," Matthew replied with a rakish look. "Though sin is somewhat more restricted now that I'm married."

"And hardly 'sin' within the bounds of matrimony."

"Don't say that. You'll take away the excitement. I'm a Barron man, remember? I was born with the love of sin in my veins. I'll be blasted if I'm going to give up all that pleasurable titillation just because I have a wife. Especially a wife like Rachel." The rakish expression turned into a deliberately lecherous leer. "Marriage is not at all a dull institution, cousin. You ought to try it some time."

"Me? No, thank you. I think the Barrons have had enough excitement for awhile. The family couldn't stand another tempestuous romance."

Matthew gave him the condescending look of a man who has found his own happiness, and thus knows exactly what it will take to make everyone else happy.

"Romance doesn't *have* to be tempestuous. People do have normal courtships sometimes, with normal, contented marriages. There's something about a Barron male that makes him persist in doing everything the hard way, especially when it comes to love. If there's a straight path to something he wants, and a long way round where he can butt his head against a low stone wall—he'll take the long way. But you were always different. Never like the rest of us. You might do things the right way round for a change."

"And you might take the wheel—for the last time, Captain Barron. Lahaina is waiting. You have the rest of your life to savor being married and properly settled down. Bring your ship into anchorage, sir. Oh, and Matt . . . try not to run her aground."

He stood at the rail on the starboard side, where the approach to Lahaina would be clearly visible. An odd choice, unconsciously made, but he did not try to move. The city was still a blur, but he knew the ship could be seen from the beach. Crowds would be already gathering to greet it.

It occurred to him, as it had often enough these past weeks, that the one of the Barron men with no great passion for the sea was the one who was destined to remain a captain. Matthew would be returning to Hong Kong to manage the company's affairs in the Orient—Barron Shipping had already been renamed Barron International in anticipation of global expansion—and Jared would be bringing his wife back to their headquarters in Boston. An old seadog turned landlubber—he would probably accept it about as graciously as their grandfather had. Dominie would have her hands full.

And the one of the Barron men who least relished his bachelorhood was the one who would not be relinquishing it. There had been a time once when he had thought things were different. When he had thought . . .

But that time was long ago, and there was no going back.

People do have normal courtships, and normal, happy marriages . . . You just might do things the right way round.

Only Barron men never did things the easy way. Hadn't Matthew pointed that out himself? Not where the heart was concerned. Old Gareth had started the tradition years ago—in another century—with his ill-fated passion for a flame-haired beauty named Dawn, who had tired of waiting for him to make his fortune and married someone else.

The story was etched in family history. Even the Gareth's subsequent marriage and the birth of his two sons—young Gareth, or Garth, Alex's father, and Asher who had been killed in a fall from a horse when his oldest son, Jared, was eight—had not soothed the sting. To this day, every vessel in the Barron line still carried the name "Dawn."

Not, as Matthew was fond of speculating, because the old pirate grieved for his first love—but because he wanted her to have constant, visible reminders of the wealth she had given up.

It was Gareth Barron's grandsons who now carried on the family penchant for stormy romance and women with hair the color of fire. Jared and his dramatically striking Dominie, with long auburn tresses and green eyes. Matthew with his pretty strawberry blonde. And Alex . . .

But Alex was the one who had always been different. He rested his hands on the rail, feeling the coolness in contrast to the tropical sun. Tempered by his mother's native Virginia, he had always been quieter. More inclined to turn his thoughts inward. A reticent man in a volatile clan ... the only Barron in whose veins the love of sin did not run.

He cast a practiced eye again at the masts. The men were poised to take in the sails. It was not that he was above a bit of bawdy pleasure, God knows. A lovely lady had been known to turn an ugly port into a pleasurable memory. But casual bawdiness was kept in a strictly compartmentalized place in his view of the nature of things. It had nothing to do with love. Love meant purity and honor. And trust.

The islands had gotten closer while he was looking away. They were passing through the channel now. Lahaina lay just ahead. Graceful arcs of palm trees were outlined distinctly against the pinkish white of the sand; he could see the foam on the combers as they broke along the shore. There were more buildings now than he had remembered, but Kamehameha's old brick palace still stood near the water's edge, behind its stunted pier.

He was getting too old. He was set in his ways. His ideals had become too rigid. No woman could possibly live up to them. He should have married when he was young, and said, "To hell with the sea," and found himself a piece of land somewhere.

He leaned forward, letting his eyes rest for a moment on the shore. Ordinarily he avoided Lahaina when he was in this part of the world, finding excuses to go instead to Honolulu, where he might confer with the American consul or watch the antics of the royal court. But he could hardly do that now, with both Jared and Matthew here.

He had no more time to dwell on his dislike for that small Pacific port in the next three-quarters of an hour. All hands were needed as a ship approached anchorage, even under the most placid conditions, and Matthew, true to his personal style, was making things more exciting than usual. The sails billowed and flapped in the wind, the rigging was groaning audibly as they skimmed over the water, full speed, holding their course straight for the surf. No timid effort for the last command of the boldest young captain of the line.

Alex grinned in spite of himself. He knew the impression they had to be making. Like a great white bird, effortlessly soaring on the crests of the waves. The scudding sails came in with a slap and a flutter, giving the clipper a leaner, smarter look, and she slowed, but just slightly. The grandest vessel ever to put into Lahaina, she carried more canvas than most of the men watching from shore had yet seen. Three tall masts, main, mizzen, and fore, each with the usual complement of sails, courses and topsails, royals, topgallants and skysails . . . and above them all, the moonraker—or skyscraper—that must have seemed as if it were brushing the clouds.

The speculation on shore would have turned by now to awe. Alex could almost hear the murmurs passing through that eager throng. Men would already be pushing their canoes into the water, great hollowed-out *koa* logs, and girls would be giggling and stripping off long, colorful dresses to the horror and despair of the missionaries.

The red-and-white flag of the Barron line would be plainly visible, flapping briskly in the wind and spray. The girls would know they were not welcome on board. Barron captains ran tight ships; their men were expected to restrict raunchier amusements to their own time on shore. But they would come anyway, out of curiosity and willfulness and a spirited determination not to be left out of anything. They would swim around the vessels; they would laugh and call up to the men, and make a game out of trying to climb the rope ladders. And more than one assignation for that evening would be made before they swam away again.

The ship lurched abruptly. Alex put a hand to the rail to steady himself as he felt their course change. Matthew, with impeccable timing, had waited until the last moment, then spun his vessel around, braking to a stop, and was now giving orders to furl the sails and drop anchor. His cousin gave him a silent inward salute. Leave it to Matt. Anyone else would have keeled badly with a maneuver like that.

The vessel had already been made fast by the time the first of the dugout canoes pulled alongside. Slip ropes and buoys had been bent to the cables, yard-arm gaskets cast off from the sails, and everything securely stopped with rope yarns when Alex looked up and saw Rachel coming toward him at the railing. Her hair was misted with spray—she must have been standing in the bow—and her eyes glittered with excitement. He recalled suddenly that she had been born in the islands and was, in a way, coming home.

"Look, Alex!" She was laughing like a little girl as she thrust her hand out, pointing toward the boat in the lead. "There they are! I knew they would be! Don't they look droll?"

He followed her gaze. The canoe had been outfitted as usual with a Chinese silk umbrella, gaudily tasseled in gold. But beneath it lounged not one of the massive *alii* but Jared and Dominie, wreathed in garlands of shimmering *maile* leaves twined around their necks. It seemed to him his cousin was looking especially smug and insufferable, even for a Barron.

"So we have a happy ending, after all." Alex was surprised at the intensity of the relief that flooded over him. He had not realized until that moment how worried he had been. "I should have known Jared would rescue his lady love with all due aplomb. And look unbearably self-satisfied in the bargain."

Relief turned to amusement as the dugout drifted aft and he got a closer look at Dominie. She was wearing a loose Hawaiian-style gown in a blend of greenish hues that suited her coloring. But even those generous folds could not hide the fact that her figure was considerably more ample than before.

So Jared's smugness had not been altogether for the heroics of his rescue. The next generation of Barrons was about to begin.

Rachel was already flying down the rope ladder, followed by a laughing Matthew, who leaped after her to join the other couple in the canoe. Alex held back for a moment, feeling strangely awkward and out of place.

He was the odd man out now—they were paired off and he was by himself—and he had an uncanny sense that it would always be like that. Good old Uncle Alex, stopping by when he was in port, arms filled with presents for his nieces and nephews—always welcomed with warmth and fondness, but never quite a part of it all.

His eyes drifted toward shore again, as if drawn against his will. A knot tightened in his stomach, as always when he anchored in the Lahaina roads, and he was tempted momentarily to put things off, spend the night on board. But he did not want to put a damper on his cousins' pleasure.

He went back to where he had left his jacket, checking things out with his eyes as he went, though there was no need. Barron ships had well-disciplined crews. They knew what was expected of them and performed it.

He had not always felt this distaste for the island. Once he had looked at the swaying palms, the shimmering coral sand, the green volcanic hills in the distance, and thought he had never seen anything so beautiful. He had savored the sultry warmth after months of biting Pacific winds, had watched the whales play with their calves in the crystal-bright winter waters, and had reveled in the infectious laughter of lithe dark-skinned girls who had not yet been taught that pleasure brought shame.

But the girls had fathers and brothers, and sometimes even husbands, with an insatiable hunger for knives and mirrors and iron nails that could be fashioned into fishing hooks. It had taken him a long time to notice, but he had, and with it, the ugliness that festered like an oozing wound beneath that glowing illusion of Eden. Shopkeepers gouging sailors for what they could get . . . bars like Dud Owen's dingy establishment, which catered to the craving for rotgut and sex with the same commercial efficiency . . . missionaries who promised redemption but only on their own terms, and only at the expense of the culture they had come to save.

Even the naive, hospitable, fun-loving natives were not quite what they seemed. Alex could not forget that it was in the glorious Iao Valley that Kamehameha I had consolidated his hold over the kingdom by slaughtering his fellow Hawaiians. The stream had run red with blood for days, its gurgling flow damned by the bodies of Maui warriors.

Pretty illusions were not always what they seemed.

Alex slung his jacket over his shoulder and headed toward a ladder to descend into one of the waiting boats. He *was* getting old. Not in years, but in the way he was looking at things. And a damned sight too melancholy. If he wasn't careful, it would get to be a habit.

He'd be glad when this blasted sojourn was over and he could move on.

Chapter 5

"Rachel? Here in Lahaina?" The hairbrush hovered forgotten in Maria's hand as she turned away from her dressing table mirror. She was properly corseted now, and gowned in scoop-necked white India muslin which gave her skin a tawny look. "Rachel Todd? You're absolutely sure?"

Ilimi laughed delightedly. She took an almost childlike pleasure in surprises, and she had known exactly what sort of reaction she was going to get.

"Of course I am sure. I saw the new *Dawn* come in myself. It was most astonishing. Very *nui*—I have never seen a ship so *big*! The great white sails nearly filled the sky. Everyone was running *wikiwiki* down to the beach to see it. I was on my way to the market to pick up some Waioli oranges, but naturally I had to go, too."

"You weren't planning on swimming out to greet the sailors?" Rachel chided gently.

Ilimi's pretty face puckered with amusement. "No, no, I am much too old for such things now. I am a mother—a *makuahine* with four big sons. But I talked to a girl who did. She said that one of the captains Barron—Matthew, I believe she said—was bringing a bride. . . . She was most disappointed. She said he is a handsome, handsome man."

"A bride?" It was an instant before Maria caught on. "You mean, Rachel? Our Rachel? Married to a Barron?"

"Unless there is another Rachel Todd who is com-

ing back to the island where she was born." Glints
of mischief sparkled in bright black eyes. "And I
think that is most unlikely."

So did Maria. She set the brush down impulsively.
She had not even begun to pile her hair in the latest
fashion on top of her head. Royall hated it when she
left the house looking like a hoyden, and ordinarily
she went to great lengths to keep the peace. But Royall had been drinking the night before and would not
be likely to make an appearance until well past noon.

And even if he did, she didn't care! Maria's high
spirits flared rebelliously. Royall could be as angry
as he liked. All she cared about was getting to the
shore and finding out if the rumors Ilimi had heard
were true.

Her feet fairly flew down the narrow rutted lane
that ran along the waterfront. She was wearing thin-
soled kid slippers, hardly suitable for haste, but she
barely noticed when she skidded on slippery patches
of sand. It had been years since that day the Todds
had left Maui to become missionaries in China. She
must have been ten or eleven, Rachel nearly five
years younger, and they had been heartbroken—or
thought they were. It had seemed the worst thing
life could offer, to be parted from a friend, and they
had vowed always to stay in touch.

They had kept their promise. Letters had flown
back and forth over the years. Maria's had been filled
with gossip and girlish daydreams, culminating in
the excitement of two engagements, one on the heels
of the other. She had not been able to bring herself
to write for a long time after that. Then her missives
had been filled mostly with idle chitchat about Honuakula—the crops they were experimenting with, the
gardens, Royall's deep respect and consideration for
the land—until finally her son had been born, and
the words had flowed freely again.

Rachel had replied with the enthusiastic abandon
that characterized everything she did. Pages and

pages described her parents' mission outside the
gates of Macao, the Chinese who came in increasing
numbers every day for their help ... how she was
learning to be a nurse herself ... her hatred of opium,
and her utter contempt for the traders she felt were
raping the land she loved and its precious people.

The area was crowded with sailors and curiosity
seekers. The clouds had thickened, casting brief
patches of shadow and muting the brightness of the
sun. Boats from the ship were still pulling in, and
there were enough people coming and going so it
took Maria a moment to pick out the small group
standing at the water's edge. She noticed Jared Barron's wife first. A tall, beautiful, very pregnant
woman—*hapai*, as the natives would say—in a gracefully flowing Hawaiian dress. Then she spotted a
mass of strawberry blond hair, unfashionably loose
like her own.

"Rachel Todd—how *dare* you?" she cried as she
raced over, both hands outstretched. "I used to look
down at you. You were such a tiny thing! Now I
swear you top me by a good five inches."

"Polly? Is that really you?" Leaving the others, her
friend came several steps forward to grasp her hands
warmly. "I think it's more like six inches. You can't
be a bit above five foot five. But I'd have known you
anywhere—even though you've turned into quite the
elegant young matron ... Have you heard I'm married, too?"

Maria laughed. Only Rachel would ask such an
absurd question. She had barley been back twenty
minutes.... And only Rachel would be right!

"Certainly I've heard. Did you think I would let
myself get so far behind in the latest gossip? You are
married to Captain Matthew Barron. A blackguard, I
believe. Or was it a scoundrel? You were going to
hate him forever."

"Forever is such a long time." Little crinkly lines
formed at the corners of Rachel's soft brown eyes.

"And scoundrel was the word—and still is.... You're more than a bit of a scoundrel, aren't you, Matthew? Come and meet my friend whom I've told you so much about."

A young man materialized by her side. He was only slightly taller than she, fair-haired, with a stylish beard, and every bit as good-looking as Ilimi's disappointed friend had intimated. Maria felt a little pang as she saw him slip an affectionate arm around his wife's waist.

"Hardly a scoundrel, my love," he protested. Something in his voice caught Maria's ear, and she stiffened briefly, then relaxed. Just a Yankee edge to his accent that had caught her off guard. "Where is your wifely loyalty?"

"Would you have preferred blackguard then?" Rachel teased.

"What? Blackguard? The very idea! You malign your poor misunderstood husband." He turned to Maria with a captivating grin. "I assure you, madam, I am the soberest, most upright of gentlemen. The very soul of decorum. Did you see the way I brought in my vessel in just now? ... No? A pity. A more stately, dignified arrival would be hard to imagine."

"A pity, indeed." Rachel was obviously enjoying the jest. "Then we could have added 'prevaricator' to 'scoundrel.' ... And who is this handsome young man?" she said as a boy dashed up, skidding to a stop at the last moment, and hovered uncertainly a few feet away. "Is this your son? But of course it is! He couldn't have gotten that carrot-top anyplace else."

Maria nodded with a proud smile. "This is Mack. James McClintock Perralt—quite a mouthful, but it's a tradition in Royall's family. The first son is always James, followed by his mother's maiden name. Fortunately, it shortens nicely." She stretched out her arm, coaxing the boy closer. "This is a very old friend of

Mama's, Mack. When she was almost as little as you—if you can imagine that."

Clearly he couldn't. The idea that old people might once have been young was beyond his fathoming, and he looked up at Rachel with a curious expression, which she met by kneeling in front of him.

"Hello, Mack," she said. I am your Aunt Rachel. . . . Well, not your aunt really, but your mother and I have known each other for years and years, so it's almost the same thing."

The boy had no trouble with that. He was accustomed to the extended families of the Hawaiian culture. "Did you bring me a present?" he asked. "Where did you come from?"

Maria tried to shush him, but Rachel only laughed. "We sailed from a brand-new city called Hong Kong, all the way across the ocean. And of course I brought you presents. Heaps and heaps of them. For your mother, too . . . and naturally, for your father. But I left them all on board. We could go get them together if your mama says it's all right. Would you like to see the ship?"

He would. There was no question of that. His little face lit up. "I have to go *he'e nalu* now. Surfing. Ilimi's biggest son is teaching me. Ilimi is our housekeeper. But I could go later!" He started off in a great hurry, as if surfing had suddenly become a chore that had to be gotten through. Just for an instant he turned back.

"I like presents," he confided.

They were all laughing as he went over to where a long board had gotten half buried in the sand, and manfully struggled to tug it out. "You are buying my son with bribes," Maria accused jokingly.

"Of course I am," Rachel agreed. "I shall buy him with fondness later. I adore children. I'm going to have a dozen of my own if I can."

"A dozen might be a bit excessive, love," Matthew started to protest, but another of the ship's boats was coming in, and his attention was diverted as they all turned to watch. Besides the oarsmen, there seemed to be only a single man on board. Bending over, as if to pick up something he had dropped on the bottom. The tall woman in the green Hawaiian gown had gone forward and was standing just at the edge of the water, but it was not her immobile figure that caught and held Maria's eyes.

Jared Barron had left his wife and was wading out to meet the incoming longboat. Women passengers were usually carried over the surf by muscular Hawaiian bearers, but most men, disdaining that as weakness, plowed through the waves themselves, and his boots and trousers were already wet.

Maria realized suddenly what it was that had made her heart turn over when she had seen him from a distance in town. And what there had been in his brother's voice that jarred her so badly before.

It was not Jared's height, or the way he carried himself. Not the New England overtones in Matthew's accent. It was an actual physical resemblance too uncanny to deny.

Even before the man in the boat leaped out and came forward with a laugh and a great bear hug, she knew what she was going to see.

There were three Barron captains. And the third was the man she had tried for years to block out of her heart and her dreams.

Sandy.

If she could have turned and run away, she would have. But her feet seemed to have grown as heavy as stone, and she could not move. She could only stand there, stunned and helpless, and wait for him to look around and meet her gaze.

When he finally did, his face, after that first brief second of surprise, was as set and cold as she had imagined. Not an emotion showed, not a human feeling. Sick at heart, Maria realized that he had long since gotten over being hurt by her unintentional betrayal—if indeed he ever truly had been betrayed. He was not even angry. He just looked annoyed.

As if she were a minor irritation. A part of his past he wanted to forget—and probably had until that moment.

"Come and meet Polly," Rachel was saying. "Maria, my oldest friend. This is Jared, Matthew's brother, and his wife Dominie, who is from Paris. . . . And this is their cousin, Alex."

Alex? For Alexander?

Maria barely heard the words; they seemed to come from someplace far away, and it was all she could do to keep her composure. She had known that that was the name of one of the Barrons, but it hadn't occurred to her to associate it with the man who had made her life seem whole for a few dazzling days. She had simply assumed that the nickname referred to the color of his hair. Why hadn't she remembered that Sandy could also be short for Alexander?

It was he who recovered first.

"Mrs. Perralt," he said in the same cool tone she remembered from that terrible evening so long ago. "How nice to see you again."

"You two know each other?" Rachel was looking curiously from one to another. Maria felt numb. Her brain was working no better than her feet, and she could not frame a reply.

Fortunately, he seemed to have no such problems. "We met at a soirée given by her husband on the occasion of one of my earlier visits. That was some time ago, but it's an evening I have not forgotten."

"Nor I," Maria said, finding her voice at last. Somehow she had to get through this painful encounter without arousing suspicion. It was amazing how calm she sounded, almost as cool as he. "It is, of course, a pleasure to see you again, sir—and to meet all of Rachel's new family. But I'm afraid you must excuse me. We'll get together again, Rachel? Soon? I want to check on Mack."

"At dinner tonight," Rachel pressed. If she had

noticed her friend's abruptness, she said nothing. But then children always made such believable excuses. "Dominie has arranged a welcoming gala. You can't refuse. I've already sent someone to invite your husband—and you, of course. I didn't know I would see you here."

"At dinner, then," Maria murmured helplessly. There was no excuse that would sound even remotely convincing, and anyway Royall would already have sent their acceptance. Barron was a prominent name, redolent of wealth and power. Royall liked to rub elbows with powerful men. "Naturally I'll be there. I wouldn't miss it for the world."

She did not look back as she turned and started toward the spot where her son was still struggling with his surfboard. She didn't know if Alex Barron was watching or not, but she wasn't going to give him the satisfaction of glancing around to see. Last time it had been he who turned away, leaving her to stare after him, heartsick and longing for a chance to explain. Sure that the terrible rift between them had been her own foolish fault.

And all the time he had been planning on casting her off. Like so much jetsam the next morning when his ship sailed.

She paused a safe distance along the sand to catch her breath. She had loved him so desperately. The pain still lay like a heavy weight on her heart. She had tried, but never managed to forget him. She had longed for him all these years . . . and he was merely annoyed to see her again!

At least this time she had turned away first. This time it was he who had been left behind. It was not much comfort, but it allowed her to retain what little was left of her dignity as she began slowly to walk away from him.

Alex Barron's jaw was set as he stood a little apart from the others and watched Maria's straight, re-

treating back. All the memories he had been stifling
since the islands had drifted into view just after
dawn came back with gut-wrenching intensity. He
could picture himself again, young, much too naive,
in that shabby adjunct of Dud Owen's ramshackle
tavern, hearing the voice of a man whose name he
could not recall but whose face was clear in his mind.

*"You've met Royall Perralt, haven't you? Our largest
landowner. . . . And his beautiful wife, Maria?"*

His wife? Alex could remember standing there,
looking at her, thinking there must be some mistake.
He must have heard wrong. She was too sweet, his
lovely Polly. Too innocent of guile. She could never
be capable of such duplicity.

Then he had seen the guilty truth in her eyes, and
he had known that the mistake had been his.

He could still feel the sinking feeling in the pit of
his stomach. This was not his Polly. Not the sweetly
innocent picture of perfection that had captured his
heart and made him fall in love. Not the laughing
titian-haired angel of his dreams.

This was simply the bored young wife of an older
man, out to have a little fun. Apparently she had
realized that that wasn't his kind of amusement, for
she had taken care not to mention certain little details. Like the wedding vows she had exchanged with
another man.

The sun beat down, mercilessly hot despite the
cover of clouds. Alex could feel perspiration
prickling his skin. The breezes seemed to have died.
Everything he had ever stood for, every value that
meant anything in his life, would never have permit-
ted him the dishonor of an illicit affair with someone
else's wife. Only the choice hadn't been his. She had
taken that from him. With deliberate deceit.

She hadn't even looked more than mildly embarrassed just now, he thought grimly. She had been
shaken for a moment. He had seen that. No doubt
she had been afraid he would let something slip in

front of her friend ... but she had recovered quickly enough. God, how cool she had looked as she turned and just strolled away.

But then, she'd probably had plenty of practice over the years.

He jammed his hands roughly into his pockets. Dammit, he wasn't a callow youth anymore. Life had taught him a few hard lessons. He should be able to shrug it off. Not let it get under his skin like this. He had lost her long ago. And with her, his illusions.

She had stopped and was standing on the sand, her head turned slightly to look out over the sea. Try as he would, Alex couldn't force his eyes away. He had known he was bound to run into her. The Perralts' plantation was somewhere out of town, but there was a house in Lahaina, too, and any social occasion to which the Barrons were invited would also include them. But he hadn't known it would be so soon. Or so public, with all his family watching.

And he hadn't known how he was going to feel.

The breeze blew in from the ocean again, unexpectedly, whipping the gauzy white fabric of her dress around her legs, and making it cling provocatively to curves he remembered all too intimately. God help him, he had no illusions about loving this woman anymore. He didn't even like her very much, and he sure as hell didn't trust her.

But he couldn't help remembering the way the spray of the waterfall had clung to her hair ... how her eyes had turned soft like the blue dawn sky, rimmed with dark wet lashes, just before he kissed her ...

She bent down, and he saw that she was speaking to a child. A little boy with what appeared to be a surfboard, from which he was solemnly and importantly brushing the sand. Even if it had not been for that vivid thatch of hair, Alex would have known that this was her son. There was a special way women had with their children, and for all her obvious failings, it was clear Maria Perralt was a loving mother.

Their laughter drifted across the sand, and he felt a sudden, inexplicable tug at his heart. If things had been different, *he* might have had a child with this woman. This might have been his wife. His son.

"A charming boy," a lightly accented voice said in his ear. He had been so engrossed he had not even noticed that Dominie was standing beside him. "I've seen him before. Playing on the beach. He's the image of his mother, don't you think? Not a trace of his father, fortunately."

"You know him?" Alex turned to look at her. "Perralt?"

"I've met him," she replied, her nose wrinkling slightly. "He was born in Louisiana, so he considers himself French. His part of the family—how do you call it, his *branch*?—resides in Charleston, but apparently they consider themselves French, too. Rather odd, for they Anglicized the name Perrault—and Jacques became James. But he still likes to practice the language. Though he does not speak it, *naturelment*, like a Parisian."

"You don't sound as if you like him very much," Alex said reluctantly. He didn't want to hear about Maria's husband, God knows, but he couldn't resist a certain perverse curiosity.

"I don't actually dislike him." Dominie looked thoughtful, as if mulling it over. "There's just something about him that's not quite . . . *sympathique*. You can judge for yourself. He's not a bad-looking man, but his face has rather a . . pinched appearance. As if he were trying to pretend he hadn't just sucked on a lemon. Yes, I think it is most fortunate that the boy doesn't take after his father," she added, and drifted off to join the others.

Alex stood for a moment, alone, and tried to block out the thought that leaped suddenly, unbidden to his mind. The boy didn't take after his *father*, Dominie had said. But she meant he didn't take after— Royall Perralt.

It could have happened. Alex was surprised at the complexity of emotions that caught him off guard and left him reeling. That week and a half so long ago could have had the usual consequences.

The one thing he hadn't anticipated as the *Jade Dawn* had glided into the Lahaina Roads. He hadn't even *considered* it. But . . .

He hadn't been careful. Why should he? There had been no need. He had loved her and thought she loved him. They were going to be together forever.

If it had happened, he wondered—if a child had been conceived during that brief, impetuous affair— how old would he be now? Late March, the beginning of April . . . he would have to have been born around the turn of the year. Seven and a half then. About right. It could be.

He stopped with a jolt as he realized where his thoughts were taking him. It could be, but it could not be, too. And *not* was considerably more likely. Even if the dates exactly coincided—which was highly improbable—she had been, after all, a married woman.

She had gone from his arms to her husband's bed. She had spent her nights with him, and perhaps long sultry afternoons as well. Probably long afternoons! What man could resist the temptation of that lithe, sensuous body? Had it merely been wifely obligation on her part? Had she tolerated an older man's physical urges because it was required of her . . . or had she lusted for him, too? Had she whispered bawdy comments to him, tickled his ear with her tongue, explored his body with her fingers and lips and brazen little teeth?

Stupidly, illogically, that was what hurt the most. Alex hated himself for the feelings he could not control—he, who had never been jealous or possessive before. It was not the dishonor that cut the deepest.

Not the callousness or the deceit, but the fact that he had had to share her with another man.

Had she still been quivering from *his* caresses, had her thighs still been moist with *his* passion, when she had come to that clear mountain pool just after dawn and made a foolish young lover believe he was the only man in the world?

He must have been watching her too intently, for he became aware suddenly that Jared had sauntered over and was giving him a strange look. Alex raised his brows raffishly, trying to seem nonchalant.

"A pretty woman."

"More than pretty, I'd say," the other man agreed. "Quite exceptionally beautiful. But then I'm a Barron, and we Barron males have that notorious weakness for redheads. A pity the lady already has a husband."

There was a hint of warning in his tone. Alex forced himself to laugh.

"Come on, Jared. This is your old-fashioned cousin you're talking to. Can you seriously see *me* with a married woman?"

"No," Jared said quietly. "I can't."

Maria had managed to compose herself somewhat by the time they arrived at the hall where the welcoming party was being held. Most of the guests had already arrived. Royall, well aware of the impression it created, always liked to make a late entrance with his wife on his arm.

Lanterns shimmered with a bright, warm glow as they lingered for a moment in the doorway. Maria was aware of heads turning in their direction. Ordinarily she would have been flattered by the frank admiration she saw in more than one pair of watching male eyes.

She had dressed carefully for the occasion and knew she looked her best. Her gown had been fashioned of changeable silk, shivering dazzlingly from deep lavender one moment to silvery blue the next. A close-fitting bodice clung becomingly, dipping to a bold point to show off her long, tapering waist and dropping just slightly from creamy white shoulders. Last year's bell shape had given way to a slightly fuller skirt, gracefully swaying as she moved, and cupid's wings and velvet tuberoses were festooned in clusters of white and metallic silver, blue and deep rich red, from just above her knees to just above the floor.

Her jewels had been selected as meticulously as her gown. Rubies glittered a bit too ostentatiously among diamonds around her neck and in the rebellious curls that had been tamed into a topknot, then allowed to come loose, as if carelessly, in ringlets over her ears. She had completed the costume with a pair of long drop earrings.

Now she was feeling self-conscious, and glad that Royall always insisted she cling devotedly to his arm whenever they entered a room. It was a relief to leave the doorway and step inside. A waiter was already bustling over with a tray of champagne, and hock and ale for the gentlemen. A young Chinese Maria had not seen before—a considerable improvement over the old tars Dud Owen usually employed.

"A fruit punch for the lady, Pake," Royall said, making no effort to conceal his impatience as he referred to the hapless waiter by the native term for anyone from China. "She does not touch anything stronger. They should have informed you of that. And I can do without the rest of this slop." He dismissed the man for a wave of his hand, and, having already created the effect he desired, proceeded to do much the same with his wife. "Go and find your friend, my dear. You must have things to talk about. I'm going to see if your stepfather can't scare up something more to my taste in the bar."

Maria felt her heart sink. Royall usually behaved impeccably in public. It was the one time she didn't have to dread being with him. But he had been drinking much more heavily of late.

"Wouldn't you like to come with me?" she ventured. "For a few minutes at least. I know Rachel would love to meet you."

"Nonsense. I spoke with her when I went to accept the invitation in person. A lovely lady. I'm sure she'll forgive me if I procure some decent refreshments for myself. It's amazing the pretense one is expected to go through when there are ladies present. Not a man here wouldn't love something more potent, but none of them has the backbone to speak up."

"Not true," a new voice chimed in. "*You* are speaking, rather loudly—and I am ready to add my concurrence. A little more potency is definitely in order. . . . Ah, Maria, I didn't see you there. May I say you are looking extraordinarily beautiful this evening?"

Maria cringed as she heard that slightly affected accent. She had never cared much for Lucifer Darley. She would not have enjoyed seeing him under any circumstances, but she couldn't help remembering now that it was he whose words had shattered her world eight years ago.

"Mr. Darley," she murmured with as much politeness as she could muster. "You are much too kind."

"Mr. Darley, *Mr.* Darley," he chided. "Haven't I told you often enough to call me Luke? Ah, well . . ." He turned toward Royall with a particularly vapid look. His hair was dark, almost black, his eyes a deep shade of brown, but his skin had an almost unnatural pallor, even in that sun-drenched climate, as if he never ventured out from the shade. "What can one do with the ladies? They are so prettily obstinate. Shall we see what the bar has to offer? A whiskey perhaps? It will be my treat. Now, there's an offer you don't hear very often. I am rarely so magnanimous."

Royall seemed to hesitate. It always surprised

Maria. The two men spent a great deal of time together. Darley was a frequent visitor to Honuakula, if only for the afternoon—yet there were times she almost thought Royall couldn't abide him.

"Why not?" he said after a moment. "Whiskey is an excellent idea. Shall I lead the way or will you?"

Maria remained where she was until they were gone. The room was the same one where she had last seen the man she had known as Sandy, but it had been expanded since then and elaborately decorated. Chinese silk lanterns, red and yellow and rich saffron gold, were strung on ropes across the ceiling and dangled from hooks on the walls; the tables that had been bunched together at one side were set with cloths in similar shades. The rest of the room had been left open, for mingling now and later dancing. A band of sorts was already playing. One mediocre fiddle, one very good, and the usual assortment of sandalwood *ukekes* and hollow gourds, and a *kalaau*, with its melodic xylophone sound.

She spotted Rachel near the bandstand, chatting with a man she did not recognize. A captain of one of the other Barron vessels, she supposed as she started toward them. A sharp pain shot through her ankle, and she winced visibly. She had twisted it on her way back from the beach and kept forgetting and stepping down too hard.

She had barely covered half the distance when Doc Fred appeared suddenly and was guiding her back toward the tables with a firm hand on one elbow. She had not even noticed him, but obviously he had seen her, and he had not missed that brief flicker of discomfort. Pulling out one of the chairs, he sat her down and proceeded to examine the ankle with deft hands. It was slightly swollen, but did not seem too bad until he pressed a particularly tender spot.

"No dancing for you tonight," he said as she let out a little gasp. "I want you to stay off that foot as much as possible. I'm going back to my surgery to get some binding tape. You are to sit right here until I return. That's an order."

It was almost a relief to obey. Maria had never been one for sitting on the sidelines. She liked to be in the center of things, but she had dreaded going over to greet Rachel, knowing that sooner or later the other Barrons were certain to join them. This at least let her put things off for a while.

Having gained a moment's respite, she allowed herself to lean back in the chair and relax. A mistake, as she was quickly to discover.

She was completely unprepared when she turned her head to glance casually around—and saw Alex Barron looking at her.

Caught off guard, she could not control her response as quickly as she had intended. Even before she realized it, she had already taken note of how modishly he was dressed. A surprise somehow, though she knew it shouldn't have been. He had always had a special flair. Pearl gray trousers hugged long, lean legs, and a white embroidered waistcoat set off the darker gray of a double-breasted tailcoat which had been cut in this year's style.

A little catch came to Maria's throat. He looked every bit as handsome now as when he had appeared at the edge of a mountain pool in a loose-sleeved casual shirt with the sun highlighting his hair.

She must have turned some horrible shade of green, for his mouth twisted wryly as he sauntered over.

"Don't worry," he said none too gently. "I'm not going to say anything. Your little secret is safe with me." He was leaning forward, his hands braced against the tabletop, in an almost conspiratorial mien. "I am no more eager than you to have it bandied about that I spent the mornings of one of my earlier sojourns cuckolding some poor fool I didn't even know. Of course, I wasn't aware of it at the time, but that hardly makes it more palatable. No man likes his friends and family to find out how thoroughly he has been deceived by a woman."

Maria was stung by the harshness of his words. "The deception was not just on my part," she reminded him tartly. He might not care for her—he might be irritated to have her pop back into his life—but that didn't give him the right to look down his supercilious, aristocratic nose at her. As if somehow he thought he were better than she! "You didn't bother to mention to me that you were a Barron. You knew I took you for an ordinary sailor, and you let me go right on believing it. You may not have been a captain yet, sir—but you're far from 'ordinary' when your grandfather owns the shipping line. Even if you claim your name is Sandy."

"A not uncommon diminutive of Alexander," he retorted, surprised at the vehemence of the attack he had not expected. "Surely you've heard it before."

"Your family refers to you as Alex. Also a diminutive of Alexander . . . and the one you seem to use."

"I have used both," he said somewhat stiffly. "I was younger then. We had a crusty old Scotsman on the Barron vessels. We still do. Angus Dougal. He taught me the ropes—kept me in line, you might say. Sandy was his name for me. The men picked it up for a while."

"And that's why you used it with me?" Maria pressed. "And didn't see fit to add a last name? . . . Not, of course, because you didn't want me to know you were one of the mighty Barrons."

"There *is* a reaction to the Barron name," Alex admitted uncomfortably. Dammit, he thought, why was he defending himself when she was the one who had wronged him? "Wealth and power bring certain disadvantages. Your reputation precedes you—whether it's valid or not. . . . I met a pretty girl. I wanted her to get to know *me*. Not the person my name might have led her to expect."

"And that isn't deception?" Maria rose and forced

her eyes to meet his. It was hard, but she was never going to hold her own against him if she let herself back down. "You are a hypocrite, Captain. You set one standard for yourself and another for me. It's amazing, isn't it, the way some men twist the concept of honesty around?"

She was shaking as she left and walked much too briskly for her sore ankle across the room. He had not mentioned the real reason why he hadn't wanted her to know he was a Barron, and she had been too proud to throw it in his face. If she'd been able to track him down, she could have created an embarrassing fuss when he left without so much as a word. As it was, he had been perfectly safe, except for the few times his ship had harbored in the Lahaina roads. And the eldest Captain Barron had taken care to spend precious little time on Maui.

Her ankle was throbbing badly, and she was thankful when Doc Fred came back and led her into an alcove off the main room. She could no longer see Alex, and he could not see her as the doctor taped her ankle expertly and reminded her she was not to put any weight on it. He helped her ease her foot back into a satin dancing slipper, grumbling all the while that it was just such a flimsy contrivance which had no doubt caused the mishap in the first place.

Maria smiled. "Actually, I was wearing kid shoes. With thin kid soles. And yes, they're every bit as unsuitable for running down the road." She hesitated, a little self-conscious, then reached out and placed a hand lightly on his as he checked the bandage one last time. "You've been a good friend, Doc Fred. Better than I deserve. I don't say it very often— I never say it—but I'm awfully grateful for you."

"Here." He looked embarrassed. "What's this? You know I'm too old for sentimentality, child."

"I am not a child," Maria said softly. "And you're not exactly an old man. I wronged you very badly once. That's another thing I never say ... but if I hurt you, I'm sorry. I was very young. I didn't understand. Did you know it was months before I stopped darting around corners to keep from bumping into you on the street?"

"I noticed," he said dryly. "I would have told you it was all right. But I feared that would embarrass you even more."

"And it would have." Maria tried to laugh, but she did not quite manage. "Was it all right? Truly?"

"This was all a very long time ago, Maria," he started, then saw the anxious expression on her face and realized what it had cost her to broach the subject. "No ... I don't believe I was hurt. I have always been a realistic man. I knew I wasn't a good match for you. Your parents simply found someone better, that's all. If things have turned out well, if you are happy with your life, then I am content. If not ... I would like to believe you would come to me. I can fix more than sprained ankles. You would, wouldn't you, if something were wrong?"

Maria sensed the seriousness beneath his words, and just for a moment she was tempted. It would be so good to unburden herself at last, to spill it all out to someone who cared. But she had chosen her path long ago.

"What on earth could possibly be wrong?" she said with a lightness that almost sounded natural. "I have a husband who gives me everything I ask for, the most beautiful house on the island, a little boy I adore ... Now tell me honestly, Doc Fred, with a son like that, could any woman want more?"

The doctor did not press, but found himself sighing as she walked away, closing off any possible continuance of the conversation. He had not been quite truthful. When he had lost her, it had been like losing a beautiful dream, the best of his heart and his spirit. But the years had worked their healing. He had long since stopped thinking of her in any romantic fashion, though he had not stopped caring or being concerned.

He ran his fingers thoughtfully over his chin, feeling the stubble of a beard he had forgotten once again to shave. He was worried about her. It seemed to him sometimes he caught a desperate pain behind the forced gaiety of her eyes. But then he remembered the warmth that had come into her voice when she had spoken of her son, and he decided he was wrong.

The boy was all she needed. It was like that for some women. Having a child relegated everything else to the background. It was not a thing that he, as a man, could completely understand, but he had seen it often enough to know it was true. Her life was her son, her every joy was her son—she would not even think about herself while there was Mack to be considered.

And if it made her happy, who was he to question the nature of a mother's love?

Alex had been more unnerved by that brief exchange than he cared to acknowledge. One standard of honesty for himself and another for her? Not totally a fair judgment, but not totally unfair either. He had not thought about it at the time. Certainly it had not been his intention . . . but there *was* deceit implicit in that failure to mention his surname.

He had not meant any harm by it, Lord knows. He had been telling the truth just now. He had wanted her to get to know him first. The Barron name would have complicated matters—and it had seemed unimportant at the time. A trivial detail, lost in the scope and exhilaration of their all-consuming love. He would have told her soon enough.

Still, he had not been quite honest. Alex squirmed inwardly. His lie had been nothing to hers! He had not coolly, deliberately set out to commit adultery—and make someone else an unwitting accomplice. His lie had had no effect in the long run, but it made him uncomfortable to realize he had not been altogether blameless in that brief, ill-fated affair.

Maria had come back into the room, and Alex found his eyes seeking her out again. Damn, he thought angrily. Even when he knew better, he couldn't seem to stay away.

She stopped, and he saw her speak briefly with her husband, who had come from the direction of the bar, a glass full of whiskey in his hand. Or rather, half full, for he had already consumed a good portion of it and appeared to be well on his way toward getting drunk. Dud Owen was just passing by and paused to give her a surprisingly familiar pat on the arm.

Alex watched, puzzled. Surely Perralt was the man's wealthiest patron. Even in a rough port like Lahaina, such liberties had to be unsuitable. He was enlightened a few minutes later when one of his fellow guests remarked with a knowing snort that the innkeepers were "the little chit's" parents. Maria, it seemed, in the eyes of that small community, had married well above herself.

"Dud Owen is her father?" he asked as he joined Dominie, who was watching the proceedings with frank fascination. It had to be a far cry from the sophisticated salons of Paris, but she was gamely throwing herself into her new surroundings.

"Oh, I doubt that," she replied skeptically. "I overheard her saying that the boy is called McClintock. For her maiden name. Doesn't that mean the name of her father?"

"Owen is the lady's stepfather," Jared put in. Alex had not noticed him, but he was never far from his wife's side, especially now that she was carrying his child. "Her real father apparently shipped out of New England with the first load of missionaries in the early twenties. He died on the way, and Mama naturally arrived looking for a replacement."

Alex was aware that his cousin was watching him again out of the corner of his eye, much too sharply, and he decided it might be wisest not to mention Maria in the future. Still, it wouldn't do to drop the subject too abruptly.

"What an interesting concept," he remarked with forced lightness. "A missionary's widow married to the local whoremonger. It does give one faith in the vagaries of the world."

"Perhaps," Dominie reminded him gently, "she was just tired of being pure."

And perhaps she had never been pure in the first place. Alex found his thoughts drifting back to the one place he didn't want them to be. With a mother who found it so easy to compromise her religious background and a stepfather who sold women to sailors for cash, what chance had Maria ever had? Who had been there to teach her right from wrong?

He clamped his jaw in a determined line. He saw what he was doing and despised himself for it. He was making excuses, trying to turn her into something she wasn't. Could adultery really be considered a sin when she hadn't been taught it was shameful?

Only, if it had seemed all right to her—the natural order of things—then why had she gone to such lengths to conceal her husband from her lover?

The tables were being set for dinner. Alex noticed cards at each place with the menu written out in elaborate calligraphy. An odd pretense in that seaside tavern. He wondered whose idea it had been. Dominie was too tasteful to have arranged it. The mother who had once been the wife of a missionary? Or had it simply become customary over the years? He seemed to recall that Perralt had had cards on the table at that other occasion long ago.

The housekeeper, Ilimi, appeared in the doorway just before dinner with young Mack in tow. Apparently he was to be taken around the room to greet everyone before the meal was served. Royall obviously liked to show off his son. There was no pretense of modesty in his dark features as he watched Maria come to take the boy's hand and lead him over to the first of the guests.

He was an appealing child. They had dressed him halfway between a boy and a man, in long fawn-colored trousers, with a black velvet coat and white ruffled shirt, and his hair had been slicked back almost manageably on a well-shaped head. Alex, watching, was impressed as much with his spirit as his manners. He shook hands gravely, every inch the perfect little gentleman, but then someone said something that must have amused him, for laughter burst out and seemed to fill the room. His eyes, blue like his mother's, danced with curiosity and exuberance.

More than appealing. Alex found himself drawn to the boy, as he had been that morning on the beach. An uncanny feeling, more than a little unsettling, and he was grateful when Maria moved on, not bringing her son over to him. He did not want to feel that small hand in his. Did not want to deal with the emotions he knew it would evoke.

Then the boy turned, looking his way for a second, and Alex saw that his eyes were not blue at all but a piercing blue-gray.

Eyes that color occurred in the Barron family. Once every generation, it was said. In his generation it was Jared who had them.

The thought ran like a shudder down his spine. Barron eyes ... but he didn't have time to digest it, for Royall seemed to have seen him watching the boy and was strolling over, almost amiably, though there was something aloof in his manner.

"You seem to like children, Captain," he said casually. "You have some of your own?" Alex was reminded fleetingly of Dominie's words. A pinched face, as if he had been sucking on a lemon. The odor of whiskey was unmistakable.

He shook his head. "I'm not married."

The man looked amused. "That isn't what I asked," he said with a slyness that was not at all pleasant.

Alex glanced over at him. Definitely pinched, he decided, but lemon was the wrong image. More like the controlled tautness of someone in chronic physical pain.

"The answer is the same," he replied curtly. "I don't, as far as I know, have any children." He had always been too cautious for that. Jared had two half-Chinese sons, whom he openly acknowledged, and it would have come as a surprise to no one if impetuous Matthew had issue scattered unknowingly around the globe. But he had taken great pains to behave responsibly, and he found himself, strangely, regretting it now. "That's a fine boy you have there. You must be proud of him. He looks very much like his mother."

"So much the better for him." Royall laughed, without rancor, but without any mirth either. "Though there is a bit of Perralt in the lad. Especially about the eyes. A most unique color, don't you agree? My mother had eyes like that. She was the beauty in our family."

And that was all there was to it. Alex caught the waiter's attention and relieved him of a glass of ale. A foolish fancy, quickly dismissed. He found himself wishing, as Royall had earlier, that there was something slightly stronger on the tray.

Eyes like that ran in families. Not just his but Perralt's as well. The man knew his son—and why not? The mother had been his own wife. Alex was aware of a sharp stab of something that felt unexpectedly like disappointment.

He started in on the ale. For a moment he had actually wanted the boy. Insane, but the instinct was there all the same. He had looked at him and liked him . . . and he had wanted to believe he was his.

Not unnatural perhaps. The deeply ingrained desire of a man for a son, particularly a man who was just coming to accept the fact that he was never going to marry and father a family.

Not unnatural, but in this case, damnably stupid. No doubt he was lucky it had come out the way it did. The last thing he needed was one more tie to bind him to lovely, treacherous Maria Perralt, née McClintock. He was already experiencing too many troubling emotions as it was.

He downed the rest of the ale in one long gulp and went off in search of another. He had a feeling it was going to be a long night.

Chapter 6

Royall continued to drink heavily throughout dinner. Maria noticed that he brought a glass of whiskey with him when he sat down, and she threw an anxious glance in his direction, but she had to admit he seemed to be holding it well. For the time being at any rate. Three small tables had been pushed together, forming a large rectangle to accommodate the Barron party, among which she, as Rachel's oldest friend, had naturally been included.

At least, she thought gratefully, she was at one end of the long table, to the left of Matthew, who had been seated at the foot, and Alex was on the same side, in a corresponding position at Rachel's right. She didn't know how she could have gotten through that long, uncomfortable meal if she had had to see him every time she looked up from her plate.

The APÉRITIF AUX FRUITS DE MER splashed in elaborate letters across the top of the menu turned out to be the usual tinned shrimp. Maria, accustomed to dinners at the tavern, took it for granted, though it did sometimes seem foolish when the fresh fish the natives brought in on their boats was so much tastier. But shrimp in little cans was more expensive, and thus, she supposed, more deserving of a place at a gala fete. It had been served this time with a unique condiment made from finely chopped mangoes. Sweet and tart and surprisingly peppery, with overtones of the Orient. Dominie's influence? she wondered, and wished she had more appetite to appreciate it. As it was, she barely managed to push the food around on her dish.

Royall's whiskey was gone long before the shrimp, and he switched to wine, which he had begun to discuss with Dominie in French. He was speaking a little too loudly, but otherwise seemed gracious enough, almost voluble, and Maria was relieved to note that he showed no signs of turning sullen. Perhaps, if she was fortunate, the evening might yet go smoothly.

"There is nothing like French wine," he was expounding in that language. "The Italians think they have the idea, but their efforts are, for the most part, woefully inadequate. And Asian rice 'wine' is, in my humble opinion, a grotesque misuse of the word."

"Oh, I don't know," Dominie replied evenly. "It's a bit strong for my taste, but it does go nicely with some of the foods of the East. I believe it would have made an excellent complement to this mango sauce, for example ... though naturally I am not such a connoisseur as yourself."

"I have sometimes thought it would be amusing to start a little vineyard here," Royall went on. "French wine from French grapes—grown in the rich Maui soil. An interesting experiment, don't you agree?"

He continued to talk about particular vintages, comparing their merits, while Dominie added an occasional polite comment and pretended more interest than she clearly felt. Alex, seated across the table, found himself straining to listen. His French was passable. He could read it fairly well and make himself understood, but it didn't extend to nuances of the palate and the aroma of various wines.

"A fascinating subject," came a new voice from between the two speakers. "And most enlightening ... but I wonder, Royall, if you are not being unfair to the other ladies. And perhaps the gentlemen as well."

Lucifer Darley. Alex eyed the man with distaste, and not solely because he had been the bearer of unpleasant news years ago. An absurd name, he thought, but he supposed the blame for that could hardly be laid on his shoulders. And they did seem to call him Luke.

"Unfair in what way?" Royall gave him a sidelong look of annoyance. "Gentlemen—and sometimes even ladies—have been known to enjoy an occasional discourse on wine."

"But in French? My dear fellow! I, of course, being from England, have spoken it fluently since an early age. Europeans learn languages of necessity. The same is not always true of Americans."

Alex caught himself studying the man a little more closely. If he was indeed British, there had been no trace of it when he was speaking his native tongue. Only a slight affectation. And his French, to Alex's admittedly untrained ear, sounded remarkably like Royall's. He would have to ask Matthew about it later. Matthew was the linguist of the family.

"You are right, of course," Royall was saying, in English now. "I have been unutterably rude. I must apologize. It didn't occur to me that anyone here might not understand French."

There was something condescending in his tone and Maria cringed, but Rachel only laughed good-naturedly. "I'm afraid most of that went way over my head," she admitted. "I speak several dialects of Chinese—and Portuguese and a bit of Spanish—but French, I must confess, is not one of my accomplishments. . . . Ah, I do believe the roast has arrived. Doesn't it look delicious? Dominie, how clever of you to put this all together so quickly."

She was already signaling to the servers, and the main course and several side dishes quickly filled the table. Just as deftly she steered the conversation back to neutral ground, tactfully asking Royall about his efforts at Honuakula, which Maria's letter had led her to believe would be a welcome subject. He responded as men usually do to a charming woman's professions of admiration, and the dinner proceeded amiably.

In fact, the roast did not look the least bit delicious. Nor was it particularly tender. It always amazed Alex, considering the superb pork prepared by the natives in their *imus*, or underground ovens, that the *haole* community continued to cling to its overdone joints of beef. The wild descendants of cattle that had been left by Captain Vancouver in the final years of the last century had a gamey taste, but there was an excellent gravy, which had been prepared from the au jus, and Royall had graciously sent for fresh butter and vegetables from the garden at Honuakula. Maui potatoes, then lightly sautéed and baked until they were crusty on the outside, were as good as Alex had ever had. And he was particularly intrigued by yellowish-green slices of an oily, nutty-flavored vegetable he had never encountered before.

It was, Royall informed him, actually a fruit. It was called an avocado and had been introduced to the islands some decades earlier by the Spanish horticulturalist Don Francisco de Paula Marin. As he continued speaking, it became clear that he had more than a passing acquaintance with agriculture, and in spite of himself, Alex felt the beginnings of a grudging respect. The man was vain, he drank too much, he could be exceedingly unpleasant—but his passion for the land was genuine, and it reached out and touched another who loved the soil and everything that grew in it.

There was only one last moment of awkwardness, just as dessert was being placed on the table. A honey-flavored pudding served with plump sections of Waioli oranges in a light syrup. Nothing else, and Maria watched Royall nervously. He was usually contemptuous of dinners where only one sweet had been put out, but this time he was too busy complaining about his Hawaiian workers.

"The damned lazy bastards," he snapped, forgetting that there were ladies at the table. "I can't do a blasted thing with them. Offer them extra money and they don't show up again until it's gone. But try withholding it until the planting or harvesting is done, and they say you're too mean to live and refuse to do another lick of work. I leave them alone for ten minutes to tend to something important—*five*—and I come back to find an empty field with hoes and cane knives strewn all over the place. I can't even keep a decent *luna*."

"A *luna* is an overseer," Maria cut in, hoping to head him off. The failure of the natives to share his dedication was a familiar prickly subject, like a nettle that had gotten under his skin and continued to sting. "The workers need constant supervision, but it's hard to find a man who knows about farming in a seaport. Especially someone with a capacity for leadership."

"And the stomach for tough discipline," Royall added. His voice had calmed somewhat. "I've had eight *lunas* in the last three years, and not a one was worth his pay. I just got rid of the last of them a week ago, which mean I'm going to be hard pressed until I find a replacement. . . . And probably even harder pressed then. I sometimes think I have to watch the *lunas* closer than I do the men."

A darkly brittle expression came over his face, not quite humor but near enough, and Maria realized that the moment was past. There were no more incidents, but she was nonetheless relieved when the meal was finally over and it was time to line the chairs up against the walls for the dancing that would follow.

She did not look in Alex's direction as they all rose from the table, but she was intensely conscious of him, as she had been throughout the entire meal. She wondered what he thought of her marriage now, and the man he considered her husband.

If indeed he was thinking about her at all.

Maria caught herself sharply. She was behaving like a lovesick schoolgirl, and with absolutely no provocation. Of course he hadn't been thinking about her. He had made it perfectly clear that he had no use for her.

He hadn't addressed so much as a single word to her throughout the dinner, even out of courtesy. His comments had been reserved strictly for Royall, as if he felt somehow, manlike, that the two of them—her victims!—ought to stick together. To keep on daydreaming about him, to fancy she was even a tiny part of his life and thoughts, would be more than foolish. It would be devastating. She had to get him out of her mind.

She took a seat on one of the chairs and tried not to think about the remainder of the evening, which seemed to stretch out interminably ahead of her. The band was taking its place again on its slightly raised stand at the end of the room. Any minute now the music would be starting, and she would be left there, nursing her aching ankle. How on earth was she supposed to endure the next several hours if she couldn't even pass the time dancing?

But then, if it wasn't for her ankle, she reminded herself grimly, the Barron men would be virtually obligated to choose her as a partner. Even aloof, reluctant Alex. It would have been torture, having him so close, touching her, stirring up old memories that refused to be forgotten. At least she was to be spared that.

The music had just begun, slightly off key but surprisingly melodic, when Rachel came over to perch on a chair beside her.

"You're sitting on the sidelines?" she said, surprised. "But I thought you adored dancing. Didn't you tell me that about a hundred times in your letters?''

"More like a thousand times, I guess ... but I'm under strict orders from Doc Fred.'' Maria stuck her foot out from under the hem of her gown. Fortunately, skirts were longer this year, hiding the ugly bandage. "It serves me right for being so careless. And insisting on stylish slippers. But you go ahead. I'm sure your handsome husband is dying for a dance with his bride.''

"Hardly a bride any longer,'' Rachel protested. "I've been married for months.... And I have the rest of my life to dance with Matthew. I think, for once, he might be patient and spare me a while to chat with my oldest friend.''

"You look like a bride to me.'' Maria smiled, trying not to feel envious. "You're positively glowing. I'd ask if he makes you happy, but there's no need. I can see that Matthew Barron is the right man for you. I'm truly glad you found him.''

"So am I,'' Rachel said fervently. "I almost didn't— or more to the point, I almost didn't let him find me. But you know all that from my letters. What I want to hear about now is *you*. You left so many things out when you wrote to me. Are you happy, too? Really, really happy?''

"What a silly question.'' Maria could not quite meet her friend's eyes. Even as a little girl, Rachel had always been much too perceptive. "Wait till you come to visit Honuakula. You've never seen anything like it. I live in the loveliest place on the island. Perhaps in all Hawaii.... And, of course, there's Mack—''

"I've heard about Honuakula,'' Rachel cut in. "Everyone says it's magnificent. I'm sure I'll be impressed. But you haven't answered my question. Are you happy?''

"I think I am,'' Maria said softly. "Funny little Rachel ... only not so little anymore. Happiness isn't always pretty romance, you know. It comes in many forms. Royall is good to me, and, well, you'll understand when you have children of your own. A child is reason for joy all by itself."

Rachel nodded. "I know. I'm absolutely longing to have a baby. Matthew says not to worry. He says the children will come soon enough, and right now he's enjoying having me all to himself. But sometimes I wonder . . ."

Her voice trailed of as Royall came up and abruptly extended his hand to Maria, who was still sitting on her chair.

"I'm sure Mrs. Barron will excuse you," he said brusquely. "I would like to show my wife off on the dance floor."

Maria's heart fell as he pulled her roughly to her feet. He had covered well enough at dinner, but he was obviously drunker than she had suspected, and there was a long evening yet to get through.

"My ankle," she reminded him awkwardly. "I told you, I'm not supposed to put any weight on it."

"I'm sure your ankle will tolerate one short dance, my dear. Mrs. Barron, I hope you will do me the honor later." His hand caught her arm, gripping tautly. Maria did not look back as he led her pointedly out to the center of the floor. She couldn't have borne the pity she knew she would see in Rachel's eyes. The other dancers were already gathering, laughing and chatting as they waited for the band to strike up again.

"Please, Royall," she protested. "You're hurting me." But his grip only got stronger. Maria could feel the pressure of his fingers gouging into her arm.

"What's the point of having a beautiful wife if a man can't be seen with her?" he said bluntly. "I ask very little of you, as you well know. The usual obligations were fulfilled, thanks to the *pu'aha-nui* fruit, when you presented me with a son. All I require is a gracious hostess at my table and a consort who looks like she's actually enjoying a few social moments with her husband. Do you think you can manage that?''

Maria nodded. When Royall started alluding, however obliquely, to the one occasion during their marriage on which he had been able to perform as a man with her, she knew he was close to the edge. It was as if, by reminding her what he had done—pointedly referring to that time as the conception of *his* son—he somehow managed to get back the illusion of virility he had lost for good on their wedding night.

"Just let go of my arm," she said evenly. Royall's scenes were infrequent—in public at least—but they could be ugly, and she didn't want to be subjected to one in front of her friend. "Of course I would be pleased to dance with you. I didn't realize it was important, or I would have agreed right away."

The music was just starting. A waltz, and Maria found herself praying it would be short. With anyone else she would have loved the sweeping rhythm and graceful turns. But Royall had a habit of holding her a little too close, bending his head with exaggerated intimacy over hers, as if proving to everyone his right of possession. She would have welcomed a good rollicking reel, even it was agony every time her foot came down.

"You might try smiling, my dear." Royall's voice was brittle with sarcasm as he spun her deftly around the floor. She had to grant at least that he was a superb dancer. "I assure you your face won't crack with the strain. Or you might want to toss your head in that fetching little way you have. Your admirer is watching."

"My admirer?" Maria was surprised enough to look at him directly for the first time. There was an almost sadistic expression on his thin lips.

"The Barron bachelor . . . the tallest of the Yankee captains. He's been staring at you all evening. He seems quite taken, though he doesn't appear to like you very much. Isn't that odd? Or perhaps not. Men are frequently beguiled by women they don't like."

He whirled her a little too quickly, and Maria gasped as her ankle twisted, even with the bandage. "I think you're exaggerating, Royall," she said, fighting to regain her composure. "Or else you're making it up. You like to think everyone is admiring me because I'm your wife. He's probably bored to tears, dying for the evening to end. He seems an arrogant sort. Much too good for the likes of us!"

Royall did not reply, and Maria concentrated on her dancing. Her ankle was throbbing again. Badly. Had he been right? Was Alex Barron watching her? She despised herself for the way her heart perversely insisted on pounding faster. Even if he was, it was only out of curiosity. Or icy disdain.

More likely Royall had simply noticed that she was uncomfortable with the Yankee captain and was trying to embarrass her. He liked to play games like that when he was drinking.

It seemed forever, but at last the music ended, and Maria thought with a carefully concealed sigh that the worst of the ordeal was over. One dance would be enough: Royall was not likely to insist on repeating it. Her arm was aching almost as badly as her ankle, and she looked down to see that his hand had left an angry red mark. She would have to send someone to her carriage to fetch a shawl to hide it.

Then Royall placed a hand on her waist, guiding her to the far end of the room, and she saw that the ordeal was, in fact, just beginning. A tall man in a tailored dark gray coat was turning to watch them approach. Maria recalled that look she had seen on Royall's face, and she realized he had one final humiliation yet in store for her.

Only he couldn't know, of course, how truly humiliating it would be. To him it was just a childishly annoying jest. To get even with her for trying not to dance with him before.

"Captain Barron," he said as they drew near, "I fear we have been neglecting you. You must forgive us. With so few ladies in our small community, it is incumbent upon the married gentlemen to learn to share. I trust you will allow me to offer you my wife . . . for the next dance."

There was nothing either of them could do about it. Maria just stood there, trembling and praying it didn't show, as the first sweet strains of music filled the air again. Purer this time, the better violinist taking the lead.

Another waltz, she thought helplessly. The band was incurably unfashionable. They found something they performed passably well, and they just kept on doing it, over and over, until someone finally objected. Waltzes one night, reels the next .. it might go on all evening.

Alex reached out his arms with exaggerated politeness. At least he would not hold her too close. Maria felt his hesitance, as she knew he felt hers, but there was no way he could have refused without seeming a boor. She tried not to think what she was doing, tried not to remember who he was . . . tried to pretend it was just another dance . . .

But it wasn't just a dance, and he wasn't just another man. Her senses seemed to be heightened, distracting. She was finding it impossible to think rationally. The closeness of him, the warmth, the man-smell of tobacco and leather and shaving soap . . . She was wearing evening gloves beneath a glitter of diamonds at the wrist. Her skin was not actually touching his, but Maria felt as if it were, and she could not keep from remembering.

The music caught her up, tempting in spite of herself, drawing her along on currents she could not resist. He was a graceful dancer, and their bodies blended with the same sure instincts that had brought them together in other, much more intimate ways before. She felt him whirling her around and then around again. His hand was strong as he guided her; his hard, supple body captured the flow of the rhythm.

His hands had been strong then, too. The music intensified the memories. They seemed to swell inside her as the violins soared, wailing with the sultry breezes that wafted through the open doors. Strong but gentle as he had teased her breast . . . or brushed a wisp of hair back from her brow.

Heaven help her, she still cared for him. As much now as ever. It was as if time had washed away not the hurt and despair, but her own feeble efforts to pretend.

No matter what he did, no matter how callous he was, how indifferently he treated her, she would never stop loving this man. It was as inevitable as the misty rain that fell from summer clouds on the fertile green slopes of Haleakala. He had come upon her unawares, one dawn in a secluded glade, and she had given him her heart. She realized now, as she should have realized long ago, that it could not be taken back again. He would hold it in his keeping forever.

And he did not have even the slightest lingering feelings for her.

Her eyes drifted up, and she looked at him boldly for the first time since his unexpected return. The strength in his face seemed hardness now, and she recognized, as she had not before, the innate arrogance that went with the Barron name. There were lines around his eyes, a set to his mouth, and she sensed a certain world-weariness, as if he had grown cynical and tired of life.

Or perhaps he was simply tired of dancing with her. It was, after all, a chore that had been foisted upon him.

"You are so quick to judge," she said bitterly. "Without knowing any of the circumstances. Without *caring* to know! I would have explained—only your ship had already sailed. You weren't interested in listening."

"What was there to explain?" His voice was cool and steady. Just soft enough so passing couples would not catch the words. "You were married to a much older man. One, I imagine, not altogether to your taste. Perhaps even repellent? You sought other amusements. That's not surprising. It happens all the time."

But not to you, Maria thought miserably. You are a Barron, and Barron men don't have to settle for being some woman's plaything. . . . Only wasn't that exactly the way he had treated her!

"You don't know the first thing about me," she said, clinging to a sudden flash of anger that was more comfortable than the feelings which had gone before. "You have no idea what things were like for me then. What was going on in my so-called 'marriage'! And you don't want to. You just make assumptions—because it's easier that way. And take precious care not to ruffle the waters by questioning them."

"Feathers," he said automatically. "You ruffle feathers," and then he stopped, realizing he had been about to smile. The past had an insidious way of creeping back. Making him want to tease, as he had teased her than.

An instinct to be resisted at any cost. He hardened his voice as he went on.

"I know you are married to a drinker, madam, and I sympathize. Perhaps he even treats you badly." Alex had not failed to notice the red splotches turning to bruises on her arm. He was uncomfortably conscious of them now, of the roughness that might not have been quite accidental. "I sympathize for that, too. But you aren't the first woman to be unhappy with her husband. And you won't be the last. You have made a marriage—not a contract with the butcher. You are committed to it."

"Even if it's not a real marriage," Maria cried out passionately. "If it's just a sham? Even if I'm not really—" She caught herself abruptly, stunned at what she had nearly done. Eight long years she had guarded every word she said, taking care not to let anything slip. Five minutes in his arms and it had almost all come tumbling out. "Even if it's only a mockery of a marriage? If every day is a waking nightmare? Married is married, and that's that! No compromises in an intolerable situation. For a woman at least—though men seem to be allowed their mistresses! My life could be pure hell, and it wouldn't make any difference to you."

"It might have," he admitted reluctantly. "Once. If you'd been honest. I am human, and you are a very beautiful woman. I might have been tempted. There might have been circumstances . . " Alex tried not to look at the marks on her arm, tried not to think about them and imagine. "But you played me for a fool, madam. You cannot expect me to forget that. A man has his pride."

His pride? Maria suddenly felt tired. Her ankle was aching, though she had forgotten it for a while. Was that what this was all about? His masculine pride had suffered a glancing wound and he was sulkily nursing it? She had come so close to telling him—she had nearly blurted out the awful secret that would have put her completely at his mercy—and he was worrying about his pride!

She had not hoped for his love. She had never had that anyway. She had just been a brief flirtation for him. But it might have been nice if they could at least have been civil to each other.

"You're right," she said. "There is nothing to explain." It was just as well they were leaving for Honuakula in the morning. With any luck she would never have to see him again. "I am a worthless piece of baggage. No morals at all. A silly, evil slut. . . . It must be repugnant for you to have to dance with me."

"I did not say you were evil," he replied, searching her face with an expression that Maria could not understand. "I'm not sure I even meant to imply you were a slut. I *do* sympathize. I know your life is not easy, though 'hell' might be a bit of an exaggeration. If I have judged you, I'm sorry. But you are another man's wife, and I will not be dancing with you again."

The band continued to play until the early hours of the morning. A light supper was spread out on the tables, seafood salad, cold meat, and pastries for the dancers to refresh themselves before adjourning to waiting carriages or walking the short distance home. Being less pretentious, it was probably considerably better, but Alex barely tasted the food he stuffed automatically into his mouth. Royall had inadvertently taken his place, and he was on the other side of the table, with a disconcertingly clear view of Maria at the far end.

She looked pale, and he felt a sudden, irrational urge to say something bright and foolish to make her smile. Those few moments' dancing with her had touched him in ways he had not anticipated. He had hidden it well. He sensed she had not suspected— he devoutly hoped she had not—but all his resolve had been as nothing, and he wanted her again. Not merely in the physical way, though there was that, too, but by his side, holding his hand, content just to be with him.

You have no idea what things were like for me then. . . . My life could be pure hell, and it wouldn't make any difference to you.

But it did make a difference. Alex set his fork down, giving up the pretense of eating, and stared off into the distance. It made all the difference in the world. She was still another man's wife, but that didn't keep him from caring. Desperately.

He had been so stupidly jealous before. It had torn at his gut, imagining those warm, sensual arms—and lascivious legs—opening hungrily to her husband's caresses. Now he was haunted by the sickening picture of her lying rigidly in bed, forced to submit to sexual advances that made her skin crawl night after degrading night.

It was an aspect of marriage for some women that had not occurred to him before. He found it more than a little unsettling.

"Well, what do you think, Alex? Doesn't that sound reasonable to you?"

The voice seemed to come out of nowhere. Alex jerked his head up to mind Matthew regarding him with amusement.

"Sorry ... you caught me woolgathering. Or rather, gathering together some odds and ends I'm not sure were tidied up on deck. A sea captain's proclivity—which doesn't concern you anymore, since you're no longer one yourself." Jared, across the table, was throwing him strange, sharp looks, but he didn't catch on in time. "What was that you were saying?"

"I was just telling Perralt there that he ought to find someone to help him out for a few weeks while he looks for a new *luna*. With this climate he could get another crop of cane going while the existing fields are being readied for harvest. But to do that, he'd have to have two crews working at the same time."

Alex was a little surprised that Matthew had broached the subject. His young cousin had never shown any interest in agriculture before. "No doubt," he agreed. "But I believe it was pointed out earlier that a seamen's town is hardly fertile ground for finding a farmer."

"I was thinking more of—oh, say, a captain between voyages. One perhaps who had spent some time on a certain plantation owned by his mother's people in Virginia. How about it, Alex? You've said often enough that you have more of a feel for the land than the sea. A few weeks away from the ship would do you good. I can remain captain long enough to get the *Jade Dawn* reprovisioned."

Too late Alex saw the trap he had unwittingly walked into, and he knew he wasn't going to be quick enough to come up with an excuse. Jared was still watching him, and for the first time he was grateful that his cousin had caught at least a glimmer of how he felt about the beautiful young wife.

"Have a heart, Matthew," Jared protested gamely. "Alex just set foot on the island this afternoon. By all means, see to the *Jade* yourself. You were probably little enough help on the way here. But surely the man who did the lion's share of the captaining has earned some time to himself. I seem to recall a partiality for Honolulu. No doubt there is a certain *lady* . . ." He let the words trail off with a suggestive inflection. "If a Barron is to come to the rescue, I expect it will have to be me."

"You?" Matthew's face puckered with good humor. "You know less about the land than I do, brother . . . and that is pathetically little. You might be able to discipline the men, but you wouldn't have the vaguest notion what to tell them to do. Or whether they were doing it correctly. Besides, in case you've forgotten, your wife is in an, uh, delicate condition. Fortunately, she seems disgustingly healthy, but I find it hard to believe you'd risk taking her so far from medical care."

"Nonsense," Dominie broke in. "I'm pregnant, not 'delicate'. Why does everyone persist in treating me like some fragile flower that will wilt if one so much as breathes on it? . . . But I must agree, my love," she added, turning with a good-natured look to her husband. "You really don't know the first thing about crops."

They continued to discuss the matter among themselves for several minutes, almost as if the subject of their debate were not even there. Alex noticed that Matthew seemed to be instigating it, which he found strangely out of character until he felt a light hand on his arm.

"I'm afraid for her, Alex," Rachel said in a hurried undertone, and he realized that all this had been arranged between them. "I don't know what's going on—Maria won't talk to me—but I have a terrible feeling. He's more than just unkind. She hurt her ankle, and he made her dance anyway. Did you see that awful bruise on her arm?"

Alex nodded reluctantly. It had made him uncomfortable when she had draped a shawl casually over her shoulders. As if she were used to concealing things.

"It's a party, Rachel," he reminded her. "The man's been drinking. That kind of thing happens. It needn't have been intentional."

"They say he drinks often. And he's been drinking more lately ... She's my friend, Alex. I don't want her left alone with him. We couldn't think of any other way to get someone out there. I truly am afraid."

Alex was afraid for her, too. A cold feeling settled in the pit of his stomach when he thought about it, and he knew he could not abandon her. There was still a bond between them. He didn't want it, but it was there. He had felt it on the dance floor—he felt it now—and he knew he would never be able to live with himself if something happened to her and he had not tried to help.

He owed her that much. She had hurt him once, but she had given pleasure, too, and pretty dreams, and he could not forget that. He was going to regret it. He already regretted it. It was going to be a hellish several weeks, but his blasted Yankee conscience would give him no rest.

"Why not?" he called out recklessly. "A little time in the cane fields will no doubt, as Matt pointed out, do me infinite good. I'm all yours, Perralt—if you want me."

The carriage wheels jolted and rumbled over the rough dirt road. Maria sat rigidly, facing forward, and tried not to listen to Royall's irregular breathing. He was sprawled out on the seat across from her, thoroughly and drunkenly asleep.

The night was dark and nearly silent. She could feel rain, but it was not yet falling. Except for Royall's snores, she almost felt alone in the world. The waterfront bars never closed, but the noises were sporadic now, fading as they left the town behind them. The carriage lantern swayed and flickered; tall grasses showed gold and green on one side, the sand whitish coral on the other.

He was coming to Honuakula.

Maria's heart constricted, and she felt strangely light-headed. As if she were going to faint. The one thing she had not in her wildest dreams imagined. She had been so sure he was out of her life forever; she would never have to face the feelings his reappearance had awakened in her. Now suddenly the world seemed to have turned upside down, and she was not even sure how she felt.

The air was hot, humid with the oppressive heaviness of the ocean, and she was finding it hard to breathe. Her stays dug into her flesh; the shawl, even in darkness, still rested secretively over her shoulders.

Part of her longed for him to come. The immature, illogical part that had surfaced tonight. Just to see him, to have him there ... to hear his voice ... She was not ready to give up the fantasies that had lain dormant so long. Her heart would be empty without them.

But another part—the sensible, thinking part—was frightened at the prospect. Maria gripped the side of the carriage, holding on for all she was worth. There was no possibility that anything would happen between them. Nor did she want it to now ... but she couldn't help remembering the way he had looked at her just as the dance was ending. Even a little kindness and she would be shattered if he left again.

When he left ... and then her heart would be empty forever.

Royall muttered something and stirred in his sleep. Maria glanced at him with the first twinges of apprehension. They were already approaching the house. It didn't look like he was going to be able to get up by himself. The servants were going to have to carry him in. Again.

Lighted windows showed just ahead, and she hoped that Mack was sound asleep. The rain began to patter softly on the roof of the carriage, not enough to blow in through the open sides. A single candle was always kept glowing in his room—he didn't like the dark—and she detected no sign of motion behind his window. Safe then—at least she hoped so. She didn't want him to see his father being carried drunk to bed.

He was growing so fast. It seemed to her he had already begun to pick things up. He would find out soon, and she would have to figure out what to do then. But she couldn't deal with it tonight.

Mack ...

Her fingers released their death grip on the side of the carriage, and she leaned back, relaxing somewhat. The rain was still barely a drizzle, hardly intruding on her thoughts. Of course—Mack. How could she have forgotten?

She had been going about everything the wrong way around. She had been thinking of herself, trying to figure out what *she* wanted, what would be right for *her*. But she was a mother now. Not a silly girl falling in love for the first time. There were more important things than the state of her poor, fragile heart.

The carriage stopped, and the servants came out, anticipating what was rapidly becoming a regular duty. The rain had let up just for a moment; the road was barely damp. Looking up, Maria still saw nothing moving behind that candlelit window. At least for tonight, her son would be spared. It was up to her to keep him safe tomorrow.

And all the tomorrows to come. It was as if a weight were falling from her shoulders with the shawl that floated unnoticed to the carriage floor. Now that she had made up her mind, it seemed almost easy. There would be no turmoil when Alex Barron showed up at Honuakula to prove his talent with the soil. She was past all that.

She would be polite when she had to be—she would make peace with him if she could—but the feelings she had glimpsed briefly tonight would remain buried inside her forever.

All that mattered was Mack. His happiness, not hers. If she had to sustain a sham marriage to keep his world intact, then that was what she would do. If she had to say good-bye to every dream she had ever had, that too was possible. Nothing would ever jeopardize her child's welfare. Not even the love she had finally dared to admit to herself.

The servants had disappeared through the doorway with their cumbersome burden. The house was quiet and cool as she stepped inside.

The First Pure Light of Today

Today dawns
With the first pure light,
Sharp-edged shadows
Stretch across the earth;
Life reawakening
In a burst of golden brightness.

Chapter 7

Honuakula sprawled across vast open meadows and wooded slopes, acre upon acre of cultivated cane fields, avocado groves, and forests thick with false staghorn ferns and red-flowering *ohia* trees, stretching almost to the ocean. The house itself stood alone on a surprisingly barren hilltop. Royall had chosen the site for its majestic view and isolated splendor, which left one seeming to hover in the clouds. A single gray-trunked *kukui* tree soared to a height of nearly eighty feet in the side yard, its silvery-green leaves and delicate white blossoms whispering softly in the breezes, and rows of yellow hibiscus had been planted in artificial symmetry along the sides of the road that wound up from the base of the hill.

The building was too large and ornate for its setting. Royall liked his money to show, and the restraint with which he had treated the natural surroundings was more than balanced by the ostentation of his house. It was not without grace, however, and a kind of stately beauty, for it had been patterned after the great plantations of his native South. White-pillared *lanais*, or verandas as he persisted in calling them, swept across the front and along both sides, which contained the sleeping quarters and the servants' wing. The cookhouse was in a separate structure, as was the plantation office and Royall's library—in reality, his bedroom, though it was not altogether a misnomer, for an entire wall of shelving was crammed with books and treatises devoted to his one true passion, agriculture.

It was shortly before noon on the morning after the party when Alex Barron appeared in the mud of the road, his work clothes and personal effects stowed in a pair of bags hitched to the back of his saddle. Royall was sober as he stood on the steps of the veranda and waited for him. Debauchery had taken its toll on his face, but he was hard and tanned, and looked ready for work. He wasted no time with pleasantries, but signaled a stable boy to take care of the baggage and, mounting his own horse, showed his new *luna* the way to the fields.

Maria did not know if she was relieved or disappointed as she lingered in the doorway and watched them ride off. The gray clouds had drifted away in the night, but they were billowing back, and it would soon be raining again. She had been preparing herself all morning for that moment, and it was a bit disconcerting to realize that she was not quite pleased with how easily it had gone.

There had been a brief nod in her direction—apparently the eldest of the Barron captains had also decided on polite formality—but otherwise no contact between them. She might just as well have lounged in a warm, soothing tub and not bothered to worry at all.

Maria was to see little of Alex in the days that followed. Their paths crossed occasionally but only briefly, and then from a distance. She would catch him looking at her sometimes, but when she looked back, he would turn away and go on about whatever he had been doing.

He was, she had to admit, treating her exactly the way she had hoped—and she was finding to her discomfort that she hated it. A perverse reaction, and utterly unreasonable. She had sworn to herself that she would keep her feelings under control—and she would!—but they were still there, and she was beginning to realize just how hard it was, this task she had set for herself.

They spoke only once during the first week he was there. It had been raining off and on most of the morning, hot tropical downpours, and the paths were slick with mud. Maria had just started for the icehouse to get some fresh butter, which was kept in a cool underground chamber to prevent it from turning rancid, when he appeared abruptly around a corner, heading in the same direction. It was too late to avoid each other, and they walked a short distance together, straining somewhat for conversation as they chatted about the plantation.

The name Honuakula, Maria explained, meant yellow or golden earth. "That was the native name for the hilltop before Royall built the house. As the story goes, it was filled once with great splashes of yellow hibiscus, though I doubt they ever grew wild here. Those along the road were planted later. More likely the name came from tall golden grasses rippling in the wind. At any rate, Royall decided to keep it. He thought it had pretty ring."

"Ah, that explains it," Alex replied casually. "The hibiscus borders were put in to go with the story. I thought they looked out of place. All the other vegetation seems indigenous."

"Actually, it was Claudine who wanted them. Royall's wife. His late wife—she was supposed to have been killed in a shipwreck or something. He talks about having them taken out, but I can't imagine Royall destroying any plant, however inappropriate, once it has taken root. . . . The only thing here before the house was that *kukui* tree. Candlenut, you would call it. The bark and juice are used for tattoo dyes, and the nuts strung together and burned for light. Royall likes to use them as decoration when we have a dinner party. But sparingly. He always worries about fire."

Alex let his eyes drift from the tree back down the

hillside. The last droplets of rain glittered like dew on the fields, and the ocean was blue and serene in the distance. "A lovely place," he said, then added unexpectedly: "I hope you are happy here."

He sounded sincere, and Maria tried to ignore the ache in her heart as he took his leave and strolled carelessly away. He seemed to have softened toward her. She sensed none of the contempt that had been there before. It was almost as if they were coming to terms with each other. She might even be able to make him understand . . .

But it would do her no good! Setting her attention back on the icehouse and the butter she had come to fetch, Maria forced herself to forget the foolish fancies that persisted in taking hold. He might understand, but he would never love her the way she longed to be loved. The illusions of the past were over now, and she had to let them go.

And she couldn't accept it if he did.

She had little time, fortunately, to brood about Alex and what he might or might not be feeling, for her duties kept her busy. There had been an experienced housekeeper when she arrived at Honuakula as a young bride, but Royall had wanted his wife to take her place as mistress of the plantation, and she had been almost desperately anxious to please him. With all the strain between them, it was the one way she could make things at least partially right and find a tenuous common ground on which they could meet.

It had not been easy the first few months—she had had no idea how much work was entailed in running a gracious home—but now she took even the most daunting of her chores in stride.

Her day began with the household ledgers. Royall kept the plantation books, but she was expected to mark down every rial spent on bolts of calico, lamp oil and lucifer matches, iron cooking kettles, pewter platters, sandalwood soap, chamberpots with little pink and green raised roses, and saleratus or soda for baking a cake. Not a simple matter for a woman who had had little formal schooling, and it was only recently that she had stopped counting on her fingers and her sums came out the first time without having to do them over and over on a separate scrap of paper.

After the books were finished, there was laundry to be supervised, linens to be pressed and put away, food supplies to be checked and inventoried. Weevils always seemed to be getting into the flour—it was almost impossible to find tight enough containers—sugar beans had to be selected at just the right stage of ripeness from the garden, and eggs not used immediately boiled and pickled in brine with cloves.

Furniture was oiled weekly and rubbed to a high gloss. Many of the tables and chests were island-crafted, exquisite pieces of carved *koa* or *lehua* wood, but Royall liked the dark elegance of mahogany, which required extra care, and had imported much teak from the Orient. Silver had to be polished, crystal kept shining, floors swept, and mats and carpets taken out to be beaten—a never ending challenge that always seemed to demand something more. Much as Maria adored them, she had almost as much trouble coaxing her native servants to stick to their tasks as the master of the plantation had with his workers in the field, though she was careful never to broach the subject with him.

There were certain things that set off Royall's temper, even sober, and she had long since learned to avoid them.

It was not all work, however, for the hours that might have gone slowly were brightened by an unprecedented number of visitors, some more welcome than others. It made her skin crawl to have to play hostess to Lucifer Darley, who had taken to dropping by with increasing frequency, but it was always a pleasure to see Doc Fred. Maria used to suspect that his main attraction to Honuakula was pretty Ilimi, whose husband had effectively ended their marriage by renouncing Christianity and taking a new wife. But Ilimi had been transferred to the town house, and he still showed up at least twice a week. "To see to the welfare of your workers," he said, though Maria had a feeling the old fraud was really checking on her.

Even her mother, who had an intense distrust of horses, had ridden out several times. And Rachel appeared almost daily, sometimes with her husband or brother-in-law, but generally alone.

It was over an hour's ride from Lahaina, but she said it did her good. And anyhow, as she explained to Maria, she had to find something to do with herself now that Matthew was spending all his time on the *Jade Dawn*.

"You have no idea how many things there are that have to be done to a ship," she said in mock exasperation. "New masts need to be made, old ones repaired . . . the shrouds or the rigging, or whatever it is, seems to be falling apart! It's amazing, all the hours that are required."

"Sounds like running a household," Maria replied with a knowing chuckle. "It makes me exhausted just listening. We'd better sit down. Shall I send for some tea? Or would you prefer a pitcher of mango juice?"

"Both. There's more dust on that road than in all of Macao. And it rained yesterday! I can hardly wait for the dry season. I'm thirsty as a—what? A camel? . . . Are camels thirsty?"

Maria laughed as she clapped her hands to summon one of the servants who had been hovering nearby, doing nothing as usual when the *wahine* of the house wasn't watching. It was good to have Rachel back. Maria hadn't realized how much she had missed having someone to chatter and giggle with. Especially since her friend seemed to have picked up her reticence about discussing certain subjects and had stopped asking awkward questions. Or maybe she had just gotten tired of probing for answers that didn't come.

"You haven't admired my new outfit," Rachel said with a puckish look after the servant had gone and come back—with tea only, no mango juice. It might be coming later, and then again, it might not. "I had it made especially for riding. Now tell me the truth, don't you think I've become unutterably stylish?"

She jumped up and whirled around to give Maria a good look. Unique would have been a better word. A split skirt, rather like a Hawaiian *pau*, had been cunningly cut from dark green twill to resemble a conventional riding habit. But with it she was wearing a loose bodice with long, flowing white sleeves and what almost appeared to be a man's white waistcoat. It was charming, it was whimsical—her young husband had no doubt been sorely distracted from his work on the ship—but à la mode?

"You look adorable," she said. "I greatly admire your imagination. But fashion, I fear, like French, is not one of your accomplishments."

"Or riding." Rachel grinned good-naturedly as she plopped back down in her chair. "We only kept one horse in Macao, and if my brothers weren't fighting over it, it was hitched up to something or other. I thought I'd improve with practice, but I ran into Alex on the way up and he said, very kindly—so like Alex—that he really thought I was doing quite 'nicely'. Have you ever noticed about that word *nicely*? It's what people always say when they don't want to tell you the truth. How is Alex doing, by the way? I barely had a chance to speak with him."

"I wouldn't know." Maria stared down at her cup, though there was nothing left in it. Alex always made a point of being nowhere nearby when Rachel came to the house, though he stopped and greeted her sometimes on the way in or out. Perhaps too much of a point, she thought, and added hastily: "I hardly get a chance to speak with him myself. He and Royall are out in the fields all day, even when it rains. Until well past sundown. Then they spend their evenings poring over books in the library. . . . But honestly, Rachel, sometimes *nicely* really does mean nicely. I do think your riding has improved greatly."

" 'Greatly' ?" Rachel rolled the word around in her mouth.

"Indeed," Maria insisted, meaning it. Rachel rode as she did everything else, with great spirit, and while she would never win any applause for style, she was turning into an enthusiastic horsewoman. "All that practice is paying off. You'll have to keep at it . . . while you still can. When you find yourself 'with child,' as they say, Matthew is certain to become overprotective—as he keeps accusing his brother of being—and refuse to let you ride."

"You don't suppose," Rachel said, her face suddenly turning thoughtful, "that riding could actually keep one from *getting* pregnant. I mean, if Jared is that concerned about Dominie now . . ."

"Don't be a ninny," Maria said with feeling. She loved to ride herself, and it hadn't kept her from conceiving and giving birth to a healthy child. "Dominie is two or three months from due, I'd guess . . . and Jared really is overprotective. He's only let her come out here once—for lunch—and then he insisted on bringing her in the carriage. It must have been a bumpy ride. Much harder on her than a horse's gait. I sometimes wonder where God kept the common sense when it came time to hand out attributes to men."

"Well back of pride," Rachel agreed. "And pigheadedness. Probably off in a bin somewhere to save for the women who have to keep them in line. . . . Still, I do worry, you know. I suppose it's silly. Matthew says it is. But I've been wanting a baby such a long time, and it just doesn't happen."

"You haven't been married 'such a long time.' You haven't even known Matthew a long time, so don't fancy I'm making sly insinuations. Everyone doesn't get pregnant on the first try, for heaven's sake."

"I suppose not," Rachel agreed dubiously. "But it *has* been more than once." She flushed slightly. "Considerably more. Matthew and I . . . well, we do enjoy being married to each other. But I can't seem to get pregnant."

"You should present your friend with a basket of *pu'aha-nui* fruit," Royall said from the doorway. The interruption was unexpected, and Maria felt color rising to her cheeks as she realized he had been standing outside on the *lanai*, listening to all the details of that intimate conversation. He hadn't even the courtesy to pretend he hadn't heard.

"*Pu'aha-nui?*" If Rachel was offended by his boorishness, she managed to keep her composure remarkably well. "I don't believe I've heard of that. It's a fruit, you said?"

"From a shrub of the same name. It produces large serrated leaves and clusters of white or lavender flowers—but you're not interested in the botanical details. The fruit is legendary among the natives. They claim it aids in conception, and they may be right. It worked for us, didn't it, my dear?" He turned to Maria with a calculated leer. "And on very nearly the first try, too. . . . Well, I'll leave you to your chat, ladies. I just came to pick up something from the office."

But the office outbuilding was on the other side of the house. Maria felt cold and sick inside as she stared after him through the open door. Quite a distance away. He must have been purposely spying on her. Checking to see how much she was telling her friend. Had that humiliating crudeness been a none-too-subtle reminder to keep her mouth shut?

"I'm sorry," she said miserably. "Royall doesn't

usually act like that. Truly. I'm afraid sometimes we forget our manners, living so far from society."

Rachel laid a hand on her arm. "You don't have to apologize. You're not responsible for what he does just because he's your husband. You must not think that any of this is your fault. And besides," she added, deliberately lightening the mood," he may have done me a favor. I'm going to have to get some of this *pu'aha-nui* he suggests. Do you think it might really be effective?"

"I doubt it," Maria replied shortly, recalling all too vividly the one occasion on which she had consumed it. "I imagine it's just superstition."

"Well, I don't suppose it would hurt to give it a try. . . . I just hope it doesn't taste too vile. There are limits even to *my* desire for a child."

The conversation drifted on to other subjects, and Rachel prattled away for a while, a little too brightly, before taking her leave, much earlier than usual. Maria was grateful for her friend's tact as she strolled out onto the *lanai* and watched the cloud of dust disappearing down the road. She didn't think she could have pretended any longer. Royall's behavior toward her had grown colder over the years, and harsher, but it seemed to her of late he was setting out to be deliberately cruel.

It was almost as if, for him as for her, life had become unbearable, and something was ready to snap.

It was just past midday. There were almost no shadows, and the air was heavy and still. Not a whir of birds' wings could be heard; not a subtle rustling of silvery *kukui* leaves. A movement showed down the slope, and Maria turned her head to see Alex bending over to check the posts on a fence.

She did not mean to let her eyes linger on him. She had long since learned it was foolish and unprofitable. But her heart was hurting; life seemed lonelier than usual, and she gave in to the moment's temptation.

She had forgotten sometimes how good it was to look at him. Tall, lean, strong. She remembered that body so well. Fluid of movement, masculine as he stooped easily, then straightened, arching his back to work the cramps out of his muscles. He wore his clothes well. Even the rough gray work shirt looked good on him, open at the neck. Maria was too far away to see, but she could imagine wisps of hair curling up from his chest. And dark pants, rough, too, fitted snugly to his legs and thighs . . .

All the longings she had ever felt, all the dreams she had tried so hard to deny, came over her suddenly, and she knew that she wanted him. Desperately. Just as she knew she could never have him.

She did not realize she wasn't alone until she heard an ominous creak behind her. Whirling nervously, she saw Royall watching her, his face black with barely leashed anger.

"I see the attraction goes both ways," he said coarsely. "You watch the Barron bachelor as hungrily as he watches you. You really should learn to control your expression better. . . . I trust you're not planning on taking this naked passion any further."

"What difference would it make?" Maria snapped back, too tired to be cautious. She might be too embarrassed to argue with him in front of her friend, but she didn't have to put up with this in private. "You don't have any feelings for me. Not even possessiveness. Nor would you have any right to, as I don't need to remind you. I could have a dozen affairs, and you wouldn't lose an hour's sleep over it. . . . I seem to remember there was a time when you *wanted* to push me into someone else's bed."

He caught her wrist abruptly, making her gasp as he jerked her toward him. Maria was startled to smell liquor on his breath. Just faintly—but he didn't usually take even a glass when he was working in the fields.

"There was a time when I wanted a son, but I have him now. And I didn't need another man for that, as you will recall. . . . You do recall, don't you?" He gripped her more tightly, sending sharp pains up her arm until she nodded. "Good. I wouldn't want you to forget that. Everyone sees you as my loving, devoted wife. I don't expect you to make a public mockery of me with another man. Any man. I assure you, you'll pay dearly if you do."

"I'm paying already," Maria said bitterly. "I'll be paying for the rest of my life—or yours, whichever comes first. Do you seriously think I'm frightened by your threats? What more can you do? Rape me again to prove you're a man?"

"Rape?" He wrenched her wrist so hard tears came to her eyes. "It isn't rape when the woman's asking for it . . . and you were asking, sweetheart! You were practically panting for it. You have the soul and body of a slut—anything in trousers makes you want to lie down and spread your legs. But God help you if your trashy behavior disgraces me."

Maria tried to pull back, but it hurt too much. "Don't worry," she said, as placatingly as she could. "I have no intention of tarnishing your precious public image."

His fingers finally released their hold. Her wrist was throbbing, but she didn't dare rub it with her other hand. His eyes seemed to be burning into her.

"Just so I make myself perfectly clear. The man is a Barron. He's used to getting what he wants—and arrogant enough not to care who he steps on to do it. Since what he wants appears to be my woman, I'd be a fool to trust him."

"If that's how you feel," Maria said slowly, "why do you keep him here? Why don't you just have the servants pack up his belongings and send him on his way?"

He looked faintly surprised. "Because I need him, of course. He's good with the land, and good with the men. I'm just getting the new fields started—we'll double our production. I'm not about to jeopardize the future of Honuakula for some petty personal grievance."

Honuakula . . . Maria stood alone on the shadowed *lanai*, shaking, as he strode off without a backward look. Everything for him always came down to Honuakula. There was something almost abnormal about the attachment. He was consumed by it. The plantation was more than a plantation to him, the land more than earth and stone. It sometimes seemed to her that he loved it as another man might love a woman.

A fly settled on her hair, and she raised her hand automatically to brush it away. She was surprised to find her wrist so sore she could hardly bend it. Royall had never touched her before, never turned rough, unless he was heavily into the bottle. Honuakula . . . the one passion of his life, the one thing he truly cared about. The earth mistress he had brought to life himself out of empty, golden fields.

For the first time Maria understood the man with whom she had spent eight years of her life. The fly was back, buzzing around her head, but she barely noticed. She could go to blazes for all he cared. He had been blustering before, indulging his male vanity. She could run off, with or without another man, and he would survive quite well. Perhaps his cruelty was even an unconscious effort to try to drive her away. The public disgrace would be tolerable as long as he had Honuakula.

And Mack.

The thought struck her with an almost physical jolt. Had she said before that there was nothing more he could do to her? The heat was oppressive, even in the shade, and Maria went back into the relative coolness of the house.

If Royall's plantation was an obsession, so was *his* son. He would no more give up the boy than he would give up the land. She could leave—he would not lift a finger to stop her—but if she tried to take Mack, he would track her to the ends of the earth.

Mack was the tie that would hold her forever to him. And Mack was the weapon he would use to keep her in line.

Alex threw himself into his work with an abandon that did not allow him to give more than a passing thought to the wife of the man who had now, ironically, become his employer, though it had been agreed between them that no money would change hands. It was not a hardship for him. He loved the feel of the rich Maui soil as it trickled through his fingers, loved the fertile smell of it clinging to his nostrils. He loved plowing and planting and watching the first green shoots sprout out of the earth. This was where he was at home, where his heart felt at peace, as it never had on the sea.

With Royall Perralt, he had come to a kind of uneasy truce. There was no pretense at liking on either side. Alex had not failed to notice the other man's brittle sharpness, his utter inability to compromise or be kind to anyone except his small son, just as he sensed his own Yankee rigidity and natural aloofness was meeting with similar responses of suspicion and distaste. But they respected each other's knowledge and talent for the soil, and it formed an unspoken bond between them.

He had spent his first afternoon and most of the next day working with Royall and a full crew in the existing fields. Being used to tobacco and cotton, the sheer greenness of the cane had surprised him. It had looked to him like a giant field of grass, waving and glistening in the sun, and the wind that had shivered through it had almost made it seem to sing. Nearly as tall as a man already, it had seemed so dense, Alex couldn't imagine anyone getting through it without a machete or cane knife.

Crude roads with deep ruts from wagon wheels ran between the fields. When Alex had dismounted and gone closer, he could see that the cane had been planted in long rows, making it possible to move up and down, though not across.

Here he had learned his first word of plantation Hawaiian—*hana*, which meant work. Hoe *hana* was the tedious, muscle-wrenching chore of weeding the seemingly endless rows, which began as soon as the first sprouts appeared and continued constantly until the stalks were thick and crowding each other, and a canopy of green leaves blocked out the sun.

Sometimes it almost seemed as if the weeds grew faster than the cane. The *kanakas*, the Hawaiian workmen, ever on the lookout for a chance to rest, had been glad to lean on their hoes and give him their frank opinion of the chore. Alex had quickly gotten a picture of their workday. Four hours in long, straight lines, even when it rained, then a break for lunch, then four hours again. Bending constantly, no talking, no stretching; the only pauses allowed were to sharpen their tools. Backs were stiff and aching when it finally came to *pau hana*, or work over, the end of the day.

Even more rigorous than hoe *hana* was the task of stripping dead leaves from the tall stalks, *hole-hole*, spelled with an *e* but pronounced, as usual in Hawaiian, "holy-holy." Over the next few days, Alex was to watch the workers, bundled in heavy clothing to protect their limbs and faces, make their way through row after endless row, and wonder how they endured it.

It was brutal, sweaty work. The leaves that filtered the sun also kept out the breezes and held in the moisture from the rain, and the air was close and steamy. An almost sickeningly sweet smell attracted swarms of wasps, and the monotonous sound of their droning was punctuated by a rhythmic *slash-slash*, *slash-slash* of the workers' knives. Even with the protective gear hands were cut so badly by the spiny leaves it made Alex wince to look at them.

He had been surprised to find that most of the *hole-hole hana* was done by women. He would have thought it a highly unsuitable task for what he had always considered the weaker sex. But when he questioned Royall about it, the other man only laughed.

"I thought so myself," he admitted almost jovially. "But I can't get the men to do it—and I don't wonder! It's damned beastly work, but they want the money so they send their women. It's turned out well all around. The *wahines* are better workers."

"It doesn't bother you?" Alex ventured cautiously. He had learned to be careful not to appear critical. "Using women like that?"

"Why should it? They don't whine like their husbands. Besides, I have to pay the men one rial— twelve and a half cents—a day. The women work for half—what the devil?"

His expression changed abruptly. Without another word he raced over to one of the thicker growths of cane. Before Alex could even react, he had grabbed a native workmen and, spinning him backward, threw him roughly on the ground. Cursing vehemently, he stomped at something under his feet with almost fanatical fury.

The other workers were already gathered around, ominously silent, by the time Alex reached the spot. The Hawaiian was nearly double Royall's size, but he came up like a rag doll when the older man clutched him by the shirt front and dragged him to his feet.

"You blasted s.o.b., you know damn well that's not allowed! Get the hell out of here. You're through. Your *wahine* can pick up your pay."

"But Mistah Ginnis . . ." the man protested weakly "he say—"

"I don't give a damn what Ginnis said," Royall cut in coldly. His rage was controlled now but nonetheless ugly. "I fired Ginnis two weeks ago. He doesn't give the orders around here. I do. And I want you off my land. Now."

The only sound was the shuffling of the man's feet as he inched backward, not daring to turn until he was sure he would not be grabbed and flung to the earth again. At a look from Royall, the others went back to their tasks, working with considerably more energy than usual.

Alex threw a curious glance at the ground and was surprised to see what appeared to be the remains of a crude pipe.

"He was—smoking?" he said.

Royall turned to him with an icy look. "The last *luna* allowed smoking at the ends of the rows. That's one of the reasons I got rid of him. And every one of these blasted *kanakas* knows it! Look at all those dried leaves. It's a tinderbox in there. One careless spark, one gust of wind . . ." He shuddered visibly, almost as if he could feel the flames on his own flesh, and Alex sensed for an instant a fear that ran deeper than reason. "Fire is always the enemy in a cane field. Any man who doesn't realize that is a fool. . . . And I don't suffer fools gladly."

Alex was to remember afterward that look on Royall Perralt's face and wonder if he should have taken it as a premonition. Had the first germ of a thought flashed through his mind at that moment? But the words had seemed sensible, the precaution not unreasonable, and he had dismissed it from his mind.

The man might have overreacted, but he knew his workers. If he had not created that violent scene, he might not have made an impression, and someone might have lighted up in the cane fields again. With disastrous results next time.

Chapter 8

The rains turned lighter at the end of June. The dry season would begin soon, not a prudent time for planting, but Royall was putting in irrigation ditches to bring water down from the streams in the hills, and he gambled that he could get it there in time. Three new fields were to be cleared and harrowed, plowed and planted, in as many weeks, and Alex found himself working as hard as he ever had in his life.

The end of each day saw him drenched with sweat. Even when it rained, it wasn't cool, and then he worked ankle-deep in mud, cursing the teams of oxen as they slid and balked at the ends of long chains fastened to stumps imbedded in the earth. Stones were hauled away by wagon loads to be used in building, tree roots and fallen trunks had to be cut up for firewood for the mill, and all the trash cleared and removed so the fields could be plowed.

He was gaining a better appreciation for Royall's harsh assessment of his *kanakas*. They were big-hearted people. God knows, he enjoyed their songs and stories, but not one of them seemed to have even the slightest interest in work, and he had to watch them closely or he'd find half his crew wandering off.

There were only two men he could count on: a wiry, leather-faced old salt who had been recruited for a brief stint as plowman, and a young Chinese who answered, as did most of his countrymen in the islands, to the name of "Pake." Pake knew nothing about farming, but he was quick and clever and eager to learn, three qualities Alex was coming to appreciate highly.

Plowing started just as the last of the rain seemed to be ending. It was exhausting labor, but he thrived on the challenge. Holding the heavy plow behind eight plodding, dun-colored oxen, throwing his weight against one side or the other to keep it steady, breaking up clod after clod of heavy red-brown earth, took all his skill and concentration. His hands were callused by the end of the first afternoon, his muscles aching, but he felt more alive than he had for years, and he understood with every fiber of his being the passionate devotion Royall Perralt felt for his land.

He did not have time to worry about Maria, which was just as well, for there was little he could do except try to keep an eye on her husband. She was safe enough during the day. As long as Alex could see or hear another crew working anywhere on the plantation, he knew she was all right. There were some advantages to having workers who dropped their tools to sing and swap tales the minute the boss was gone. And he made sure he kept Royall up as late as possible every night, questioning him about the cane or debating some esoteric agricultural theory that necessitated searching through one scholarly treatise or another. But beyond that he was helpless.

Sooner or later he had to go back to his own cottage, and then it was out of his hands. He could hardly intrude on the privacy of their bedroom. He had already figured out that Royall slept most nights in his library, but that didn't mean he wasn't making an occasional foray to visit his wife.

Alex hated himself for the sickening feeling that rose with his gorge at the thought. It was asinine, there was no justification for it—the man was her husband, he had a right to do whatever he wanted in her bed—but he could see that she was desperately unhappy. He couldn't have her himself. Honor would never allow him to become enmeshed in a tawdry affair with a married woman, but it frustrated every proud male instinct in him not to be able to protect her.

At least the man wasn't drinking. Alex paused to look up at the sky and was worried when he saw no trace of a cloud. He wasn't all that sure the irrigation scheme was going to work out. When Royall was sober, he didn't seem to exhibit the brutish tendencies that had alarmed Alex that first night, but there was a new bruise on her wrist.

She had said she'd gotten it twisted in the rope while she was drawing a bucket of water. But she had said it too quickly, glibly, and Alex had been reminded of the way she had draped a shawl over her shoulders on an especially warm evening. She's used to making excuses, he thought. She has done this before.

Damn. He wished the *luna's* cottage weren't so far from the main house. He wouldn't even hear if she cried out. And which of the servants would dare to go to her aid?

The noon break was ending, and Alex forced his mind back to the task at hand. He could hear the workers returning, Pake bringing them safely in tow. The young Chinese had proved invaluable, getting things out of the natives with a combination of wheedling, flattery, and threatening to run to the boss-man that even Alex could not manage.

"Good," he called out. "You're here. Let's see if we can plant some cane."

The afternoon passed swiftly. Royall appeared several times, briefly checking on their progress and supervising the arrival of a new wagon load of seed cane. On one of his stops he had young Mack proudly perched on the horse in front of him.

Alex enjoyed the boy's visits, and even Royall relaxed somewhat when he was there. His energy was boundless. He always seemed to be brimming over with excitement—clearly he reveled in his father's attention—and full of endless questions. Every third word from his mouth seemed to be *why* or *how* or *what*.

"Why is it called *seed* cane? It doesn't look like seeds. Where does it come from? How did it get here? What are you going to do with it?"

His mind flashed quickly from one thought to another, rarely pausing for answers in between. Royall was surprisingly patient with him. It was called *seed*, he explained, because it was used to make new cane, as flowers came from seeds you put in the ground. The first cane had been brought to the islands by the Polynesians in their canoes, but now it grew wild on the hillsides.

Most of the cane in their fields, he told the boy solemnly, came from native gardens, but it didn't do very well after a while. So he had sent for some special cane. All the way from Tahiti. He knew about it because that was what they had grown on his family's plantation in Louisiana.

The field had been plowed in long, raised ridges, with valleys several inches deep between. Now he brought Mack over to the end of one of them and leaned down to pick up a length of the new cane. Eager as Royall had been to begin planting, Alex noticed that he took time to make everything clear.

"You cut the stalks in pieces like this," he said, holding it up for Mack to get a closer look. "About two or three feet long. You see these little lines that go all the way around? Feel how bumpy they are. They're called joints. That's where the new sprouts will come from."

The boy's face was rapt with curiosity and a sense of his own importance as he watched Royall make a deep furrow with his hoe and lay the cane in it lengthwise. "Why are you planting it in that funny hill?" he asked, reverting to his favorite form of expression. "Is that an *o'o*? Ilimi has one just like it she uses in the garden. Where did it come from? Who made it?"

"The cane is planted in low mounds so it won't rot if there's too much rain," Royall told him, starting with the first question. He covered the cutting with about two inches of dirt, then made another furrow a foot away and repeated the procedure. "The water runs down the sides. That way the cane won't get soggy and be ruined. The *o'o* was made in our own shop. Right here on the plantation. But the first ones were made by the natives. For digging. They got the idea from blubber spades on the whaling ships."

"What's a blubber spade?"

Alex grinned as Royall continued to answer his son's questions, thoroughly and without patronizing the child. He planted a few more cuttings himself, then gave the hoe to Mack and stood to the side, adding only an occasional comment as the next length of cane found its way into the earth.

He remained for several minutes, watching, but mostly silent, until his attention was distracted by a commotion down the field. Two of the *kanakas* getting belligerent, and he sprinted over to head off a fight.

Mack pretended not to notice, but he was obviously aware that his father was gone. He worked very slowly and very seriously. Taking up the *o'o* again, he ran it along the shallow ridge in a straight, careful line, then laid the cane in just so, his face puckering with concentration as he checked to make sure it was perfect. Alex felt a sudden constriction in his chest as the boy looked up and he caught sight of piercing blue-gray eyes.

It was like looking at Jared again, he thought, when they were both about that age. Except for the hair. Jared had been blond. Even the shape of the face was similar. Barron men all had the same features . . .

and he found himself wondering again as he had that first time he had seen the child on the beach.

Royall had said that his mother had the same eyes. But it would have been a long time since he had seen her, and memory had a way of changing things. And even if she did, they were still a Barron trait. There had to be at least a possibility, and Alex realized suddenly he had to know.

It was a damn-fool impulse. Even if he could be reasonably sure—and, God, how could he?—there was nothing he would be able do about it. He could never be a part of the boy's life.

More likely he would just prove it was impossible. He arched his back unconsciously, feeling the aching in his muscles. At least that would put an end to it once and for all. At least he would know. Anything was better than tearing himself apart with suspicions. How old would a son of his have to be? Seven and a half, born around New Year's. It ought to be easy enough to find out.

He strolled over, feeling nowhere near as casual as he looked. "That's an excellent job of planting, young man," he said. "You're going to make a fine farmer one day." He squatted down, patting the soil with one hand. "Definitely first-rate. I can't imagine many boys your age doing as well. How old are you now? About seven?"

Blue-gray eyes glowed with pride at the compliment. "Almost eight," he said. "Do you really think I did good?"

Eight. Alex's heart seemed to stop. Too old ... but "almost eight" could mean anything to a child. They were so eager to grow up at that age. They started being almost eight the day after they turned seven.

"Well, that is a big boy. Almost eight, you say. Your birthday is soon?"

"October second," the child replied—and Alex had his answer. Three months too early. He was no stranger to pregnancy and childbirth. He had younger sisters, and they all had children of their own. A baby born that early could hardly have survived.

"Almost eight," he agreed, and gave the soil one last appreciative pat before standing again. "Yes, I think you did very good indeed. You're learning fast, Mack. Your father must be proud of you."

He did not get quite the response he had expected. "I try," the boy said earnestly. "I try most awfully hard. Do you really think he's proud of me?"

I think he'd be a fool not to be, Alex thought, but he did not put it quite that way out loud. "Yes," he said. "I'm sure he is."

He was aware as he walked away of an indescribable sense of loss. He had wanted the boy. It surprised him, but he was too honest to deny his feelings. He had wanted even the intangible bond that would have been between them if there had been just a chance.

All the time he had been with her, he thought—all the time he had been making love to her, she had been carrying another man's child. A great hollow seemed to echo inside him, never quite recognized before, but once seen, he knew it could not be ignored again.

He caught himself with an angry grimace. Damned if he wasn't turning into a sentimental buffoon. He had never been mawkish and self-pitying before. Reality was reality, and the sooner he faced it, the better off he was going to be. He had met a woman . . . and he had loved her . . . but that was over now.

In a few weeks, the fields would be plowed and the *Jade Dawn* ready to sail for Boston. He would do what he could for her in the meantime, but after that it was going to be up to her friends. He would always care. There was no bitterness left in his heart toward her—he would always hope that things had turned out well—but he would be off with the morning sun, the trade winds swelling his sails, and Maria and her son would be left behind forever.

The irrigation channels were finished almost exactly on schedule. Water ran from cold crystal streams high in the hills, through a dense green jungle of ferns and *maile* vines to the lowlands where the thirsty soil of Honuakula waited to drink it in. The main ditch was already filled; all that remained was to throw open the gates the next morning. Royall, not trusting the *kanakas* even when they had been working under his strict supervision, was planning on spending the last evening by torchlight, checking out every inch of the main and feeder ditches before the water came gushing through.

It was an impressive undertaking. Even Maria, who had been left out of the planning and knew only what she had overheard in bits and snatches of conversation, recognized as she rounded the last rise and drew near that it had been brilliantly planned and executed. She had come, on Royall's orders, to fetch his dinner. One of the servants could as easily have brought the Hingham bucket packed with pickled eggs, cold ham, oranges, and cake, but he liked to display her, even in front of field hands, as the perfect, devoted wife. And because it was easier than trying to argue—and, in fact, not an unpleasant walk—she had not tried to demur.

She had to admit, as she stared at the complex pattern of still empty channels, it was worth coming to see. The main ditch was located at the highest elevation: from it a feeder ditch ran down the slope through each of the three fields that had recently been planted. Not straight but spiraling, creating an odd corkscrew effect. Alex's idea, and there had been much joking about it among the workers. The new *luna* was *pupule*, they said. Crazy. He couldn't even plow a straight line. But Maria, studying it now, realized how clever he had been. If the water had run

directly downward, it would have all have surged to
the bottom, leaving the land above as dry as ever.

"Boss-man one smart *haole*." Pake grinned broadly
as he stopped for a moment beside her. Maria knew
he was not referring to Royall. "Plenty big hills in
China. Plenty plenty water ditches. Long long time.
All round—like *haole* ditches. All work plenty good."

Round was not exactly the word Maria would have
used, but she nodded in agreement. Curving was
more like it. An ancient method, used for "long long
time" by the Chinese. She wondered if Alex had read
about it somewhere, or if he had simply come up
with the idea in his own head. She supposed she
would never know.

Mack had come down from the house to have a
look at the wondrous new waterway, and Maria felt
a catch in her throat as she saw Alex's tall form bending over him. He seemed to genuinely like the boy.
There was more than kindness in those gentle, laughing features, and Mack was responding with a clear
case of hero worship.

Then she saw what they were looking at, and she
couldn't resist a smile. A sailor off one of the ships
in the harbor had given Mack a Galapagos turtle,
and it had become his favorite pet, outranking even
his precious pony and the sheepdog that Royall actually approved of. When he had gotten it, it had been
so small he could hold it in his hand. Now it was as
big as a platter and apparently nowhere near ready
to stop growing.

"He comes all the way from South America," she
could hear her son saying as she drew closer. "His
name is Mickey. Young Doc says he is going to live
a very long time. Turtles live absolutely forever. So
we called him McThuselah. He likes to eat taro."

Maria could see the thought processes working on
Alex's face. Puzzlement turning to a faint twitch of
his lips as he recalled Methuselah's 969 years, and

realized that a child with a given name like McClintock would have heard the word somewhat differently.

There was still a trace of humor as he looked up and saw her. Mack, forgetting all about his pet, came running excitedly to greet her. Unfortunately for poor McThuselah, he picked that moment to wander over to one of the shallower ditches, and getting a sniff of something that obviously appealed, waddled happily down the sloping side. Royall, who had been standing a few yards away, leaped forward with a muttered curse and snatched him out.

"What the hell is *this* doing here?" he bellowed angrily. "Dammit, Mack, this is an irrigation ditch, not a playground for your pets! I've half a mind to make turtle soup out of it." He tossed the creature irritably away from him. It landed with a loud splat on a patch of mud and skidded several feet before coming to a stop.

Mack gave an anguished cry and would have rushed to the rescue, but one look from his father stopped him. His lips were quivering, and his little face seemed to close up, an expression Maria had seen more than once lately, though never to that degree. He's beginning to notice, she thought helplessly. There would have to be explanations soon. More excuses.

She was relieved when Alex, unaffected by Royall's livid glare, strode over to the turtle, still lying on the ground, and picked it up. "He seems to be all right," he said after a quick inspection. "No bones broken—or should I say, no broken shell? I think he's going to be fine."

His voice seemed to break Royall's hold over the boy, who came to look at his pet with stricken eyes.

"He isn't moving," he said dubiously.

"Of course not. He's too smart for that," Alex told him. "He's hiding inside his shell until he's sure it's safe to come out. . . . But your father's right, Mack. This is no place for your pets. They get in the way.

Pake! Take this little intruder up to the house. I'm sure one of the servants will know what to do with it."

"Why don't you go with him, darling?" Maria put an arm around the boy's shoulder as Pake came over and took the turtle with a knowing, somehow reassuring look. "Mickey will feel much better if you're there with him."

The boy hesitated for a moment, then went off trustingly with the young Chinese, his heart filled with hope for his beloved pet. Maria didn't dare say anything. Royall was standing too close. But she tried to thank Alex with her eyes, and thought he understood.

"The boy has to learn." Royall's voice was as cold as it was controlled. "He's too old to be so careless. I can't have that damned turtle getting into the ditches and clogging things up. If I see it around here again, it *will* go into the soup kettle!"

As if something the size of a serving platter could do any harm, Maria thought. It wasn't the turtle that had brought on that rage. He had seen the boy talking to Alex, seen the adoring look on his face, and it had frightened him. He was a man jealous of his possessions. And to him a child was a possession.

"A simple scolding would have sufficed," she said wearily.

"He'll understand about these things when he gets older. Farming is in his blood. He knows it's the land that's important. . . . I'm afraid my wife is overtired, Barron," he said, turning to Alex. "Household chores do seem to take a toll on her. She's not as strong as she might be. I wonder if you'd be good enough to escort her back to the house."

It was not a question. Alex inclined his head slightly, but did not shape his reply into words. Another command performance, like that dance at the welcoming gala. He eyed the man with distaste as his back retreated into the distance. It was almost as if he were setting her up. Coaxing her to be friendly so he could berate her for it later.

"Is the turtle really all right?" Maria asked softly.

"I don't know," Alex admitted. "I hope so. I didn't see any damage to the shell. If there's anything to be done for it, I expect Pake will have it all figured out and tended to by the time they get back to the house."

Maria smiled wanly. "Mack loves animals. He always has. Royall can't understand that. He has a feel for the land, but he's never cared much for living things. Unless they're useful. I think he looks on it as a weakness."

Alex pulled out a handkerchief and wiped his hands, which had become encrusted with dirt. He had always loved animals, too—there had been a parade of them over the years, tolerated by extraordinarily patient parents—and he realized that even now he was still trying to form connections between this boy and himself.

"Come on," he said, tucking the handkerchief back in his pocket, "I'll see you home."

"It's all right. Royall's gone now. You really don't have to. It's barely dusk. I think I can get back without tripping over my own feet."

"It's no problem. There's nothing to keep me here anyway." They started up the road together. "I've gotten as much work out of the crew as I can for one day. I have to concede, they do give new meaning to the word *lazy*."

Maria caught the careless lightness in his words, and she knew he was trying to take her mind off Royall's ugly scene. "They really don't have much incentive to work, you know. A rial a day is lovely, but how many fine new outfits of clothing can anyone possibly use?"

"Especially since they only seem to wear them to church," Alex agreed. He had been amazed, the first time he had come to the islands to see the people all rigged out in their Sunday finery. The men in satin waistcoats, silk stockings, and black evening pumps, the women in velvet and damask *holokus* with great flowered hats, the gaudier the better. "But there are other things to spend one's money on besides tail-coats and bonnets."

"Not for the Hawaiians ... except maybe a fish-hook or two. They don't have the same feeling for 'things' that we do. Private ownership isn't a concept the ordinary Hawaiian really understands. And why should he? He doesn't even own his land. All that belongs to the king, who doles out great chunks to the chiefs, or *alii*, in exchange for loyal service. Just to earn the right to use small tracts of it, the common-ers—the *makaainana*—are required to labor for the *alii*. To have to labor for the *haoles*, too, holds very little appeal for them."

"But isn't that all the more reason to work and make money?" Alex argued, finding himself more interested in the subject than he had expected. "If life is that precarious, it wouldn't hurt to save a little something for a rainy day."

"Spoken like a true Yankee." Maria laughed. The sound was soft and musical, stirring up memories in Alex. "But saving is exactly what Hawaiians learn not to do. Look at it this way. Suppose a man slaugh-ters a hog and salts some of the meat—or some extra fish he has caught—and sets it aside. Along comes the king, or one of the chiefs, and he says, or she— many of the *alii* are women—'That looks good. I want it. Give it to me,' and he has to. . . . Or if he is lucky and gets to keep it, then all his friends and relations show up for the *luau*, the great feast, he is expected to give! So why not just enjoy everything while you have it and not worry about tomorrow?"

They had reached the place where the road cut one way up to the house, the other to the *luna's* cottage. Alex stopped to look at her one last time. Dust seemed to swirl up from the dryness; there was no wind, and it settled lightly on her hair. The sky was just turning red behind her, a rich, shimmering glow, and she was very beautiful.

"You told me once I didn't have any idea what your life was like," he said. "You told me I was too quick to judge, and you were right. I'm sorry, Maria. If I could take away the pain, I would.... I loved you so much once. Ah, God, I loved you."

He hadn't meant to say the words. He hadn't even realized he was thinking them, but they were out of his mouth and he couldn't call them back. Conflicting emotions flickered across her face. Disbelief and hope and a deep, inexplicable pain.

"But not enough to stay with me," she said softly.

Alex stiffened. "There's no future for a man with a married woman. I *had* to leave when I found out."

"You were planning on leaving even before that," Maria reminded him, trying not to let it hurt too much. There was love ... and love. And if the kind he had to offer was not what she craved, that was not altogether his fault. "I went to you the morning after—after that awful night. But the *Shadow Dawn* had already sailed. You weren't a captain yet. You were the grandson of the owner, but I don't suppose mighty ships move on a grandson's whim.... You knew all along you were going to be leaving that day. And you never said a word."

"Is that what you thought?" He was staring down at her, his face dark and unfathomable in the waning light. "That I cared so little I would slip out of your life like a thief in the night? Without even having the common decency to face you and say good-bye? By God, if you believed that—!" He took a step forward; his hands were under her elbows, tilting her up so she had to look at him. Was that passion she saw in his eyes or anger? Or a mingling of both? His voice suddenly sounded strange and muffled. "What makes you assume I wasn't a captain?"

Maria felt the first stirrings of something she didn't

dare acknowledge. She had assumed because she hadn't known he was a Barron. And later it hadn't occurred to her to question.

"You were . . . too young."

"I was the youngest captain on the line. The youngest Barron Shipping had ever had. Jared bested me by a couple of months the next year, and Matthew beat us both out later. . . . The *Shadow Dawn* was my first command. I wasn't exactly popular with the men when we sailed out of Lahaina. I roused them out of quite a variety of beds and bunks, and they had only a few hours to ready the ship."

"Then, you really did love me?" She barely whispered the words.

"I did," he said, and he was drawing her against him. Tightly, holding her with arms that were even stronger than she had remembered. "And I do."

Maria was not even conscious of opening her mouth to receive his kiss. She knew only that he was there and she was waiting, hungry, longing for him. It was as if some force outside herself, stronger than her own will, had taken over and held her hard and trembling against him.

He loved her. Maria felt his words wash over her. Again and again. Even the dizzying passion of his kiss was no more overwhelming than that sweet revelation. He loved her . . . and he always had. There had been no cruel betrayal. Her dreams had been real, her instincts true, if only she had had the faith to believe in them.

There would be no tomorrow for them, as there might once have been. Even the excitement of that long-yearned-for kiss could not quite block out reality. This one precious moment was all they could ever have. But he loved her. The knowledge of that surged hotly through her veins. He loved her, and her heart and body clung to the fleeting rapture she had thought would never be hers again.

His eyes were blazing as he released her. Maria

recognized now what she saw in their depths. Not anger or passion, but the anguish of having to give her up forever.

"Stay away from me, Maria Perralt," he said hoarsely. "Stay away, or God help us both, I won't let you go next time."

Chapter 9

The only motion was a flicker of light on the windowpane. Outside, the night was black and almost eerily silent. Maria held her breath and waited for the pain to go away. It shot with a burning sensation through her side, and for a moment she was frightened. Then it subsided, and she dared to let herself breathe again.

He had never hurt her this badly before. She caught a glimpse of her reflection in the mirror above the dressing table across the room. Even from that distance, even with the shadows, she could see the bruise forming on the side of her face.

He had never hit her so many times. Or so viciously. Maria started to tremble all over again, as if he were still there. She hadn't even detected a reek of whiskey this time. Always before, he had been drunk or drinking. She had known when to be cautious, to stay out of his way. Tonight there had been no warning.

She had gone out to sit on the *lanai* after dinner, alone, to sort through her feelings and let herself relive the bittersweet memory of what had happened with Alex that afternoon. More than ever, she had realized there could be nothing else between them, but the lingering taste of his lips had been like a soothing balm, and she had remained for a while, cherishing and savoring it.

When she had returned, she had found Royall waiting for her in her room.

One look at the black rage on his face had been enough to tell her what had happened. He had seen! He had been on the road behind, or somewhere on a nearby hill, and he had seen her with Alex.

"I warned you what would happen," he said in a low, vibrating tone that was more terrifying than if he had shouted and blustered. "I told you that you would pay if you made a mockery of me. Slut! You couldn't even sneak off in the bushes for your sordid self-indulgence! You had to satisfy your randy urges right in the middle of the road where everyone could see you!"

"What . . . ?" Maria struggled to remember where she had last seen him that afternoon. Hadn't he been headed in the opposite direction? "What were you doing there?"

"What was I doing there? This is my land. My plantation! Why the devil shouldn't I have been there? Half the *kanakas* were probably using that road to go home. . . . Good God, what if Mack had come down and seen you? Throwing yourself into the arms of the hired help like some debauched wanton? You are a sad excuse for a mother, madam. I would get nothing but sympathy if I were to send you away."

Maria's blood ran cold. Too late she saw the trap he had set for her—and she had walked right into it! He had suspected her feelings for Alex. That's why he sent them off together. He had been planning on following, hoping to catch her at something.

And he had probably brought a couple of the *kanakas* along just in case.

"You think *you're* an ideal father?" she lashed out, hiding her fear behind a sudden burst of anger. If he thought he was going to get her son away from her without a fight, he was badly mistaken. "You're *no* kind of father. As we both know! And no kind of man! Go ahead, make a scene. All the sympathy will be on my side when I tell everyone how pathetic you were in my bed. How you tried and tried for hours and couldn't do a thing! There are a couple of previous marriages to back up the story. I wonder if Claudine mentioned anything before—"

Maria didn't even see his hand come out, he moved so fast. She was still reeling from the first blow to the side of her head when he struck her again, knocking her brutally to the floor.

"Harlot!" he cried, his voice almost squeaking with the violence of his rage. "Whore! Blasted, fucking whore!" He gave her a sharp kick as she lay on the ground, then kicked her again, the toe of his boot gouging into her side.

Maria thrust out her arms, helplessly trying to fend off the blows. He was completely out of control. She sensed he was taking out all his frustrations on her, all the inadequacies he had ever felt in any woman's bed—she had been a fool to taunt him about his manhood—and she was terrified for an instant that he was going to kill her.

But the fury seemed to abate almost as quickly as it had come. As if somehow, with those few swift blows, he had managed to revitalize his tarnished masculinity and proved himself potent and virile again. His face was pale but utterly devoid of emotion as he stood in the doorway of the hall and looked back at her.

"I trust, madam, I have made my point. Further indiscretions will be suitably punished."

Maria curled up in a tight ball after he had gone, trying to shut out the pain and make it go away. She had not known he was capable of such savagery; she had not even imagined that the small abuses he had practiced before could escalate into this terrible orgy of blind, brutish rage. She moved her arms tentatively, then her legs, relieved to find that everything seemed to be working. No bones broken—*no broken shell*, she thought with an unconscious sob, and longed for the comfort of Alex Barron's arms, strong and sheltering around her.

By the time Maria managed to crawl over to the chair and pull herself up, she was already feeling somewhat better. He hadn't hurt her, after all, much worse than usual. Only a few bruises, no serious damage. But he had frightened her badly, and she knew it would be a long time before she felt safe again.

A slight sound came from the French doors that led out to the *lanai*. Abruptly Maria snapped her head around, terrified that he had come back. But she saw only a little boy, his face pressed against the glass, wide blue-gray eyes filled with horror and fear.

"Oh, Mack ..." She ignored the pain in her side as she flew over to the door and knelt reassuringly beside her son. "It's all right, darling. Truly it is. Don't look so scared. Mama has just been clumsy again—you know how clumsy Mama is. It was a nasty accident, that's all. It's only a bit of a bruise."

The child did not react, almost as if he had not heard her. Tears glistened in his eyes but did not flow down his cheeks.

"Is he mad because of Mickey?" he said in a small, hoarse voice. "Because I brought Mickey to the water place? Is that why he hit you?"

Oh, God. Maria felt as if she had been struck all over again, hard in the stomach. He had been there all the time. Watching through the French windows while his papa beat his mother.

"No, darling, no ... this has nothing to do with you," she said hastily. "Papa was angry with me. I said something I shouldn't—and he lost his temper. He didn't mean to hit me. It was mostly an accident. He was just trying to ... to punish me. You know, like we punish you sometimes when you are naughty. Only it got, well, a little out of hand ..."

She stopped, hating herself for what she was doing, and Royall for having put her in such an impossible situation. She was lying to her child now. Defending a man for brutalizing a woman! But how could she hope to make him understand what was happening when she didn't truly understand it herself. He was so young.

"I won't pretend what your papa did was right, Mack," she said. "It wasn't. But people can't always help themselves. I don't know what happens. It's like a demon gets inside them and takes control. Papa has a fondness for brandy, I'm afraid. And *okolehao*. Drink does bad things to people."

"He wasn't drinking tonight," Mack observed. His eyes were still solemn, but he seemed to have decided to drop the subject. "I came to tell you Mickey's all right. He stuck his head out of his shell. Just like Captain Alex said he would. He wanted some taro. Mickey is really awfully greedy."

Maria felt the tension draining out of her. The questions would continue to come—she knew he would never look at his papa in quite the same way again—but at least for tonight he seemed to have accepted her explanations.

"There, you see, it's an omen." She put her arms around him. It didn't even matter that it hurt. She barely felt the pain. All she wanted was to hold her son and keep him safe. "McThuselah's all right, and I'm all right. Everything's going to be fine, darling, I promise you. Everything's going to be just fine."

And it would. Maria held that fragile little body against her breast, soothing herself as much as him. She was walking a fine line now between calculated risk and disaster, and she knew it. She could not afford even the slightest misstep.

But there would be no missteps. Somehow—she didn't know how, but somehow—she would make things better for her son's sake.

"Don't you dare tell me you ran into a door, or a tree branch fell on you!" Rachel Barron's thin, heart-shaped face was flushed with indignation, and her brown eyes snapped as she stood on the *lanai* and looked at her friend. "There's only one thing that could have made a mark like that ... and this isn't the first time he's hurt you. You've got to stop denying it. Pride's pride, but this is getting silly. I'm your oldest friend! If you can't talk to me, who can you turn to?"

Maria tried to smile, but she was too tired. She had been up all night, and the bruises were still hurting. Not sharply, just dull aches that never quite went away.

"Somehow I didn't think a tree branch would be very convincing.... No, I'm not going to pretend anymore. You're right, I do need someone to talk to. Honestly, Rachel, I don't know what's gotten into him. We don't ... well, we've never been close, but it's only recently he's gotten so—so ..."

She struggled for the word. Rachel looked her in the eye. "Violent?"

"Not exactly. Not until last night. Just a little ... rough sometimes. And then only when he was drinking. It's like he doesn't know his own strength." She faltered, unable, for all her claims of not pretending anymore, to admit the extent of what this man had done to her. "I don't think he really meant to hurt me. He just—"

"He didn't mean to *hurt* you?" Rachel made no effort to control the incredulity in her voice. "He had to smash his fist into the side of your head to leave that bruise. Hard! You don't do that without hurting someone. The man's a monster!"

Maria shook her head wearily as she sank down on the most comfortable chair on the *lanai*. It was not just pretense. With the cold light of dawn, she had come to a realization of her own share in that horrible nightmare.

"It's more like a sickness, I think. He gets so obsessed sometimes ... and it was partly my fault. I said something awful to him. Really nasty. He went wild with rage."

"And that makes it all right?" Rachel fairly spat out the words. She couldn't bear to stand there and watch her beautiful, spirited friend meekly accepting what was clearly unacceptable in any civilized society. "I know you, Maria McClintock. If you said something nasty, you must have had provocation. Even if you didn't—even if you were the most hateful, despicable woman in the world—that still doesn't give him the right to strike you."

She went over to her friend and knelt passionately on the chair beside her.

"Listen to me, Maria. No man has a right to do that to a woman. *No* man. For any reason! This is not your fault. Not the smallest part of it is your fault! It's never a woman's fault when she is beaten by a man. There's no justification for that . . . But it is her fault if she lets it keep on happening again and again. You have to put a stop to it. You know that, don't you?"

Maria leaned her head against the high chair back and stared off into the distance. Of course she knew. Any fool would know after that painful beating. Every instinct urged her to abandon the brocades and diamonds she had never wanted anyway and leave with nothing but the clothes on her back. Only it wasn't quite as simple as that.

"What would you propose I do?" she replied. "Go running to Mama, who would only remind me that Royall is my husband. I made a commitment to him, remember? For better or for worse. This, apparently, is what they mean by 'worse.'"

"Women have been known to leave their husbands," Rachel reminded her. "A drastic step, but you'd be better off alone than living like this. . . . And marriages have been known to be, uh, set aside."

Maria raised a brow, almost amused in spite of herself. "Why, Rachel Todd Barron—and you a reverend's daughter. Don't tell me you advocate divorce?"

"Reverends' daughters can be practical, too." Rachel twisted her feet out from under her and sat straight on the chair. "No, of course I don't believe in divorce—but there are extreme circumstances sometimes. Like a man who beats his wife. Some things a woman cannot be expected to tolerate. Divorce is an ugly word. There's a taint that always lingers, especially for the woman. But you could go someplace else if you had to. Someplace where no one would know you."

"And find some man and coax him to fall in love with me ... and just not happen to mention my 'tainted' past?"

"I wasn't thinking of 'some man'," Rachel replied very quietly. "I was thinking of Alex."

Maria's head snapped up, and she stared at the other woman. "You know? He told you."

"I've known from the beginning ... and, no, Alex didn't say a word. I knew from the first time I saw him look at you. And you at him. I took very unfair advantage of his feelings, but I was frantic with worry about you. He was, too. . . . I don't know what happened all those years ago, when you knew each other before, and I'm not asking you to tell me. But I know Alex loves you. Very much. He wouldn't give a fig about the taint of divorce. The Barron fortune would protect you from the worst of it anyway. People are never quite so unkind to the rich."

The *taint* of divorce ... ? Maria tried not to let herself get caught up in her friend's naive enthusiasm. If Rachel only knew how desperately she longed for just that particular taint. It wouldn't even be a real divorce, only a legal formality, since the "marriage' it would be dissolving was in every way a sham. It all sounded so tempting. So very tempting.

"What about Mack?" she said softly.

Rachel looked surprised. "Mack would go with you, of course. Alex adores the boy. He would never expect you to leave him behind."

"And Royall? Do you really think he would just stand aside and let me take Mack away from him? The law will be squarely on his side. You know as well as I do that women who walk out on her husbands are lucky if they even get to see their children again. Society is not very kind to wayward wives, whatever their reason. Even if I could bear to be without my son—and I couldn't!—there's no way I would ever leave him alone with Royall."

A troubled look came over Rachel's face, and she was silent for a minute. This was obviously something she hadn't considered.

"The man is a wife beater," she said at last. "Surely no court would entrust him with the care of a small child. . . . And he wouldn't want this sort of thing bruited around. Royall is very concerned about his reputation, I think. The threat of a public battle ought to make him back down."

"If you believe that, you don't know the first thing about Royall Perralt. No one defies him. And he holds on to what is his." There were plenty of things he wouldn't want bruited about, as Maria well knew, but that wouldn't keep him from fighting. "Mack is his future. The Perralt name going down through the generations in Hawaii. A founding family continued. . . . His dreams for Honuakula require an heir. That's not something Royall will ever give up."

"He might not have a choice."

"What, here? In Hawaii? Royall has amassed a certain power in this part of the world. The most important of the *alii* are his friends. How do you think he got all this land? He's taken great pains to cultivate them. It will pay off for him now. A few 'presents,' and the king's court will be eating out of his hand."

"There are other courts," Rachel reminded her. "Other countries. . . . This is going to keep on happening, Maria. It will be worse next time. Much worse. Whether it's a sickness, as you say, or the evil that I sense, this has gone way beyond rough. Sooner or later he's going to kill you. You have to get away. Find someplace where you can work things out."

"The results will be the same anywhere," Maria said unhappily. She wanted to believe every bit as much as Rachel did. More, but she didn't dare let herself get carried away with impulsive daydreams. "Royall is already trying to make it look like I'm an unfit mother. He set me up with Alex—no, not *that*, but it will look bad enough. The scarlet woman runs off with her lover, and deprives the poor, wounded husband of his son. What male judge on earth isn't going to side with the husband?"

"Even if he beat his wife?"

"His adulterous wife. No doubt the slut deserved it. A man's pride can take only so much. You know as well as I, I wouldn't stand a chance."

"Lawyers can be awfully clever," Rachel insisted, but Maria noticed that her voice had lost some of its confidence. "There must be all sorts of things they could try. You'd have the wealth of the Barrons behind you. Royall's personal fortune is a pittance to that. The possibilities are endless."

But possibilities weren't enough. Maria got up and went over to the rail. It looked so beautiful, so benign, the land Royall had tamed with his sweat, and for which he would willingly have traded his soul. Or hers. There might be something the lawyers could do. She might find a court that was fair and compassionate. But she might not, too.

She looked at the ocean, placid and cool against the horizon, and thought of the ship that would be sailing off again all too soon. She would be a fool to put her faith in lawyers and courts. The stakes were too high.

If she lost, she would lose more than the right to see and love and hold her son. If she lost, she would have to turn him over to Royall. Maria remembered that little face pressed against the darkened windowpane, the horror in his eyes, the tears he could not shed. Even if Rachel was right, even if she *was* risking her life—and there were ways to minimize the danger—she couldn't abandon her child.

What would happen the next time Royall was displeased with him? What would become of his turtle then, and all the wild birds with the broken wings? As long as she was there, the brunt of that savage rage would fall on her. And she was wiser now, shrewder. She knew how to protect herself.

"You don't need to worry about me. Honestly." As she turned to her friend again, she managed a crooked smile. "You are making much too much of this. It's only a bruise, and it doesn't even hurt anymore. I'll just have to learn to be tactful. It will be a new adventure for me. . . . Royall hasn't always been like this. It's only lately. Things have been difficult . . . And I really did provoke him, you know."

Rachel sat for a long moment, watching her in silence. She would have protested further, but a quiet resolution had come into Maria's clouded blue eyes, and she knew it was hopeless.

Tact would hardly be a new adventure for her. Rachel knew that with more than a woman's instinct. Maria had had to be tactful every minute of every day, and cautious, and now it seemed she would have to be afraid, too.

She was going to need all the tact and all the resourcefulness she could muster. And more than her share of luck. Rachel's heart broke for her. She had never felt more helpless, but in a terrible way she understood and admired her friend's stubborn courage. If this were her son, the child she had hungered and prayed for, would she have done any less?

The irrigation channels were ready to be opened early in the afternoon. Alex had been surprised when Royall had not shown up for work that morning, then apprehensive, as an hour had passed and there had still been no sign of him. After another fifteen minutes of fruitless waiting, he had sent Pake to the plantation office to see what was wrong.

The Chinese had come back a short time later, pig-tail flapping behind as he ran, a broad grin spreading across dirt-smudged features.

"Boss-man plenty drunk drunk," he had reported cheerfully in his usual singsong pidgin. "No come out. Door locked. Houseman say stay long long time. Day, maybe two. Maybe week!"

The brightness in his voice had left no doubt as to his feelings about the boss-mans' potential absence. Royall was not popular with any of the workers, especially the Chinese. Of the few he had managed to recruit from another sugar operation on Kauai, only Pake had been loyal enough to stick it out for more than a few days.

And that "loyalty," Alex suspected, was more a shrewd desire to learn about irrigation so he could figure out how to siphon off some of the water for his own vegetable garden.

He straightened up from the feeder ditch, where he had been making a final examination of the crude wooden gate before letting the water in. Royall's absence still bothered him. The irrigation system was far too important to him; he had been keyed up for days, thinking and talking of little else. It was the wrong time to lose self-control.

But the man *was* a drinker, and the bottle didn't always wait for a convenient moment. Alex shrugged off his doubts, deciding he was worrying too much. Still, he took the precaution of sending a couple of the *kanakas* to watch the office door from a discreet distance and let him know if Royall emerged.

At least he wouldn't have to worry about their slacking on the job. This was just the sort of "work" they relished. They would pull out their pipes, squat on the ground, and begin to exchange stories. And probably do a few drolly accurate imitations of the boss-man and his *luna* while they were about it. If Royall was up to something, he would have plenty of warning.

In the meantime there was more than enough to keep him occupied. Alex took the spade himself and cleared the dirt from the makeshift dam that held back the water, muddy now in its earthen pond. His boots and work pants were drenched above his knees, his shirt spattered as the water gushed out, splashing with encouraging force against the wooden barrier that led to the feeder ditch. Raising his arm, he gave Pake the signal to wrench it open.

It gave with a grating sound, surprisingly sharp, and the water spurted into the feeder ditch, filling it and lapping against the smaller gates at the end of each of the furrows. One by one these were opened, too, and the life-sustaining moisture oozed out. A trickle at first, then slowly rising, following the ridge in a graceful curve, overflowing onto the soil. When one section had been thoroughly drenched, that gate was closed and the next lifted.

Alex felt a surge of exhilaration. It had been his plan. Carefully thought out, every contingency prepared for, but he had not been certain until he had actually seen the water soaking into the earth that it would work. It was an important moment in the history of the islands, and he was not too caught up in his own emotions to realize that and be excited at having however small a share in it. If the climate could be tamed, water brought from the hills—perhaps one day even from the rain forests on the far side of Haleakala—the land would be not only as beautiful as any place on earth, but productive beyond imagining.

"Hey, Pake," he shouted, clapping him on the shoulder with the camaraderie of men who have worked together and triumphed over great obstacles, "you got a name?"

"Sure." Those dark eyes were almost as bright as his own. "Chang. You call me Chang."

Alex was still feeling the thrill of the water, almost as if it were coursing with the blood through his veins. It was not a surge now, no longer even a trickle, just dark patches of wetness seeping into the ground. The main gate was brought down again, so the water would build up in the reservoir, and the furrow gates carefully secured. Nothing but mud was left in the bottom of the feeder ditch. He had already started to make the final inspection before calling it *pau hana* for the day when he looked up and saw Rachel running down the road that led from the house.

Surprise turned almost instantly to alarm. She would not have sought him out in the fields if something wasn't wrong. Leaping out of the ditch, he started racing toward her.

They met almost at the place he had tethered his horse to a stake driven into the ground. It took her only a few terse sentences to tell him what had happened.

"I can't make her even consider leaving," she concluded. "She's afraid for the boy, and she has good reason. but, oh, Alex, we have to do something."

"Blast the man!" he cursed bitterly. "I'll see him in hell for this!" He was already loosening the horse's reins, swinging into the saddle. "He's going to answer to me. And the law—if he's lucky!"

"Alex, be careful," Rachel called after him, already having second thoughts about her decision to come to him. Alex was the gentlest of the Barrons, the least impulsive, but he could be as headstrong as the others when he felt his cause was just. And the Barrons were famous for their raging tempers. "The man is her husband. If you get him stirred up, there's no telling what he might do. You could make things even worse for her!"

Her words were lost in the wind behind him as

Alex rode like a madman up the hill. He drove his mount with a savage frenzy, paying no attention to the ruts in the road, taking reckless chances that could have destroyed them both. All he could think about was the woman he had failed to protect. He didn't even know how badly she was hurt. He hadn't thought to ask, and he was tormented now with visions of her lying somewhere, pitifully broken, gasping for air and near death.

He knew he was being irrational. Rachel would never have left if Maria were mortally hurt, but still he was afraid. Terribly, coldly afraid, as he had never been in his life. It was agony for a strong man to feel so utterly helpless. If he lost her now—if he lost even the hope that was all he could have—it would be like losing a part of himself.

He was relieved, when he reined in his horse and hurriedly dismounted, to see her standing alone on the *lanai*, staring off into the distance. Then she turned, and he was sickened by the livid mark on her face.

"*He* did this to you?" He covered the ground in a few long strides and was up the steps, drawing her into his arms, longing to succor and shelter her. All pretense at caution was gone now. He didn't care who saw, or what they thought of him for loving a woman who belonged to someone else. "By God, I'll kill him with my bare hands! And that's too good for the bastard!"

"Oh, Alex . . ." Maria forgot all her resolves as his arms closed around her. Strong and comforting, as she had longed so desperately to feel them. She did not even try to resist the tears that streamed down her cheeks. "He wasn't even drunk. He's never hurt me before when he wasn't drinking. I was afraid. He was so angry. . . . He *hated* me so much. He just kept hitting me, and then I fell . . . and then he kicked me . . ."

"Damn," Alex muttered, feeling clumsy and infuriatingly inadequate. Her tears were a taunting rebuke. Where had he been when she needed him? "What kind of man beats a woman? Does it give him some sadistic thrill, knowing she can't hit back? Why, in God's name—"

"He saw us," Maria said miserably. "He saw us kissing. He doesn't *care*. He doesn't have any feelings for me, but he wanted to punish me anyway. Maybe because I can love, and he can't . . . Oh!"

She broke off abruptly, stiffening and pulling hastily out of his embrace. His arms had felt so good— she had needed to cling to him—but how could she have let herself forget, even for an instant, where she was? And what the consequences of carelessness could be?

"If he catches us . . . You shouldn't be here! This is insane! Alex, please, you have to go. He could come back at any minute. He doesn't always stay in the fields."

"Not a chance," he assured her. "He may not have been drunk last night, but he sure as hell is now. He's been holed up in his room since this morning. Pretty thoroughly soused, from all accounts. I left a couple of men at his door just in case. They'll come and warn me if he tries to go anywhere."

The anxiety eased in her face, but Alex noticed that she did not come into his arms again. The bruise seemed even darker now, perhaps because her skin looked so pale. He ached to hold her, comfort her, tell her again how much he loved her, but he knew she would not let him.

"He had it all planned," she said. Her voice was so soft he could barely hear her. "He wanted me to kiss you. He wanted to catch us. That way he could make it look like I wasn't a suitable mother. What kind of influence is a degenerate, loose-moraled woman—an adulteress, for heaven's sake—on an impressionable young child? He wanted a reason to send me away. To make sure I never saw my son again."

"Well, he outsmarted himself this time," Alex said grimly. "You're leaving, all right, but not because he ordered you to. Pack your things, and the boy's. I'm taking you to town tonight. A kiss is not adultery— and he can't even prove that much. We're going to fight him, and we'll win—"

"But we can't! Don't you see?" Tears still glittered on her lashes, but she was not crying anymore. There was a firmness in her eyes, and a conviction that made Alex suddenly uncomfortable. "And he can prove the kiss. I think he brought some of the native workmen with him. They won't like it, but they won't defy the *alii* if they're asked to swear to it in the king's court. . . . No one is going to believe that a man and a woman who kissed so passionately in public weren't doing much, much more in private. I *will* lose my son."

Alex half turned away, glancing around as if to check the area behind him, though he knew there was no possibility Royall would be there. He *had* seen a pair of *kanakas* wandering around, now that he thought back on it. Shortly after she had left. And they had given him strangely sheepish looks.

"It needn't come to that, Maria," he said.

"It needn't?" Her voice was filled with longing and pain. "Do you hear yourself? It *needn't*—but it might. I can't risk that. . . . I love you very much, Alex Barron. If there were any way I could go with you now—any way—I would, and you know it. But there isn't. My son needs me. You have to accept that."

There was enough finality in her voice that Alex, like Rachel before him, knew she had made up her mind. All the arguing in the world wouldn't move her. As long as there was even the slightest chance— and the chance was more than slight—that she would lose her child, she would never leave that house. He would have to find some other way to keep her safe.

At least, if the house man was right and Royall really could be expected to remain in his room for "maybe week," he had a little time.

"All right," he said. Dammit, he couldn't even smash his fist into the man's face! "I don't like it—I hate it like hell—but I love you enough to respect your decision. For now anyway."

Alex spent the night outside, still dressed in his work clothes. He had not even allowed himself a few minutes to go back to the cottage and change. Dried mud was caked to his shins and thighs as he took a seat on the ground, his back against the trunk of the *kukui* tree, and made sure he had a clear view of the door and windows to her room.

She had left a lamp burning, as if she were afraid to be alone in the dark, and he longed to go to her. Longed to hold her, reassure her, make love to her, but he knew he could not. She did not want him there. She had told him as much, and he understood why, but that did not stop the aching need to be close.

Damn the man. *Damn* him! He was her husband—and he took that as a license to pummel her with his fists and boots. What was he going to do next time when his rage got out of hand?

Alex choked back the helpless frustration that rose like bile, bitter in his mouth. He wanted to give the bastard a taste of his own medicine, wanted to kick the door in and show him what it felt like to be beaten to a bloody pulp. But unless he was prepared to kill him—which was not altogether out of the question, the way he was feeling now—he couldn't lay a hand on him.

He wanted to protect her. He needed to protect her, but she wouldn't let him. And God help him, he knew she was right. Royall, being a man—and no doubt the "wronged" party in any court action, no matter what he had done—did have the power to

take away her child. She would never survive that.
Nor could Alex live with himself if he caused it to
happen.

The boy was more important to her than her own
happiness. Her own life. She would do anything for
him, give up anything to keep him safe, and Alex
could not fault her for that. He loved her because of
what she was. Because of her capacity to feel and
care, deeply, fiercely. He would not have her be any
other way.

If the boy were mine, he thought—and caught himself abruptly. The boy was not his. He was Maria's.
The decision was hers. He had promised to respect
that, and he would.

The air was warm, even as midnight eased slowly
toward dawn. Alex drifted off briefly, half dozing,
still half awake, his mind working constantly on the
problem even as he tried to catch a few minutes'
sleep. A faint sound disturbed him, and his eyes
jerked open, scanning the darkness. The light was
still flickering peacefully in her window. A small animal foraging through the thin, crackling layer of
leaves on the ground. He heard it again, then even
that was gone. Nothing else seemed alive in the
night.

There were things that could be done. He relaxed
again, feeling the sturdy pressure of the tree behind
his back. He would have to see about getting more
men out here. Men he could trust. With Royall "in-
disposed," there would be no one to question his
decisions. It was getting on toward time for cutting
and milling the original fields of cane. Extra hands
would be needed.

The thoughts were coming faster now. Two Barron
vessels to draw on, and the *Jasmine Dawn* due any
day on the outward trip around the Horn. He might
take Angus Dougal off the *Shadow*, where he had
been serving as first mate. He was a Scotsman. He
had a way with the soil and knew how to keep his

eyes open and his mouth shut. Yes, Angus definitely. Neither Jared nor Matthew would object if he took them into his confidence.

He hadn't wanted to before. He had been so blasted afraid of baring his feelings, naked in front of his cousins, though they had probably already figured it out. But his pride could go to hell now, and gladly. Nothing mattered but Maria.

He was going to need someone inside the house. For that, he would see if he couldn't arrange to bring back the housekeeper, Ilimi. They said she was sweet on Young Doc Fredericks. Maybe he'd be willing to help. He always seemed to keep a watchful eye on Maria.

Yes, there were things that could be done. . . . Alex let himself doze off again, more deeply this time, no longer feeling as impotent as before. He loved her, and he would protect her—whether she wanted him to or not. There was no way on earth anyone was ever going to hurt her again.

It was nearly dawn when he awakened. The first gray light barely illuminated the sky, and the house and outbuildings were still black in shadow, only their outlines distinguishable. A thin line of color was just touching the horizon in the east, and he turned to look at it, relieved that the night had passed without incident. He almost missed Maria as she slipped quietly from the house to the stable.

Even in that faint light she was lovely enough to make his heart hurt. An almost ethereal vision in a flowing Hawaiian gown. All the warm colors of the rainbow swirling together, reds and pinks, vermillions and golds, and a skirt split for riding. Memory caught in his chest and throat, making it hard for him to breathe.

She had been lovely then, too, beyond anything he had ever seen or imagined or dreamed. He remembered his first sight of her, the misted spray of the waterfall floating like a cloud around her, blue eyes daring to meet his. Remembered the accepting warmth of her arms, the way she had looked later, dressing to leave him, the regret that mingled with lingering passion on her lips as she opened them to tell him good-bye.

He had loved her then. He had thought he loved her as much as it was possible for a man to love a woman, but he had not even begun to understand . . . and he knew suddenly where she was going, that silent figure in the morning light.

And he knew he was going to follow her.

Chapter 10

The water felt cool and cleansing. Maria tilted her face up into the tumbling cascade and let it pour over her, washing away the pain and ugliness. It had been many years since she had come to this place. The memories had always been too intense; she had been afraid of awakening old feelings, opening old wounds. But now she needed to envelop herself in a sense of *him* again.

Alex Barron . . .

She brushed her hair back with her hands and wished she had thought to bring a bar of soap. The scent of sandalwood mingling with the wet smell of the water—even the thought of it brought back that day when he had first come to her. When she had not even known yet who he was.

The bruise on her cheek was not hurting anymore. It had not seemed so bad when she looked at it earlier in the mirror, barely a lingering trace, and there was only a slight discoloration on her hip and upper thigh. She had been fortunate this time. Extremely fortunate. Would fortune be as kind again?"

Maria threw back her head, shaking off the dread and fear with the water that streamed through her long flame-bright hair. It didn't matter what happened tomorrow. She would not worry about tomorrow, or the day after—or all the days after that. He really did love her! He had told her so, and he meant it. All the doubts had been no more than her own foolish inability to believe. She had not dared let herself dwell on it at Honuakula; the heat, the dust, the oppressive atmosphere, had been too heavy to allow her even to dream. But here in this special place, which was theirs and theirs alone, her heart still had the courage to soar.

His love was real and true—and it always had been. Maria felt the warmth of that sweet realization caressing her with the cool caress of the water. She had not been wrong in her first instinct.

She had not imagined that look on his face when she had turned, all those years ago, and seen him staring at her. Desire, yes ... there had been that, and amusement in his smoky gray eyes, and all the arrogance for which the Barrons were justly renowned. But the bond between them had been real. He had been caught up in the same magnetic force that had drawn her inexorably to him.

She had not imagined the physical thrill that passed like a current from his body to hers the instant they touched. She had known then—and should have known always, if only she had trusted her heart—that she would belong to him, and he to her, forever.

If she turned now, she thought as the water spilled over her, soothing, sensual ... if she turned, she would see him there, all the years gone and yesterday come back again. It was a sweet illusion, hard to resist, and Maria felt her body twisting around, treacherously, aching for what it could not have.

For a moment she thought her eyes were playing tricks on her. Or her memory. He was standing almost where he had been before. Tall, with the sunlight behind him, pink just fading to gold and shimmering in his hair, making him look almost fair.

There was no amusement in those smoke-clouded eyes now. No maddening, half-mocking laughter. Only the desire, raw and haunted—like the expression she glimpsed sometimes in her own lonely mirror.

Not an illusion, then . . .

Maria realized suddenly what it was that had compelled her to turn. She had felt him there. She had
sensed the sheer power of his gaze scourging her
naked flesh, the feverish longing that reached out to
touch and inflame her own. She must have made a
sound, a cry of joy or welcome, or perhaps she took
a step forward, for he was in the water suddenly,
his clothes drenched, plastered against his hard male
body, and he was taking her in his arms.

There was no conscious thought or will in their
coming together. It was only instinct now, all the
pent-up emotions they had fought so long catching
and holding them, clinging, to each other. He was
kissing her, burying his face in her hair, murmuring
things she could not understand, his voice was so
muffled with passion. Maria felt him lifting her
strongly, impatiently, carrying her onto the bank.

Water was dripping from his shirt and trousers,
her skin and loose wet hair. She did not resist as he
pulled her down, but sank eagerly with him, hungering for the feel of the grassy earth beneath, the virile
force of his body coming to claim her. Their need for
each other was frenzied and consuming. He did not
even take time to remove his clothing, but drove
himself into her deeply, urgently, and, almost with
that first savage thrust, utterly fulfillingly.

The moment of their joining was complete for both
of them, and they lay for a long time, exhausted and
silently content, in each other's arms. Maria sighed
and nestled closer, luxuriating in the warmth and
almost incredible tenderness that followed their
tameless passion. The sound of the waterfall was like
a splashing melody in the sultry summer air. She had
forgotten what heaven it was to love and be loved.
To know the sweet perfection of a man's devotion,
the gentleness of kisses so soft they could hardly
be felt.

It was some time before it occurred to her that

he was still mostly dressed, though in considerable disarray. A very undignified sight, and she found herself, quite inappropriately, tempted to giggle.

"Why, Captain Barron," she said, "are you always so impetuous? I swear, you sweep a girl right off her feet."

He was smiling as he sat up and let his eyes drink in the loveliness he had so long denied himself. "I am never impetuous," he replied. The silken softness of her skin, the curve of her mouth, were beginning to tempt him again. "I've been waiting eight years for this. Eight very long years. I'll be damned if I know why. And you're not a girl anymore. You're a woman. A very ... beautiful ... woman ..."

He punctuated his words with little kisses in each of the pauses. Her temple, then her earlobe, then the hollow at the base of her throat where she could feel her pulse beating faster. Every nerve ending in her body began to tingle, just from his touch, and she disentangled herself with a soft laugh. She knew only too well where such behavior was likely to lead.

"I am a woman now," she agreed. His hands were stroking her hair back; his lips found the nape of her neck and he was nibbling gently, very disarmingly. "But I *was* a girl when you knew me before. An extremely foolish girl. I should have told you the truth. I—I meant to ... but I was afraid. And then it was too late."

He heard the seriousness in her voice and stopped teasing. "It doesn't matter, Maria. You were young, and so was I. We were both foolish. Lord, I must have seemed smug! My values, *my* standards, were the only ones that could possibly be right. You were bound by a commitment I didn't even begin to understand, but ... married is married, at least for a woman. Isn't that how you put it the night we danced? You are a lovely dancer, by the way ... I didn't admit it, but I was finding it very difficult to concentrate. You fit wonderfully in my arms."

His voice had turned soft, his face, too. Maria knew if she let him kiss her, she would not say what she had to.

"You are avoiding the subject, Captain."

"In favor of much more interesting topics . . . like how very womanly your breasts have become." He was not actually touching her, but it felt as if he were. His eyes were caressing, boldly and quite tantalizingly. "Not that I wasn't very fond of them before, mind you. Girlish innocence has its appeal, too. . . . Dammit, Maria, I'm trying to apologize! And not making a very good job if it. Smugly perfect men such as I don't get a lot of practice. You were his wife. As far as I was concerned, that meant you had to stick with him. I didn't stop to think what kind of nightmare it might be for you."

"But that's just it," she said softly. "I wasn't his wife. I'm not his wife now. I never have been, except maybe . . . for a little while."

Alex caught the faint hesitance in her words and pulled back, puzzled, to look at her. She was not Royall Perralt's wife, she had said, and for a moment he thought he must have misunderstood. Then slowly he realized what she was trying to tell him.

Royall had obviously been making his bed in the library for some time. Except, presumably, for a brief period—"a little while"—at the beginning of their marriage. She didn't mean she wasn't legally bound to the man. She meant she was not his *real* wife. Their marriage was not a true or complete one in the deepest sense of the word.

"I know you're not sleeping with him," he said, rather more gruffly than he had intended. "And I won't lie and pretend I'm not glad. I have enough male pride—or is it vanity?—to want my woman exclusively to myself. It makes me sick to think of his hands on you. Even before, when I believed it was over between us, I was consumed with jealousy, imagining you loving him . . . kissing him back."

She shuddered, a visible reassurance, dispelling whatever doubts he might still have had. "He only touched me twice like *that*. The first time he—he raped me. That's why we got married."

"He raped you?" Alex was too aghast to conceal his horror and disgust. "And you married him after that? Your parents allowed it?"

"They insisted. My mother anyway. Royall was very rich and . . ." She faltered, having trouble going on. It was hard, making herself think back on that time, the memories were so brutal. "He—he was careful not to—to leave anything in me. It was in one of the rooms above the tavern, and he thought I was a whore. I guess he doesn't like mingling his bloodline with the lower classes. There wouldn't have been a child, but I was . . . well, I was ruined anyway. So when he offered to set things right . . ."

Her voice trailed off. Alex stifled the anger that rose in him. He was more appalled than ever, but this was not a time to concentrate on his emotions. His pain. He laid a hand on her cheek, tilting her face up to look at him. He knew he wasn't going to like what else she had to say, but he sensed it was important for him to hear it.

"You said he touched you . . . like that . . . twice."

Maria nodded, silent for a moment, willing herself to continue. "Royall has a . . . problem. He's all right with whores, he says—and he must be. He managed with me that first time. But there's something about the idea of a wife—of *having* to perform with her, I guess—that makes him, well . . ."

"Impotent?" Alex said quietly.

"He just couldn't do anything. No matter how he tried. At first I felt sorry for him. It was unpleasant, of course, but . . . he was very honest about it. He told me everything. I knew how degrading it must be for him. But then it got really awful."

"He did succeed one more time," Alex said, recalling the little boy with the cruelly deceptive Barron eyes, three months too old to be his son.

"He wanted to get me pregnant." Her voice was almost toneless, breaking only momentarily as she forced the words out. "He fed me fruit. *Pu'aha-nui.* It's supposed to make you conceive. I get sick if I even look at it now.... He—he dressed me up like a prostitute ... and made me do things ..."

"Shhhh ..." Alex drew her into his arms again, soothing, longing to comfort. He had heard all he needed and then some. Later he would vent his anger and curse the man who compensated for his own pathetic inadequacies by raping and beating women. But now she had been subjected to enough. "That was a long time ago, love. It's over. You can tell me about it someday, if you need to, and I will listen. Or you can just let it go and forget it. It isn't important now."

Her expression changed, and he thought for a moment she was going to cry. But she smiled instead. Weakly, but gamely.

"I know. Don't look so alarmed. I hardly think about it anymore. It's only sometimes ... it comes back for a moment. But all I have to do is remind myself that you love me, and it goes away again."

Her lips were parted, an unconsciously sultry look, as captivating as it was ingenuous. Alex had forgotten how young she still was, inexperienced in the wiles of love. He was surprised to feel his body beginning to respond, though he had thought the seriousness of the conversation had dulled his ardor, and hers. But the little tremor he felt as his hand ran slowly down her arm was not one of distaste.

"I want to make love to you again, Maria," he said hoarsely. "I want to lay you on the ground and feel myself inside you."

"I thought you might." Her gaze dropped impudently to the front of his trousers, still unfastened

from their previous haste. There was no mistaking
his renewed desire.

"It's all right?" He wanted to say "It won't remind
you of the bestiality that was forced on you before?"
but could not bring himself to utter the words aloud.

"No, not quite all right." She hesitated, and Alex
was furious with himself with the protesting ache
that swelled in his groin. He would stop if she
wanted—he would never do anything to hurt her—
but, God, he didn't want to! "I think I would prefer
it if you took your clothes off this time. . . . And since
they're already wet, why don't you drop them in the
pond? They really are disgusting. You look like
you've been playing in the dirt."

"In the mud," he said, and laughed as he looked
at her in the golden sunlight, which was streaming
down on silky-skinned limbs and rounded, womanly
breasts. Dawn had gone with their first passion, and
the morning was warm with the scent of fern and *maile*,
and an elusive, lemony hint of wild hibiscus. The laughter healed whatever hurts memory had brought, and
Alex was aware of an unexpected sense of contentment
mingling with the desire as he stripped off his shirt and
watched it sink slowly beneath the surface of the water.

He loved her more than life itself. The discovery
did not surprise or alarm him; it was merely the inev-
itability he had been too mule-headed to acknowledge before. He loved her more than anything that
had ever mattered to him. More than his Yankee
pride or precious honor. Loved her enough to surrender even his soul to be with her again.

Nothing had changed for them. He knew they had
only these few fragile moments, and then she would
go back to her legal entanglement with another man.
He was moving beyond the pale of society now; he
would be condemned even by the people he loved,
but he did not care. His need for her, the depths
of his passion, drove everything else from his heart
and thoughts.

He could feel her eyes on him as he removed his boots, then his trousers and socks, which joined his shirt in the rippling mountain pool. He sensed that she was enjoying his body, as he enjoyed hers. That she liked the hard muscles in his shoulders and chest, the flatness of his stomach, the lean hips and masculine thighs of a man whose work was physical and kept him strong and trim.

It excited him, the frank boldness of her gaze, no coyness or false modesty as he turned and she let him catch her watching. Her lips were slightly parted; her tongue darted across them, not altogether unconsciously this time, and every masculine instinct reacted, instantly and fiercely. An open, sensuous woman, honest about her desires. A woman who would always be his equal, in bed or on a grassy mountain knoll.

She must have known what he was thinking, for she raised her hand and let her fingertips brush his chest. A little less confident than her eyes. A tentative half caress.

"Go ahead and touch me, love," he urged. "I want you to touch me everywhere. Just like I want to touch you. Here . . ." His fingers were on her breasts, fondling lightly but very expertly, teasing her nipples into sharp little peaks. "And here . . ." Strong male hands ran down her sides, stroking her hips, bolder now, her thighs, their smooth inner skin moist and warm with her need for him. "And here . . ." He placed a hand between her legs.

"Oh . . ." The sound that escaped Maria's lips was halfway between a gasp and a moan. He did not move; his hand was just resting there, but she thought she would die from the sweet longing it evoked. He knew her so well. Even after eight years he remembered exactly how she liked to be touched. "I do want you, my darling," she murmured. "So very much."

"I hope so," he responded. Laughter reverberated

somewhere deep in his voice, but there was passion, too, and every instinct in Maria's body thrilled to it.

"You remind me of someone I used to know," she said. He was lying back on the ground, coaxing her closer. Maria leaned over him for a moment, fascinated at the way the shadows of her body muted and softened his face. "His name was Sandy."

He was drawing her down now, beside him on the ground. Every sinew of his taut male body felt hard and provocative against the pliant contours of her own yielding flesh.

"Did you love him?" he asked. The words were low and seductive in her ear.

"Very much."

"As much as you love me?" He was cupping her buttocks in his hands, pressing her against him. Maria could feel his virile male desire. His breath was hot on her lips, promising a kiss that did not come, and she longed for it with a sudden urgency that took her breath away.

"No . . . I could never love anyone as much as I love you."

It was her mouth that found his, a hungry suppliant; she could no longer bear to wait, and he did not disappoint her. Sensing she did not want gentleness, he wasted no time with tender preliminaries. His tongue was rough as he explored that warm, willing cavern, demandingly and very thoroughly ravaging every inch of it. Maria's own tongue responded with an eagerness born of eight long, empty years, tasting, savoring, feeling the texture of him.

His mouth still clamped on hers, not letting go for an instant, one hand still hard on her buttocks, Alex let his other hand become even brasher, more intimate. He was possessing her breasts now, no longer toying and fondling, but claiming, arrogantly, surely, knowing the feverish heat he was arousing within her. Maria felt as if her flesh were on fire, her breasts, the smooth mound of her belly. Every touch, every

looked at her. His face was ashen, and there was hate searing in his eyes. I've never seen him so angry, not even later. I—I couldn't bear to stay there any longer. I just turned and ran down the path. Her laughter followed me all the way to the house. . . . And the sickening sweetness of her perfume. I couldn't get it out of my nostrils for days."

She was beginning to shake. Alex could feel the tremors running through her body, and he gripped her hand tighter. He longed with every fierce male instinct to hold and comfort her, but he knew only time could assuage the ugliness of the memory. He was so wrapped up in his concern for her, it was a moment before he realized the impact of what she had just said.

"But if this is true, if Claudine really *is* alive, why in God's name did you stay with the brute another minute? I would have thought you'd be wild to get away. This was your chance to be free of him."

Maria looked up and gave him a wan smile. Alex was surprised to see tears in her eyes. "Where would you have had me go? I had no money of my own. No one who wasn't too afraid of Royall's wrath to take me in. And what should I have said? That I had seen Claudine, living and breathing—and spitting malice? But there was no proof! Royall paid her off . . . as she had known he would. And he'll keep on paying as long as she stays under cover. He came to my room an hour later, maybe two, and told me exactly what would happen if I tried to betray his secret. Any of his secrets. He had things to hold over my head—but that doesn't matter anymore . . ."

She slid into the pond and let herself glide effortlessly out toward the center, needing for a moment to get away from him and the painful questions she herself had provoked. Her hair streamed out, a red fan in the sunlight behind her. It took Alex only a single stroke of his powerful arms to reach her.

"The devil it doesn't!" He caught her roughly and

forced her to stand beside him in the deep, clear
water. She might have been too intimidated to fight
back all those years ago when she had been alone,
but she had him to take care of her now. "This is
exactly what we're looking for. Don't you see? If we
can prove Claudine is still alive, that means we can
be together. . . . Did you even try to find her, Maria?
Did you ask if anyone had seen her?"

"Of course. I may have been young and very foolish, but I wasn't altogether witless." The waterfall
was only a few yards away; Maria could feel ripples
splashing against her breasts gently, like the lingering traces of his caress, and her heart ached. He still
didn't understand what she was trying to tell him.
"I have friends among the Hawaiians. I was able to
make inquiries without being obvious. But the fog
was so thick. Only one man saw her, or thought he
did. Old Kaholo, Ilimi's grandfather. But she was
wearing a long cloak with a hood that concealed her
face. He could make out only an indistinct outline."

"Did he see where she came from?" Alex pressed.
"What direction she went afterward? It might still be
possible to pick up her trail. At least we'd know
where to begin."

His hands were gripping her shoulders; there was
so much force and purpose in his voice, Maria was
almost tempted to let herself hope. It would be so
easy—if she didn't remember the one thing that had
not yet occurred to him.

"She didn't leave any trail. Do you think I didn't
search for one? She came from a small ship in the
cove. At the base of the road that leads up to Honuakula. Kaholo thinks there was a man pacing the
beach, waiting for her to return, though it might only
have been one of the crew. But the woman didn't
come back down the hill. Kaholo was there all the
time. He was hoping the fog would clear. He wanted
to go fishing. He thinks the man may have gone up,
maybe to check on her, and come back again. There

were shadowy figures. He couldn't be sure. But he didn't see a woman."

"He might have missed her," Alex said thoughtfully. "He might have turned his head or dozed off for a minute." She gave him a sharp look, and he realized she had explored all this before. She knew the old man better than he, and the depths of his passion for fishing. "Or she might have taken off the cloak. He could barely make things out, you said. He might have mistaken her for a man."

"No. . . . I saw her, remember? She had on a very bright red dress with a full, flowing skirt. If she had been on that path, Kaholo would have seen her. It's almost as if she vanished into thin air. . . . Royall was drunk for two days and a night after that. He wouldn't even open his door to take a tray of food. When he came out, he reminded me what would happen if I dared to defy him. Then he shut himself up again, and we didn't see him for two weeks."

That must have been some bender, Alex thought. And no wonder. What a hell of a shock, having his past thrown in his face after all that time. And by a taunting bitch with a cap of brown hair who couldn't resist rubbing it in!

"No one vanishes into thin air," he said. "Royall was shrewd enough to make sure she wasn't seen again. And Claudine was greedy enough for blackmail to let him. He spirited her off the island somehow, maybe with the connivance of the man in the boat. Her current lover? . . . But he has to have some way of getting funds to her on a regular basis. The last thing he wants is to have her show up again. If I could just have a look at the plantation records . . ."

Her fingers touched his lips, lightly stopping him. She was smiling the same smile again. Only now he saw it was sad.

"I tried all that. A long time ago, when it might have made a difference. It wasn't any good. I could never find a way to prove I wasn't Royall's wife. But

at least I knew it myself. I was—truly—free of all
earthly ties when we came together. So you see, I
didn't trick you into adultery, though I know you
believed that for many years."

More than believed, Alex thought. He had clung
to the anger and shame, and he was a little surprised,
now that he had finally learned the truth, how unimportant it seemed. He had agonized so long over the
stain on his rigid Yankee honor, it had almost become a part of him, like a third arm or eye. Then he
had discovered he still loved her . . . and everything
else had slipped away.

"I've already admitted I was an inflexible ass. And
a fool to boot. I should have had more faith in you.
I won't make the same mistake again. I'm going to
take you back to town—maybe to Honolulu—and
keep you safe until we can find the proof we need."

"You still aren't listening to me," Maria said softly.
"It's too late. If I'd had the courage to tell you everything in the beginning . . . if you hadn't sailed away
so rashly, perhaps . . . But that was a long time ago,
and this is now. I cannot go with you, anywhere,
because of Mack."

Alex stiffened, misunderstanding, as Rachel had
before him. Could she possibly think he didn't have
room in his heart for the child that was a part of
her? "I meant Mack, too, of course," he said gruffly.
"There will be no problem with me about the boy. I
thought you knew that."

"With you, no, but there will be a problem with
Royall. Even if we can prove I'm not married to
him—which is by no means certain—Mack will still
be his son in the eyes of the law. A father has
rights. . . . And I'm still going to look like the loose
woman cavorting with her lover, right out in the
open where her child could come along and see. Royall has influence. No court in the islands, either here
or in Honolulu—"

"Then we will have to find a court elsewhere."

The water splashed around them, icy fingers stroking their skin. Alex felt her shivering, and he brought her back on the bank, wishing he had a blanket to wrap her in, even though the sun was blazing by that time. "We can have this matter settled in the U.S. All we have to do is get away before Royall catches on. You're probably an American citizen. You were born there, weren't you? What state? . . . Never mind, it isn't important now. Have I ever told you about my uncles?"

"Your uncles?" She looked up, startled. He was relieved to see that he had distracted her.

"My mother's brothers. In Virginia. As raunchy a pair of old bachelors as you ever set eyes on, but they're clever. And very tender-hearted, though they go to great lengths not to get caught at it. The older one, Uncle George, read law with Thomas Jefferson years ago in Williamsburg. Uncle Eddie wanted to, too, but he could never apply himself to anything for very long. I'll send a letter off with the next ship heading for the eastern coast. If anyone knows what our legal position is, it's Uncle George."

"He may be clever, but he can't change the facts." Maria felt suddenly very tired. His arm was insidiously tempting around her, coaxing her head down on his shoulder. She wanted so much to let herself believe. "And we don't have a legal position. Any court is going to look at Mack and see Royall Perralt's son. Legal marriage or no."

"What if he were my son?"

Maria's head jerked up, and she stared at him helplessly. There was something in his voice that frightened her. She had waited so long for that question. She had seen him watching the boy and wondered why he hadn't asked it before.

"Oh, I know he's not," Alex said abruptly. "Don't look so stricken. I can count on my fingers as well as the next man, and Mack told me his birthday was October second. I don't have any unreal expectations.

But with those eyes ... it *might* be possible. I expect I could produce my cousin Jared, if necessary, for the court."

The audacity of it took her breath away. Maria knew now what it was that had frightened her before. That reckless Barron spirit. He was so much readier to gamble than she. He wouldn't even consider the possibility he might lose.

"That would make me look even more shameless than ever," she reminded him. "Bearing a child to a man who was not my husband? The world would not look kindly on that.... And Royall, whose name is on the birth certificate, would still be the legal father."

"Not if we find Claudine. Are you sure he knew she was alive when he married you? You couldn't have misinterpreted what you heard?"

"No, it was very clear."

"Then he was lying through his teeth when he spoke his marriage vows. That's deliberate fraud. His behavior will be at least as subject to question as yours. And you were very young. How old? Seventeen?"

"Fifteen," she said, "when I married him."

Fifteen? Alex cursed himself inwardly. She could have been no more than sixteen then, barely seventeen perhaps, when he first laid eyes on her. Bitterly hurt by life and looking for compassion ... and what had she gotten from him? Summary condemnation and an empty space in the harbor where his ship ought to have been.

"He's going to look like the bastard he is. A fraudulent marriage leaves him no legal claim to the child. And he won't even have the claim of blood when I convince the court that Mack is mine."

The words came out with a little more emotion than he had intended. Maria felt as if her heart were breaking. She sensed the longing he could not quite bring himself to say, and she knew it was unfair. He deserved more than that.

"Alex ..." she said softly, but his mouth twisted wryly, and he stopped her before she could go on.

"There are times I've wished he were. I won't insult your intelligence by pretending I haven't. I look at him, and I keep feeling ... a connection. Idiotic, I suppose. Men are such fools, aren't they? Always hungering for what they can't have.... But if he were mine—if there were even the slightest chance— I swear before God, I would get him out of this mess. And you! I'd carry you onto the *Jade Dawn*, over my shoulder, if I had to—kicking and screaming all the way—and set the cannons toward the shore. And heaven help any man who tried to take either one of you away from me!"

The passion was raw in his voice. He made no effort to conceal it. Maria's heart was bleeding now. The two people she loved most in the world, her lover and her son. How cruel to be forced to choose between them.

She hated herself for what she had to do, but there was no say she could let him go on even thinking like that.

"And sail off into the sunset ... and just keep on sailing and sailing. Forever. Royall would be bound to come after us. You know that. We'd always be wondering where he was, whether he was one step behind us, what kind of plans he was making.... Always afraid to set foot on shore, the cannons aimed and ready—that's not the life I want for my son, Alex! ... Or for the man I love."

"I know that." He said it quietly, with neither the anger nor the resignation she had alternately expected. "I was just telling you what I would do if Mack *were* my son. And you couldn't stop me. We wouldn't spend one more night on this blasted island. Only he's not mine, so we'll play by your rules. But that doesn't mean the game is over."

Maria heard the calm assurance in his voice, and

she longed, treacherously, to believe him. "You make it sound so simple."

"In a way it is, love. The clue to everything is Claudine. It'll take longer than I like. I'm not comfortable keeping you here. But all we have to do is find her, and everything else is going to fall into place."

"*All* we have to do?" Maria ached for the feel of his arms around her. It would be so good to let go and just trust in him. "You forget. I tried to find Claudine before. and failed. And that was eight years closer to the afternoon she disappeared."

"But you didn't have Alex Barron to help you," he said, and then his arms *were* around her, comforting, tantalizingly virile. In spite of herself, Maria dared to hope, just a little. "Royall was shrewd, I admit that, but no man can accomplish the impossible. He had to get Claudine off the island somehow ... and he had to bring her somewhere. Probably close. He didn't have a lot of time to prepare. Honolulu maybe. She might have been using another name—her maiden name?—to keep from attracting attention. Did you check in Honolulu?"

"No," Maria said, and the germ of hope started growing larger. "I didn't think about Honolulu ... and her name used to be Doral." Perhaps, after all— just perhaps—there might be something they could do. But she still had to keep him from being reckless. Running away, guns and cannon blazing, would destroy whatever small chance they had.

"You see." He was sounding particularly pleased with himself. He had obviously noticed that she was weakening. "I told you. You need Alex Barron to help you. ... And there are a few other things he might do for you, too."

"Oh?" His tongue was playing with her ear, little darting, licking motions. It was very hard to think when he was distracting her like that. "And just what might those be?"

"I think I could arrange to show you."

Chapter 11

Maria had only known once before in her life what happiness truly was. For the next ten days, while Royall was closeted in his room, having his own brooding love affair with the bottle, she dared to let herself savor once again the sensations she thought she had lost forever. Even the uncertainties of the future could not diminish the joy she felt as she and Alex spent nearly every waking minute together.

Each morning they would slip out separately just as dawn was painting the earth with an iridescent pinkish glow and meet in their secluded glade. He would be waiting when she got there. Maria would slip from her horse into the warmth of his embrace, and her heart would rejoice all over again that somehow they had found their way back to a love which was as magic and fulfilling as ever.

There, with the gentle murmur of the waterfall and the birds trilling and whistling in the trees, they reminded each other what it was to share not just the physical passion that brought them to such sudden, soaring heights, but the quiet moments as well, the laughter and the little teasing endearments that helped to heal the hurts and make the fear go away.

Or they might take their horses and race along the beach. Maria loved to ride. Sometimes it almost seemed to her she was a part of her beautiful, feisty-spirited mare, Kanani. Alex, with his easy skill in the saddle, was more than a match for their playful exuberance, and with combers crashing against the sand, great rolling billows frothed with white, they dared to let the wind stream their hair out behind them. She would leap from her horse and run along the edge of the surf, not even caring that her slippers and the hem of her gown were getting drenched. And he would catch her—as she had known he would—and tell her he loved her.

Then he would show her, in the most explicit way possible, with the pounding of the waves beating like her own heart in her ears, and everything else would be forgotten. Their time together might be short, to-morrow and its prospects tenuous at best, but for those few brief moments the world stood still and now was forever.

They had only a short time to spend alone with each other, for Maria always insisted on being back when her son got up. Alex, whose attachment to the boy was somewhat more comfortable now that he had admitted his feelings, was not inclined to object. He was finding himself looking forward to the little family gatherings in which he was always included.

He was also somewhat guiltily conscious of the fact that he was about to deprive Mack of a father, however inadequate the man was, and he was deter-mined to form a solid relationship with him before that happened.

Sometimes they would breakfast on a grassy knoll next to the house. A simple picnic repast—fresh man-goes and spiced apples from New England, cold chicken instead of steak, bread still warm from the oven and thick *kiawe* honey, all spread out on a red plaid blanket. Mack was plainly in little-boy heaven. This was a special treat, shared previously only with his mother, and his childlike heart was thrilled by the attention of a grown-up so important even the other adults seemed to look up to him.

Afterward they might go for a short walk, usually down to the stable, where Mack was allowed to keep his assorted menagerie, which he delighted in show-ing off to a kindred spirit. The present collection in-cluded several lizards, three cats, a well-trained sheepdog, a mangy mongrel whose future at Honua-kula was apparently extremely dubious, and a Ha-waiian goose with a broken wing, nearly mended now and ready to be released back into the wild. And, of course, the infamous McThuselah.

"He really was hiding," Mack confided solemnly. "Just like you said. He wasn't hurt—he was just scared. He wanted to make sure it was all right be-fore he stuck his head out again."

"A wise turtle," Alex agreed. "But you know, Mack, I think it might be a good idea if McThuselah went into town for a while. It's going to be busy around here when we start cutting and milling the cane. We wouldn't want him to get in the way. I'm sure one of my cousins could put him up."

He had expected an objection, but the little eyes that looked up at him were knowing beyond their years. "That would be good," Mack agreed. "I was most awfully worried about him. I was thinking I might ask Young Doc, but he has way too many animals already. He always says so. He's a vetram-arian, you know."

Alex threw a quizzical glance at Maria. He had deciphered "vetramarian" easily enough, but some-how that wasn't quite the kind of practice he had associated with Fredericks.

Maria laughed. "Of necessity. There's no one trained in animal doctoring around here, so the sick cows and horses and dogs all come to him. He al-ways seems to have at least half a dozen furred or feathered boarders. . . . And thank you for McThu-selah. I'm sure he'll be much happier away from the commotion in the fields."

"It'll just be for a few weeks, Mack. You'll have him back soon," Alex promised, and made a mental note to be sure the boy's pet was taken along no matter how abruptly they left the island. It would help to ease the pain of transition.

Middays brought leisure again, for Mack was busy with his schoolwork. A tutor made the long ride from Lahaina every day except Sunday, and at Maria's insistence a grass-thatched classroom had been erected and several of the native children invited to share his studies. Royall had not been crazy about the idea. The dark-skinned *keikis* were hardly what he considered suitable playmates for a young Perralt, but he had thought it advisable not to voice his objections since education was a subject on which the missionaries were especially uncompromising. He had noticed that the sons of these men and women of God were branching into commercial ventures with startling success. Royall always considered it expedient to stay on the good side of successful men.

Alex paid only scant attention to the workers in the fields. Their chores were routine now: hoe *hana* in the newly planted patches of cane, *hole-hole hana* in those that were about to be cut. He had brought in eleven of his own people, including Angus Dougal and a wiry, sharp-tongued Cockney named Alf Shirl, who knew nothing about farming but had a definite flair for getting work out of men. With each of them heading a crew, and Chang going back and forth between them, sharing the quite astonishing amount of knowledge he had managed to accumulate, little was required of Alex beyond an occasional visit to make sure everything was running smoothly.

The rest of the time he spent with Maria. They might stroll out to have a look at the fields together, or drop in at the schoolroom, where the din of excited voices attested to the skill of the young tutor and made Alex think with a pang of his own rigid Yankee upbringing. But more often they simply sat on the *lanai*, sipping mango juice in the warm afternoon and talking quietly.

For Maria this was an especially precious time. As

treasured in its own way as the mornings when their bodies came together, feverish and wild with the passion that had built up through the long night. Or the stolen moments in the evening when they would wander into the darkness beyond the flickering windows and kiss and ache with longing . . . and remind themselves how soon the dawn would come again.

It was a time of pretending. Maria was aware of that, but she could not have dispelled the illusion even had she wanted to. It was almost as if this were her husband. As if he had come back to her after a long day in the canefields and was perching in his customary fashion on the veranda rail, staring off into the distance, not feeling the need to talk, as married folk sometimes did. And she was the lady of the house, comfortable with the silence, just sitting with him, waiting for their son to return, whooping and giggling with excitement from school.

Their son . . .

Maria glanced at his profile, craggy and beloved against the sun-shimmering golden fields. Her heart yearned for everything she wanted to share with him.

"Whatever happens," she said softly, "always know I love you."

He turned back to look at her with steady gray eyes. "What's going to happen is that we will locate Claudine . . . and she will help us prove what Royall has done. In court—your way, my love. Then you and I, and your child, will be a family. Forever."

"You make it sound so pretty." Maria drew her legs up and curled her arms, childlike, around them. She loved him for trying to keep up her spirits, but she knew that even his determined optimism had to be wearing thin. "And so positive. But . . . it's been several days now. Have you even found a trace of her?"

Alex shook his head reluctantly. At her insistence, he had not confided in his cousins, but both Jared and Matthew had been asked to make discreet inquiries about Royall and any "questionable" financial transactions he might be involved in.

"I know he's getting money to her, but I can't figure out how. He's blasted cunning—I'll give him that. Every one of his business associates in Lahaina is completely legitimate. Nobody's picking up extra cash to shift funds on the sly. The transfer must be taking place somewhere else. Maybe in Honolulu."

"No." Maria frowned slightly, wishing she could be more hopeful. "Royall hates Honolulu. He's only been there three times in all the years I've known him."

"Then whoever's getting the money has to be coming here. Probably from Honolulu. Anyone else showing up on a regular basis would attract too much attention. The payments have to be made in cash. Royall wouldn't want any records."

"It sounds reasonable," Maria admitted, getting caught up in his confidence in spite of herself. "But surely something would have been noticed. You did say all his acquaintances were legitimate. Doesn't that include the ones from Honolulu?"

"It wouldn't have to be someone he knows well. A packet of money could change hands in a dingy alley at dusk."

"Yes ... but wouldn't that be awfully hard to track down?"

"From here maybe. But it might be easier at the other end. In Honolulu. This man has ties with Claudine, don't forget. We know her maiden name. Doral. And she's not the sort of woman who would have escaped notice if she was ever there. As for her lover, or whatever he is, I'd be willing to bet he's young and good-looking, with an oily sort of charm. And probably French. We'll have to find a way to get to Honolulu without making Royall suspicious. Maybe you could—"

Maria stopped him before he could finish. "I told

you, Royall hates Honolulu. I've never even been there. He wouldn't consider allowing me to go. If you really think it's necessary, you'll have to make the trip by yourself."

"It's necessary, all right." He came over from the rail and sat on the chair beside her. In a way, he wasn't being altogether reasonable. It would probably make more sense to send Matthew. He was the one who was fluent in languages, and the trip was almost certainly going to require a conversation with the French consul. But this was too important to entrust to anyone else. Even his cousin. "I have to go, but I'm not letting you stay here alone. I'll figure out some way to get us both there, love. You have my word on that. And we *will* learn what happened to Claudine."

There was so much assurance in those strong Yankee features, Maria almost found herself daring to believe. It *might* work ... but eight years was a long time to try to pick up a trail. There were hundreds of ways Royall could be getting money to his real wife. If she hadn't died in the meantime and saved him the trouble.

"What makes you so sure," she said quietly, "that Claudine will cooperate even if we do manage to find her? She might just as well lie and say that Royall didn't know she was alive until she showed up at his door. That he had married me in good faith."

Alex did not look the least bit disconcerted as he stretched long, lean legs out in front of him.

"Why would she do that?" he said softly.

"Royall did pay her, you know."

A faint smile touched the corners of his lips. "Then I will just have to pay her more. Two things strike me about Claudine Doral Perralt. Greed ... and spite. If she can line her pockets and hurt Royall at the same time, I imagine it will give her great pleasure ... The one aspect of the business that probably won't be the least bit satisfying to her is knowing she's telling the truth.''

Alex lived in dread of the day the door to the plantation office would open and Royall would come strolling out again. It was not that he wasn't prepared. Every possible precaution had been taken. On the pretext that it was stifling hot, even in the dead of night, he had slung his hammock between the *kukui* tree and a stake in the ground, and Ilimi was back in the house again, with her oldest boy and two of her nephews.

Someone would always be there. Always awake, always watching, and yet he could not shake an uncanny sense of foreboding. An instinct, utterly unbased on logic, that something was about to happen.

When Royall finally did appear it was almost an anticlimax. He was extremely pallid and looked much older, as if recovering from a serious illness, but there was nothing threatening in either his demeanor or his words. Indeed, just the opposite. He was cool and stiffly polite, his manners exaggerated almost to the point of caricature, as he paused at the steps of the *lanai* and reminded Maria that the end of the cane season was always marked with a festive celebration at Honuakula.

He hoped, he said, she was not neglecting to make suitable arrangements, and added almost nonchalantly that the Barrons would naturally be welcome at the gala. Then he sauntered off toward the stable.

As if nothing had happened, Alex thought bitterly. As if he hadn't beaten the mother of his own son and gone off on an alcoholic binge for the better part of two weeks! He longed to challenge him, to shake him out of his cold complacency. It galled almost beyond endurance that he couldn't stuff the bastard's teeth down that thin, aristocratic throat. But he had promised Maria he would at least try things her way, and that was a promise he would keep. As long as he could.

Maria saw the strain he was trying to hide, and it frightened her even more than the potential of Royall's violent rage. She felt sometimes as if she were walking on a wire stretched across a chasm, and the slightest breath of wind would dash her onto jagged rocks beneath. Whatever it took, she had to keep him from losing control. She had to guard every word, hide her worst fears, even twist the truth around to keep from igniting the spark that might set him off and destroy their hopes forever.

But she also saw the depth of his need to protect her, and in spite of herself she could not keep from responding. For the first time in her life she felt truly cherished. It seemed almost a miracle that he loved her enough to respect her feelings, even though his masculine pride was chafing with frustration.

The first cane had already been cut the day before Royall reappeared to take his place as master of the plantation. Maria was surprised and secretly pleased when Alex encouraged her to come out and watch them work. She knew he was primarily concerned with keeping an eye on her, but she had never been invited to take more than a cursory interest in Honuakula before, and she found herself truly fascinated as the long months of planting and hoeing culminated in the frenetic energy of the harvest.

A number of temporary workers had been hired. Strong-shouldered, muscular-armed sailors from several ships in the harbor, not just the Barron vessels, were gathered with the usual natives when Maria arrived in the morning. The patches of cane stood like dense green rain forests, glittering in the sun, twice the height of even the tallest Hawaiian. Gloves were pulled on, and files used to make the first sharpening of the machetes or cane knives. Then the files were tucked back in belts and waistbands, and the men took their positions.

On command, they all began moving, a silent, co-ordinated army, bent nearly double, knives flashing as they assaulted the long rows of cane.

The work was sweaty and demanding. Sharp splinters caught in the workers' clothing and burrowed painfully under their skin. Speed was important, but so was thoroughness. The cane had to be cut close to the ground, where the best juice was. Too *mauka*, too high, and too much of the sugar was wasted—*poho*—and tassels had to be lopped off the tops of the long stalks and thrown methodically into the furrows for fertilizer.

Clouds of red brown dust rose, swirling and choking, nearly engulfing the field. The cutters tied the bottoms of their trousers to keep it out, and stopped frequently to mop their faces with faded red and blue handkerchiefs and clean the chocolate-thick dust out of their noses and mouths.

In what seemed only minutes the entire field was leveled, and the men were returning in a long, sweeping line. Maria watched, intrigued by the speed with which they gathered up the stalks, tied them into bundles, and tossed them onto waiting carts, each hitched to three yoke of sturdy, dust-encrusted oxen.

The carts, Alex told her, as they walked companionably together, catching up with one of the lumbering loads that had left a few minutes before, were designed and built on the plantation. Imported wagons were too flimsy to withstand the rutted roads and the weight of the cane. They carried one ton apiece and moved at the rate of a mile an hour, which since the mill was about that distance away, meant a round trip every two hours, or, counting loading and unloading time, three trips a day.

Even the road was dusty. Maria's skirt had turned a dull brown color, and her corset felt tight and almost unbearably restrictive. It seemed so absurd, the clothes one was expected to wear as the mistress of a great plantation. She wished she had had the nerve to put on one of her loose Hawaiian garments.

The mill was already in operation when they approached. Smoke was pouring out of tall stone chimneys, and the sound of water rushing over the mill dam mingled with the groaning and splashing of the wheel. A heavy odor, sweet and pungent, like fermented molasses, hung in the air.

Inside, everything was dim. The light from the huge open doors through which the wagons rumbled was supplemented by sputtering lanterns dangling from rough-hewn rafters. Dark-skinned workers, naked to the waist, were grouped around a pair of granite rollers, each weighing three and a half tons, which had been shipped all the way from China. They were just being set in motion as Alex and Maria entered. One of the men pulled a long lever; two others jumped on the flywheel, and the massive rounds of stone began their cumbersome revolutions against each other, much more slowly than the water wheel which propelled them.

There was, Maria noticed, no slacking here. A tall, very wide Hawaiian was already bringing a load of cane stalks from one of the carts. He started to feed them, several at a time, between the slowly grinding rollers. Cane juice, flecked with dirt and bits of stalk, poured down a long wooden trough into a bucket at one end. As soon as it was filled, one of the workers hauled it off and another was set in its place.

Maria's eyes were shining as she watched. "Come on," Alex said, gratified by her obvious interest and eager to share the knowledge he had only just acquired himself. "Let me show you the clarifiers. This is where all that muck you saw coming out of the grinding wheels is removed."

He led her into a large room, even dimmer than the first and stiflingly hot. Most of the light came from open ovens under a number of large vats filled with steaming liquid. Here the cane juice was mixed with milk of lime to coagulate the impurities and allow them to be separated out.

"Milk of lime?" Maria asked curiously.

"That's a fancy name for powdered lime and water. The process is a little trickier than it sounds. If there isn't enough lime, the sugar won't form into grains—but if there's too much, it turns dark and is less valuable. Since no two batches of cane have the same sugar content, the workers have to have a good sense of what they're doing. The men here are highly skilled and well paid."

Maria was suprised to see two Chinese among the others. There were quite a few of them scattered around the islands, Alex told her, and more coming in every day. Chang was far from alone. Several *pakes* had, in fact, worked at a sugar mill on Kauai, and a couple of them had even started their own operation.

"Royall doesn't like having them around," he said. "He doesn't trust them, but they have the experience and they're good at the job. He has no choice but to hire them and pay an attractive wage."

Maria noticed that he formed Royall's name with obvious distaste, and she hastened to change the subject. "You put the cane juice in those pots, then? And mix it with milk of lime and boil it?"

"That's an oversimplification ... but yes. And 'boiling' isn't quite accurate. We barely allow it to simmer the first time. After it cools, the scum is taken off the top, and we put it on the fire again. It does boil then, but only for ten or fifteen minutes. When it settles, the clarified juice can be drawn off the top. What we call 'boiling the juice' actually takes place in the boiling house."

"Which you are going to show me now," Maria teased. It was hard to miss his enthusiasm for the work he had originally taken on with reluctance.

"And which you are going to regret," he said with a good-natured grin. "It's the closest thing to hell on earth, in terms of temperature anyway. I don't even care to spend time there myself—fully clothed."

Maria was to find out all too quickly that he had not been exaggerating. The barnlike area into which he brought her now almost made the previous chamber seem cool. A steamy blast of heat hit her in the face, nauseatingly sweet, a sickening blend of sugar, burning cane trash, and human sweat. The shimmering red haze from a large brick oven gave an unearthly glow to the setting.

It took Maria's eyes a moment to adjust, and she was startled to see Royall materialize out of the eerie half-light. It had not occurred to her that he would be there, though it should have, and she made an instinctive move to clutch Alex's arm for support. She caught herself, but not quite in time.

His face seemed to darken, turning almost purple in the intense heat. For a terrified instant Maria thought she saw the same anger and hatred that had driven him to strike her before. But then he turned away, shrugging almost carelessly, and she realized she must have been wrong.

Still, she was just as glad she had not worn the comfortable native gown, after all, and she forced her attention back to the room. Now that she could see better, she picked out five shallow iron pots bolted together in a long row in the oven. They descended in size from about six feet in diameter. Several Hawaiians, nude except for the traditional *malo* or loincloth, were tossing fuel onto the flames and using long paddle-like implements to skim the surface of the boiling juice. Their skin was glistening with sweat, almost as if it had been oiled.

Steam rose from the pots, half obscuring the violently bubbling liquid, and logs and cane trash snapped and hissed as they sent up plumes of smoke. As the juice grew thicker, Maria noticed that the level sank below the rim of the kettles, making it difficult to skim. At a signal, the smallest pot was abruptly emptied, and each of the others scooped deftly into the next down the line, bringing the liquid to the rim again.

By the time the juice was "struck" from the last pot, Alex explained as he led her, mercifully, out of the room, it had reached the proper temperature for crystallization, about 288 degrees. This was the most critical part of the process, and Royall insisted on overseeing it himself, not even stepping out for a few minutes.

All that was left after that was to cool the juice and let the molasses drain off. A time-consuming affair, but some fellow was said to be experimenting with a centrifugal device that could spin it off in minutes.

"It's not only the juice that needs to cool," Maria said, ruefully aware that perspiration was plastering loose tendrils of hair to her brow and neck. She could just imagine what she looked like. "I'm glad you showed it to me. It was truly fascinating ... but I can see why nobody would want to spend any time in there fully clothed. Especially a woman, with all these petticoats and silly contrivances! I think I'll go back and soak in a nice cool tub ... and don't look so worried. Royall is safely occupied. Besides, both of Ilimi's nephews will be there, and they are huge."

Alex smiled. "You must allow me my protective instincts, love," he said in a quietly vibrating undertone. "Even if you don't allow me to act on them." Maria sensed that he longed to touch her. Just lightly, a brush on the arm or the cheek, but he turned instead and walked back into the mill.

The air felt wonderfully refreshing. Even the dust and sultry summer winds were welcome as she followed the narrow path that led through the remaining stands of mature cane to the main road. Chang detached himself hurriedly from a group of workers and trotted up beside her, offering in a mixture of pidgin and almost proper English to walk with her to the house.

"Chang go there anyway," he said with his perpetual eager brightness. "Have job for boss-man. Big important errand. Chang almost forget. Plenty bad bad. Lucky thing missus come along, make him remember."

Lucky, indeed! Maria smiled, but she did not protest as they started together up the dusty road. She knew very well what Chang's "big, important" errand was. Don't let the "missus" out of your sight.

Another example of Alex's protectiveness, but she could not bring herself to mind.

It was getting so easy to depend on him. So very easy to believe all those optimistic promises. They *would* find Claudine, he kept telling her, and slowly, without even realizing it sometimes, she was beginning to trust. They would find her, and everything else would follow from that.

It was an insidious feeling, creeping up on her when she least expected it. She was finding it harder and harder to remind herself that it all might come to an end one day. That she might have to say goodbye and watch from the *lanai* as great white billows of canvas disappeared into the horizon.

She did not know if she could ever go back to the way things had been. It frightened her even to think of it, and the idea of sailing off on the *Jade Dawn*, cannons blazing, the devil take the consequences, was beginning to hold a dangerous appeal.

It occurred to her that it was not only Alex Barron's reckless impulses she had to guard against, but her own.

Chapter 12

It was the first cool morning in months. Summer was fading into autumn, and hints of briskness gave a welcome bite to the breezes that blew *mauka*, upland, from the ocean.

Maria followed the road as it wound down the gentle slope toward the last of the fields that had not been cut. A pretty morning, and she was enjoying being alone for a change. Only three stands of cane still remained, defiant splashes of emerald brightness separated by dirty brown lanes. Even these would be leveled within the hour, and milling finished by sunset tomorrow. The day after that people would be arriving from as far away as Honolulu for the celebration that traditionally marked the end of the harvest.

She paused at the edge of the cane field, just at the place where the narrow lane cut through two leafy green patches. The sound of busy workers drifted through the dense foliage, but here everything was almost incredibly still, and she was conscious, as rarely before, of the sheer pleasure of solitude. She loved Alex for caring so much—and everyone else to whom he had obviously communicated his anxiety—but there were times she positively craved a few minutes to herself.

Even her mother had shown up two days earlier. Maria had been astonished when Lena Owen had appeared on the *lanai* and announced she was staying. "To help with the party," she had said, but

Maria knew that she, like the others, had been alarmed by Royall's increasingly erratic behavior.

In a way, she was touched. For Lena to leave her wayward husband alone in the rooms over the tavern was a major concession. Proof that for all her reticence on the subject, she did truly love her only child.

But love or no, two days of her mother's relentlessly cheerful chatter—and the prospect of Lord knows how many to come—was daunting, to say the least, and Maria had snatched the opportunity to slip away when no one was looking.

She frowned slightly as she glanced back at the house. It was not that she was really worried, but Royall had been drinking heavily again. She had heard some of the men talking about it. He had shown up several times at the mill smelling of *okolehao*, something he had never done before. And he rarely came out of his rooms now before noon.

So much for Alex's theory that he had to oversee the boiling house himself, though it did seem strange that he would trust the men he had hired, no matter how competent they were.

Well, at least she wouldn't have to worry about him for a while. Maria shook off the uneasiness that had come over her and started down the path between the stands of cane. According to Ilimi's oldest nephew, Royall had been snoring so loudly before he could be heard all the way to the stables. He was famous for the volume of his snores when thoroughly drunk. The men were always joking about it, and doing devastatingly funny imitations. He had caught them once and they had been soundly punished. Royall did not take kindly to being made fun of.

"Missus!"

Chang appeared suddenly at the far end of the long path, his face bright and eager, as if even with all that work, he was truly thrilled to see her. Maria could just picture the excuses rolling over in his mind, tempting him to pick one or another, and she was sure her precious solitude was about to end when a sudden commotion sounded somewhere on the other side of the field. A loud crash accompanied by what appeared to be splintering wood.

Chang jerked his head toward the noise, then abruptly back at her, and Maria saw dismay spreading across his features. Should he go and check—or stay and take care of the boss-man's wife, as he had undoubtedly been ordered? An agonizing dilemma.

"I'll be all right, Chang," she called out, raising her voice to be sure it carried, though in truth everything seemed almost eerily silent at the moment. "I'm heading that way myself. I'll be along in a second. You'd better go and see what happened."

He hesitated, then whirled around, and Maria laughed out loud as she watched him scurry down the path and disappear off to the right. For a young man as conscientious as Chang, and devoted as he obviously was to Alex, it had been a cruel choice. It seemed only fair to relieve him of it.

She did not, in fact, move quite as quickly as she had implied to Chang. It was warm beneath the patches of cane, but not unpleasantly so, for a slight breeze wafted down the path, and she was relishing her last moments of privacy. She could already hear voices, new ones joining in all the time, shouting and cutting each other off, and she knew the bedlam she was going to find when she finally reached them. Here it was just peaceful enough to make her want to tarry.

She was startled to catch sight of a figure in dark clothing bending or squatting to the right of the path some distance ahead. One of the Chinese? With all the protective clothing the workers wore, it was hard to tell.

Her first thought was that Chang must have come back, but she quickly realized she was wrong. There hadn't been time for him to run all the way around the field and back down one of the rows. And with the stalks crowded so thickly together, he could hardly have cut across.

The man jumped up abruptly and, without looking back, scurried over the path into the stand of cane on the left. Almost as if he had sensed her there. Maria stared after him, puzzled. His manner seemed furtive, guilty somehow, but she didn't have time to dwell on it, for just at that instant a brown-and-gray-mottled streak cut across the path in the opposite direction and plunged into one of the long green rows.

Mack's mongrel! Maria felt her heart sink. Royall hated him enough as it was. If he found out the animal had gotten into his cane, he would give him to the Hawaiians to skin and roast in their *imu*.

Without stopping to think, she hurried anxiously toward the spot where she had just seen him. When she thought she was about there, she began squinting down one shadowy, tunnel-like row after another. She had to find him and get him out of there before anyone spotted him and reported back to Royall.

The light was green and eerie, making it difficult to see more than a few yards. Maria hesitated helplessly. She wasn't even sure which row he had gone down. How on earth could she possibly guess where he was? He could be almost anywhere. There was no point trying to whistle or call. He was hopelessly untrained and wouldn't come to anyone but Mack.

Then, just as she began to fear she would never locate him, she caught sight of a faint movement in one of the deep green-canopied furrows. The dog? She was sure of it, and began to move stealthily toward him. He was lying down, attacking something between his front paws, gnawing at it with a sound that was audible now.

A bone?

Maria drew in her breath, barely daring to inch

forward, and prayed that she was wrong. If he had a bone and she tried to get close to him, he was likely to go after her just as ferociously with those same strong teeth. But if he was still there when the men came through with their cane knives, Royall was certain to learn of it, and Mack would be devastated. She had to find some way to coax him out of there.

She must have made a sound, for the dog's head snapped up. Maria was aware of eyes gleaming out of the semidarkness for the briefest fraction of a second; then, snatching up the bone or whatever it was, he began to lope away from her.

She gulped with dismay as he disappeared into the luminous green shadows. He was heading right toward the place where she had heard the commotion before. Dozens of eyes were certain to be watching when he burst into the open. She could only hope Royall would stay in his rooms for a good long time today.

Could Alex's cousins be persuaded to take the dog in, too? she wondered. Hardly fair to ask. Dogs required more care than turtles, and even Mack admitted, in his less possessive moments, that he was a stupid, surly beast.

The mongrel was out of sight now, but Maria continued to follow, though she knew there was no hope of stopping him. She might as well go back, she supposed. But she was probably almost halfway anyhow.

Distances were illusive. It was even darker here. The air was unpleasantly close. Green leaves met overhead, forming a high arched roof that shut out the sun, and she was more aware of the heat than she had expected. Wasps swarmed all around almost languidly, a steady buzzing drone. She could barely see them. Just little specks floating in the shadows.

A faint glow seemed to shimmer ahead. Maria sensed as much as saw it. Surely she ought to be reaching the end by now. That looked like light—but high off the ground, halfway to the tops of the tall stalks. The wasps were more persistent now, landing in her hair, and she shook her head to try to get rid of them. They clung, tenacious but not threatening. As if the sultry humidity made them too lazy even to sting.

An acrid odor of smoke cut through the sweetness of the cane. Much too strong for the distant mill chimneys, Maria thought, feeling the first twinges of alarm—and coming from the wrong direction. Throwing a hasty look back over her shoulder, she was horrified to see thick puffs of smoke rising from the path she had just left.

Fire! She began to race down the long cane-walled row, trying desperately not to panic. The man she had seen before. That was why he had acted so guilty. And made sure she didn't get a look at his face. He had been hunkered down, puffing on his pipe. Breaking Royall's strictest rule.

He must have dropped it in his haste to flee. The smell of smoke was sharper now; it was stinging her nostrils and bringing tears to her eyes. Maria tried to run faster, but she kept tripping on the uneven earth in her fashionable kid slippers. Dead leaves formed a thick mantle underfoot, treacherously slippery, and she stumbled frequently. Her hands were badly scraped, her knees bruised and aching as she struggled to get up again and again.

Why couldn't she see the end of the path? She was aware of something in there with her. The mongrel, as frightened and frantic as she. There ought to have been light by now. The smoke wasn't that dense. *Why couldn't she see it?*

Then, abruptly, she came to an unexpected barricade. Groping with her hands in the terrible dim haze, she identified loose stalks of cane. A haphazard heap of it several feet high. Now the fear was overwhelming. It swelled in her chest and made her heart pound. This was what she had heard before. One of the wagons had toppled over, spilling a load of cane on the ground.

And it was directly in her path!

She tried to scramble up the pile instinctively, irrationally, but all she did was slide back again. There was nothing to get a hold on. Some of the stalks had come loose in the fall. Others were still tied in bundles, but they broke under her weight and kept tumbling down with a horrible hollow clatter.

She could hear the dog snuffling beside her. It seemed unnatural suddenly, the way he never barked. She saw that he was trying to dig his way underneath one of the dense walls of living cane. A chance perhaps, and she attacked the stalks herself, tugging and beating frantically with her hands.

But the growth was thick and solid. No way she could possibly get through without a machete, and Maria realized suddenly that she was going to die. Cruelly, painfully, alone in that seething jungle of cane. The fire had almost reached her. She started to scream. No one would hear her. No one would help. The minute the men had seen that black cloud rising, they would have run in fright from the fields, but she had to do something.

The smoke was so thick, it was burning her lungs now. She could hear the crackling of the flames just behind her. The heat was intense and terrifying.

Alex had just finished unloading a mass of wet, crushed cane in the open-sided shed where it would be dried to make fuel for the ovens, and decided on impulse to drive the cart down to the fields himself. It wasn't his job. He had no business being out of the mill with Royall absent, but he enjoyed the challenge of handling the oxen and needed some time to clear his head.

He didn't like the way Royall was drinking. The stench had been so bad the previous afternoon, it was almost as if he had deliberately doused his clothing in cheap native liquor. He had never been like that during harvest before, everyone said. Never even touched a drop.

Alcoholism had a way of getting worse, of course, but it was a change in the pattern, and changes made Alex distinctly uncomfortable. He had overlooked similar signs once before, and he was blasted if he was going to make the same mistake again. One of the oxen balked, and he scowled distractedly, trying to keep his mind at least partly on the team. Maria would be all right until after the party. She was never alone, especially with her mother there. Alex had been pleasantly surprised when Lena Owen showed up. But he was going to have to start putting men on Royall's door again.

As he rounded the last grove of *kukui* trees and came in sight of the field, two things struck him almost simultaneously. Dark smoke surging up in the air, and the overturned wagon, now abandoned by the men.

Damn! One of the workers must have been smoking again. He should have paid more attention to Royall's fears. His eyes ran quickly over the area, assessing the damage. They were going to lose the remaining three stands of cane. Nothing could be done about that. Or the wagon. At least the surrounding fields had been cleared. The fire wouldn't spread.

It was then that he saw Chang racing toward him, arms flailing wildly in the air, his face distorted with alarm.

"Missus!" he kept shouting. "Missus!" over and over again, and gesticulating toward the fire. Alex realized with a rush of horror what he was trying to tell him. Maria was in that field. Somewhere near the place where the flames were spreading rapidly.

His feet were frozen for an instant with fear. She was there, but he didn't know where. He had no idea how to find her, what to do for her, when suddenly his ears picked up muffled cries from behind the load of fallen cane.

Leaping forward, he covered the ground in a furious sprint. The wagon was unhitched, lying on its side, badly broken. Alex clutched it, grasping one end in desperate hands, trying with almost superhuman strength to drag it out of the way.

Angus Dougal was beside him suddenly. His good Scottish nose had distinguished the scent of fresh-burning cane from the smoke of the mill, and he was lending a powerful shoulder. Alf Shirl followed a second later, and several of the men, but all of them together could not budge that sturdy cart with its ton of cane.

The fire was blazing now, a hot breath on their skin. There wasn't much time. "Up, laddie," Angus said urgently. Alex glanced over and saw him cupping his hands into a foothold.

Without a second's hesitation he inserted his boot and felt himself being thrust up by the strength of the other man's arms. Shirl followed almost immediately, boosted in similar fashion, and Alex realized instantly what they had in mind. With Angus and some of the others holding the wiry Cockney, Shirl's work-hardened hands holding him, he could lean over the edge on the other side without worrying about tumbling off.

Out of the corner of his eye, he saw that Chang had picked up a cane knife and was frenziedly hacking the living stalks on the side. Good man! he thought. One of them was sure to reach her, and he made a silent pledge that the Chinaman would have his own sugar operation or anything else he wanted when this was over.

Maria had managed, even in her terror, to stack some of the loose cane in a solid pile and climb on it. Not high enough to get to the top, but with Shirl clutching his belt, Alex was able to stretch out and catch her hands. The same slippery stalks that had impeded her before were helping them now. At a shout from Alex, the men pulled them up and over, and it was barely a second before they all landed in an undignified heap on the ground.

At almost the same instant Chang cut through the tall stalks, and a terrified mass of singed gray-brown fur shot yelping across the fields. Mack's blasted mangy pet! She must have gone in after him, and it had nearly cost her her life.

They were scrambling now to get away from the fire, which was already consuming the last of the cane and lapping hungrily around the wagon. Every instinct in Alex's body hungered to take her in his arms and hold her. It tortured him that he could not. She was smudged with smoke and coughing as they reached safer ground some distance away; her eyes were red and teary, but she had never looked so dear to him, and he had never loved her more.

Angus's warning "Laddie" was soft in his ear, and he knew he must have made a move. But, ah, God, it was hard to stand there in front of everyone and try to look like he was just glad he'd been able to rescue his employer's wife!

He did not know if he could have restrained himself, even with Angus's hand on his arm, if Lena Owen had not suddenly come flying down the road from the house. She was still a handsome woman, but her hair was in wild disarray, her face splotched and crimson. She was gasping for breath as she reached them.

Ignoring the others, she went directly to Alex.

"Where is Royall?" she said.

Alex felt his blood run cold. In all the fear it hadn't even occurred to him to wonder . . . His lips opened, but he could not form the words.

It was Angus who answered. "The man is nae here, but it dinna matter. We have the situation well in hand. See, your lass is nae hurt. Only a wee bit dirty. She could do with a good wash back t' the house."

Lena glanced at him briefly, then back at Alex, her dark eyes still searching his face. Still asking the question apparently only he could hear.

"Royall is drunk," he said shortly, with none of the Scotsman's tact. "He's locked up in his room. He hasn't been out all morning. . . . Take Maria home, will you? The fire's about burned itself out, but the smoke is still thick. She probably could do with a bit of a wash."

"He's right, Mama." Maria made a gallant attempt at a smile. "I feel like Mack that time he was mining for gold behind the icehouse. And it really is hard to breathe with all this smoke."

Her voice was so hoarse, it hurt Alex to listen to it. But Lena seemed reassured, and without further discussion started back with her daughter in the direction of the house. Alex watched them go with a helpless sense of rage and frustration. *He* should have been the one walking beside her now, a steadying hand on her waist. It should have been *his* place to comfort and care for her, and he cursed the circumstances that made him stand there like a blasted fool and pretend she meant nothing to him.

And pretend damned poorly. He was aware of the men watching him, and he had little doubt that every one of them had figured out his feelings. That Angus knew, and no doubt disapproved, had been clear from that quietly urgent "Laddie" before. But it was also clear that his heart was with the young man he had taken under his wing all those years ago, and Alex wondered which rankled most. The disapproval or the pity.

Where is Royall? He shifted his gaze unconsciously toward the house. The image of another day in the fields came back. That almost pathological horror and fear he had glimpsed in Royall Perralt's face at the mention of fire.

Or had it been ... fascination?

Alex shivered in spite of the sunlight and residual heat from the fire. Had a diabolic thought been planted in his brain at just that moment? A cunning way to revenge himself on the woman whose very existence was a constant reminder of his own masculine failings?

Had Lena's instinct been right, and this wasn't an accident?

Unlikely. Alex turned his attention back to the fields. The fire had destroyed the cane in a matter of minutes, and finding no more fuel, died down to hissing embers. There was no way to plan something like that. Royall couldn't have known that Maria would even be there. Or that the dog would go rushing down one of the rows of cane—or that a wagon would tumble over conveniently at the end. There were too many unpredictables.

An accident, then. He went back to the place where he had left his cart. The oxen were jittery, but they had stood their ground. Leaving some of the men with shovels in case the fire flared up, he sent the rest back to their chores and started with a sharp crack of his whip up the road toward the mill. No point leaving the cart now. There would be no more cane to haul. It looked like the milling was going to be finished ahead of schedule.

An accident ... but it made him nervous all the same. He didn't want Maria around there anymore. He was going to have to get her to Honolulu a little sooner than he had planned.

Chapter 13

It was such a lovely, cheerful afternoon, Maria found it hard to remember the fierce violence of the fire only two days before, and how very near she had come to losing her life.

The air was still, much warmer than expected, but not unpleasant. She paused on the steps of the *lanai* and surveyed the broad, sweeping lawn that ran around three sides of the house. Brightness and laughter were everywhere. Ladies twirled lace-trimmed satin parasols, more decorative than functional, and spun around coyly to show off new gowns, green- and gold- and lavender-sprigged dimity and fine book muslin in all the latest pastels. The men were only slightly less vivid as they called out to old friends they had not seen for as long as a year. The dark greens and grays of slim-waisted day tailcoats, aided in more than one instance by a tightly laced corset, were accented with jonquil, buff, and flora blue waistcoats and an occasional muslin cravat as piercing and vivid as the sky.

The guests had begun arriving the afternoon before, especially those from the other islands. Maria had pulled herself together enough from her recent ordeal to play the part of the gracious hostess, though it had been more of a strain than she had expected. Royall had not appeared. She had tried to make his excuses, but she had noticed several sly looks being exchanged, and she knew that everyone had guessed, quite accurately, where he was. Indeed, when Alex and some of the men had gone to his room after the fire, they had found him sprawled out as expected, snoring loudly and stinking of *okolehao*.

He had not appeared all the next day, and Maria had been half afraid he would not show up for his own party. That would have been something to explain away! But he had opened his door this morning and ventured out looking surprisingly fit. Now he was strolling around, greeting everyone by name and slapping one acquaintance after another jovially on the back, as if this had just been another successful harvest and nothing were amiss.

Maria let her eyes run over the area one last time, making sure no detail had been neglected. She loved parties, but she was a nervous hostess, always afraid her efforts wouldn't meet Royall's exacting standards, though, in fact, her dinners and balls were already becoming legendary among the social elite of the islands.

Tables had been set for the staid and less limber on the *lanai*, and in the shade of the graceful, spreading *kukui* tree, but most of the younger guests were grouped on blankets scattered around the grounds. Each contained a single girl, pretty or plain, some of decidedly mixed blood, who was holding court for several doting admirers. Maria smiled in spite of herself. There were definite advantages to a society where males outnumbered the females.

The buffet was well stocked and running smoothly, with servants bringing fresh items every few minutes from the kitchen. Dinner would be more extravagant, served late in the afternoon when the air had cooled and strings of *kukui* nuts were lighted to ward off the encroaching dusk, but no one needed to go hungry in the meantime. Long boards had been covered with gaily patterned lengths of calico, and food for every taste was crowded on top. Cold chicken and ham and slices of yesterday's roast beef; imported French cheeses still cool from the icehouse; big bowls of mangoes, bananas, and plump Waioli oranges; slices of cucumbers, and avocados in a vinegary sauce that kept them from turning brown; spiced pears and dried apples; little frosted cakes from the new cook her mother had found, who was working out surprisingly well for a change; and, of course, slices of crisp-crusted white bread in which Maria took special pride, for flour in that climate was more often weevily than not, and baked goods were always a treat.

Scattered throughout the area were large buckets filled with ice, brought by ships that sailed down from cold northern waters. Jugs of fruit juice were kept in them, ostensibly for the ladies, though it was so refreshing many of the gentlemen were helping themselves, too, often spiking their glasses with stronger spirits.

Royall's one concession to his southern heritage, Maria thought. Among the fine French brandies and champagne, he had included several bottles of rum and some apparently excellent American whiskey which he had no doubt learned to appreciate in Charleston. The trays of hock and ale usual at such gatherings were conspicuously absent.

Maria felt an uncomfortable prickle on the back of her neck, as if someone were staring at her, and she turned to see Lucifer Darley a short distance away. The sly, amused look on his face made her skin crawl. Like a reptile! She had not seen him arrive, though she had known, of course, that he would be there. He hadn't missed an occasion at Honuakula for nearly as long as she had been mistress of the plantation.

He lifted his hand and gave her a mocking salute, as if tipping the brim of an imaginary hat. Really, the man was disgusting! she thought. He obviously knew exactly how she reacted to him and was enjoying it. Maria gave him a curt nod and turned abruptly, looking for something to distract her attention. The last thing she wanted was to get stuck in a conversation with someone like that.

Fortunately, Angus Dougal had just arrived, neatly but most unfashionably dressed, and looking more than a little out of place. Ordinarily mates from ships in the harbor were not included at such affairs, nor of course were the field hands. But Maria had been pleasantly surprised to learn that the taciturn Scotsman had been acting captain of the *Shadow Dawn* a short time earlier, which gave him the tenuous veneer of respectability required for an invitation.

"Mr. Dougal." She hastened toward him, stretching out her hands, which she sensed both pleased and embarrassed him. "I'm glad you could come. I haven't had a chance to thank you. You saved my life, you know. Mr. Shirl said it was your idea to boost men up on the wagon—though he did mention that he caught on himself very quickly."

Angus saw the twinkle in her eye and chuckled. He was finding it unexpectedly easy to like this feisty, courageous woman, and he was beginning to understand young Alexander Barron a wee bit more than was altogether comfortable.

"I have nae doubt o' that. There na' a drap o' modesty in the man's body. . . . But you ha' nae need t' thank me, lass. Someone else would ha' thought o' it soon enough. It was na' so clever. Just good common sense."

"It was clever enough," Maria insisted. "I wouldn't be alive now if it weren't for you. And Alf Shirl . . . and Chang whacking away with his cane knife. I've never felt so . . . trapped in my life." She heard the tremor in her voice, and forced back a note of lightness. "It's amazing, isn't it? The predicaments some women get themselves in. A fire on one side— a broken cart with a ton of cane on the other? I couldn't have arranged things more perfectly if I'd sat up all night working on it."

"Well, then," he said quietly, "you'll just ha' to be more careful, will you na'?"

There was a thoughtful expression on his face, and Maria had the uncanny sense that the words were not carelessly uttered. "Yes," she agreed, "I guess I will," and wondered if she had just imagined it as she turned to welcome a new arrival. It might have been a casual comment, but she was uncomfortably aware that everyone was thinking what a strange coincidence it had been, her happening to be in that patch of cane just as the fire happened to erupt.

As if somehow it weren't an accident—though of course, it had to be. Her eyes scanned the gathering, trying discreetly to pick out Alex, though he didn't seem to be there yet. There was no other reasonable explanation for it. And she had caught the man smoking herself!

She spotted a tall figure in the shadow of the *kukui* tree, and her heart gave a little jump, but it was only Jared Barron. They were so alike, those two, and even Matthew, though he lacked a good three inches of the others' height and was considerably fairer. His beautiful French wife was with him, looking cool and graceful though she must be due to deliver in a couple of weeks. Maria started over, eager to speak to them.

She was almost there before she realized that Royall was with them. She had not seen him standing off somewhat to the side, but his voice was clear as he turned and caught sight of her.

"Ah, there you are, my dear," he said as casually as if this were last year's party and all the unpleasantness hadn't exploded between them. In spite of herself, Maria had to admire his icy aplomb. He would have made a superb actor. "Have you come to greet our distinguished guests? Captain Barron here has just been telling me there's trouble with one of their vessels. The *Jasmine Dawn*, is it? She's flying a yellow flag."

"Hello, Dominie," Maria said. "How lovely of you to brave the bumpy roads and come all the way out here. Jared. Yes, I've heard. Some of the other guests have been talking about it. Malaria, they say."

Jared nodded his agreement. "Only a dozen of the men have come down with it, but naturally the quarantine applies to the entire ship. Unfortunately, we're low on cinchona bark, and the local doctor doesn't seem to keep a supply. Just as well, perhaps. If the men survive, they'll be less susceptible to blackwater fever later. Still, we're worried. Alex dropped by to check on them a couple of times last week. And, of course, yesterday afternoon."

"Really?" Royall turned toward Maria with a strangely speculative look. "I hadn't realized he was spending so much time in town."

"Nor I," she echoed honestly. She had known that he had gone someplace the day before. She had seen him ride off after the guests began arriving, and he hadn't returned for nearly three hours. But if he'd found time to get away before that, she'd have been amazed to know when. "I suppose he felt he had to go. Especially if they're out of this—whatever it is."

"Powdered cinchona bark," Royall said dryly. "It comes from Peru. It's been used for over a century in treating malaria. . . . What a devoted captain. And the *Jasmine Dawn* isn't even his ship."

Jared gave him a pointedly cool look. "We all have an interest in every Barron vessel. I'd have gone myself, but with Dominie's . . . well, it would hardly be appropriate. And Matthew, of course, has the same potential concerns for his wife."

"Yes," Royall agreed. "It would be a pity—wouldn't it?—if one of you were to come down with the disease."

He made no effort to hide the malice in his voice. Maria was too horrified even to be embarrassed. He wanted Alex to fall ill with malaria! He was *willing* him to get it, as if the sheer force of his malevolent hatred could somehow make it happen.

Was there a possibility? Something tightened in her chest, and she felt the first unpleasant hints of warning. Was that how malaria was spread? Could one catch the disease just by getting close to someone who had it? She would have to ask Rachel. She knew about things like that.

Suddenly she felt bone-weary and almost at the end of her patience. Dinner hadn't even been served yet, and she was already wondering how she was going to make it through the long evening and night that lay ahead.

Alex had been in town the afternoon before, but not to visit the *Jasmine Dawn*, which had in fact been tended to quite efficiently by Jared. The afflicted men—three in all—were doing much better, thanks to the ample supply of cinchona that was always carried by every Barron vessel on tropical routes, and he had not felt the need to stop and get a report on their progress.

Instead he had spent his time having a brief conversation with the man who was facing him now over a cup of dark, extremely vile-looking liquid. He had given up the *luna*'s cottage for some of the overnight guests, and was bunking in the stable. The smell of hay and horses mingled with an odor that could most kindly be called pungent.

"You're sure you want to go through with this?" Doc Frederick's voice was low and cautious. "It's harmless enough. There shouldn't be any serious effects, but it's going to be unpleasant."

"I don't see that I have any choice," Alex replied grimly. "What's in this stuff, anyway?"

"The Hawaiians call it *koko'olau*. In its usual form it's an invigorating tea. Brewed that strong, it should cause flushing and mild perspiration. I've added a couple of other local nostrums to heighten the effect.

The natives have a particular fondness for cures they can see. It gives them confidence to watch sweat draining the diseases out of their bodies."

"I take it you don't have any faith in the idea yourself." Alex put the cup to his mouth and forced himself to drain it. The concoction was somewhat bitter, but not as bad as he had expected.

"I've tried it on a few occasions," the doctor said. "I never dismiss native remedies out of hand. Many of them are remarkably effective. But I haven't seen sweat cure anyone yet—though in most cases it doesn't seem to do any harm. . . . You having any reactions? It tends to act fairly quickly."

Alex shook his head. There was a mild sense of something, but he had the feeling it was more like anticipation. When he had stopped in at Fredericks' medical office yesterday, he had been terse and to the point. He wanted an excuse to disappear from sight for a while, and the only thing he could come up with was a disease that would warrant quarantine. Preferably malaria, since there was already a yellow flag in the harbor.

"Are you sure this is going to work? It will give me all the right symptoms?"

"Enough of them," Doc Fredericks replied, noting with satisfaction that little beads of perspiration were beginning to form at the younger man's hairline. "Redness and sweating anyhow, and there may be some warmth. But you won't be fever hot. You don't want to be touched by concerned hands. And you're going to have to fake the chills."

Which shouldn't be too hard, Alex thought as he got up from the cot and went over to get a bottle green broadcloth coat that was hanging on a peg on the wall. All he had to do was remember what had nearly happened to Maria the day before yesterday, and the convulsive shuddering would come without effort.

"How long does it last anyway?"

"A couple of hours. You'll feel it wearing off. You're going to have to find an excuse to come back and brew some more. I have it measured out in packets."

"I can check on the horses or something," Alex said, slipping on his coat as they headed out the door and started up the path to the house. "That should be easy." He was surprised at how warm the light-weight jacket felt. Almost steamy inside. His armpits were already drenched, and the hair on his chest prickled with dampness.

They were perhaps halfway to the house when he stopped and faced the other man.

"I don't suppose you approve of me, Fredericks. I doubt most of the people here do, and I don't much give a damn anymore. But I swear to you—I care about Maria. I am not going to let her be hurt. Ever. By anyone."

"It's not my place to approve or disapprove," the doctor said quietly. "I've never set myself up to keep track of the foibles of mankind, God knows. I agreed to help you, and I will. . . . I heard about the fire."

"The fire was an accident," Alex snapped; then, regretting his brusqueness, he added more evenly as they continued on toward the house: "It's set all our nerves on edge, but I don't think there's anything more to it than maybe an omen. . . . I haven't told you how much I appreciate your taking time for all this. I know how busy you are. Mack says you're a 'veterarian' as well as a purveyor of human care."

"Vetra*mar*ian," he corrected. "Mack is most emphatic about that. He's a good boy. I've always had a special fondness for him. I was present at his introduction into the world, you know. What a flurry that caused! He *would* come early, the impatient little rascal."

Early? Alex felt his pulse race illogically. Get a grip on yourself, Barron, he told himself firmly. That potion you drank must have fogged your brain. Early doesn't mean three months.

"He seems a sturdy lad to have been born prematurely," he ventured cautiously.

"I wouldn't exactly call the birth premature. Just a week ahead of schedule—but it was blasted inconvenient! Right in the middle of the holiday dinner."

"I didn't know there was a holiday on the second of October," Alex said, then realized as he caught a sharp look being cast in his direction that he was giving himself away. Having a fondness for the mother didn't usually extend to learning every detail about her child, though the doctor did not push the point.

"Ah, well," he said, "Hawaiians have holidays all the time. If it isn't a sacred *hula* for Laka, the favorite sister of Pele, then it's a *luau* celebration for Lono, the god of growing things and harvests. Any excuse will do. . . . I think we're about there." They had reached the edge of the broad lawn and were preparing to mingle with the other party goers. "Are you ready for your performance, Captain Barron? I must say, you look the part."

Alex did indeed look feverish. Maria, halfway across the yard, was alarmed the instant she saw him, and it was all she could do not to let her anxiety show. Malaria? She knew so little about it. Just that it was a terrible recurring disease. Even if you survived the first bout, it could kill you the second or third—or tenth—time around. Especially if the dreaded blackwater fever set in.

But flushing and a bit of perspiration didn't automatically mean one had malaria. Maria forced herself to be sensible as she went about her chores, overseeing the delivery of food from the kitchen and making sure all the guests were comfortable. It could be almost anything. A nasty cold perhaps, or even a reaction to all the smoke he had breathed in. She had been feeling ill herself a good part of yesterday.

Still ... She tried to keep herself from looking at him too openly, but she could not. Just as she could not quite control the fears that were gnawing at the back of her consciousness. Reason told her she was being foolish. There were a dozen much better explanations than the dreaded malaria. But all she could think of was the evil expression she had seen on Royall's face before. The sheer hunger he had felt to make this awful thing happen.

One of the serving maids stopped her with a question, and Maria almost forgot for the next few minutes as she busied herself with matters at hand. They were running low on fruit drinks. The day had been much hotter than expected. She had the kitchen help dilute orange juice with well water and flavor it with Honuakula sugar and mint from the garden, and cold vegetables needed to be dressed for salads and attractively arranged in large calabashes.

She did not have time to stop and think. The dread was still there, but it was safely submerged, and she might have managed to keep from dwelling on it if she hadn't happened to look over at the side of the house. Royall was standing alone, staring off at something in the direction of the *lanai*, his eyes dark and glowing—and filled with such raw pleasure, it was almost obscene.

Her heart catching in her throat, Maria turned to follow his gaze.

Alex was sitting in a chair at the edge of the *lanai*, a little apart from the others. Even from a distance she could see that he was shivering. He was trying to conceal it—his shoulders were set, his jaw clenched—but he was clearly in the throes of a debilitating chill.

Were chills a sign of malaria? There was a hideous sinking feeling in the pit of her stomach as she looked back at Royall. That was not simple pleasure

she had seen in his eyes. It was gloating. He was
sure Alex had the disease now, and he was gloating!

Before, he had been willing him to come down
with it. Now he was consciously willing him to die.

Someone touched her arm lightly but firmly. Maria
jerked around to see Rachel standing next to her.

"I don't think there's anything very much wrong
with him," she said quietly. "He may have some
sniffles tomorrow, but I doubt even that."

"Malaria . . ." Maria reminded her hoarsely. "They
say there's malaria on the *Jasmine Dawn*. And Alex
was there."

"Briefly, I heard." Rachel was looking thoughtfully
at the small group seated on the *lanai*. Jared and
Dominie were there, and a couple of well-to-do businessmen who were apparently old friends of Alex's
from Honolulu. "Malaria means 'bad air.' It seems
to be carried on something in fetid marshlands with
rotting vegetation and poor drainage. I've never
known anyone to get it from casual contact with an
infected person. The three men on the *Jasmine* picked
it up in the South Pacific. None of the rest of the
crew has come down with it."

"I thought a dozen men were ill."

"Three . . . and I don't believe Alex has a fever.
His face is red and he's as lathered as an overworked
horse, but he really doesn't seem ill. Don't forget, I'm
a nurse. And that bout of shuddering was all wrong."
She looked around to see that her reassurance was
having no effect on her friend, and added gently:
"Would you like me to find out for sure?"

"Please . . ." The word barely came out, and Maria
reinforced it with a nod of her head.

"All right. Give me a minute, then just saunter
over casually. If I don't make an enormous fuss about
getting him immediately into a proper bed—not that
makeshift cot in the horse barn—you'll know everything is all right."

*   *   *

Alex was feeling none too pleased with himself as he leaned back in the chair and reviewed in his mind the grossly overdone convulsions that had wracked his body before. Quaking at will was not as easy as it sounded. He could only hope Royall had been too far gone to notice anything out of order. The man had started drinking again about noon, but he seemed to be pacing himself with uncharacteristic control.

Alex ran his finger along the inside of his shirt collar. It was uncomfortably sticky, and he wished he could take off the starched black cravat and white Marseilles waistcoat. The trouble with the blasted potion was that it whetted the appetite. And ravenous hunger was hardly a symptom of malaria.

Fredericks had had the foresight to have a couple of sandwiches and some bananas waiting in the stable when he went back to brew more tea, but that had been easily an hour ago. It was agony watching Dominie pop one frosted cake after another into her mouth and talk about how lovely it was to have an excuse to eat as much as she wanted.

He was startled to feel a cool hand on his forehead, and another coming from behind to rest efficiently on one cheek. "Why, cousin Alex," Rachel said in a low voice bubbling with laughter. "Not a hint of fever. What a fraud you are. Those shudders were almost comical. I'm afraid you'll never find a career on the stage."

Alex knew better than to try to demur. He had not shared his plan with anyone except Jared, whom he had needed to spread a few convenient lies about the seriousness of the disease on the *Jasmine* and the lack of healing cinchona, but he should have known better than to try to fool a dedicated nurse like Rachel.

"Young Doc warned me not to allow any concerned hands on my brow. . . . Why do they call him *Young* Doc, by the way? He has easily a decade on me."

"Because there was an Old Doc once, of course. I remember him from when I was a little girl. He had the most wonderful parties on Christmas, with presents for all the children.... What are you up to, Alex?"

The last words were whispered, almost in his ear. "Nothing that need concern you," he said in an undertone. "Just do your part and see that we get Maria to Honolulu. ... And, for God's sake, try to look a little worried about your poor, ailing in-law. Royall is coming this way. In case you haven't figured it out, this little charade is for him."

"I'm not totally without a brain in my head," she replied, tartly amused. "Or without a certain talent for persuasion. Maria will be on her way to Honolulu by this time tomorrow. Just watch.... Royall," she called out, raising her voice slightly, "I've been telling Alex what a delightful gala this is. He seems a bit under the weather. I thought he might be coming down with a fever, but he says he's fine."

"Probably just a slight indisposition." The blatant malice was no longer apparent, but Royall did not take his eyes off Alex as he found an empty chair and sat down. There was a nearly full glass of what might have been either whiskey or brandy in his hand, though he didn't seem to be touching it. "I'm sure it's nothing serious."

"Hardly." It was all Alex could do to keep from squirming under that intense scrutiny. Luckily he didn't have to throw another fit of chills. "It takes more than a little discomfort to slow me down. We Barrons are tough."

"And stubborn," Rachel said, laughing. "I told him he ought to rest, but, no. ... Oh, here's Maria. Do come and sit with us. I really am amazed at how clever you are! I've been to all sorts of festive occasions thrown by some of the biggest trading houses in Macao, and none of them has been anywhere near as exciting. I suppose this is the beginning of your season here."

Maria looked at the other woman's relentlessly bright expression and felt as if a heavy weight had been lifted from her heart. But she was careful not to let anything show as she made an effort to keep her gaze from straying toward Alex.

"We don't really have much of a 'season' in Lahaina. I'm afraid we're terribly provincial. There'll be a number of parties throughout the fall and winter, but fun would be more the word for them than stylish."

"But you will be going to Honolulu, of course," Rachel persisted. "For fittings for your new dresses. I do envy you. It will be so exciting, choosing all those fabulous outfits."

Maria stared at her in amazement. Rachel knew perfectly well she never went to Honolulu—and since when had fashion been exciting to the reverend's daughter? Alex's idea, she realized suddenly . . . and knew even before Royall spoke that it wasn't going to work.

"The dressmaker comes here," he said stiffly. "To Honuakula. My wife does not go to her."

"Really? How quaint," Dominie interjected in the most ingenuously scandalized tone Maria had ever heard. "In France, nobody who is anybody—even from the most remote villages—would dream of not going to Paris to have a new wardrobe prepared. A dressmaker who *travels* . . . ? Ah, but I am over-stepping the bounds of good taste." Her face took on a prettily apologetic look, halfway between sincerity and pity as she lapsed, seemingly unconsciously, into French. "I forget myself. That is France. This, of course, is someplace quite different. I must learn to be more tolerant."

The words struck a snobbish core in Royall. Maria saw the emotions playing on his face and marveled at the brilliance of what had obviously been a carefully prepared scheme. The one thing that could have touched him—and the one person who could have done it. Dominie, with her impeccable French background.

He took a long, slow sip from his drink, as if measuring it out, then another, and let his eyes run speculatively from the beads of sweat on Alex's forehead to the dampness at the front of his shirt to hands that were shaking genuinely now. From hunger as much as the stimulant in the tea.

He must have liked what he saw, for his lips shaped into a thin smile. "Why not?" he said almost casually. "I defer to *madame*'s judgment when it comes to fashion. The dressmaker who travels is undoubtedly of inferior quality. Besides, it will do my wife good. I'm sure you heard of her recent . . . problem. She could use a week or two to relax and pull herself together."

He could not quite keep the venom out of his voice now. Or the gloating Maria had sensed before, and she felt her stomach twisting into knots again. He seemed so sure Alex was ill. Could it be Rachel who was wrong?

Certainly she didn't seem to have any doubts. In fact, Maria had to admit, she was looking positively delighted.

"But that's fantastic!" she cried, clapping her hands like a little girl. "I would love to go with you . . . only I'm hoping I won't be wearing quite the same size dress this winter." She turned to Royall with a smile so dazzling it might almost have been natural. "I must thank you, sir, for your advice about the, uh, fruit. I think perhaps it may have lived up to its reputation. I have an idea, Maria! Why don't you let Mack come and stay with me while you're gone? I'm sure Royall will be busy cleaning up, or whatever one does after the harvest. And it will give me a chance to get used to having a child around the house."

Alex sat back in his chair and watched admiringly

as Rachel quickly wrapped up the loose ends. She had not been mistaken when she said she had a talent for persuasion. Within minutes it had been settled that the boy would stay with her and Matthew, and the two Honolulu businessmen, who had not been sitting there entirely by accident, were pressed into service to bring Maria back with them in their private schooner to Honolulu. Everything was going as planned.

Alex let his eyes drift back one last time to Royall. He was just sitting there quietly, absolutely no expression on his face now. But Alex knew exactly what was going through his mind as he raised his glass and slowly drained it.

He was drinking to the imminent demise of the eldest Captain Barron. And he was reveling in it.

He was going to be damned disappointed when it didn't come off.

Dinner emerged from the *imu* as the sun settled low in the sky, and the earth was bathed in a deep golden glow. Maria had decided on a Hawaiian-style feast, a *luau*, with local ingredients prepared as the islanders had since long before the coming of the first white man. The guests gathered around as the earth was uncovered from the underground pit, and the massive *pua'a*, a pig of more than a hundred pounds, its cavity filled with heated rocks, was lifted out. Servants dipped their hands in a bucket of cold water and, reaching inside, grabbed some of the rocks and tossed them away, then dunked their hands hastily back and repeated the process until they were all removed.

With the tender, shredded *kalua* pork came *laulaus*, little bundles of butterfish and tender taro shoots wrapped in *ti* leaves; sweet potatoes and bananas, hot from the oven with the steam still rising from them; and raw fish marinated in lime juice and dressed with coconut milk and salt water. For the less adventurous she had provided plump roast turkey, and plenty of chicken simmered in wine from a recipe Dominie had suggested, and, of course, the fresh vegetables and garden greens for which Honuakula was justly renowned.

Only the ubiquitous *poi* was missing. Maria, virtually raised by the Hawaiians, loved to swirl her fingers in a calabash of the starchy, purplish goo, pop them into her mouth, and suck them off with noisy relish. But she had long since learned it was a taste most Europeans did not acquire, and she served instead boiled rice and bread left over from earlier in the day.

Royall remained with his guests throughout the early part of the dinner, but he was drinking steadily, downing whole glasses of whiskey at once and snapping his fingers impatiently for the servers to bring him another. By the time the strings of *kukui* nuts were lighted, casting little sparkling glimmers like fireflies in the gathering darkness, he had already disappeared. One of the men Alex had stationed to watch the plantation office came back to report that he had locked himself in again.

Another change in the pattern, Alex thought uncomfortably. Royall Perralt had always been almost pathetically concerned with what people thought of him. He would never have displayed drunkenness so openly at his own festive gala before.

It was as if he had moved onto a different plane. As if all the standards by which he had lived his life previously were gone, and it occurred to Alex that it was just as well he was getting Maria out of there. He had no idea what was coming next, but he didn't want her around when it did.

Mack had come out to join them for dinner. Alex noticed that he was quiet while his father was still there. The rapport he had sensed between them earlier in the cane fields was gone now, and the boy seemed subdued, almost wary. But as soon as Royall left, he began chatting exuberantly with Jared and Dominie, plying them with his usual questions.

It wrenched Alex's heart to watch him. He was too young to have to deal with his father's alcoholism and cruelty, but in a way it was a relief to see the wall that had come up between them. It would have been excruciating, tearing Mack away from the man if there had been any feelings of love or closeness. As it was, he would be ready to accept a stepfather.

"Why are all the Barron ships called *Dawn*?" he was asking Jared. "That seems a silly name. Don't they sail at night, too?"

"They do," Jared conceded. "But they aren't named for the time of day. They're named after a lady my grandfather loved and lost a long time ago."

Mack gave him a dubious look. Clearly that sounded even sillier. "Why would anyone name a ship after a lady?"

Even Maria laughed at that. With Royall gone, the atmosphere seemed to have eased for everyone. "Because grown-ups get very foolish and sentimental sometimes, darling," she said. "It's a kind of softening that comes with advanced age. You'll be afflicted with it yourself one day."

Alex was relieved to see that the color had come back into her cheeks, and she looked almost relaxed with her son. He had not discontinued the medicinal tea—he didn't want the wrong reports getting back to Royall if he sobered up before morning—but he had cut the dosage and was feeling considerably more comfortable, though he was still careful not to eat anything but a little soup. Vegetable instead of turtle, in deference to Mack.

"Perhaps you would like to come out and visit one of the *Dawns*," Jared was saying to the boy. "The *Jade Dawn*, I think. It's the biggest and grandest of the Barron ships. Though the *Shadow Dawn* was Captain Alex's first command. He gets quite possessive about it sometimes. . . . I could show you all the instruments and how they work. You might want to be a sea captain yourself one day."

"No," Mack said, then, remembering his manners, added, "Thank you, sir. I want to be a planter. I'm sure the sea is very interesting, but I like the land myself."

"Of course you do," Jared said quietly. "Just like your father."

Alex did not miss that subtle emphasis on the final word, and he knew what his cousin had to be thinking. With those eyes, how could he not? He didn't have the appropriate dates to realize it was impossible.

The music began a moment later, distracting the foolish, sentimental grown-ups, and Ilimi appeared to take Mack to bed. The one good fiddler on the island had been retained, with only native rhythm instruments to back him up, and the first strains were almost incredibly sweet as couples began to pair off and move out onto the floor.

Alex watched hungrily as Maria began to dance with a foppish gentleman in a flowered silk waistcoat and azure cravat. A waltz again, and he longed to feel her in his arms, swirling and tantalizing, tempting him to forget everything else, but he knew he had to wait his turn. He couldn't afford to call attention to himself by being too forward now.

The dancing took place in the house, but all the long French doors were open, and couples moved back and forth into the cool shadows of the *lanai*. Alex stood alone on the lawn and watched as Maria appeared and disappeared from view, and tried not to mind too much that she was sharing these lovely, intimate moments with men he did not even know. She would be his tomorrow night. And every night after that.

It was late by the time he finally managed to steal one dance with her. Many of the guests had already departed. Others were bedded down for the night, and the *lanai* was nearly deserted. Only the fiddle remained, wailing plaintively into the darkness. All waltzes now. No complicated arrangements that required more than two dancers.

The candlenuts had long since burned out, replaced by lanterns scattered at sparse intervals, and there were patches of almost impenetrable black at the ends of the *lanai*. If I kiss her now, Alex thought, no one will see—but he did not dare take the chance. There was too much at stake.

Maria felt the tenderness in the hands that touched her, just lightly, holding her the prescribed distance away. All very proper, all superficially correct, but she sensed that his heart, like hers, was beating faster and he was remembering things that were far from proper and correct. The music seemed to be playing for them alone, and they swept in and out of the light and flickering shadows as if the rest of the world did not exist.

"This is the second time we have danced," Alex said softly. "But it will not be the last."

"You had me almost frantic with worry, you know," she scolded, only half teasing. "I had no idea what you were doing. I was sure you were coming down with something awful."

"You had me a little worried yourself. You weren't supposed to catch on so quickly. I wanted you to be able to react naturally. I was afraid Royall would be watching you."

"It wouldn't have mattered." He was turning her around very slowly, losing the rhythm of the music, drifting somewhere behind it like dried leaves on an autumn wind. "He hates you so much . . . he *wanted* you to be ill so badly, he would have believed it no matter what. I think that's why he felt safe enough to start drinking again. He thought God or fate had taken care of you for him."

Alex sensed her anguish, the fear she was trying to hide, all the more vivid because it echoed his own.

But it didn't matter anymore. They were going away now, and except to collect the child, they would not be back again.

"The next time I hold you in my arms," he said, "we won't be dancing. And there will not be all this space between us."

Tomorrow Bright
with Dreams

Sunset to
Dawn again;
Tomorrow rises
Out of the ashes of yesterday,
Bright with dreams
Yet to come.

Chapter 14

Honolulu was far from the most attractive place in the islands. Maria recalled, as the schooner drifted slowly through a natural channel in the coral reefs toward the waterfront, that the early missionary wives had complained bitterly about the heat and dust. For all its lack of superficial appeal, however, the city had a deep, protected harbor that made it a magnet for commercial interests, and the business of the royal government was conducted there. Maui might have been the playground of the kings and their mistresses and sisters—who were sometimes one and the same—but when it came time to create new laws or deal with the upstart foreigners, they invariably returned to their brash, ugly capital.

Maria did not see the ugliness as the schooner dropped anchor and canoes pulled alongside to ferry them across the last bit of water. She did not see rows of grimy thatched huts sprawling out along a muddy beach, or the tangle of cheaply constructed grog shops and brothels and billiard halls crowding inland behind them. She saw someplace completely new for the first time she could remember. Someplace she had never been before.

And she saw the chance to be free for at least a few days.

Powerful Hawaiian arms carried her from the dugout to the shore to protect her dainty ankle boots and fashionable India muslin skirt. A representative of Barron International's small Honolulu office was there to meet her as her feet touched the ground. Captain Barron, he said—Captain Alexander Barron—had sent word ahead that she would be arriving, and they had managed to procure a small house for her.

It was not, he was afraid, very fancy. Not at all what she was used to. But it was the best that could be arranged on short notice and was located along a particularly fine stretch of nearly deserted beach.

Maria did not in the least mind that the house wasn't fancy. She wouldn't have minded anyway—all she wanted was to be with Alex again—but she was much too fascinated with the sights to even think about where she would be staying. She had been just three when she and her widowed mother had arrived on Maui. She had not been off the island since, and she leaned out over the side of the carriage now and craned her neck to take everything in. The dingy taverns and seedy dance halls gave way to more respectable dwellings as they left Nuuanu stream behind and followed the broader avenue off to the right. Sturdy buildings appeared now, surrounded by planted yards with jagged-leaved coconut palms and *lehuas* and banana trees set amid glossy green hedges bright with red and golden hibiscus.

The "particularly fine beach" the young man from the company office had told her about was called Waikiki and had long been a favorite of the kings and the *alii*. The ride from town had taken considerable time, and it was just turning dusk as the carriage wheels clattered onto the last rough length of dirt that passed as a road. The sand was shallow but extended some distance, shimmering like a satin ribbon in the sunset glow, and a striking *pali*, or cliff, loomed majestically at the far end.

It was a breathtaking, magical sight. Maria could almost see the giant royal Hawaiians striking along it in days gone by, bold and naked except for *maile* leis and garlands in their hair, and the red-and-yellow-feathered capes and helmets they fancied.

The house was as plain as her escort had promised. It had been erected, apparently, by a wealthy businessmen for picnic outings with his family and an occasional night away from the sweltering summer heat of the city. It had not been intended for prolonged use, but it was open and very clean, and Maria found it enchantingly natural. Woven partitions divided the space into a semblance of rooms, and unglazed windows let in the breezes and the rhythmic sighing and crashing of the surf.

She had half expected to find Alex waiting, but the house was empty as they stepped onto straw mats that covered a rough wooden floor, raised slightly from the sand beneath. The young clerk, she noticed, remained with her, chatting politely. Obviously he was under strict orders not to leave until Captain Barron arrived. Maria was sure he must have better things to do with his time and hoped for his sake that the wait would not be a long one.

In fact, it was less than an hour when the first echo of hoofbeats sounded down the road.

Maria rose from the low, comfortable chair in which she had been sitting and went over to the open doorway. It was dark by this time—lanterns were already flickering inside—but there was enough light from a rising moon to see Alex Barron dismounting from his hired horse and looping the reins over a post at the end of the short path.

She did not even notice the clerk slip tactfully outside to return to the waiting carriage. Alex was there. She could think of nothing else. He was there, and she was in his arms, and he was kissing her, long and very hard. It was just as well that the young man from the company had not dallied, for her lover's hand was sliding impudently into the neck of her dress and he was fondling her breasts.

Maria was only half conscious of the little incoher-

ent moans of longing and pleasure that slipped out
of her mouth as he half released her. Not quite letting
go, and definitely not stopping what he was doing
very effectively under her bodice.

"Does that mean you missed me?" he said wickedly.

"Not at all," she replied with a tart toss of her
head. "I didn't think of you once all day. Whatever
gave you such an idea? ... And I am not turning into
a mass of quivering jelly inside just because you ...
Ah!" He had managed to work one breast out of her
dress, though the neck was modestly high, and was
sucking her nipple ravenously into his mouth.
"That's not fair, Alex. You know what that does to
me?"

"Shall I desist, then?"

"Try it—and die!"

He was laughing as he raised his head. A wonderful, deep, rich sound that promised all sorts of lascivious delights. "Do you know what I was thinking on
the ride out here?" he asked slyly.

"You were thinking I am a wild, wanton creature,
and you couldn't wait to get your hands on me!"

"That, too," he conceded. "And another part of my
anatomy. Not on—*in*. But I was thinking that we
have had exactly twenty-one mornings together. Like
this. Assuming three, uh, encounters each time, that
makes a total of sixty-three."

"Oh, I think I can remember a couple of times
when there were four ... encounters." She was very
aware that her bosom was still wedged half out of
her dress. His deep gray eyes had turned almost
black in the shadows and were devouring her
hungrily.

"Sixty-five, then," he said. "Sixty-six for good measure ... and we have never once made love in bed.
I think that's an oversight that should be remedied,
don't you?"

"I do," she started to say, but he was kissing her

again, ravaging her mouth with his tongue, and she could not get the words to come out.

They did not, after all, make it to the bed. Their knees gave out together, and before they knew it they were on one of the woven straw mats. Maria's skirt was up around her waist. Eager hands were clutching her sheer linen drawers, tearing them in his urgency to get at her. She whimpered again, softly, desperate with the need to be filled and tormented by him. Her own hands were helping, freeing him from the front of his trousers, and they came together in a sharp, breathtakingly swift surge of satisfaction.

It took some time afterward to disentangle themselves from the various articles of clothing that encumbered them both. They were still laughing and kissing, enjoying the amazing power they had over each other's bodies, as skirts and pants, shirts and petticoats, all ended up in a heap on the floor. Alex's hands were not quite as deft as he struggled to help loosen the corset strings and free Maria from her whalebone prison.

"Confound it, this thing is downright unnatural," he grumbled as he noticed red marks where the stays had gouged her flesh. "It wouldn't offend my sense of style in the least if it were to go back in the satchel and stay there. I hope you brought something more sensible to wear."

"I didn't have much time to pack," she reminded him. "I brought mostly *very* sensible Hawaiian gowns. I only have two other proper dresses. To wear when we go out. . . . Or perhaps 'other' isn't quite the word," she added with a rueful glance at the crumpled mass of white India muslin. "I'm afraid that will need considerable attention before I can wear it again."

"I wasn't planning on spending a lot of time *out*," Alex replied pointedly. He let his eyes run rakishly down her body, accenting his meaning with insolent clarity. Maria felt her flesh turning warm, searing every place that bold gaze lingered. No matter how many times they were together, it would never cease to astound her how quickly her body began to get ready for him again. "I'd be just as happy if I never saw one of those proper gowns. I much prefer the native outfits ... with nothing underneath. You might want to slip one on now."

"What?" Maria gave him a calculatedly surprised look. "You mean, you want me in clothes? You're not planning on showing me the bedroom?"

He pretended to look shocked. "You're insatiable, woman."

"I don't think so," she said softly. "I think I could be satiated quite easily ... if you put your mind to it. ... You did promise me a bed, you know."

The bed, as it turned out was large and very opulent, covered with a gaudy red silk spread, but Maria was only dimly aware of it. Alex had picked her up in his arms and was carrying her into a quiet niche with no windows on any of the exterior walls. Then he was laying her down, and Maria caught a startling glimpse of his bronzed, muscular back in several mirrors which were angled in the most peculiar manner.

The coverlet felt sleek and sensuous against her bare skin. She had a fleeting thought that the young clerk must have been naive—or painfully polite—when he told her the house was used for family outings.

There was no lantern in the room, but light spilled through the wide opening from the central area onto Maria's limbs and torso as she lay on the bed, waiting for him to come to her.

He did not move. He had straightened up again and remained standing at the edge of the bed, gazing down at her. His face was hidden in shadow, but it excited Maria just to imagine the expression on it.

"Spread your legs," he said hoarsely, all the passion she had sensed throbbing deeply in his voice.

"I want to see you opening yourself to me ... and know that you are mine."

Maria obeyed almost instinctively. He was rising to the occasion, literally. It was fascinating—and tantalizingly provocative—to watch him grow hard and rigid for her. She would not have been surprised, or disappointed, if he had driven himself into her, roughly, immediately, without any preliminaries.

Instead he knelt between her legs. One hand rested on either side of her hips.

"I am going to kiss you, Maria," he said huskily. "All over your body. I want to make love to you tonight every way a man can love a woman."

Maria shivered as he brought his mouth slowly downward. Only he didn't kiss her all over. He had found the space between her legs; she could feel the warmth of his breath, shocking her for just an instant. He was still teasing, circling with little tender kisses around the soft, moist hair.

Then he claimed the warm flesh hidden in that tangle of curls, and he was inside her, as never before. Maria could hardly bear the agony of longing for him now. His tongue was bold, skillful, evoking sensations that were new and familiar all at the same time, and she let herself go, trusting and surrendering to this man who would always hold her body and her heart.

They did not leave the house all the next day. Alex had arranged to have food delivered in large straw baskets, which were left at the edge of the lane that led from the main road, and they did not see another soul. They did, in fact, make use of the bed, which was considerably more comfortable than the scratchy mats on the floor, and had all those funny mirrors to suggest quite titillatingly interesting ideas.

But they also found quilts and cushions to make a comfortable resting place on the shrubbery-sheltered *lanai* with a breathtaking view of the waves, and it seemed a shame to let such a cozy invitation go to waste.

Seventy-three now, Maria thought contentedly as they lay together late the next afternoon and watched the first reflections of sunset color and brighten the water. Though she might have missed something in her count. She smiled softly to herself as she thought of the intensely compelling ardor that never seemed completely to go away. It was such heaven to wake up in the middle of the night and begin kissing and caressing, and the next thing she knew he was hard inside her in the enveloping darkness.

Alex went out several times during the next few days, but only long enough to ride into town and back again. He had hired a half dozen men to circulate with descriptions of Claudine, both on Oahu and the other islands, and he wanted to collect their reports and interview some business associates he thought might be able to help.

The results were always discouragingly the same. Claudine had been vividly remembered from that one brief visit, which took place anywhere from five to ten years ago, depending on who was doing the remembering, but no one had laid eyes on her since. There wasn't a man in the islands, apparently, who couldn't recall every detail about how she had looked and what she had said. Or who could recall even vaguely the man who had been with her.

She must have been quite a piece of goods, Alex thought, to have made such an impression on the masculine population. Raw sex oozing out of every pore, no doubt, though she didn't seem to have followed through on any of those implied promises. Perhaps because she had been with her lover? Only one man had been rumored to be close to her. A defrocked priest, of all things!—and he had moved inconveniently somewhere up in the hills.

Maria saw Alex's increasing frustration every time he returned, and she knew he had to be more discouraged than he was letting on. All his hopes were centered now on the French consul, who was off on vacation and would not be back for several more days. If that didn't work out—

She shuddered even to think about it, and she sensed that he did, too. But because she could see he was putting on a bold front to keep her spirits up, and because she loved him so much, she tried to relax and just enjoy their short, precious time together.

Alex had managed to get hold of a closed carriage, a rarity in Hawaii, and he took her out sometimes for a ride. He couldn't risk being seen too often with her, but he did want her to have at least a peek at what was rapidly becoming the commercial and social center of the islands. Though, in truth, Maria didn't get a chance to notice quite as much as he had intended, for every time she got interested in something, a playful hand kept creeping up under her skirt, distracting her in the most intimate ways.

She was quite flustered by it until she realized she could do the same thing to him. And he would have every bit as hard a time keeping a properly composed expression on his face if someone happened to be passing by.

They would draw the curtains over the windows on the way home, after they had passed the last dwellings at the edge of town, and laugh as they tried to make love in the hopelessly jolting coach and finally, blissfully, succeeded.

But most of the time they simply stayed at the house. They might lounge on the *lanai*, watching the changing aspect of the ocean, so calm one day, thunderous and pounding the next, or enjoy lunch from the baskets under a grove of mango trees in the side yard. Early in the morning, or just before dusk, when the sun was less scorching and the breezes mellow, they would walk hand in hand from one end of the long beach to the other.

After they had become confident that no one else frequented the area and their seclusion was complete, they threw their clothing on the sand and raced into the waves, shrieking with laughter and splashing water all over each other as they frolicked naked like natives in the surf.

They did not touch when they came out, though they both ached to, desperately, but picked up their scattered garments and walked the few yards across the sand to the cottage. There was always a possibility that someone might ride by, and engrossed as they would be, the sound of approaching hooves might elude them.

They were not quite as subtle as they imagined. One look at the melting softness on Maria's face, the ramrod-stiff emblem of Alex's manhood jutting out like a declaration in front of him, and even the birds in the trees, had they been able to speak, could no doubt have told exactly where they were going. And what they were about to do.

Maria had occasion to wear one of the three proper gowns she had brought with her only once. The French consul finally reappeared, and Alex decided on impulse to take her with him when he paid a visit to the man. It was said he was a crotchety sort. The vacation had been with his wife and several ill-behaved children, and he was reputed not to have returned in the best of humor. The presence of a woman, especially an attractive one, might serve to soften him somewhat.

Alex chose her outfit himself. It was the most flagrantly feminine of the gowns, a sapphire blue silk that would have been more at home in the evening than the afternoon, snugly fitted with a bodice just low enough to show off creamy skin and a long, elegant neck. She looked, Alex thought, as the carriage pulled up in front of a whitewashed, coral-based building, stunningly beautiful, and he was as proud of her as if she were already his wife.

He was to be glad he had had the foresight to bring her. François Léberge was not a patient man, and he had a Frenchman's innate distrust of anything "foreign." He spoke English fluently, but only when he had to, and this was not one of those occasions. The man before him might be a Barron, offspring of one of the most influential families in the shipping and trading business, but it was he who had requested the interview. If Alex wanted something from him, it would be on his terms. And in French.

Alex's command of the language was halting at best, and Maria was little help in that regard. Royall had engaged a tutor for her briefly, but he had tired of it after a time, and while her accent was excellent, she had almost no vocabulary. Between them they could manage only the most basic questions, and Alex had no doubt the session would have been terminated after a few perfunctory minutes if the man's eyes had not been entertained by the hint of cleavage that showed temptingly in the round neck of Maria's gown.

It galled him to have to tolerate the lewd thoughts that were twisting those thin lips into an unmistakable leer. Next thing he'd be salivating, like an old dog waiting for his food dish to be put down. But they needed information only he might be able to provide, and restraining the impulse to tell him to keep his eyes where they belonged, Alex concentrated on asking about Claudine.

Yes, Léberge affirmed, he remembered her distinctly. The description had been most accurate, and of course with a woman like that . . . He let his hands flutter suggestively. The sound of screaming came from somewhere deep in the house, children whining and quarreling with each other.

"She came about her papers. She was born in Louisiana just before the territory was sold to the Americans. All she had was a letter from the parish priest testifying to the date of her baptism. She needed official proof that she was a French citizen."

No, he went on, he didn't recall exactly when this had occurred. Seven years ago, he thought. Perhaps eight. It would be in his records someplace. He would look it up tomorrow and send it to the company's office. He didn't have time for it now.

"I have no idea how long she was here," he replied in response to Alex's next question. "A week. Maybe a little less. Naturally, I didn't keep track of her movements."

I'll bet, Alex thought, but he was shrewd enough to keep it to himself. "Did she happen to mention where she was going?"

"I don't recall," the other man started, then broke off thoughtfully. Not because he was trying to remember, Alex sensed, but because he was trying to decide whether he wanted to be bothered telling them. Maria smiled encouragingly, making up his mind. "I believe she said she was going to Maui. To pay a call on the French planter there. Perhaps she wanted to be invited to one of his famous parties, though why I can't imagine. I hear they are very overrated."

Maria caught the wounded snobbishness in his voice and realized he felt slighted because he had never been invited himself. It did seem strange, now that she looked back on it, that Royall with his obsession for everything French would not have cultivated the consul.

"Was she alone?" she asked.

Both she and Alex were encouraged when Léberge shook his head. At last, someone who actually remembered the man with Claudine.

"But naturally no," he was saying. "Women like that are never alone. There was a man accompanying her. Her brother. His name was Lou, I believe. Louis. Something like that. His papers were in order, so I had no dealings with him. It would not be in my records."

Her brother? Not exactly what Alex had been expecting to hear, though in a way it made sense. "Do you recall what he looked like?"

Léberge shrugged. A very expressive French shrug. "I did not especially notice the man. Why should I? There was nothing exceptional about him. . . . Dark hair, I think. Dark eyes. Hers were very dark. I seem to recollect that he was extremely pale. Almost unnaturally so."

Alex tried not to be disappointed. Dark hair, dark eyes, fair skin—the description would fit a good percentage of the population. It was no more than he should have expected. With Claudine around, the man's gaze would hardly have been directed at anyone else.

"You didn't see her again? After she left the island to visit the planter on Maui? Forgive me for pressing, but it is of some importance to *madame* here." He made his features as grossly suggestive as the French consul's, all but giving him a knowing wink. "It is a matter of the, uh, honor of her husband. Between us men of the world, I am sure you can understand. She is, you see, the sister of my fiancée. It is most essential that we find out if this woman ever returned to Honolulu."

Léberge threw a speculative look at Maria, as if comparing her with the woman who had clearly led her husband astray. On the whole, Alex thought, somewhat surprised, he seemed to side with Maria.

"If she did come back from Maui, I didn't see her," he said with what sounded like genuine regret. "Of course, her papers were completed, so she didn't need me anymore—but I think I would have heard about it. We are a small community, and she caused a certain amount of . . . talk." He hesitated, an oily slyness lighting up his eyes. "You might try speaking with Monsieur Badeau. *Père* Badeau he was then. Still wearing his black robes. The lady appeared to have a certain—how shall I say it?—fascination for his priestly calling. She seemed the sort. . . . If you will excuse me, I'm afraid I have other duties to tend to. I wish you luck on your quest, *Madame*."

His face had taken on a tight, pinched expression. Why, he's jealous, Maria thought. Claudine's interest in another man had piqued his pride just enough to make him spiteful. If he could cause trouble for her by helping another pretty woman, he would be more than happy to do so.

He looked so French at that moment, and so like Royall, she wondered if it was a characteristic of the species. Then she remembered Jared's lovely Dominie and realized she had been exposed only to the worst of the Gallic males.

They stayed barely a few seconds longer. Just enough time for Alex to get directions to the home of Monsieur, formerly *Père*, Badeau, and then they took their leave.

It was a relief to get out in the hot, dusty air again. A child's petulant howling followed their carriage for some distance as it rumbled down the street.

Alex was quiet all the way home. He rested one hand on her knee, but otherwise showed an uncharacteristic lack of amorous playfulness, and Maria, sensing his need to retreat into his thoughts, was careful not to intrude.

He continued to be quiet throughout the candlelit dinner that followed, with the smell of sand and salt water drifting through the open windows. But his mind was active, and he kept replaying the conversation with the French consul over and over, trying to sort it out, and annoyed with himself when he couldn't make the pieces come together.

There is something missing, he thought. Something he ought to be able to see and couldn't.

He leaned back in his chair and stared out through

the window. The moon was nearly full, and the sky glowed a deep, luminous blue. Maria had cleared off the table and thrown away the banana leaves they had been using as plates. Now she was scrubbing it almost as neatly as if she had never had a houseful of servants.

The man was Claudine's brother. That had surprised Alex, though he realized it shouldn't. If Lou or Louis or whoever he was had been picking up the money for her, he had to be someone she could trust. Lovers for women like Claudine Doral came and went at regular intervals. But a brother would be part of her life forever.

That they were from Louisiana was harder to fit into the pattern.

Alex got up and went over to the window, restlessly staring out into the moon-bright night. Royall must have met Claudine after he left Louisiana, or she would have known about his reputation. Stories like that got around, and she was just the type who would delight in listening to them.

Of course, it could be a coincidence. Common backgrounds tended to bring people together. It gave them a way to pass the time. On shipboard, for instance. It could have happened that way.

Still, there was something that wasn't quite right. Alex couldn't put his finger on it, but he knew it was there. Something about Louisiana perhaps. Damn. He wished he could make his mind work!

He turned to discover that Maria had left while he had been engrossed in his thoughts, and the large central room was empty. Strolling over to the woven-straw partition, he found her just where he had expected. She had heaped a pile of towels in the center of the bed and was perched on them, stark naked, biting into the first of what was obviously intended to be a mango orgy.

She had told him once that you should never eat mangoes with your clothes on. Alex could see why.

Her chin was already smudged with the pulpy juice. Any second now, it would be running down her arms.

She grinned as she looked up and saw him.

"But they taste heavenly," she insisted. "You are looking very serious, my love. I thought I ought to give you a little time with your deep male musings." She paused for a moment to wipe the corner of her mouth with one of the towels. Her voice was very quiet when she went on. "We didn't really find out anything today, did we? Just that Claudine went to Maui eight and a half years ago, which we already knew. And no one saw her come back.... Only, of course, she isn't still there."

"At least we can prove she was alive then. If the consul comes up with the records he promised, we can pinpoint the date. That would invalidate your marriage."

"Not exactly," Maria said softly. "We can only prove someone using Claudine Doral's name and matching her general description was seen in Honolulu at the time. No one actually knew her as Mrs. Royall Perralt. He wasn't having his famous parties for people from all over the islands while she was living with him.... And even if we could satisfy the court, there's still no proof that he *knew* she was alive. His marriage to me might have been made in good faith. He could still have a claim on my son."

Alex came over and sat on the edge of the bed beside her. "When you overheard her with Royall that time," he asked, "were they speaking French or English?"

"English. I wouldn't have been able to understand everything if they weren't." She took another bite of the mango and looked thoughtful. "It didn't occur to me to wonder at the time. I don't know why.... I suppose she did it to annoy Royall. She seemed to enjoy hurting him. Obviously it worked. I've never seen him so angry. Not even that time I was terrified he was going to beat me to death."

"Think carefully, Maria. What was her accent like?"

"French, of course." She was watching him closely, puzzled by the question. "Very slight, but definitely French. Probably Louisiana, though I don't suppose I'd know the difference."

"Like Royall's?"

She shook her head. "No. Royall was raised mostly in Charleston, though there *is* something of the same quality ... Perhaps because he grew up speaking French at home. But Royall doesn't really have an accent, not even a Carolina drawl, except sometimes when he's drinking. He just speaks very—oh, I don't know—carefully. As if he were trying to erase all the traces of his past. . . . Why? Is it important?"

"I'm not sure." He was on his feet again, pacing the floor anxiously. Time was almost up for them. "There's something that keeps nagging at the back of my mind. I almost get a hold on it, and then it's gone again. A fact I half remember, a thought that had occurred to me once ...? I just have the feeling that everything's there if only I had the wit to see it."

He stood in the doorway, feeling frustrated and helpless as he looked out into the empty, lamplit room where they had made love when they first came into the house. He was grasping at straws, and he knew it. He wanted to believe the solution was somewhere in his mind because there was no place left to search for clues. Except one defrocked priest who probably didn't know any more than the others.

Claudine Doral had appeared on Maui on a foggy afternoon, and no one had laid eyes on her since. Only Maria was right: she wasn't still there. A woman like that could hardly have been kept hidden for eight and a half years.

Royall had to have gotten her off the island somehow. But he couldn't have smuggled her onto a ship in Lahaina, even in the dead of night. Someone would have seen; someone would have talked later. Nor could he have transferred her from a private vessel to a larger merchantman in Honolulu. Or Hawaii or Kauai. She was too distinctive. She would have been noticed.

It was as if she really *had* vanished into thin air. Only Royall Perralt was no magician. There had to be something obvious. Something he was overlooking.

"Maybe I should just challenge him to a duel and get it over with. That would be one way to settle things."

Maria shuddered. "Don't say that, even in jest. Royall is an excellent shot. He might kill you."

Alex turned slowly back to look at her. He had, in fact, meant the words as a dark jest, but he was surprised to realize for the first time he was seriously considering the possibility. He was a strong man, but not a violent one. It had never occurred to him that he might be capable of cold-bloodedly calculating the destruction of another human being.

"I'm not bad with a gun myself," he said quietly.

"But you don't practice every day." Maria saw the determined set to his jaw, and it frightened her badly. "Marksmanship is very important to Royall. He looks on it as a masculine skill. He sets up targets—or sometimes he has the servants throw things in the air—and just shoots at them for hours. Whenever there's nothing happening in the fields. He started teaching Mack more than a year ago."

"A year?" Alex said, shocked. "But the boy couldn't have been much over six. That's too young."

Maria nodded. "The sound was so loud, it terrified him. You should have seen his face. But he's so in awe of—of Royall. He wanted desperately to please him. And he's really gotten quite good. He hardly ever misses now.... Royall had a small rifle made especially for him. He's threatening to take him hunting. You know how Mack adores animals."

Her anguish was apparent. Alex longed to comfort her. She loved the boy so intensely, she couldn't help overprotecting him sometimes.

"That's not altogether a bad thing, love," he reminded her gently. "A man has to learn to provide for himself and his family. There are times when hunting is necessary. Better to learn to do it properly. A clean, skillful shot does not cause unnecessary pain."

"I know that, but he should learn from someone who's kind. Someone who will teach him to do things properly and respect the lives that he takes. Not just go out and kill for pleasure."

Alex saw the tears she was trying not to shed. He came back to the bed and reached out to take her hand. "He will learn the right way, I promise you. Kindness will always be part of his life. . . . I'm afraid I've been selfish. You're missing him, aren't you? We've been gone nearly two weeks. You've probably never been separated so long."

Maria managed a weak smile. "I'm not quite that possessive a mama. I've always tried not to cling to him just because there was nothing else in my life. He loves going with Ilimi's boys when they visit their grandfather, sometimes for days. . . . But he really does have a sympathy for animals, you know. He keeps making pets of them. Royall can't stand that. When Mack was about five, he made him go out and watch his favorite chickens being slaughtered. He wanted him to develop 'backbone.' "

"Lord," Alex said with feeling. "That must have been awful. How did he handle it?"

"Actually, very well. At least outwardly. Only I noticed he didn't eat chicken for a long time after that. Except when Royall was around."

"I can understand how he felt." Alex grimaced wryly. "I wasn't that much older, just twelve, when they shipped me out to sea as a cabin boy. My grandfather, whose word is law in the family, chose a sealer for my first vessel. Not, I think, because he wanted to toughen me up. Or give me 'backbone.' It was just the next available ship. But it was a hell of a choice for a boy who had always loved animals."

"A sealer?" Maria saw the hardness that had come into his face, and it surprised her. It was so unlike him. "I don't know what that is."

"A ship engaged in seal hunting," he replied shortly. "The early China trade was poorly balanced—from our point of view. They had all sorts of things we wanted to buy, and we couldn't find anything to tempt them. Except quaint little chiming clocks. And after two or three ship loads the novelty starts to wear thin. We were leaving all our money on foreign soil, and traveling with empty holds half the way. Then some of the traders got the idea of raiding breeding grounds in the Pacific for seal and sea-otter pelts."

"Which did tempt the Chinese, I take it."

"Fur is a sign of wealth and position in China. Especially in the colder northern climates. A fine fur-lined coat might be passed on from father to son. It was quite profitable for a while—until we got too greedy and the seal population was exterminated on one island after the other. Then the big houses turned to opium, but that's another story.... Do you know how seals are killed?"

"No," Maria admitted, not at all sure she wanted to find out. But she sensed his need to talk, and he had always been supportive of her. "How?"

"With a club for the most part. A stout three-foot length of wood. An experienced hunter might use guns on some of the males. They can be ferocious fighters. They'll take a stand against the enemy—or break for the water, followed by their harems. A man would be a fool to get close to them. But clubs are good enough for the females and their cubs. You just smack them on the nose to stun them, then stab and skin them on the spot. It's all over in a matter of minutes."

He was still holding her hand, even tighter now. To draw rather than give comfort this time, and Maria was glad to be there for him.

"I can still see it," he said in an awful, hollow voice. "And hear it. The pandemonium was incredible. Sailors chasing the poor, hapless creatures all around, shouting to confuse and separate them. Terrified seals bellowing with rage and fear, running in all directions, dropping everywhere ... and big-eyed pups yelping pathetically, trying to find their mothers. I was nearly as frantic as they to get out of there."

"It sounds horrible."

"It was more than horrible. It was senseless slaughter. It wasn't even efficiently organized. The beach was a shocking sight the next day. The skins were cured and stacked, but there was no use for the carcasses, which were left to rot in the sun. They were so thick in places, you couldn't even see the ground. The stench was unbelievable.... Luckily, Angus Dougal was on the ship. I was the first of the Barron 'laddies' he took under his wing. He found me other duties on board. I never witnessed the actual killing again, though, of course, I heard it, and it haunted my nightmares for years.... When we got back to Boston, he gave my grandfather an earful about his lack of judgment."

"That sounds like Mr. Dougal," Maria said, chuckling in spite of herself. "I can just picture him confronting the infamous Gareth Barron. Tyrant and former pirate."

Alex was smiling. She could barely see his face. His back was to the light coming through the doorway, but she sensed that the momentary savagery of the memory had eased.

"It had its effect. Even tyrants listen sometimes. They kept me on land for the next three years, and I never went out on a killing ship again.... But I never developed the great Barron passion for the sea.

I stand at the helm of a mighty clipper, and I don't feel the things my cousins do."

"Perhaps you wouldn't have anyway," Maria reminded him.

"Perhaps ... and perhaps it doesn't matter. It was good, clean work, and after that first voyage there were times I actually enjoyed it. But I never quite got used to the idea of seal fur being used for adornment. It was years before I could even look at a lady with a fashionable cape or muff. So you see, I do understand how Mack felt. If I had had to stand by and watch my pet chickens being slaughtered ... Ah, but I'm doing it again, aren't I?"

"Doing what?" He had raised his hand. Maria was very conscious of it on her cheek, just next to the smudge of the fruit she had been eating.

"Trying to forge some sort of impossible bond with your son. We are so alike—we think alike, we feel alike—therefore there must be some *physical* bond between us. Utterly irrational, of course. My mind gave up the idea a long time ago. It accepts the truth, but something in my heart ... I *will* be a father to the boy, Maria. I swear that to you. Not just a stepfather, but a real father. In every way that counts."

There was no mistaking his longing, not merely for her, but for her son, and Maria felt her own heart swell until she was sure it would burst. She had been so unfair to him. She had thought once that she had to make a choice between the two people she loved most on this earth, but she knew now that choosing was not possible.

She had to share the burden. And the risk. She had failed to trust him once, many years ago, and it had cost her dearly. She had to be brave enough to trust now. Without reservation. Even if it meant putting her fate, and that of her child, completely into his hands.

"Alex, there are things we need to talk about—"

"Hush, love," he said softly. "Not now. You are

very messy. Did you know that? You have fruit all over your cheek ... and your pretty little chin ..."

"Yes, now ..." Maria protested, but he had started to lick the pulp and juice off her face. First from her cheek, then her chin ... then all around the edges of her mouth. Little erotic flicks of the tip of his tongue.

"No," he said, and she could not protest again. He was already drawing her down on the bed, trying to find space between the mangoes and the bunched-up towels, and her body was already beginning to respond. There would be time to talk afterward. She could tell him then the secret she still held back—the one thing she had kept from him, as much for his protection as her own or the boy's—but her thoughts were getting all muddled together, and she couldn't make sense of them anyway.

She let her arms twine around him, and her legs, greedily enclosing him, reveling in the warmth of his body. Then he was coming into her slowly, tantalizingly. Her hips arched up to hasten his entry, and everything else was forgotten as they became again one single being in that sweet, perfect place that only lovers can reach.

Later, when she remembered again, the lantern had gone out, and it was dark and very quiet. She touched her lips to his brow, but he was sound asleep and it seemed a shame to wake him.

Chapter 15

Maria was feeling more than a little guilty the next morning. Alex had left a short time before to question the man who had once been a priest, and she had not tried again to tell him what was on her mind. She was glad now she had not given in to her impulse the night before. She had made the right decision—she was sure of that. She *would* tell him everything, and soon. But the timing was not right.

The house felt close, and she wandered out onto the *lanai.* Even here the air was hot and sultry, with the promise of a tropical downpour though the clouds were still scattered and far away. They would be going back tomorrow or the day after that. Unless this man Badeau had something for them, which was unlikely, they had failed in their quest. They would return to Lahaina with nothing more than they had had when they left.

A sound caught her ear and she turned around. A little bird she did not recognize was sitting on a branch in one of the mango trees, singing into the sunlight. He looked so cheerful, and Maria wondered what it would be like to feel that free.

She had been wrong before. She could acknowledge it now. She had thought by her sacrifice she could somehow shelter her son and the man she loved. But there was no shelter from the storm that was rising. They would have to face it together, like the family they were.

Only they couldn't afford to take any chances.

She left the *lanai* and walked barefoot across the sand to the surf line. They would do it his way—they had tried hers, and it had not worked—but they still had to be cautious. She couldn't risk the possibility that Alex might do something rash and foolish. They had to go back to Maui as if nothing had happened, gather up Mack and such of his toys as they could arrange, and bring him onto the *Jade Dawn*. With the cannons pointing toward the shore if necessary.

Then she would sit down with him and tell him the truth.

The ocean was unusually calm. The waves barely lapped against the shore, leaving only the faintest froth of white as they ebbed back again.

I keep trying to forge some sort of impossible bond with your son, he had said . . . only the bond was not impossible. He had felt the connection because a connection was there. A father's instincts might not be as deep and sure as a mother's, but they existed, and they had not played him false.

"It's not fair, Mama!" She could still hear Mack's voice, brimming over with hurt and indignation. "All the other boys get presents twice, and I only get them once!"

It was Christmas and he had just turned five. There was always a special party for the children on that day. Old Doc had brought the custom of the *tannenbaum*, the Christmas tree, with him from his native Germany. Usually just a coconut palm in a pot, but it was decorated with candles, and the *Weihnachtsmann* always appeared with a sack full of gifts. After his death, his younger associate had continued the tradition, gradually adding smaller parties for individual youngsters on their birthdays, which had led to Mack's plaintive wail.

"You're quite right, Mack," Young Doc had agreed. "It's not fair, being born on Christmas and not have a special day all to yourself. I'll tell you what—I don't need my birthday anymore. I'm much too old for such things. What do you say I give it to you? How does the second of October sound?"

And that was how it had begun. In all innocence. Mack's eyes had shone with excitement, he had declared himself "most awfully delighted," and from that time on, his birthday had been celebrated at the beginning of October.

Maria had not set out to deceive Alex. She had known what he had to think when he first saw Mack, and she had expected the obvious question. She had been surprised, and a little relieved, when it had not come. But it had never even occurred to her, until he blurted it out himself, that he might know Mack's official birthday.

She had intended to tell him then. She had started to tell him—the words were half out of her mouth. But then he had told her what he would do if the boy *were* his son, and the cannons on the *Jade Dawn* and the thought of a life of perpetual flight had frightened her into a waiting game. Not fair perhaps, but she had not known what else she could do. Then.

Now she understood that he had been right all along. Even if it weren't for Royall's increasing violence, there was no going back to the way things had been before. She could not subject herself again to that same brutal treatment; nor could she allow Mack to fall under the malignant influence of a man who was incapable of even one generous instinct.

If they had to run—and keep on running forever— that was just the way it would be. She could not deny herself the lover who filled and completed her heart. Nor would she deny her son the father he deserved.

Alex sat for a moment, his hand resting on the saddle in front of him, and looked at the house that was so different from what he had expected to find. It stood alone in the center of a small clearing, nearly overrun with ferns and flowering tropical vegetation.

Great, gnarled *hala* trees, their roots rising stilt-like out of the soil, pressed in on three sides, but there was enough space to let the sun come streaming through in brilliant golden shafts.

It was not a large house or particularly impressive, but there was a sense of almost decadent lushness in the greenery and the rich velvet draperies that could be glimpsed behind glazed windows. Clearly Père Badeau had not fallen from the priesthood into a pit of poverty.

Alex wondered where he got the money to live on, then decided, on second thought, he didn't really want to know. There were some things better left unexplored.

The door opened, and a man stepped into the sunlight. He was tall and slender, with the well-etched, disturbingly handsome features of a frank sensualist. Dark circles of debauchery showed faintly under his eyes; the lids were half closed, as if too heavy to hold up, and a voluptuous mouth hinted at cruel mockery, but these only served to heighten an impression of sybaritic self-indulgence that had no doubt been the ruin of more than one woman.

He seemed an appropriate match for Claudine Doral. Alex could see why she had chosen him over the French consul.

"You are looking for me?" To Alex's relief, he spoke English, though with a heavy accent.

"If you are Badeau."

"I am." He inclined his head, just slightly, and beckoned with his hand. It was a peculiarly graceful gesture. "Please to come inside. I can offer you a cup of Arab coffee. Or perhaps you would prefer something stronger?"

"Stronger," Alex said. He did not ordinarily drink so early in the day, but it occurred to him that the man might be readier to open up after a whiskey or two.

The hedonistic opulence he had sensed outside

was heightened as he stepped into the single room that seemed to encompass the entire ground floor. The furnishings were dark and beautifully carved, upholstered with wine red velvet and glowing sapphire brocade, which picked up the deep jewel tones of an exquisite Oriental carpet. Every inch of the walls seemed to be covered with sketches and paintings, startlingly, sometimes grossly, erotic, but stunningly executed. Alex was surprised to see several easels set up over a bare section of floor at one end of the room.

"My name is Barron," he said. "Alexander Barron. I'm captain of the *Jade Dawn* in Lahaina."

"I am acquainted with you, Captain Barron." Badeau had gone over to a magnificent *koa*-wood cabinet. "By reputation. I like to know what's going on, though I don't get out much myself." He turned, a bottle of dark amber liquid poised in his hand and a frankly inquisitive look on his face. "Many people seek me out ... for many reasons. You do not seem to be one of them. I would be curious to discover why you are here."

"I need some information," Alex replied. "About a woman named Claudine Doral. I believe you knew her several years ago."

One eyebrow shot up. A satirically amused look, as if he were deliberately trying to be offensive. "In the biblical sense?"

Alex felt himself bristle. "In any sense," he said curtly. "I'm trying to trace her whereabouts."

"In any and *every* sense." The man seemed unruffled as he handed Alex his drink in a cut crystal glass so clean it sparkled. "Claudine was a very ... interesting woman. She was—how does one put it— *très agréable.* ... Now I am more curious than ever to know why you are here. What is it you want from me in connection with this woman?"

Alex took the glass and cradled it in his hand. "I want two things, which you probably won't be able to give me. I want to prove that Claudine Doral was alive eight years ago, which would make a certain man a bigamist. And set another woman free. And I want to know what happened to her after she left Honolulu and made a brief trip to Maui."

"Ah, an *affaire de coeur*. You wouldn't know it to look at me, but I am a romantic." He took a long, thoughtful sip from his drink, seeming to evaluate it, as if it had not come from his own bottle. "I can't help you with the latter, I'm afraid. She did mention going to Maui. She seemed quite pleased with something she was planning to do there. Claudine could be a cat sometimes. Where she went from there I have no idea. As a matter of fact, I expected her back here ... But I think I might be of some assistance to you in the first matter."

He set his drink down and went over to the far end of the room, where a large cabinet was set between two of the easels. Pulling open a long, shallow drawer, he began to rummage through what appeared to be a number of pencil and pen-and-ink sketches.

"Ah, here we are." He selected several and began to spread them out on the table that separated the studio area from the living quarters. Alex set his own drink down and went over to look at them.

Even without having met the woman, he knew that this was Claudine. The cap of brown curls was distinctive, fitting snugly over a well-shaped head, and her lips were petulant and slightly parted. There was a blatant sexuality about her that seemed to leap off of the slightly browned paper. Alex could almost smell it. She was lying on her back in various poses, one or both knees up, legs spread wide apart, her hand playing suggestively between them.

"That was her idea," Badeau said. "I couldn't have gotten her to stop if I'd wanted to ... and I didn't. She said she was bored just lying there. She was quite a randy little thing."

"I get the picture," Alex cut in, trying not to be shocked. He had seen and sometimes enjoyed art of an amorous nature before, but this was almost painfully explicit. Every genital detail was clear and precise. As was her hand, and exactly what she was doing with it.

"Not quite. I think there's something you may have missed." Badeau was tapping the corner of one of the sketches with a long, elegant finger. "CLAUDINE DORAL" and "1833" were printed in a sloping hand. "I frequently title and date my sketches. If my sacred word that I drew this in the year indicated isn't sufficient, I daresay you could take it to almost any man on the island and get a statement from him. Claudine caused quite a flurry."

Alex grasped the possibilities instantly. He could also show it on Maui and obtain letters swearing that this was the same woman who had been Royall Perralt's wife. It wouldn't settle the question of whether the marriage to Maria had been one of good faith, but it might be enough to persuade her to take her chances with the law.

But somehow he couldn't imagine himself going to a friend or business acquaintance, plopping one of those pictures down in front of him, and saying, Do you know this woman?

'I was thinking more of something that could be presented in court," he said dryly.

The other man laughed. It was not, Alex was surprised to hear, an unpleasant sound.

"Fortunately, I have others of a more neutral nature." He went back to the drawer and began riffling through it again. "She had quite an interesting face. It appeals to an artist. There are several sketches just of her head, and . . . yes, this should do. My favorite, alas, but it is the best representation . . . I might be persuaded to part with it."

"Name your price," Alex said quietly.

Black eyes were fixed on his face, assessing him

for a long, probing moment. "One thousand dollars." When Alex did not flinch, he laughed again. "I should have asked for more."

"You should have," Alex agreed. "The money will be delivered tomorrow morning from the Barron office in Honolulu. If you've made yourself familiar with my reputation, as you say, you know I can be counted on to keep my word." He took the sketch the other man handed him and glanced down at it. Just the image of her head, as he had said—tilted slightly away, but even then he was struck by the force of her sensuality. And the greed that almost seemed palpable.

For what? he wondered. Men or money? Or both?

"Tell me," he said casually, "what was it about you that appealed to her most? The fact that you were a priest or an artist?"

"Both, I think ... though that is not why she came to see me." His mouth was forming into the faintest semblance of what might have been a smile. The cruelty was even more evident now. "Claudine was fascinated with anything forbidden, and priests are forbidden. Or they are supposed to be ... though I imagine by that time she had already learned it is not always so. But she especially liked having her picture drawn."

"She seems the sort who would enjoy being the center of attention," Alex ventured.

"Certainly, certainly, though that is not all there was to it. She liked looking at something on a piece of paper and knowing it was her. It appealed to her vanity. I promised she could pick one out to take away with her. That's why I was surprised when she didn't come back. Ah, well ..." He shrugged, as if it were of no consequence. "I daresay she changed her plans."

Alex took the sketch out into the living area and placed it on a low bookcase that contained leather-bound volumes in French and Spanish. He could hear Badeau behind him, gathering up the other drawings and putting them back in the drawer. He was just as glad to be away from them. They were not merely lewd. They made him feel that he needed to wash his hands, even though he hadn't touched them.

He picked up his drink and took a sip. Not whiskey but brandy, and particularly fine. He had a good idea now how the former priest supported his sumptuous lifestyle. Did he just sell pictures, or did he provide pretty girls as well? And slender, doe-eyed boys?

"You said she had another reason for coming to see you?" He was surprised, as he turned, to find Badeau a short distance away. The man had moved so stealthily, he hadn't heard him.

"She wanted something from me, of course." He refilled his drink, glanced at Alex, got a shake of the head, and went over and sat on one of the chairs. "There was some problem with her citizenship papers. She had lost the proof of her birth. In the territory of Louisiana before it fell out of French hands."

"I understood there was a letter from the parish priest."

"*Mais certainement.*" Badeau raised the glass to his lips with an almost feline expression. "But not before she came to me. She needed someone who knew about such things, you see. I could prepare the letter for her in the proper form. It would appear authentic. Consul Léberge is not a man of extraordinary mental capacity. . . . And it was not altogether unscrupulous. I could tell by her accent that she had come from there. I was happy to do this little favor for her."

Alex swirled the glass around in his hand and stared down into the translucent liquid. If Claudine had gone to such lengths to authenticate her papers, she must have been heading someplace French. But that, of course, was before she had seen Royall. Her traveling arrangements might have been considerably altered.

"And she, I'm sure, was happy to do a little favor for you in return."

"Naturally ... though not what you are thinking. The sketches were the favor. Claudine made quite a unique model. The *artiste* was tempted. Oh, there was the other, too. She was here, and not averse ... though I must say it was rather a disappointment. The excitement of Claudine, you see, was in the anticipation. Not the reality."

Alex turned away with distaste. He had no sympathy for the real Mrs. Perralt, but the idea of a man speaking in such a way about a sexual conquest was abhorrent to him. A small religious picture rested in a gaudy brass stand on top of the bookcase, its mediocre conventionality a stark contrast to the other art in the room. Alex stretched out a curious hand to take a closer look.

The instant he touched it, it snapped apart, as if on a spring, revealing something considerably less holy inside. The painter was not as talented as Badeau, but he lacked nothing when it came to imagination.

He heard a soft laugh behind him. "A little trinket from Canton. They are clever, are they not—the Chinese?"

"No doubt ..." Alex found the release that snapped the obscene surprise shut again and turned back to the man in the chair. "I understand Claudine was traveling with someone. Her brother, apparently. Louis Doral. Did you happen to meet him?"

"Her brother?" Badeau looked genuinely surprised. "I would not have thought so ... though there was perhaps some superficial resemblance. Mostly in the coloring. But theirs seemed an, um, different sort of relationship. Ah, well. That would explain quite a bit, wouldn't it? ... Louis? No, I don't think so. Lou, perhaps. An Americanized nickname."

"Could you give me a description of him?"

"I can do better than that." He picked up a sketch pad that had been propped against his chair and began with a few deft strokes to flesh out an informal portrait. The likeness was already recognizable when Alex came up from behind to take a peek at it.

Damn! His eyes widened as he stared at the supercilious features taking shape beneath that skillful pencil. It had been so blasted obvious. Right under his nose all the time. The logical explanation—the only logical explanation—if he had just had the sense to see it!

He must have made a noise, for the man was looking up at him with a curious expression. "I take it *cet homme sans charme* is not a stranger to you?"

Alex half nodded. "You have a certain talent," he admitted grudgingly.

"Such brilliant hands—and such a warped mind. You do not understand it, heh? . . . But I do, and that is what counts."

Alex hardly heard the words. As he stood there, looking down at the picture, another thought, completely unrelated, came into his mind. He might be able to find Claudine through her brother . . . but there might, after all, be another solution to the problem.

"I think perhaps you could do something else for me," he said softly. He had stepped back toward the door, where he could see the man's venal features clearly. "I would make it worth your while."

"Ah, you pique my curiosity again, Captain Barron. There are depths to you, I think, that do not show. Just what is it you want, for which you are ready to pay what will surely be a high price?"

"The cost would not be mine alone, Père Badeau. You have sold many things to many men. I wonder, would you be willing to sell your priestly honor?"

Dark amusement glowed in even darker eyes. "For how much?"

"Another thousand dollars tomorrow when the first payment is made," Alex said. "And a thousand dollars again every month for as long as you live."

Badeau leaned back in his chair. He was letting the laughter play on his lips now. "I already sold my soul a long time ago. Next to that, my priestly honor is of small import. What can I do for you, Captain?"

It was nearly sunset when Alex returned to the house on the beach. Maria took one look at the smugly pleased expression on his face and knew that, against all odds, this last desperate venture had succeeded.

"You found her?" she said incredulously. "You found Claudine?"

"No, but I think I probably can." He laughed as they went together into the house and he kissed her warmly. This was the longest they had been separated since coming to Honolulu, and he had missed her. "At least I found her brother ... but we may not need her anymore."

He took the drawing of Claudine out of a spare sketch pad Badeau had given him, along with several letters which he had spent most of the afternoon accumulating. The ex-priest had not been exaggerating when he had said that Alex could go to almost any man on the island for the sworn statements he needed.

Maria required only a quick glance through the documents. She had not neglected to pick up the name and date in the corner of the sketch, and she caught the implications immediately. Claudine Doral had been alive when she had been captured by an artist's pencil in 1833. At least half their problems were solved.

But she couldn't forget that there was still one major obstacle in the way.

"We've talked about this before," she said cautiously. "It's not enough to prove that Royall committed bigamy when he married me. We have to prove that he knew it, and his vows were deliberately fraudulent. Otherwise he can still try to get Mack."

"Not if you were married to someone else when the boy was conceived. And born." Alex saw the way she was looking at him and laughed again as he pulled another sheet of paper out of his pocket, where he had placed it for safekeeping. "I believe this says it all quite clearly."

Maria's hand was shaking as she read through it once, and then again, to make sure she had not been mistaken.

"But ... this is a certificate of marriage. Between Gareth Alexander Barron and Maria McClintock. In the year of our Lord 1833 ... I didn't know that was your name."

"It's a family tradition. The oldest boy in every generation is always Gareth. They ran out of convenient nicknames, so I was called Alex. You will notice, my angel, that it's dated very early in January. We will have to alter the logs of the *Shadow Dawn* somewhat, but I wanted to allow plenty of time for the blessed arrival.... Naturally, when you learned how Royall had deceived you, you were terribly distraught. But since the marriage was not legal, you consoled yourself with another husband."

"It doesn't seem to have worked out very well," Maria remarked dryly. In spite of her trepidation, she was filled with admiration for the cleverness of the plan. It just might succeed, though there were a few things they were going to have to figure out. "It seems we were together only a short time. What happened anyway? Why did we separate?"

"Who can remember?" He gave her a teasingly vague look. "A quarrel perhaps. I thought I caught you flirting with another man. At any rate, I was too young to settle down. I sailed off for more glamorous horizons and left you, poor child, to fend for yourself. With no one else to turn to, you were forced to put up with your reputed husband's evil charade."

"You make yourself sound horrible," Maria said.

"No doubt ... but I have straightened out and am ready to do the right thing now. Surely the world will sympathize.... The point is, love, this is all we need. Not only will I be Mack's actual father in the eyes of any judge—I will be his legal father, too. There's not a blasted thing Royall can do about it!"

"I don't know, Alex ..." Maria studied the paper she was still holding in her hand. It *was* clever, but he almost made it sound too simple. "A forgery like this? Wouldn't it be awfully easy to expose?"

"A forgery?" He pretended to be highly indignant. "A forgery, you say, woman! Do you seriously believe I am capable of such skullduggery? Bribery, yes. Blasphemy, certainly—but never heinous forgery! This is a genuine document, I will have you know. In Père Badeau's own hand. And, in fact, if there's any blasphemy, it is his as a priest. He has been induced by a certain transfer of green matter to recall most vividly the ceremony at which he presided some years ago.... And since the payment is to be made in installments, I expect his memory will continue to be sharp. I wonder if he's costing me more than Royall is paying Claudine and her brother."

Maria glanced back at him, startled. With all the things he had been throwing at her, she had nearly forgotten. "You said you found the brother. Where? In Honolulu?"

"No, back on Maui. Clinging to his victim like a wart. They always say the best place to hide something is in plain sight. He was so obvious we never saw him.... Not Louis. Monsieur Léberge misremembered the name. He wasn't, after all, paying attention to the *man*. Or Lou ... but a very similar French name. Luc."

"Luc? You mean, like Luke? Lucifer Darley?"

"I always thought that sounded like a phony

name. Even the initials are the same. Do you remember when I told you there was something nagging at the back of my mind. About accents—or Louisiana, something like that? I almost got it when you said that Royall always enunciated very clearly, as if he were trying to erase his past. Darley spoke like that, too. I recall noticing it once, and thinking his French sounded peculiarly like Royall's. I meant to ask Matthew about it, or Dominie, but I forgot."

"Lucifer Darley . . . You know, it does make sense. He was always around, though Royall never seemed to like him. And that would explain why the French consul wasn't invited to any of our parties. He would have recognized Claudine's brother. I did think that was odd. . . . But how he is getting the money to her? I don't believe I've ever known him to leave the island."

"He wouldn't have to. We checked on all of Royall's contacts and business acquaintances. But it didn't occur to us to check on his. There are any number of ways he could be sending the money out."

"I suppose so," Maria conceded. "But still, it does seem strange, doesn't it? He can't ever have seen her again. She *is* his sister. He might have made a voyage occasionally, every year or two to visit her."

"Maybe he doesn't like her very much," Alex suggested. "That's entirely possible. Maybe he enjoys the climate in the islands too much to leave. Or maybe he just gets seasick. It doesn't matter, Maria. All that matters is that you are safe now, and I am going to take you—and Mack—away with me."

Maria felt the tenderness in his hands as he eased the picture from her gently and set it down. He was trying to coax her closer, and she longed to respond, but she knew that the haven he seemed to be offering was not quite as secure as he pretended.

"We're not safe yet," she reminded him. "Any of us. We still have to go back for Mack. Royall can be very dangerous. If he finds out what we're up to . . . I wasn't exaggerating before when I told you he could handle a gun."

"I know," he said quietly. "That's why I want you and Mack on board the *Jade Dawn* when I go to see him."

"You're going to see him?" The alarm seemed to burst inside her. "No, Alex, that's much too risky! He's going to be wild with rage. There's no telling what he might—"

"I have to, love. Royall's got to know what we've found out . . . and what we're prepared to do about it if he tries to make trouble. Otherwise, your worst nightmares are going to come true. He is perfectly capable of hounding us to the ends of the earth. The only way we will ever be free is to face him down. Now . . . Don't look so frightened. I'll take my cousins with me, and Angus Dougal, and half the men from the ship if it will make you more comfortable. And *both* of Ilimi's massive nephews."

Maria tried to smile and only half succeeded. He was right, of course. She knew that. Royall had to be faced sooner or later, and sooner was better. She could not deny that. . . . And, after all, Alex would have plenty of men with him.

She turned away and began busying herself setting things on the table for dinner. Surely there wasn't anything Royall could do to them now. She forced herself to move briskly and confidently. He had been defeated, and soundly. It was over. She was being foolish, clinging to her fears just because she had lived with them so long. She had to learn to let go.

She did not manage to look quite as cool as she thought. Alex, watching, saw her concern, and he wandered out onto the *lanai*. Not so much because he was restless, but because he didn't want to add to the tension she already felt by letting her see that he shared it.

The weather was hot and threatening. It was still

almost unbearably humid, but the rain didn't seem to want to come. Alex stared off into the blue-black darkness. Somewhere beyond that impenetrable wall of night lay the island of Maui and the child Maria loved more than her life.

They would be there by sunset tomorrow. The end was in sight. No more insurmountable barriers, no mountains to climb, only a little brush to be cleared away. He ought to have been easy in his mind, and yet . . .

He squinted into the night, as if somehow it would help him to see it. There was still something that didn't feel right. As if he had a part of the puzzle— most of the puzzle—but the key piece was missing, and he couldn't make out the subject.

It does seem strange, doesn't it? She is his sister . . . and he can't ever have seen her again.

Only no one had ever seen her again. Alex felt his stomach tighten, and he couldn't figure out why. Not the brother who had at least financial ties with her. Not the debauched priest with the lewd sketches that had piqued her vanity so much. Not all the men in Honolulu whose eyes were still bulging out of their heads eight years later.

She had gone to Maui one oppressively eerie afternoon and vanished into the fog. She had not left, she had not stayed—she was neither here nor there, like the kind of riddle children love and adults have forgotten how to solve.

A flash of lightning erupted in jagged streaks across the sky. Far enough away to seem unreal. With the faint rolling thunder came at last the detail that had been eluding him. The puzzle was whole now. He could see it clearly.

God help him, it was all so simple. A fool could have seen it. Or a child, whose mind had not yet been clouded by *ifs* and *maybes* and *might have beens*.

Alex shivered even in the steamy heat. He knew now what had happened to Claudine Doral. And why he had not been able to find a trace of her.

Chapter 16

The air on Maui felt cooler and fresher. It was early morning, and breezes from the ocean blew through Maria's hair as she stood in the garden of the house Matthew and Rachel had rented on the outskirts of town.

It was a pleasant place. The *wiliwili*, or coral trees, were still graceful, though they were long past the time of their beautiful blossoming, and *ilima* shrubs had been planted close together to form an ornamental hedge, but Maria missed the rich, sweet scent of her mother's rose garden in the small stone house on the hill. She had expected to go there when she returned. It would have been perfectly safe—Royall would not hear until later in the day, if even then, that she was back—but Alex had been adamant. He would have preferred sending her immediately to the *Jade Dawn*, but knowing she would never agree until she had come to shore and gotten her son, he had compromised on placing her for the night with his cousin.

Maria frowned unconsciously as she glanced off to the right, across the road and down the long beach toward the place where the *kuleana*, the homestead settlement of old Kaholo and his immediate family, was located. She had been a little uneasy when she had arrived late the afternoon before and discovered that Mack would be spending the night and part of the next day there. Alex had stayed below deck on the schooner which had brought them back from

Honolulu. He had not dared leave until after dark, when he could slip unseen to the doctor's house, where he was supposedly either recuperating or dying from an attack of malaria, and Maria had come alone to what she had expected would be a welcoming hug from small, excited arms.

It was not that she objected to Mack's spending the night at the native compound. He had been there many times before. Old Kaholo delighted in rousing his great-grandsons at dawn to take them fishing, and Mack, whose fierce love of animals did not extend to scaly creatures, perhaps because he had been exposed to the sport so young, was always thrilled to be included. Rachel, knowing that his mother had allowed the treat before—and not expecting her back so soon—had naturally said yes. As Maria would have herself ... and yet she couldn't help wishing he hadn't gone.

It was not a reasonable reaction. Alex wasn't going to be coming for them until later anyway. He had wanted to interview Lucifer Darley first. She might as well let the boy enjoy a few carefree hours, but somehow it made her uneasy again. Perhaps because everything was making her uneasy that morning.

"I am just missing him too much," she said with a forced laugh. "I guess I'm turning into an over-possessive mother, after all."

"We can get him back if you choose," Ilimi replied with a curious look in her direction. She had brought out a tray with tea and breakfast fruits which she was laying on a small table, though Maria had made no effort to come over. "I could send one of my lazy, good-for-nothing nephews to fetch him for you. There is nothing so terrible about a mother missing her son."

Maria shook her head. "They'll be on the water by now. Happily spearing fish or dragging them up in their nets."

"Then the nephews can find a boat and paddle

out. It would do them good to work for a change. They can find more excuses than anyone I know to lie on the beach and wait for their mother to bring them *laulaus* and big bowls of *poi*."

Maria tried not to smile. Ilimi's assessment of her nephews was not far off the mark, though in truth, she herself was remarkably nimble at finding excuses to get out of her chores. "No, let him have fun while he can. It would be a shame to spoil his morning."

"He'll be back very soon anyway," Ilimi agreed, obviously approving of Maria's decision. "Two hours, maybe three. You will hardly have time to miss him anymore." She lingered at the table, clearly looking for an invitation to sit down and chat. She had not objected when Maria offered to lend her to the Barron household—she liked Rachel's bright, cheerful manner—but the reverend's daughter was not accustomed to the ways of the island and had not yet learned that work should be tempered with pleasure. "Is there anything else I can bring you?" she ventured tentatively.

"No," Maria started to say, then looked thoughtful. "Well, yes ... perhaps. You might ask if Rachel needs you for anything. If not, I'd like you to go to the doctor's and see if Captain Barron is there. Alex. I want to make sure he's all right."

A sly twinkle appeared in Ilimi's bright eyes. "He does not have malaria, you know."

"I know ... and you are not to breathe a word of that to anyone! As Doc Fred has no doubt admonished you. ... Oh, and Ilimi, I want you back here right away. No finding reasons to distract the good doctor in his work, do you hear?"

The young native woman was laughing as she made her way back toward the door to dispose of her tray. Obviously, she was glad to have a chance to get away for a while, and Maria couldn't blame her. The house had been unexpectedly crowded since last night. Barely an hour after she had arrived, Jared and Dominie had suddenly appeared and asked if it would be a great inconvenience if they stayed there.

It was, of course, extremely inconvenient. The house was not large, and they would be cramped, but no one had seemed the least bit surprised. The baby was due any time now, as Rachel had explained.

"You know what a fussbudget Jared is, and I think even Dominie is getting nervous. Much better for them to be close to the doctor."

But the doctor was only twenty minutes farther from their own, more comfortable house. And Dominie didn't have a nervous bone in her body when it came to her pregnancy. Maria knew that the Barrons were closing in around the woman who was loved by one of their own. As soon as Mack returned, they would close in around him, too, and she would not have to be afraid anymore.

She turned her head to see Ilimi just entering the house.

"You're sure he'll be back soon?"

Ilimi grinned. "I know my grandfather. If there's one thing he loves more than fishing, it's eating what he has caught. He'll be back in time to make a great *hukilau* for lunch. . . . I can still send one of the nephews, you know. Why not? Mack will not mind when he learns you are home."

"He'll learn soon enough." It was a temptation, but Maria resisted. "A couple more hours won't matter. He's fine where he is. Get along with you now. I gave you an errand to run. And remember, no tarrying!"

She picked up a cup of tea from the table when she was alone again, but did not sit down. Instead she carried it over to the *ilima* hedge with its tiny yellow-orange flowers which were so prized for royal leis. He *was* fine where he was. Royall didn't even know she was back—and anyway, he would never hurt the boy. Mack was his obsession, his dream for the future of his precious Honuakula. The Perralt name, if not the Perralt blood, living on through the ages.

She was surprised to feel that the cup was shaking. She had to clutch it with both hands to keep the tea from spilling. There was no immediate threat to Mack. She had never been afraid of that. She was going to have to get a hold of herself. As long as Royall didn't know he was about to lose the boy, Mack wouldn't be in any danger.

And Royall couldn't know that. She managed to steady the cup enough to take a sip of the cooling tea. Royall believed he held all the cards. He thought he was winning. He was so sure of it. All he wanted was to get drunk and gloat.

She was just letting her fears get the best of her. Maria finished the tea and set the cup back on the table. She had to steady her nerves before she saw her son again. She didn't want to upset him. The days ahead were going to be hard enough as it was.

The sun glinted off a mariner's brass telescope high on a green hill overlooking the town. A dark, slender man hunkered down in the tall grasses that hid him from below and held the lens to his eye for some minutes.

A soft hiss of satisfaction escaped his lips as he lowered it again.

So, she was alone in the garden. There was no expression on his face, but Royall Perralt's black eyes gleamed with unnatural excitement. He had seen the arrival of the schooner in the harbor the afternoon before, and watched from that same slope as they had paddled her in a native canoe to the shore.

He had kept the glass trained on the doctor's house, too. Many times in the days that had passed. There had been much coming and going, but nothing out of the ordinary. He had not seen *him* come out, though naturally he had not been watching every minute.

It was rumored that he was very ill. One couldn't trust rumors, of course ... but if he were able to get around, would she have been alone in the garden? It might be he was near death.

That would be good. The thought warmed his insides like a glass of fine brandy. Very good. It would make things much simpler. But it was not necessary for what he had in mind.

He snapped the telescope shut. No time to be wasted now. They thought he was stupid. It gave them such overbearing superiority to look down their noses at him. Poor, weak, witless Royall. They thought he wallowed in drink until he had half lost his mind and had no idea what he was doing anymore.

They didn't know that drink could be a man's shield as well as his solace. Especially a man who knew how to control and ration his habit. He had never gone on binges when he couldn't afford it. Didn't they realize that? Hadn't they wondered when, suddenly, all his restraint had disappeared at once?

But then they thought he was stupid. He started back, still crouching, to where he had left his horse. It hadn't occurred to them that he might be cunning enough to fake his drinking. That he might let them see him with a drink surreptitiously in his hand. Might douse his clothing in *okolehao* like a whore with her cheap perfume. There was something to having an enemy who thought you were stupid.

He tucked the telescope into a special loop on his saddlebag and tightened it. The horse started and whinnied. Royall jerked the reins sharply to silence it, and led it partway down the slope on the other side before mounting where he could not be seen from the shore. Kaholo hadn't liked being told the night before that he would have to leave the *haole* boy behind the next day when he went fishing. The feisty old Hawaiian wasn't good at taking orders. But he had not dared refuse a friend of the governor of the island. And Royall *was* the boy's father.

His father.

Even the word rankled as Royall urged the horse down a grassy field toward the path at the bottom of the hill. He should have been the boy's father. He had been so sure that confounded *pu'aha-nui* fruit was going to work. He had paid enough to the native charlatan who sold him the secret. He had *counted* on its working. It had been disgusting, forcing himself to touch her ... trying to pretend she was the kind of woman he could tolerate. It made his skin crawl even now to remember it.

The horse balked, as if he had pulled in the reins. Royall slapped it sharply on the flank. The damned nag. He could never get it to respond. Maybe he would just shoot it and leave it up on Haleakala when he was done with it. He had always liked the frisky mare, Kanani, better. Now, there was a spirit he could get his hands on.

All that humiliation—on both sides—and for what? She had whimpered and looked put upon, but if she had only known, he had felt every bit as sick and degraded as she. Still her body had not responded. The fruit had been no more than a taunting mockery.

She had conceived quickly enough with *him.* Royall could taste the bitterness, sour in his mouth. He didn't know how long the affair had lasted. Perhaps only a single tumble in the dirt somewhere. He hadn't even been aware of it at the time. But it had been enough. Her body had swollen like a balloon when that bastard had stuck his arrogant male member into it and left a part of himself behind.

God, how he longed for the child to be his. He even pretended sometimes, when he forced her to admit what she knew was not true. Sometimes he almost believed it.

He *would* believe it one day. And one day, in a way, it would be true. When they were all gone, and there was no more interference. He would mold Mack into an image of himself. He would make him a Perralt. And then he would really have a son.

The horse balked again, and he started to curse, then forced himself to cool down. Anger had a way of clouding the mind. He couldn't afford that luxury now. It would all be over soon enough, and then he could revel in the anger. And drink himself into a stupor for weeks if he wanted.

The plantation came into view. Royall held the horse back for a moment to look at it with the same inexpressible longing that always filled his heart when he saw it. They didn't understand what it meant to him. No one had ever understood. The fools. The rich fertility of the earth was just a passing prettiness for them. No one cared as he did. No one ever would, except maybe the boy someday when he grew up just like his father.

They all thought it was what a man did with a woman that brought the richness into life. And what a woman did with a man. The physical coupling of two bodies in a sweaty moment of sex. The mere idea was coming to repulse him more and more. He wasn't even finding gratification with prostitutes anymore. The last time he had gone to the brothel, it had taken the slut hours to arouse him, and she had had to work for her money. No doubt she had spent an equal amount of time laughing and complaining to the others afterward. He would not subject himself to that again.

He had known the exquisite thrill of pure sexual ecstasy only once. Little droplets of sweat broke out on his forehead, and his hands started to tremble. He had gone to that priest on Oahu. A lewd, decadent, scornful man, but it was said he had pleasures no one else could offer.

Royall had expected a woman of extraordinary skill. He had stated most explicitly that that was what he wanted. But the degenerate had taken one look at him through knowing, hooded eyes and brought a slim-hipped, silken-skinned boy instead. And his body had been drained and fulfilled for the first time.

The intensity of the experience had frightened him, and he had not gone back. All his passion was for the land now. For the pungent-scented earth he caressed with his labor. There were better ways to sweat than in some whore's bed. For the fecund, furrow-tracked soil he sowed with the seeds of his own deep longing. It was that golden mistress he would leave to his son.

He prodded the horse with his heels, and they started forward again, pausing only once where a narrow trail branched off the main road. His eyes followed it briefly, across the interior of the island toward the slopes of Haleakala in the distance. The House of the Sun, as the natives called the extinct volcano. Only now the summit was already half hidden by enveloping clouds. It was going to be foggy. Would that make it easier, he wondered ... or harder?

He stopped just long enough to take one of Mack's jackets out of the saddlebag and tangle it in the branches of a low shrub a short distance down the trail. Bright red. Very noticeable. He made sure it was secure, so it wouldn't blow away if the wind picked up.

It was a nuisance. They would have to take the long way around when he came back with the boy. He didn't want Mack to see it. But that was only a minor annoyance. Everything was going smoothly.

He slipped the horse's reins over a hitching post, unlocked the door to the plantation office, and went through it into his library-bedroom. The walls were dark and confining. He glanced around with distaste. A man shouldn't allow himself to be shut out of his own home. He had been stifled in that small, dingy prison far too long. He wouldn't be sleeping there again.

There was a chest on one wall, next to a small writing desk. Royall opened a drawer, took out the paper he had prepared, and looked it over one last time.

Yes, perfect. . . . He could almost see the expression on her face when she read it. It would suit his purpose admirably. He placed it in the center of the writing desk and propped it up just slightly so it couldn't be missed.

All that was left now was to pick up the boy. What a stroke of fortune that he happened to be in the native *kuleana*. That had alleviated the need for all sorts of elaborate ruses. He ruffled his hair with one hand and pulled his shirt half out of his belt as he went back and unhitched the horse.

A good touch that. He was never tousled. Even when drunk, he was almost compulsively fastidious. Whoever met him at Kaholo's compound would be surprised by his appearance. He would have to take care to behave erratically. And, of course, he would tell them he was taking the boy hunting. They all knew how Maria felt about that. She coddled his weaknesses shamelessly.

She would find out about it in the short time it took for someone to run along the beach to town. Royall's lips turned up in a thin smile for the first time that morning. He did not see how he could fail. . . . And she would find out alone, for the man, even if he was recovering, was not with her. She would be too frightened to take the time to go for him.

She was so predictable. He swung into the saddle and headed the horse toward the beach. She had always been predictable.

He knew exactly what she was going to do.

Alex stood in the spacious entry hall and waited while a surprised servant summoned his master.

They were not, he gathered, used to receiving callers so early. He had the feeling it would be a few minutes.

He let his eyes wander around the room, barely taking it in. He had not said anything to Maria on the trip back from Honolulu about what he suspected. No, more than suspected. What he almost certainly knew for a fact, and he was beginning to have second thoughts about his reticence. He had not wanted to worry her, but he hadn't put her on guard either, and it occurred to him now that perhaps he should have.

She was feeling a false sense of security. He had realized that the afternoon before when she had actually thought he was going to let her leave the schooner and go alone to the empty little house on the hill. She had been so sure Royall would not learn of her arrival until at least the next day. She had not felt the need to be cautious until then, and he had almost given in to the instinct that had warned him to tell her. If she knew the truth—if she knew how much Royall Perralt *really* had to lose—she would not be complacent, even for a moment.

But it had seemed somehow foolish. It still did, in a way. He was, no doubt, being an alarmist. Royall was probably locked up in his room, drunk and oblivious to everything else. There was no point upsetting Maria until he had to.

Still, he was glad he had insisted that she stay with his cousins. The Barrons were intensely protective of their women. They would take care of her.

It had been some minutes since the servant had gone, but still no one appeared. Alex jammed one hand in his pocket and tried to relax as he took in the entryway again, with more attention this time.

Lucifer Darley, *né* Luc Doral, maintained a handsome lifestyle. His taste seemed to run to French *empire*. Several small tables and the only chair in the hall were all from that period. Through an open double doorway leading into a larger parlor, Alex saw more of the same arranged around a vividly patterned Chinese rug in the center of the room. The paintings on the walls were neither as skillful nor as unique as those displayed by the defrocked Père Badeau, but some of the artists were recognizable, and they did not come cheap.

Apparently Darley had struck at least as good a bargain with his "patron" as the former priest had with him.

"Captain Barron." The voice came from a doorway behind him. Alex turned to see Darley wearing a burgundy silk dressing gown that made him look even more waxen than usual. "I must say you surprise me. I had not expected a call from you. Especially so early. It did not seem, in our previous brief meetings, that you were particularly interested in anything I might have to say."

"No . . . ?" Alex kept his features deliberately neutral. "That just shows how deceiving appearances can be. As a matter of fact, there are quite a number of things you could say that I would find extremely interesting . . . *Monsieur* Doral."

There was barely a fraction of a second's pause.

"I beg your pardon?" He was so cool Alex almost had to admire him. "I'm afraid you have mistaken my name. It's Darley, not Doral. And as I am not French, the *monsieur* is not appropriate."

"Louisiana was French territory once." Alex kept his eyes on him all the time, but the man did not flinch. "I understand from the consul that you have retained your citizenship . . . and I have had the advantage of seeing a sketch of you. Drawn by a remarkable, if somewhat unconventional, artist. So, you see, it would be foolish to keep up the pretense. They say you are Claudine Doral's brother."

"Do they?" A flicker of response showed just for an instant. More amusement, it seemed, than trepidation. "Well, maybe they are right . . . and maybe they aren't. But you didn't come all the way over here so early just to bandy words. What is it about Claudine you wish to know? I assume it is she you came to see me about?"

"You could say that," Alex replied evenly. "There are several points on which I hoped you might enlighten me. She was a very unusual woman, your sister. Everyone seemed to notice her ... until one foggy afternoon. That had me puzzled for quite a while. I kept wondering how Royall managed to smuggle her off the island without anyone seeing. Then I realized, of course, he didn't."

"No?" Darley managed to maintain a look of polite boredom, but his voice was not quite steady.

"No. Claudine Doral came to Maui—and never left again. Royall killed her. . . . What I don't know is whether you helped him."

Maria could not quite shake the feeling that something was wrong. The garden was still pleasantly warm, the scent of the flowers enticing, but she kept remembering how silent Alex had been on the voyage back from Honolulu. And all the long evening that had preceded it. Much too silent. He had been so exuberant when he had come back from his interview with the former priest. Then he had changed abruptly, turning introspective.

Almost as if he were keeping something from her.

The sense of dread came back again, stronger now. As if the situation had somehow grown more dangerous—which meant more dangerous for him, since he insisted on taking all the risks on his own strong shoulders. He had told her he was "just tired," and maybe that was it. But it would be like him to try to protect her.

She threw a nervous glance down the empty street. Still no sign of Ilimi. She had been gone nearly three-quarters of an hour now. Not alarming in itself. Ilimi never hurried if she could find an excuse to do otherwise. But something could have happened.

Maria started toward the house, then changed her mind and came restlessly back to the garden again. Matthew and Rachel would be enjoying their breakfast. They could do without her anxious face and forced, cheerful prattle. Dominie had been feeling queasy and gone upstairs to lie down. The first pains might come at any moment. Jared was no doubt hanging over her with the most suffocating solicitude. He was getting so nervous, Doc Fred had absolutely forbidden him to be anywhere near the room when the delivery began.

Why was it always the strongest men who were most intimidated by the process of birth? Maria never failed to be amazed. Her own gruff, burly stepfather had fallen apart when Mack was born. He had alternately paced and blustered and bellowed, sticking his head in the door so many times to bark out orders he had had to be removed from the house. She had been able to hear him all the way out in the stables—and she had not even been his daughter!

Perhaps it was because they felt so helpless. Men were such foolish creatures. They always had to be in control. They faced wars and duels with the coolest courage. They could fight their way out of barroom brawls and take on a shipload of pirates—but they turned pale and threatened to keel over when their wives went into labor.

Ilimi appeared suddenly at the end of the road. Maria's heart gave a little thump, and she hurried through the gate to meet her. She was surprised to hear a noise from above and see that Jared had opened the window and was leaning out.

Even at his wife's bedside, he had been keeping an eye on her. If Maria had not been so worried, she might have laughed. God forbid the Barrons should let their women take care of themselves! . . . Well, it would probably be good for him. It would keep his mind off Dominie and the pain he could not take on himself no matter how he wanted to. There were some things even the fiercest male pride couldn't accomplish.

"You found him?" she said as she reached Ilimi and they began to walk together toward the house. Jared was no longer hanging out, but she noticed that he was still near the window, watching her. "Alex was at Doc Fred's? You talked to him?"

Ilimi shook her head. "He was already gone when I got there. I waited a half hour, but he did not come back. I knew you would be angry if I stayed longer."

Maria choked back her anxiety. He had probably just gone to see Claudine's brother. He had said he would . . . but she hadn't expected him to go so early. What if there *was* something else?

"I've changed my mind, Ilimi," she said. "I want Mack back here. Try to find one of your nephews. Or better yet, both of them. But don't take too much time. If they're not around, go yourself. . . . And bring as many of the men back with you as you can. Don't walk alone along the beach."

She had expected Ilimi to laugh, but her dark, pretty face was surprisingly serious. "Fred was worried, too. I don't know why. He wouldn't say anything to me. But I knew he was worried. Yes, I think it is best we bring the boy here."

Maria stared helplessly after her as she disappeared down the street, moving much faster than usual. Ilimi was never alarmed. She had the easygoing Hawaiian way of taking everything in stride, and she never picked up on other people's moods and foreboding.

If even Ilimi was concerned, there had to be something wrong.

She was afraid now. Terribly, coldly afraid, and she didn't know why.

* * *

The man was good. Alex had to give him that. He had turned ashen for a moment, a sick gray color oozing up from under his natural pallor, but he had recovered quickly and was looking remarkably poised.

"I think perhaps we ought to sit down," he said, and led the way into the parlor. There was a small grouping of chairs at the end of the room, and he selected one, indicating with an almost nonchalant gesture for Alex to do the same.

Not a hint of nervousness showed. His hand was steady as he opened an ornately lacquered Chinese box, removed a long, slender black cigar, tapped the end on the table, and put it between his lips, all without a word.

"You're avoiding my question," Alex said. He took a seat, not quite feeling comfortable enough to lean back. There was no way of knowing what to expect. "*Were* you in on the killing?"

"No," Darley replied. He touched a match to the tip of the cigar and drew in a mouthful of smoke. He seemed to relax as he let it slowly out again. "She was already dead when I got there. I was waiting at the boat. Claudine had talked a certain gentleman into lending it to her for a pleasure jaunt. She was very good at that. She had gone up to see Royall by herself. She wanted to have a . . . chat with him."

"She wanted to blackmail him," Alex cut in shortly. "He had remarried, thinking it was safe, and she threatened to expose him. A charming little scheme, but apparently it backfired."

Darley looked amused. "I shouldn't have let her go alone, of course. I knew better at the time, but . . ." He waved the cigar carelessly in his hand. A peculiarly affected gesture. Almost effeminate. "Claudine could never resist being just the tiniest bit nasty. She knew how to drive the knife in and give it that extra little twist. . . . I was worried when she didn't come back after a while. She was just lying there, on the floor. Very still. I had never seen Claudine still before, even when she was asleep. Her head was at the strangest angle. I think her neck was broken."

Alex felt a chill, but he did not say anything. He simply watched and waited for the other man to go on.

"He didn't intend to kill her, you know. He might have if he'd thought of it. But he just lashed out. It seemed to surprise him that he was capable of such physical force. He had never laid a hand on her before. He was much too afraid of her tongue. . . . It looked like he had hit her several times. Kicked her, too. . . . But he was quivering like a frightened child by the time I saw him. Just standing there, shaking violently. A most opportune moment to arrive."

"Opportune?" Alex made no effort to hide his distaste.

"For me," Darley admitted. "Royall is really a timid man. Bullies are like that, have you noticed? Especially the kind that beat up on women. He was just beginning to realize what he had done, and he was terrified. It made him very susceptible to suggestion."

"And you, of course, were more than happy to suggest a thing or two."

"Of course . . . though it was not altogether to his detriment to listen. He really wasn't thinking clearly. He was so desperate for a drink, I practically had to wrench the bottle out of his hand. He didn't seem to realize what would happen if someone came and saw her sprawled out like that. It was hardly a convincing 'accident.' The side of her face was all bashed in. . . . I wasn't going to tell on him, naturally. It wouldn't have been in my best interests. But it was essential to get rid of the body before anybody else got a look at it."

The smoke was cloying, even in that large room. Ordinarily tobacco was an aroma Alex enjoyed, but it was turning his stomach now. He would just bet Darley had offered not to tell! A Royall arrested or hanged or whatever they did in the islands was not a Royall who would be available to pay blackmail year after endless year.

"So you helped him dispose of her . . ."

"Me?" Darley laughed. "I'm greedy, but I'm no fool. I was back on the boat a few minutes later and headed for Honolulu. If he was going to be caught dragging the body out and loading it onto his horse, I didn't want to be anywhere around. . . . Actually, I didn't think he would pull it off. Drinkers usually make a mess of things. I was quite surprised when he succeeded. I understand he went on a hell of a toot after that."

Not exactly unreasonable, Alex thought. With Claudine making vicious taunts about his impotence and Darley putting the squeeze on him over her still warm body, it would have been a wonder if he hadn't gone on a "toot."

"I don't suppose you know where he buried her?" he ventured cautiously.

"Oh, I rather think I do." Darley looked strangely pleased with himself. "He told me he took her up on Haleakala. To the rim of the crater. I don't know the exact spot, of course. I wasn't there. But Royall isn't very hard to figure out. . . . He likes to organize picnics a couple of times a year. There's a special place he always goes to. It takes the better part of a day to reach it. You have to camp overnight. Not very convenient, but he seems to take particular enjoyment in it. Almost like a private joke."

He paused to see if the other man was listening. Alex was, though he was too appalled to comment. It was not what Darley was saying that seemed so monstrous. Claudine no doubt had deserved the end she had gotten. It was the almost complete lack of emotion in his voice.

"I might be wrong, of course," Darley went on,

"but it seems to me he throws sly glances at one particular spot. A little depression between two shallow rises. There's a silversword growing there now. I expect he likes that. Royall has always had an affinity for ephemeral plants. I don't know why. Perhaps because of his madness. He *is* mad, you know. And getting madder all the time."

Alex could not control his disgust any longer. "Good God, man, this is your sister we're talking about. Don't you have any feelings for her?"

"Why should I?" He seemed faintly surprised. "Claudine was a very tiresome woman. I had long since ceased having any 'feelings,' as you call them, for her. And by the way, you are wrong."

He paused to take a deliberately slow puff of the cigar. Smoke twisted thick and sinuous around his face.

"Claudine was not my sister. . . . She was my wife."

Chapter 17

"Your . . . *wife*?" Alex sat in his chair and gaped at the man opposite him. Claudine Doral had been his wife? Surely he had to be jesting.

But the dark eyes that looked back at him were only mildly amused.

"That surprises you? I would have thought you more astute, Captain. If you have seen a sketch of me, you must have seen one—*several*—of Claudine. Except for the dark hair, we don't look much alike."

No, Alex thought—they didn't, though he sensed a certain resemblance in temperament. Claudine was sensuous, Darley almost bland, but they both had distinctly quirky twists to their minds.

"You're telling me she was already married to you when she met Royall?" he said. The implications were more than a little chilling. "She didn't, I gather, bother to get a dissolution before she coaxed him to the altar."

"Now that would be an interesting development, wouldn't it?" Darley gave a careless shrug. The cigar still dangled foppishly from his fingers. "Also very foolish. I should have said—Claudine was my wife *briefly*. She had already caught a glimpse of much greener pastures. An elderly man with a great deal of money, which she offered to share if I would agree to divorce her. She had, naturally, given me ample cause."

Alex watched him warily. "I take it the green pastures didn't materialize."

"Alas, men did have a way of tiring of Claudine. I am a prime example. Fortunately, we drifted to New Orleans where we encountered Royall. Or rather we saw him there and heard all about what happened— what *didn't* happen, actually—on his wedding night. He was very vulnerable. . . . and it was rumored that he could function with a little help in the whorehouses. If you've seen the sketches, you know Claudine can be enchantingly sluttish. It was worth a try. We managed to book passage on the same ship that was taking him to the Orient."

Alex watched as Darley flicked the ash from his cigar onto a gold-rimmed china dish and stared down at it. "The plan seems to have worked," he ventured.

"But naturally. Claudine could be very flattering when she wanted. She plied him with her charms and made him feel like a man again. He wasn't, of course. Royall really likes boys. So do I on occasion, though I prefer women more. But I am not afraid to explore the depths of my character. Poor Royall was horrified. Repelled. He looked on it as a weakness and tried to pretend he was something he wasn't, especially to himself. It was quite comical."

The callous mockery made Alex's skin crawl. The possibility hadn't occurred to him, but it made sense now that he thought about it. He might almost have pitied the man if he hadn't so despised him. A homosexual in a world that abhorred deviations, desperate to keep up a facade. The strain must have been unbearable, and the loneliness.

"When did she marry him?" he asked curiously.

"Right after we arrived in Honolulu. I made her hold out on the ship. Not an easy thing for dear Claudine to do. He was a challenge, you see. She could hardly wait to wriggle into his bed. Royall always thought that she was afraid he wouldn't marry her if he 'had' her first, but I was the one who was really worried. That he wouldn't make it and the whole deal would be off! As it turned out, I was right. Royall never cared much for Honolulu after that. They left a few days later and didn't come back. At least not together."

"I can imagine," Alex remarked dryly. "I don't suppose it was pleasant for either of them, though Claudine seems to have known what she was getting into."

"Ah, well, Claudine was never very realistic, particularly when it came to herself." The ash on the cigar was growing long again. He held it almost to his lips but did not take another drag. "Her vanity suffered a nasty blow. I imagine that's why she had to keep taunting him. She really thought he was going to find her irresistible. She couldn't imagine a man not getting hard just looking at her, which most of them did."

"So she left him?"

"In a way . . . though not the way you mean. The house at Honuakula had been built by that time. Claudine liked being the mistress of a great estate, especially since she could get everything else she wanted on the side. There *are* advantages to being a rich man's wife. Royall got tired of being cuckolded. Word was starting to get around. He paid her a handsome sum to leave. . . . And me, of course. I had taken a place on Kauai. Conveniently out of the way, but close enough for sisterly visits."

More "on the side," Alex thought, but he didn't bother to say it aloud. "Let me guess. You ran out of money and came back to the well for more."

"It was inevitable. With Claudine's extravagance and my taste, how could it be otherwise? Regrettably, the well was dry." He did not sound too upset. "It was to be expected, I suppose. Royall had let it be spread around that Claudine ran off with another man. He was under no obligation to take her back, and he didn't see any reason to part with more of his money. . . . We realized, of course, it was no use.

Not being inclined toward self-torture, we saw no point in beating our heads against a wall. We did not try to contact him further."

"Until you learned that he had decided to risk marrying again."

"By purest coincidence." He waved his hand expressively. The cigar ash was precariously long, but he made no move to flick it in the dish. "We just happened to meet someone who had been in the islands, and he mentioned a French planter who gave the most fabulous parties. And a beautiful, very young wife with flaming red hair. . . . The prospects were too enticing to resist."

Alex was finally beginning to catch on. Things were coming together that hadn't made sense before.

"That's why she went to the French consul. Not because she'd lost the papers that proved her place of birth. She had them, all right, but they were in her maiden name. She needed something to make it look like she had been *born* Claudine Doral."

"There was a great deal of money at stake." Darley seemed to be fascinated by the ash on his cigar. He was holding it away from him, staring at it, as if wondering how long it could last. "We were safe, of course. We could prove the divorce. But Claudine had been spending time openly with me. As her supposed brother. It would have been awkward, to say the least . . ."

The ash finally fell, landing on the expensive carpet. Darley simply sat and watched as it burned a dark brown stain in the colorful wool.

"I'd be more careful if I were you," Alex remarked caustically. "The well is drying up again. Or hasn't that occurred to you? Now that Royall's crime is about to come out—and I assure you it is—you won't be able to bleed him any more. You might want to hang onto the possessions you have. Or keep them in good condition to sell."

Darley did not look the least bit perturbed.

"Ah, but I'm sure I can find another source of income. I'm afraid it's you to whom the obvious hasn't occurred. If Claudine was *my* wife, then her marriage to Royall was invalid. Which means he was free when he married the current Mrs. Perralt. I have eyes in my head ... I see the way you look at her. You *do* want her entanglement to another man to be null and voidable. Or haven't *you* thought about that?"

Alex had, in fact. It was the first thing that had come into his mind—until Darley himself had set things right.

"But she *wasn't* your wife. You had already divorced her. Which makes her marriage to Royall completely legal."

"Yes ... but you have to prove that." He ran the tip of his tongue unconsciously over his lips, but otherwise did not move. Like a cat fixing its eyes on its prey. "Claudine won't be able to help you. Even if you dig her up—and I might be wrong about the place—all you're going to get is bones and hair and the ruins of a red satin dress. And there's only one other person who knows when—and *where*—the divorce took place.... So you see, I think I can manage to keep myself in carpets. Assuming, of course, we are able to come to terms."

Alex glowered at him with loathing. He longed for nothing so much as to spit in his face, but if he wanted Maria's freedom he knew he was going to have to buy it. Funny, he thought—it had galled less to pay a debauched priest for a lie than this man for the truth.

"It's a pity Claudine is dead," he said through his teeth. "You make a perfect match."

"Yes, well ..." Darley smiled. It was not a nice smile. "Life is like that, isn't it? We must make do with what we have. And I think, if I read your expression correctly, what we have is an agreement."

Everything seemed to happen at once. Just as Maria went back into the house to wait for Ilimi,

Jared came down the stairs, roaring at the top of his lungs that Dominie was having her first contraction. Matthew, hurrying out of the dining room, followed by Rachel, took one look at his brother's chalky face and offered to go for the doctor.

"I don't think you'd make it," he said with a grin. "We can't have Fredericks wasting valuable time trying to resuscitate you somewhere on the street."

He took off at a good sprint. Maria knew, for all his bravado, that he had to be imagining what it was going to feel like when his own wife finally delivered the child she longed for so desperately. At that rate, she thought, he'd be back with the doctor in less than half an hour, and she had never known a baby to be born faster than that. Jared just stood there, looking bewildered for a second, then turned and started up the stairs after Rachel.

"Just stay out of the way, Jared," Maria heard her saying from the landing at the top. "I've assisted at plenty of births. I know what I'm doing. It will probably be hours yet ... You're not going to faint on me, are you?"

Her voice drifted away, and Maria was aware suddenly of how empty the house felt. It was only an illusion. She wasn't really alone. She knew that, but a vague uneasiness kept coming back and troubling her. As if some instinct were trying to warn her. It was so tangible she could almost feel it, deep in her bones.

The others had been gone only a minute or two, perhaps not even that—she could hear sounds coming from upstairs, but the voices were muffled— when she glanced out the window and saw Ilimi hurrying back up the street, almost running. With her was a young boy of nine or ten whom Maria recognized as part of Kaholo's *kuleana*.

Alarmed, she hastened toward the door.

"Where's Mack?" she cried as she threw it open

and stepped out onto the *lanai*. "Why didn't you bring him with you?"

She was being illogical. She was even aware of it. There had hardly been time to run all the way to the compound and back, but she was certain now that something was wrong.

Ilimi's first words confirmed it. "He is with his father. I met this one"—she caught the boy by the ear and jerked him toward her—"on the beach just at the edge of town. Old Mokihana, Kaholo's favorite wife, told him to come and find you. He was to say to you that *Kane* Perralt had taken the boy away with him."

Maria fought back the panic that threatened to engulf her. It was just a coincidence. It didn't mean anything. Royall still looked on Mack as his son. It was only natural that he'd want to see him, especially if he were coming out of one of his lengthy drunks.

"What did he look like? Mr. Perralt? *Kane* Perralt?" She tried to appear calm as she turned to the boy. "I want you to tell me everything that happened. . . . Did he say where they were going?"

She must not have succeeded, for the boy's face was the picture of pure terror. His mouth kept opening and closing, like a dying fish, but nothing came out. Ilimi finally had to answer for him.

"He looked very strange. Not right at all. *Pupule*, this one said."

"Plenty *pupule*," the boy echoed, finally finding his voice. Maria tried desperately not to jump to conclusions. Natives used the word *crazy* for anything from stark madness to something they simply didn't understand.

"His hair was a terrible mess," Ilimi went on. "And his clothes. As if he had been sleeping in them, but there was no smell of *okolehao*. No one has ever seen him look like that before." She took a deep breath. She was no more anxious than the boy to tell her young mistress the rest, but she knew she had to.

"He said he was bringing Mack hunting. They were going back to Honuakula to get his clothes and the guns. And then they were going up on the mountain."

"Hunting . . . ?" Maria paled. Royall had threatened it often enough. It was no surprise. She had known it would come, and soon. But she didn't like his being out with Mack and a gun. Not now.

"They are fools!" Ilimi spat the words out with an angry glare at the boy. "They knew from the night before that this was going to happen, but did they do anything? No! If I had been there, I would have stopped it. . . . But you! You didn't dare defy him! He is too important. You were afraid."

"It's all right," Maria said, trying to reassure the boy and think at the same time. "It isn't his fault. Really, Ilimi, it isn't. He's just a child himself."

She threw a helpless glance back through the open door at the cool interior of the house. She had to do something—but couldn't ask Jared to leave Dominie. Not just as she might be going into labor. And heaven knows when Matthew would be back. The doctor might not have been ready to leave.

"I want you to find Alex," she said, impulsively swinging back to Ilimi. "I don't care where he is. Go and get him! And Captain Matthew, too. I'm going to the livery stables. I may be able to get to Honuakula fast enough to head them off."

She started running down the street without looking back. Dust swirled, thick around her face, and she felt herself growing more and more frightened with every step she took. What if Mack was in trouble? What if he was frightened and needed her? She had to get to him before it was too late.

The thought caught with the dust in her throat and choked until she could barely breathe. She tried to remind herself that she had to think clearly. There was no real basis for her fear. She was just letting her nerves get the best of her again. Royall would never hurt Mack. He loved him. He might hurt her but never the boy. And he didn't even know she was back on Maui.

The livery stable was empty, dark inside and smelling of damp hay and manure. There was an attendant, but as usual he was nowhere to be seen. Maria ran her eye along the row of horses and picked out a likely chestnut gelding. Taking down a heavy, well-worn saddle, she went over to the stall and flung it on his back.

She didn't know who he belonged to, but he was sturdy and seemed to have spirit. They could have her up for a horse thief later if they wanted. She didn't have time for niceties now.

Royall *didn't* know she was here ... did he?

Maria gave the cinch one last sharp tug and led the horse out through the door she had left open behind her. He had learned that Mack was with Kaholo and his family. He might as easily have learned where she was. Gossip traveled fast in a small community. He might have taken the boy just to keep her from seeing him. It was the sort of spiteful thing Royall would do.

And the hunting might have been for her benefit, too. Because he knew it would upset her. It didn't mean Mack was in any kind of danger.

But it didn't mean he wasn't either. Maria put her foot in the stirrup and swung awkwardly into the saddle. Her skirt was full enough to fit over the gelding's stout rump, but her ankles and a good part of her calves were exposed under a froth of white petticoats.

Royall had been behaving erratically. She guided the horse down the main street toward the road that led inland. Alex had noticed. Maybe that was what had him so worried. And Doc Fred, too. He had been drinking more and more, isolating himself from everyone, not even caring any longer what people thought. She sensed that he was very close to the edge, and she was terrified suddenly that he was going to take her son over with him.

They reached the summit of the first low hill, and she urged the gelding into a gallop. Royall had said they were going to Honuakula first. It would take time to pack clothing and blankets for the cold upland nights. If she hurried, she would be there before they could leave.

Alex barely managed to suppress his anger as he strode down the path that led from Lucifer Darley's hillside home and along the road through the central part of town. He was trapped. He hated it, but there wasn't a blasted thing he could do about it. He might be able to prove Royall was a murderer, though even that was in doubt. But he also had to prove that the man had been legally married to Claudine, or Maria was still going to be tied to him while he rotted away in some stinking prison.

He headed on impulse toward the house Matthew had hired on the far side of town. No point going back to the doctor's now. Their plans were going to have to be changed. He would think about it later, decide what to do. But not until after he had collected Maria and her son and gotten them onto the *Jade Dawn* where he knew they would be safe.

As he saw it, he had two choices. He turned onto the road that led along the beach. He could persuade Darley to continue suppressing the evidence of his marriage to Claudine, which would mean periodic payments of a not inconsiderable sum. Or he could negotiate an even heftier one-time outlay to get him to divulge the details of his divorce.

On the whole, he was inclined to favor the latter. It would take pretty near everything he had, but at least it would be over. He would be rid of the parasite. He wouldn't have to dole out payments to him year after year.

There seemed to be a commotion at the house as

he approached. He had not been there before, but he would have recognized it from the description even if Matthew had not just arrived with the doctor, who was preceding him inside. His cousin was about to follow when Ilimi suddenly burst out the door, and catching him by the shoulder, began speaking and gesticulating rapidly.

Alex increased his stride. He couldn't hear from that distance, but clearly something was going on. Maybe it was just that Dominie had gone into labor—that would account for Fredericks—but he didn't like the looks of things.

Matthew saw him and moved across the *lanai* to the steps.

"It's Maria," he said tersely. "With all the excitement over Dominie, no one was watching her. Ilimi says she's gone to Honuakula. Royall got a hold of the boy somehow and is planning on taking him hunting. She's afraid . . . I think because of the guns. She went to try to head them off."

"Damn," Alex muttered. "What the devil does she think she's going to accomplish? She can't stop Royall if he's made up his mind. She might only set him off. He wouldn't hurt the boy . . . but he might hurt her."

Jared had come down, drawn by the sound of voices. He appeared in the doorway just in time to get the gist of what they were saying. Behind him, Alex caught a shadowy glimpse of Doc Fredericks on the stairs.

"Take it easy, Alex," Matthew said. "They'll probably be gone by the time she gets there. Ilimi says Royall picked Mack up quite a while before. She's not going to be able to tell which way they went. We can get to her before she has a chance to do anything. I'm coming with you, of course." He turned to the man in the doorway, "Jared?"

His brother hesitated, obviously torn. Before he

could say anything, Fredericks' voice came out of the house.

"Go on. There's nothing you can do here. It's probably just a false alarm. There haven't been any more pains. I expect the baby will wait for you to return." He came up beside the other man briefly in the doorway. "Besides, I wouldn't let you back in the room anyhow. You're one of the worst prospective fathers I've ever seen."

"You're sure?" Jared was obviously not referring to the last statement, which was indisputable.

"I'm positive. Dominie's young and healthy, and it's been a normal pregnancy. Nothing's going to go wrong. For God's sake," he said, turning with an appealing gesture to the others, "get him out of here. The woman will be fine, I'm not worried about her— but I can't say as much for him. I haven't lost a father yet, but there's always a first time."

Jared held back one last second, then seemed to make up his mind. "I hope they've got a good horse at the livery stable," he said. "I don't like the one I've been hiring."

Alex knew what it cost him, leaving Dominie like that. The doctor was probably right. Probably nothing would go wrong. But if it did, he would never forgive himself for not being there.

"I owe you one," he said quietly.

"I owe you a thing or two from the past myself," Jared responded, his strength visibly restored now that he was taking action again. "Come on. Let's get over to the stables. . . . It's going to be all right, Alex." He clapped a hand on his cousin's shoulder in what passed for affection in that undemonstrative clan. "We Barrons have been through worse than this."

Matthew was already heading down the street. He had gone back to the house just long enough to pick up his pistol, which he was tucking into his belt. Jared started to follow, with Alex behind them, when the doctor's voice came from the doorway:

"Barron?"

Three heads turned, but he was looking at Alex, and the others continued on their way. He waited for the younger man to take the several steps back to him before speaking.

"You asked about the boy's birthday," he said quietly. "I assume you had a reason. Mack was not born on the second of October. I exchanged birthdays with him. He was born Christmas Day."

Then he was back in the house again, his footsteps echoing up the stairs, and Alex was left alone with his thoughts.

Christmas Day. A week early. There was no need to count on his fingers now. He had been through that before. He knew exactly what it meant. He had wanted it all along. He had felt it. He had told himself over and over that he was a fool, but he had kept on feeling it anyway. And he had not been wrong.

Fear mingled with the longing as he thought of the boy and what might be happening to him even at that moment. If *he* knew the truth, then Royall must know it, too. He had succeeded with Maria only once after their wedding, she had said—and Alex had simply assumed that that once had been nine months from the child's birth. What if it wasn't? What if there was *no* possibility?

He had been so sure Royall would never do anything to harm Mack. What if he was wrong?

It seemed the ultimate irony to learn about the child and realize that he might lose him at the same instant. It was not just his woman he needed to protect now. It was his son. *His* son. He would lay down his life for either one of them.

"Alex?"

Matthew's voice, from the end of the street. He was near the door to the livery stable. Jared must already have gone inside.

Alex broke out of his reverie and sprinted forward.

A blasted lot of good he was going to do them, standing in the street with his mouth hanging open!

Honuakula was almost deathly quiet. Maria tugged the reins to slow her horse to an easy walk. It seemed eerie not to see anyone in the yard or on the *lanai*, or going in and out of the house and barns.

She was too late. She knew that even before she went into the stables and saw that the horse Royall usually rode was gone, and Mack's small pony. They had already packed up and left. She was too late. Whatever was going to happen would happen. She could not prevent it now.

And surely it wasn't as bad as her frantic fantasies were making it. Maria went back outside and scanned the distant slopes automatically with her eyes. No sign of motion. No way of even guessing where they had gone. To the mountain, the native boy had said. That might mean the great extinct volcano Haleakala. But Hawaiians had a colorful way of exaggerating everything. It might just mean the hills.

It was only a hunting trip, after all. She focused on that, trying to draw comfort from it. It would be unpleasant. Mack would be hurt. But life was full of hurts. He was growing up so fast. . . . She couldn't protect him from everything.

She had wanted him to learn from his real father. She had wanted Alex to take him out and share his knowledge and his compassion. But there would be other lessons, other things to share. Surely time would heal whatever hurts today might cause.

The gelding was still where she had left him. Maria had not tied him to a post, but he had not strayed, and she went over to run an idle hand down his neck. She was still standing there, trying to decide what she wanted to do, when she noticed that the door to the plantation office was wide open.

That's funny, she thought. The first hint of alarm prickled down her spine. Royall always kept the door closed when he wasn't there. He was very particular about that. He would never have gone off and left it that way.

She started toward it, moving slowly, her feet strangely heavy, as if for some reason she was afraid of whatever she was going to find inside. An odd feeling, but one she could not quite ignore.

Even when she reached it, she hesitated for a moment, listening. But everything was silent. Nothing alarming beyond that open door. She could not hear a sound as she stepped cautiously over the threshold.

Her eyes ran around the room. No one there, but she had not really thought there would be. Both of Royall's rifles were missing from the rack on the wall. Hardly unusual. He frequently took the two of them when he went hunting to make sure he had a spare. The undersized gun he had had made especially for Mack was also gone, but she had expected that, too.

What else? Maria looked around again, feeling vaguely uneasy. Nothing seemed to be out of place, but somehow it didn't look right.

The door to Royall's library was ajar. The room where he slept. Maria approached it with distaste. She could see a light burning through the crack in the door. Another uncharacteristic bit of carelessness. Royall was never careless, except when he was drinking. And the natives had said there was no smell of *okolehao* about him that morning.

She spotted the note the instant she pushed the door open. Ivory parchment with spidery black writing, propped up on the desk. Right next to the flickering lamp, and she knew he had intended her to see it.

Not carelessness after all. He had left the light for her to read by. Maria was not naive enough to believe it was a gesture of courtesy.

Her hand was trembling as she reached out. Whatever it was, she knew he meant it to hurt her. But she sensed something deeper in that carefully penned missive than merely the urge to cause pain. Something that made her cold with dread and fear.

She picked it up and read:

The night is dark and growing darker. We are weary, the boy and I, but he does not understand that yet. Life is pain. Life is loss. Life is, in the end, unendurable. When it becomes too unendurable there is the blessing of sleep.

We are going to the crater. The House of the Sun, but we are going in darkness. We will not be back.

Oh, God! Maria tightened her fingers around the paper and held it crumpled against her breast. She could almost feel the terrible despair emanating from it. There had been so many clues, if only she had been paying attention. All those changes. He had seemed to be falling apart in front of her eyes. But she had foolishly attributed it to the effects of alcoholism.

We will not be back.

His intent could not have been clearer if he had spelled it out specifically. He could no longer bear the unendurable agony of life, and he intended to end it.

And he was not going to die alone.

Fear jolted through her. There were only two things on this earth that Royall Perralt cared about besides himself. His plantation, and the child who had inhabited his warped imagination so long he had almost become his son. He could not take Honuakula with him. But he could take Mack.

Maria realized now what it was that had seemed out of place in the other room. Racing back, her heart pounding wildly, she saw the open black box on a table under the window.

It was empty, only a slight indentation in the crimson velvet lining showing where a gun had lain.

Royall's pistol. One of a pair. The other was kept in a drawer in the large desk in the center of the room. Maria tore it open, but that was gone, too. Box and all.

He had taken every gun in the house. There was not the slightest doubt in her mind now what he was planning to do. And she knew suddenly where he was going.

Not just to the House of the Sun. The beautiful Haleakala that dominated one entire side of the island. Not to a vague somewhere on the rim of the crater, but the place that always seemed to draw him again and again. With the silversword growing in the little hollow.

At least now she had something to do. The note still crushed in her hand, Maria raced back outside. It would take time to saddle Kanani, but it would be worth it. She needed a dependable mount. Now if she could only get word to Alex . . .

As if in answer to her prayers, Chang appeared suddenly on the path up from the fields. She waved broadly to attract his attention. Thank heavens Alex had persuaded him to stay on when the men from the *Dawns* had left. He was the only one she could trust.

"Take this to Captain Barron," she cried, smoothing the note as best she could and folding it somewhat more tidily. "You can use the gelding. Tell him Mr. Perralt has Mack. He's taking him up on Haleakala. To the special place where we always have our picnics. I'm going there now. Can you remember all that? . . . He'll have to get a guide to show him the way. He'll never find it by himself."

The young Chinese nodded several times in rapid succession. He looked surprised, but didn't waste time asking questions.

"I tell captain plenty good, missus. Chang remember. You no worry. Chang remember good good."

He eyed the gelding with trepidation, and Maria panicked for a moment. It hadn't occurred to her that, of course, he did not ride. But he got himself up somehow and gamely headed in the direction of town. If he didn't fall off and break his neck in the meantime, he'd get her message to Alex.

A futile hope perhaps, but there might be something he could do.

It took only a few minutes to get Kanani saddled and ready. Maria could not spare the time to change her clothes, but there was a blanket on the bunk Alex had been using, and she rolled it up and tied it to the back of her saddle. The nights were cold at higher altitudes. She might need it. She prayed she *would* need it to keep her son warm.

The majestic slopes of Haleakala rose into a thick bank of clouds as Maria turned her horse toward the trail she had taken so many times before. She could not even see the top. It was going to be foggy at least the last half of the way, That would make it harder to find them. . . . But it might make it harder for Royall to find the place he was looking for, too.

She had just reached the base of the long, winding trail when she saw Mack's bright red jacket tangled in a bush. He must have been even more upset than she thought about going hunting. He usually took better care of his things. Royall would have been furious, but luckily he hadn't seen.

She had made the right guess, then! Maria dared to let herself hope for the first time. Not really a guess, but it was a relief to have it confirmed. They *were* going in the direction she had assumed.

She stopped just long enough to pick up the jacket and tuck it into the blanket roll. Mack would be chilled in the fog without it. She was going to have to bring it to him. It was like an omen. Why else would it be there? She was going to reach him in time.

She had to reach him in time! She would not even think about what might happen if she didn't. Her young son's life depended on her. She had always been there when he needed her before. She would be there for him now.

Hoofbeats sounded like thunder, and yellow-ocher dust rose in clouds around them as the Barron men pressed their mounts toward Honuakula. They did not speak; there was no time. But urgency showed in their strained faces and the way they leaned forward into the wind.

Their numbers had been augmented unexpectedly when a man had appeared in the stable just as Alex was selecting a new horse. The stout gelding he had hired for the rest of his stay, and at a damned exorbitant price, seemed to have disappeared, and he had been approaching a long-legged roan that stood a hand above the others.

"Not that one." Dud Owen's voice had come from the doorway. "She be a looker, but lazy and mean as a snake. Ye'll spend all yer time fightin' to stay on her back. Take Rollo there. No speed, but he's got a mule's share of endurance. He'll get ye where ye're goin'."

Alex had taken his advice, noticing as he did that Owen was starting to saddle his own mount. He had given the tavern keeper a sharp look and gotten a steady one in exchange.

"I be going with ye," he said with a set to his jaw that told Alex he had been there long enough to figure out what was going on. "She be my daughter. I never took to the idea of her marryin' that one. No good, right from the start, but I didn't stand me ground. I be standin' it now. If he's done anything to Maria, it's me he'll answer to."

Alex had not failed to catch that slight emphasis

on the word *my*, but he had let it pass. He, of all people, ought to understand. Hadn't he felt the same way about Mack when he had thought there wasn't a ghost of a chance the boy was his?

"You won't get any arguments from me," he had said. "We can use all the help we can get."

The road seemed to stretch forever ahead of them. Alex gripped the reins tightly and tried to squint through the dust. He had not been anywhere near as pleased to accept the fifth member of their small party. They had been almost ready to leave when Rachel had shown up, dressed in a shirt of Matthew's and an old pair of his trousers.

They had all been aghast, Alex particularly. He knew how stubborn Rachel could be, and they could ill afford the time it would take to argue with her. He had turned to Matthew impatiently, and his cousin had put his foot down.

But Rachel had just looked back at him with an expression he had long since learned not to underestimate.

"I am a nurse, Matthew," she had said quietly. "I might be needed."

The color had drained from his face, but he had not tried to protest again, nor had any of the rest of them. They knew she was right. There was no telling what might happen in the hours that lay ahead, and it was a grimly silent group that rode single file out of the stable into the daylight.

At least they were all armed, Alex thought with what little satisfaction he could find. Except for Rachel, who did not know how to shoot. Dud Owen had persuaded them to take the extra minutes it required to send for guns. Alex had chafed at the delay. He had wanted to leave immediately, but he was glad now to feel the hard pressure of a pistol at his belt.

He didn't know what Royall was up to. It might just be a hunting expedition, as he claimed. But it might not . . . and Darley had been right. Royall *was* mad. A madman with a rifle could be extremely dangerous.

They had more than passed the halfway point when they were startled to see an astonishing sight coming toward them down the road. Chang, riding the gelding Alex had hired. Or trying to ride, for his feet had come out of the stirrups, his legs were flailing wildly on both sides, and he was hanging onto the saddle for dear life.

Jared had to ride up and grab the reins he had dropped. Fortunately, the horse was obedient and responsive, and it was easy to bring him to a stop. Chang was already talking by the time Alex reached him, repeating Maria's message and pulling out the note he had jammed into his pocket.

His English was improving every day. He could not form proper sentences, but he could parrot what he had heard, and he did. Exactly. There was no mistaking what had happened.

Alex's blood ran cold as he unfolded the note and read it. He understood, as Maria had not, exactly what it meant. "God," he said in a horrified voice as he passed it to Matthew. The man had outwitted him. He had played dumb, but he wasn't. He was damned clever. And ruthless.

Jared had moved his horse next to Matthew's and was reading over his shoulder. "Suicide?" he asked, but Alex shook his head.

"He's not the type. Royall Perralt is much too concerned with his own hide to risk putting bullet holes in it. This is all for Maria. He wanted to lure her out into the open . . . and he did."

Dud Owen agreed. His square red face was beaded with sweat. "The man be a sly one, all right, and not like to hurt himself. I don't know what he be up to with Maria, but I don't like it."

"Nor I," Alex agreed. Only he knew exactly what Royall was up to. He had separated the boy from his mother—and from the man he had to have guessed was his real father. Now it was time to make the separation permanent. "Do you know where this 'special place' is? The one Maria thinks he's taking Mack to?"

"I do." Owen cast a speculative look at the cloud-capped mound of rising earth that was the volcano in the distance. "He was always funny about it. I never knew why. Had to go there two, maybe three times a year. . . . I can find it in the dark if need be. And it may. We have a long piece to go from here."

"Then let's get moving," Jared said, keeping his voice deliberately steady. "Don't look so anxious, Alex. She's got a bit of a start on us, but we can catch up. It looks like the fog is going to be thick. She'll hit it first. It will slow her before it slows us."

Alex nodded. If it didn't slow Royall and give Maria a chance to catch up with *him*. He traded horses with Chang and watched as the young Chinese headed back to town, safely on terra firma this time, leading the steadfast Rollo by the reins.

A bit of a start, Jared had said. A bit! But she would be on Kanani, the fastest of their mounts. And Maria, frantic to get to her son, would be pushing her to the limit.

He dug his heels in the horse's flank and started forward, followed by the others. He could only try. That was all he could do. And pray God he was not too late.

Chapter 18

Maria did not know how long she had been riding. Four hours, perhaps five, perhaps six. She had been in the fog for some time now, and it seemed to be getting denser. Everything around her was almost unnaturally dark. It might have been approaching dusk, or it might just have been that the sun was shut out.

She shivered as she guided her horse around a narrow turn in the trail. She could see barely a few yards ahead. The fog was steady, not swirling, but it seemed to be concentrated, thicker in some places than others. The cold seeped into her bones. She could almost smell it.

She thought about the blanket, tempting on the saddle behind her, and longed to untie it and wrap it warmly around her shoulders. But that would mean dismounting and struggling with the knots, and her fingers were numb with cold. She didn't dare take the time. She didn't know how much time she had left.

God help her, she had no idea how far ahead Royall was, or what he was going to do when they reached their destination. Surely he wouldn't just take out his gun and—

She shivered again and looked up at the sky. She couldn't let herself think like that. She was going to reach them in time. She had to! She scanned the western horizon, trying to pick out a faint patch of brightness that would tell her where the sun was. But all she could see was a wall of impenetrable gray. She might as well have been in another world where there was no day or night. She could not even guess how late it was. Or how far she had come.

She had made good time at first. Kanani was strong and spirited and had enjoyed a good gallop across the level spaces and even up some of the gentler slopes. But the trail had gotten steeper, the mare had tired eventually, and Maria had had to rein her back more and more to an easy walk. Now, with the fog almost completely obscuring visibility, there were times they barely seemed to be moving.

Where does the fog come from, Mama? Why is it so wet? It just hangs in the air? Why doesn't it fall down like the rain?

Mack's voice. Maria could almost hear it, cutting like a knife into her heart. Question after question after exasperating question. She longed to clasp him in her arms and hold him so tightly he squirmed to get away.

He was so little. It wasn't fair. He shouldn't be in danger now. He should be playing someplace with his dogs or his turtle or whatever bird he was nursing back to health.

Oh, God . . . She shut her eyes and swayed in the saddle. She had to hang on to keep from falling. Dead leaves formed a thick, soft mantle on the ground, muffling the horse's hooves. The moisture made them slippery, and Maria gave Kanani her head, trusting her to get them safely past. She was surefooted and had been on this trail many times before.

He was so little. His face seemed to drift on the fog in front of her. The way he had looked that night in the darkness outside her bedroom window. Small and wide-eyed and terribly frightened. She hoped he wasn't frightened now. Whatever Royall was doing to him, she hoped at least he was not afraid.

The fog was so bad now, she couldn't see anything. She had to get off and bend low to the ground to make sure they were still on the trail. Fortunately, it was well marked. Several jaunts a year, sometimes with as many as fifteen or twenty people, had tamped it down. And Royall frequently made the trip by himself in between.

There was only one tricky place, and that would come later. Where the trail branched off in three separate directions. She never remembered which way to go. Left or right or straight ahead. She had always relied on visual clues. a tree she recognized, a particularly interesting rock formation—but would she see them in the fog?

She mounted again and began to pick her way down the trail, trusting Kanani even more now. The mare wouldn't get them lost. She couldn't! They had to get to Mack before Royall could do anything to him . . . if he hadn't already . . .

A wave of faintness came over her again, and she had to get a firm grip on the saddle. Was it all in vain? This desperate rush up the mountain? Had Royall already finished what he set out to do and taken that small bright life?

Maria tried desperately not to think of her son lying cold and still on the ground somewhere, the spirit gone from his pale, motionless body, but the image was horribly compelling. It seemed so real. She couldn't bear the thought that he might already be dead. That she might never seen him again, hear his laughter, never be maddened by all those incessant questions.

Stop it, she told herself firmly. She forced her attention back to the trail, fixing her eyes on what little she could see. She couldn't give in to fear and despair. She *had* to believe Mack was still all right. She had to keep on trying to reach him.

All she had now was hope. She could not let that go.

She had no idea what she was going to do when

she finally reached them. She hadn't gotten that far in her thoughts. The fog had turned so thick, it was like an icy cloak wrapped around them, and the mare balked. Maria could not coax her forward, and she had to get off again, feeling her way with her feet as she led the horse behind her. This time it was Kanani that had to trust her, and she followed faithfully.

She could not expect to overpower Royall by force. She had no illusions about that, and she had come out without so much as a kitchen knife to defend herself. If there had been a gun left in the plantation office, she would have taken it, though she had never learned how to use one. She had been allowed to watch the first few times Royall had taught Mack, but the process had frightened and appalled her, and she had not been invited back again.

She still hated guns, but it would have been a comfort to have one now. Her horror of them was nothing to her horror and fear of Royall. At least she would not have felt so totally defenseless.

She realized to her surprise that she could see again. The fog seemed to be clearing somewhat. Climbing back into the saddle, she laid a steadying hand on Kanani's strong neck. Maybe she could talk to him, reason with him. But she had never been able to get Royall to listen to her before. Or maybe she could best him with guile.

If she could slip up behind him ... It might be possible in the fog. If she could catch Mack's eye somehow, signal to him to steal away when Royall wasn't looking ... If she just could get him onto the horse with her ...

If, if, *if*! She urged Kanani to move a little faster. The trail was visible several yards ahead now, and she didn't know how long it would last. She had to make up time while she could. There was no point trying to figure out what to do when she didn't know what she was going to encounter. Any plans she made would have to be formed at the last minute.

They would have to be quick—and they would have to be good. She was going to get only one chance.

She peered as deeply as she could into the fog. Definitely darker now. Almost dusk, then. Night would be falling.

Please, God, she prayed, keep him safe from harm. I don't care about myself. It doesn't matter what happens to me. But please, *please*—keep my son safe.

It was cold in the small, flat space between the rocks where they had made their camp. Mack could feel it even with a thick, fleecy jacket buttoned all the way up to his neck, but he did not shiver. His father didn't like it when he shivered. He liked him to be strong and show he was a little man.

Royall had built a fire. It was not a big fire, but the heat was already beginning to radiate outward. He had said it would be safe. The fog was thick, he had said. No one would see the glow, but it would have to be a very small fire all the same.

Mack had been surprised. He didn't see what difference it made if someone noticed the fire or not. But he didn't say anything. He just sat and watched as Royall poked it to get it going better and then tossed on some fresh wood. It was wet from the fog and sputtered for a minute before catching.

"You're going to have to learn to start a fire one day yourself, Mack," his father said. "It's important for a man to be able to take care of his own needs. We're going to be spending a lot of time outside together, you and I. Things are going to be very different from now on."

Mack did not answer. He knew no answer was expected. Just quiet obedience. Royall was getting cooking gear out of a pack, which he had carried some distance from the place where he had tied his horse to a tree. That had surprised Mack, too. But his own pony was contentedly munching grass nearby, so he wasn't really worried.

He watched as Royall put a large pan on the fire, filled it with grease, and let it heat until it started to spit and crackle. He knew what they were going to have for dinner, and he knew he wouldn't like it. But he would have to eat it anyway.

He had killed for the first time that day. The warmth of the firelight touched him now; he no longer felt like shivering, Royall had taken him to a broad, open meadow before they had come to the fog. There had been a flock of Hawaiian geese resting on the ground. Glorious gray-brown creatures with long, furrowed necks and black heads.

Mack could still see them in his mind. Starting at the unexpected intrusion, lifting almost in a single mass into the air. Royall had ordered him to put the gun to his shoulder, his eye to the sight, and take aim.

He had had only a split second to react. He had to shoot. The force of his father's authority was enough for that. But if he shot randomly, he might simply graze one of the great birds and leave it wounded and dying in pain.

It was the first adult decision of his life. He was conscious of that, as he was conscious of the light, barred markings on the underfeathers of one of the geese as he followed its graceful motion with the barrel of his gun and pressed the trigger.

It had been a good, clean kill. The bird had stopped in midflight and plummeted to the earth.

Mack had stood for a long time afterward looking down at it. It had not seemed real to him. He had just stared at it there on the ground and not felt anything. It was still beautiful, like the goose he had cared for and just released in the wild. But it was broken and dead.

Perhaps it even *was* his goose. It was hard to tell, all limp and twisted like that. It seemed a cruel fate, to have been cared for and brought back to health only to be shot by the very hand that had fed it. Mack hoped it was not the same bird. Most probably it wasn't.

He looked up at his father through the fog and darkness and felt hatred for the first time in his young life. Royall was bending over the fire, the red radiance from beneath elongating the shadows on his face and making him look strangely sinister. Pieces of the goose were sizzling in the fat now. Mack could smell it, sickening and greasy. It was a smell he would remember all his life.

It was then that he decided what he was going to do. It was a conscious, thought-out decision, much too old for his years, but he did not know that. He would stay in his father's house until he was sixteen. Sixteen was old enough to be out on his own. He would do what he was told. He would not try to fight. Fighting only made things worse. But the day he was sixteen he would leave.

Royall seemed to sense him watching and looked down. Mack met his eyes without flinching, but he did not give away what he was thinking. He would take care of his mother. He didn't know how, but somehow he would. He would never let Royall hurt her again. He had hated it when he hurt her before. On that he would not be backing down. But otherwise he would just retreat into himself and wait. And on his sixteenth birthday he would take his mother and go away, and they would never have to see him again.

He felt better now that he had made up his mind what to do. He could even eat the goose, and it wouldn't choke him too badly because he knew one day it would end.

He was glad he had traded birthdays. That would make him sixteen almost three months sooner.

The night is dark . . .

Royall's words in his farewell note. They seemed strangely prophetic. The night *was* dark. There were moments Maria could not see anything at all, the fog was so thick, and all she could do was rein in her horse and sit quietly waiting.

Waiting and listening. Every muscle would tense as she strained her ears in the enveloping silence. It was so cold she could not feel anything but her fear. It could come at any moment, loud and shattering. The first shot would be for her son, she knew ... and Royall would not have missed. Royall never failed with a gun. If she heard it, she would know it was over.

She stiffened slightly, holding her breath, but there was nothing. Only a vast, brooding emptiness with barely a rustle of leaves in trees that were getting sparser and scragglier the higher they went. Then the mist seemed to blow away, and Maria could see again quite clearly.

The moon was full. The light was bright enough to illuminate gnarled branches, like long, twisted fingers, on trees off to the side, and the trail was more distinct than it had been for hours.

It occurred to her that the periods of visibility were getting longer. The cloud mass over the summit of the volcano seemed to be drifting away on a rising wind. Just the scattered edges remained, and those were becoming wispier. Soon they would be gone altogether, or nearly gone, and the night would be clear and brittle and cold.

Maria was surprised to see a sharp rise in the trail that she recognized. They had always had to slow to get around that rocky outcropping which partially blocked the way. She was close, then. Much closer than she had expected. She must have gone faster than she thought. Or perhaps it was simply later in the evening.

Her hands tightened tensely around the reins. Kanani protested, tossing her head, but Maria could not make herself release that death-like grip. She was frightened suddenly, in a way she had not been before. It was almost as if the night were alive around her. The fog curled damp and cold over the back of her neck, and the trees seemed to move, undulating in blue-black shadows, closing in around her.

A noise came from somewhere nearby. Maria jumped as her head jerked around. Nothing there, but she knew she had not been mistaken. Then she heard it again, a kind of muffled bark, and realized it was only an owl. A *pueo* somewhere in the branches of a nearby tree. She could not see it, but she could sense it watching her passage through the night.

She focused her eyes back to the trail, but she did not feel any easier. The cold was almost brutal now. She had an uncanny sense that someone was there, just out of sight, around the next bend in the path.

Foolish, she knew. There was no reason for it, no sign that she could see, but instinct made her want to curl up, low and tight, merging her body into that of the horse, as if somehow she could keep herself hidden.

It had almost been better when the fog was thick. She could see now that it was swirling away. She would no longer have to get off and pick her way down the path. But seeing meant she could also be seen, and she felt suddenly open and very vulnerable, silhouetted on her horse again the translucent sapphire deepness of the sky.

She came almost abruptly onto the place where the path separated. Three natural trails going off in three directions. Maria peered down them, one after another, and felt utterly helpless as she realized she had no idea which one to take. The fog was not as thick as it had been, but it kept oozing back, obscuring anything more than a few yards away. The ground was hard and stony—the tamping down of hooves over the years had not affected it—and there were no clues to tell her what to do.

She closed her eyes and tried to picture how it had been all those other times when she had ridden past this spot. But there had been people then, and laughter, and she had not paid any attention. She had not been desperate then, knowing every second counted.

She hadn't yet heard the shot that she dreaded. There might still be plenty of time. She couldn't even begin to guess what Royall's state of mind was at the moment. . . . But there might not be, too, and she couldn't afford to be wrong.

To the left. Surely they had gone to the left. Making up her mind, she guided Kanani resolutely in that direction. The path was firm as they started down it. A good sign. She remembered it had been firm all the way to that hauntingly desolate spot above the lush green rain forests that seemed to draw Royall with an almost hypnotic compulsion.

The place he loved so much he wanted to die there.

Her mouth was dry with fear now that she knew she was getting near. She was going to have to keep all her wits about her. Both her eyes and ears were straining now, not just for gunshots but anything. A word, a laugh, the reflection of a fire in the night.

Royall would not just get to the spot and end it all. That was not like him. She couldn't imagine Royall doing this thing so simply.

He would have planned some sort of ritual for his last hours with the boy. He *had* to have, for that would give her time and perhaps the opportunity that she needed. Maria clung to the thought and tried to draw strength from it. A ritual of male passage between father and son. An evening by the campfire perhaps, a chance to share the beauty of the dawn, one last glimpse of a silversword glistening in the rays of the early morning sun.

The path ended suddenly. The undergrowth was too thick to go any farther. Not a trail at all, Maria

realized, but a false dead end, and she wheeled the
mare around and started back. Precious minutes lost,
but perhaps it didn't matter that much, after all.

She had seen a silversword there. She recalled it
clearly now, in that funny little hollow between two
rocky slopes. It would barely show in the misty
moonlight. Surely Royall would wait for dawn.

He had always cherished the silverswords. Of
every growing thing, it was those he loved the most.
He had gone into rages when he had heard of groups
from ships in the harbor uprooting them and rolling
them for sport down cinder cones in the crater. It
seemed to fascinate him, the way they grew so stead-
fastly for five or ten or fifteen years, silent silvery
tributes to nature, then burst into a six-foot pillar of
glorious blossoms and died.

He would identify with them now. Tonight, his
final night, would be the time for him to send forth
the flowering shaft that marked the end of his own
life. His last vivid farewell to the earth. They would
be kindred spirits. He would not want to die without
seeing his silversword again.

And as long as he was still alive, her son would
be all right. She did have time.

It took no more time than five minutes to find her
way back to the break in the trail again. Right this
time, she thought. She was reasonably certain now.
They hadn't ridden straight ahead. She distinctly remembered a turn.

She had gone only a short distance when she
caught sight of a spot of red on the ground.

She *was* going the right way. She didn't even have
to dismount to see it. The break in the fog left everything almost startlingly clear. Mack's glove. It
matched the jacket he had dropped before.

Too much carelessness. Maria prompted the mare
forward again, cautiously this time. Very slowly. He
might have dropped the jacket—or the glove. But not
both. It had to be deliberate. He must have sensed

something wrong and was leaving a trail for her to follow. How many other clues had she missed in the darkness?

If he sensed something wrong, then he must be frightened. Her mother's heart ached for what he had to be going through. But if he was frightened, he would also be alert. He couldn't possibly know what Royall was doing, of course. There was no way, at his age, he could begin to understand, but he would at least be observant, perhaps looking over his shoulder for her.

And Royall had no idea she was anywhere around. She might be able to get him away.

Kanani snorted lightly and shook her dark, damp mane. Before Maria could steady her, she heard a whinny from somewhere in the darkness. Soft but not very far away.

She was almost there, then. She paused, trying desperately to see into the night. But the fog had closed around her again, and she couldn't pick out landmarks to tell where she was.

Only the faint outline of the path showed several feet ahead. Maria started forward, then stopped again. Kanani's hooves sounded almost unnaturally loud. She could hear every *plop* as they landed on the solid earth.

If she had heard that whinny, Royall must have heard it, too. He had to have the horse hitched close to his camp. Was he wondering now what had made it restless?

She slipped off the mare's back onto the ground. She could feel the cold and moisture through the thin soles of her shoes. There was a small shrub nearby— what Mack liked to call a "tree," though in reality there were no trees on that desolate stretch of landscape—and she hooked the reins onto one of the branches. Not as sturdy as she would have liked, but she would have to take the chance that Kanani wouldn't break loose.

She couldn't afford to risk riding any farther. She would have to go the rest of the way on foot.

The camp was dark now and very cold. Mack could almost feel the silence around him as he woke and sat up in the roll of thick blankets that made his bed. The fire had died. There was no more red glow, and he could only see a little bit in the moonlight that filtered through the mist.

He did not like the dark. Mama always left a lamp burning for him at night, but he hadn't dared ask his father even to keep the last few embers alive in the fire. His father did not like weakness. Being afraid of the dark was weak.

He crept out of his blankets into the center of the clearing, where there was at least a little more light. He did not know what had awakened him. He thought he had heard a noise. But there wasn't anything now, and he knew he must have imagined it.

He often imagined things in the night, but it had never mattered so much before. Mama had always been there to take care of him and tell him not to be scared.

Royall's bedroll was empty. He had not even spread it out. It was just lying, folded on the ground next to the ashes that were already getting cold. It occurred to Mack suddenly that he was alone. It was not a pleasant feeling. The shadows all around the camp seemed even darker now. There were things in them. He couldn't actually see them, but he was sure they were there.

Wild animals perhaps, or ghosts. He had not yet reached the point that he could distinguish between them, especially in the dark. He remembered suddenly where his father had put his guns. Beside the pile of blankets, and he went over to be near them just in case. He was very good with guns. His father always told him so. He could protect himself from whatever was out there.

One of the guns was gone. The one his father had kept in a special holster at his belt. Mack supposed he must have taken it with him wherever he went. Maybe back to get something from the horse. It made him feel funny somehow. His father wasn't afraid of the dark.

But the other gun was there, in the box. Mack opened it to make sure, and then decided he might as well take it out. It was cold and not quite as comforting as he had expected. He scanned the shadows again with his eyes. They seemed awfully big, and he felt very little and very alone. He wished he were safe at home and Mama were there. Mama would laugh and hug him and tell him it had all been a nightmare.

He really didn't like the dark. And he didn't like being all alone in the night.

Maria inched slowly forward. She recognized where she was now. About a quarter of a mile from the campsite. That fretful whinny had seemed much nearer. She had thought she was almost on it when she heard it before. But sounds were deceptive on a foggy night.

She tried to picture the path in her mind. The light was fading in and out, never very clear. A narrow crevice just ahead, with rocks jutting up on both sides. They had had to ride through it single-file. Then the trail cut sharply down for perhaps fifty or sixty feet before leveling off again. A clump of bushes just beyond, barely half the height of a man, and a last gentle downward curve into the campsite.

There was another cluster of shrubbery this side of the crevice. Taller and sturdier. Maria stretched out a hand as she reached it to guide herself past and was startled to feel something move.

She stopped with a gasp. She could hear something breathing now. Heavy and harsh, not human, and she realized that what she had taken as a thicker patch of scrub was Royall's horse.

They *were* there. She was certain of it now, if she had had any doubts before. They were somewhere just ahead ... but why had he hitched his horse so far from camp?

She had the sudden, idiotic sense that it was he who had been leaving the trail for her. Mack's jacket first, Mack's glove, then finally his own horse, to make sure she didn't get confused in the fog.

But that was crazy. The last thing he wanted was someone following him now. Especially her. He had to know that she would try to get the boy away from him.

She eased her way slowly through the close-walled crevice. It took more concentration on the other side, getting down the steep slope. She had to half crawl to keep from setting off a noisy hail of rocks and dirt. She did not even notice until she got to the bottom and glanced back over her shoulder that the fog had dissipated again. Even the brown streaks in the earth stood out distinctly.

It was an uncanny sensation, frightening somehow, but she had no premonition that she was not alone until she heard a low masculine laugh coming from somewhere behind her. Whirling around, she saw Royall emerging from the shadows of the small patch of shrubbery.

Even in the moonlight she could see the amusement in his eyes. He was holding a gun, leveled at her.

"I'm so glad you could come, my dear. I was beginning to get worried. I thought perhaps you were able to resist my little invitation, after all."

Chapter 19

Maria was too startled even to be afraid for a moment. A bitter wind picked up, blowing her hair back from her face, but she didn't feel anything as she stared at him in the eerie blue light.

"Where's Mack?" she said dully. "What have you done with him?" But she already knew, even before he laughed again. The same blood-chilling sound she had heard a moment before from the shrubbery behind her.

"What have I done with him? Why, tucked him in, of course . . . safe in his bedroll back in the camp. He won't know anything until tomorrow. He won't ever know what *really* happened. You will just have disappeared from his life. Such a pity. We'll always wonder what happened to you."

The brittle edge of sarcasm was not lost on Maria. "You've been planning this. . . . It was all a scheme to get me out here. You never meant what you said in that note."

"The night is dark and getting darker? Ah, but it was dark, you know. There were times I felt I was tumbling into an abyss. That part was true enough." He shifted the gun in his hand, as if it were heavy and he was getting tired of holding it. "But all that's over now. It's going to be light very soon, thanks to your charming cooperation. . . . You really don't know me very well, do you?"

"No," Maria replied numbly. The fear was coming now. She could feel it choking her until she could hardly breathe, but she knew she had to keep him from seeing it. He was the kind of man who fed on fear. "I played right into your hands, didn't I? How very foolish of me. I should have known you would never do anything to hurt *yourself.*"

"It's too bad we couldn't have gotten along better." He was studying her strangely in the moonlight. Maria could feel his eyes assessing, as he had sometimes in the weeks before their wedding. Only now she sensed he found her lacking. "It really was your own fault. I gave you everything you could possibly want. A house, servants, jewels—wardrobes full of clothes! Do you think it was any more pleasant for me? It was a bad bargain on my side, too. I opened my heart to you once. I was brutally honest, but did that make any difference? No, nothing satisfied you!"

The sudden brittleness in his voice terrified Maria. He was getting angry, and she couldn't let that happen. Keep him talking, she thought. You have to keep him talking—and she willed her mind to work.

"I was very young. I didn't understand. It was all so confusing. Especially after I found out about ..." She let her voice trail off, not certain how far she dared to go.

He filled in the word for her. "Claudine? Yes, that did give you ammunition, didn't it? And you didn't fail to use it. ... I wouldn't have minded about the affair. I always knew you were a trashy slut. That's what appealed to me briefly. You could have had your roll in the hay or wherever it was and welcome. At least it gave me the boy I wanted. But when *he* came back ... well, I couldn't let that happen, now could I?"

"You knew all along," she said slowly. "You guessed. Right from the beginning. That Alex is Mack's real father."

His face tightened, as if even the words hurt. But

his voice was calm as he went on. "I thought at first it was the other one. Jared Barron. With those eyes, it was a natural conclusion. And there was a certain resemblance. But you didn't seem particularly interested in him. You hardly noticed he was there. Then the cousin showed up . . . and it all fell into place."

"So that was why you had me dance with him. At the welcoming gala."

He dipped his head in a faint acknowledgment. "Very clever, my dear. I see you're finally beginning to catch on. Yes, I wanted to observe you together. I needed to be sure. Your behavior confirmed my suspicions. . . . I told you once that you really should learn to control your expressions better. It will prove your undoing. . . . Actually, I believe it already has."

Maria shivered, and not from the cold. "I should have caught on, shouldn't I? It seems I am not so clever, after all." She had known he was setting her up, but she had thought it was only petty spite. How could she have been so blind? Heaven help her, she was paying for it now. "That's when you decided to invite Alex to Honuakula, isn't it? You thought if we spent time together, day after day, we would succumb to temptation and you could catch us together."

"Hardly. I didn't invite him. The idea was pressed on me, as you will recall. If I had had a choice, I wouldn't have had your lover anywhere near the place. But it would have looked strange, wouldn't it, refusing such a generous offer? Especially with the Barron eyes recurring so obviously in my own small son. People would have talked. . . . And it might have worked out, after all. You did succumb, and I did catch you—once."

"Might have?" Maria sensed something ominous in the words, though she wasn't quite sure what. "It probably would have worked—almost certainly it would have if you'd kept at it. What changed your mind?"

"You, of course.... That night I came to your room and you taunted me with being, as you so coyly put it, *no kind of man.* So very typical. Like every tramp I've ever known! A 'man' to you is something attached to a stiff organ that's always ready to be shoved between your legs!"

He made no effort to control the dark rage burning out of his eyes, and Maria sensed he was near the edge. There was very little time left now. Had Alex gotten her desperate message? she wondered. How long would it take for him to find a guide and get through the fog and darkness? He had to be at least an hour behind her. Maybe two.

And even if he wasn't—even if somehow he had managed to catch up—he wouldn't know she was a full quarter of a mile from the camp. He wouldn't be cautious yet. The sound of hooves would echo through the stillness. If she was going to get out of this alive, she had to think of something for herself. And quickly.

"You punished me for that," she reminded him, trying to sound cooler than she felt. "Did you think I didn't learn my lesson? You almost beat me to death."

"I would have," he replied. Maria noted to her relief that some of that terrible, rigid anger seemed to have subsided. "I wanted to. But I was wiser by then. I knew what I was capable of ... and what the consequences might be. I'd have had a pretty time, wouldn't I, trying to explain my wife's battered body bleeding on her bedroom carpet? Besides, there was a much more satisfying way of accomplishing the same thing."

"The ... fire?" Maria gasped at him, too horrified for a moment even to remember her present danger. "It wasn't an accident then? But ... it had to be!"

He had let the gun drop somewhat. Now he leveled it again and shifted it on his palm, as if practicing his aim. "You are so unimaginative, my dear, and so boringly predictable. I knew when your mother showed up why she was there. And just how you were going to react. You never could tolerate her prattle for more than an hour or two. I was sure by the second morning you would be dying to slip off alone ... And where else would you go but to the fields, where you might catch a glimpse of *him*? The shortest way is via that little dirt path between two patches of cane."

"But even so ..." Maria said doubtfully, "I don't see how you did it." She took care to make her voice sound almost admiring, a grudging sort of flattery as if she couldn't help herself. "You might have been able to topple the wagon. But you couldn't possibly have known that the dog would be there—or that I would chase after him between two rows of cane. There was no way you could have arranged all that."

The ploy seemed to be working. She could almost see him preening. If she could just keep him talking a little longer, she might be able to think of something. Maybe if the fog rolled in again ...

"But of course I could," he replied, unable to resist boasting. "I told you, you are too unimaginative. The dog was staked, of course. Actually, it was the second morning he was there. I had thought you might come sooner. And the bone was already in the cane across the path. He was salivating to get at it, but quietly. You must have noticed how he never barks. I simply waited until I saw you, then took care of the wagon. It had been rigged so it would fall with a single blow of the maul. All I had to do then was run down the rows, cut the hound loose, and wait for you to do exactly what I expected."

"As you said," Maria remarked bitterly, "I am so predictable." He had used her love for Mack, and it had worked. As he as using it now. "But why such an elaborate scheme? Why didn't you just cosh me over the head and leave me where the flames would get me?"

"Because it would have been too risky, of course," he replied disdainfully. "Someone might have come along before I could get the fire started. It would have been almost as awkward as trying to explain my wife's being bludgeoned to death in her bedroom. It was all well and good to pretend to be drunk and snoring. Quite amusing really, imitating the *kanakas* doing their famous imitation of me. But it would have been something else to try to *prove* where I was if you were discovered murdered. Besides . . ."

He paused, fixing her with the coldest look Maria had ever seen.

"You took great pleasure in tormenting me once. Reminding me I was not—by your definition—a man. I thought it might be interesting to give you a taste of torment, too. I didn't want you to die too easily."

He didn't want her to die easily? Maria felt sick inside. It was all she could do to keep it from showing. There was madness in his words, but it was a cunning kind of madness. Desperate and frightened, she let her eyes run surreptitiously over the desolate earth that surrounded them. Nothing to help her there. He had chosen the spot well. She would never make it up the fifty feet or so to the crevice in the rocks. And even if she managed to duck into that clump of shrubbery, he could easily beat her out again.

"So," she ventured warily, "when the fire didn't work, you decided to entice me up here. Just you and me . . . and your gun."

"It seemed an appropriate place." A trace of amusement lingered on his lips. "One wife, two wives—it's all the same now. It does appeal to a certain sense of the macabre. Leaving you here with her."

"With her? ... Oh!" It was more a gasp than a word. A long, deep intake of breath. Too late Maria realized what it was that had bothered Alex since that last evening in Honolulu. He had already figured out what had just occurred to her. "Claudine. You killed her! That afternoon she came to blackmail you. And buried her here."

"In that little hollow where the silversword started to grow," he conceded. "A pity. Darley figured out where I put her. He's sly that way, but he can't keep a secret on his face any more than you can. And, of course, he would have told. ... I had to uproot the plant to dig her up. She's not far away, but no one will ever find her. You'll be with her soon. ... It really *was* too bad. I hate destroying beautiful things."

His voice was tinged with regret for the first time. Not for the woman he had already killed, or the one he was menacing now, but for the silversword that had just ended its brief, ephemeral life. Helplessly Maria looked around again, not even trying to be subtle this time. Where was the fog? It had come and gone so many times before. Sometimes so thick. Now the moonlight was frighteningly clear.

"This isn't going to work, you know," she said, bitterly aware that she was grasping at straws. You didn't reason with a madman, but she had to try. It was all she had left. "You're going to get caught. I sent your note back to town. The one in which you threatened to commit suicide. Everyone will know how you tricked me up here."

"My suicide note?" Royall raised one curving brow, mockingly quizzical. "Ah, you must have gotten hold of a page out of one of the stories I've written. How careless of me to leave it out. I usually keep everything locked in a drawer. I've been dabbling for some time now. The sort of dark fiction one would expect from me. This particular tale is portrayed from the woman's point of view. A very selfish woman. An ancient Hawaiian ... She can't keep her son, you see. So she is going up to the volcano to leap with him into the flames. Just to keep his father from having him. . . . It's amazing how selfish some women can be, isn't it?"

The irony of his words were not lost on Maria. His eyes had grown hard and cold, and she realized suddenly that they had come to the end. And there was nothing she could do. Still no sign of the fog. No sign of anyone coming to help. She was going to die in that cold, dark place.

"Royall ..." She heard the pleading in her voice and hated herself for it. It wasn't going to do any good. It would only add to the sadistic satisfaction he already felt.

"I'm afraid you're growing tiresome, my dear." His voice was smooth now, almost oily. "We really must be getting on, don't you think? I've left the boy alone much too long. You wouldn't want me not to take proper care of my son."

"He is not your son," Maria said quietly and willed her eyes to meet his. She might not be able to defend herself, but at least she could deny him the pleasure of watching her squirm. "He is Alex Barron's son. You know it, and I know it. There is no point pretending between us."

"I know it now," he admitted calmly. "But I will not know it tomorrow. Tomorrow he *will* be my son."

He was raising the gun as he spoke. Very slowly, savoring the moment. Maria felt her body go tense with fear. Was it going to hurt? she wondered. And Mack ... what was going to happen to Mack? Would Alex somehow find a way to take care of him? If only she knew her son would be safe ...

The shot came before the gun was halfway to her breast. Too stunned for a second even to move, Maria just sat there and watched as Royall spun around with a hoarse grunt. It seemed forever, but it could only have been the barest fraction of a second. The front of his shirt looked as if it had been blown away. A massive patch of bright red was already spreading as he dropped to the ground and his fingers released their grip on the weapon.

Maria turned to see Mack standing beside the low clump of bushes. His face was so pale it looked almost blue in the moonlight, and his eyes were scrunched tightly shut. He was still holding the twin to his father's pistol.

Oh, God, Maria thought helplessly ... Oh, God. Her life spared, but at what cost to her son? At almost the same instant a second explosion rent the air. Loud and somehow even more nerve-shattering than the first.

She spun around just in time to see a spray of dirt being sent up by a bullet several feet from Royall's body. Alex was already coming down the slope, half running, half sliding, his gun still poised in his hand. With one quick look at Maria to make sure she was all right, he gave Royall's body a cursory examination, kicked the pistol aside, and tossed his own after it.

"Good work, Mack," he called out to the boy, who was still standing absolutely motionless beside the low cluster of bushes. "You missed, but you startled him enough so I could get in a shot." He came over and slipped the gun out of his hand. "You're a hero, boy. Do you know that? You saved your mama's life. I could never have done it without you."

Mack's face slowly unscrunched, and he opened his eyes.

"It was dark in the camp," he said. "I got scared. I didn't want to be alone anymore."

He looked so little. Maria longed to go to him, but she did not want to take that moment from Alex. She had already cheated him out of far too much. She had cheated them both. They needed this time of bonding now.

"Quite right," Alex was telling him. "I would have done the same thing myself. No one likes to be alone in the dark."

"Did I really miss . . . ?" Blue-gray eyes were wide and hauntingly frightened. "I am very good, you know. I hardly ever miss."

"Everyone misses sometimes," Alex said gently. "It was dark, and there was still a little fog left. . . . Didn't you see how he jumped right after you shot? That meant you surprised him. And a lucky thing, too."

Mack shook his head. "I didn't see anything," he admitted. "I had my eyes closed.'

"Well, there you have it." Alex's voice was soft and kind. "It's very hard to hit something with your eyes closed." He reached out his arms, and Mack came to him, letting his head rest on his shoulder. Not crying—he did not cry anymore—but shaking all over.

Maria could resist no longer. The space between them was gone suddenly, and she was holding her son, crushing him against her breast, and Alex's strong arms were enclosing them both.

The mist had almost completely disintegrated ten minutes later when Jared arrived, drawn by the shots. Dud Owen was almost immediately behind him, the alarm on his broad, ruddy face turning to unconstrained relief as he caught sight of his stepdaughter. If Maria hadn't been so exhausted, she might almost have smiled. Beneath that bluff, brash manner lurked a tender heart. Somehow, over the years, he had obviously dropped the "step" from the way he felt about her.

Matthew and Rachel appeared a short time after that, and they were all together briefly before Jared took his leave. Now that he was sure everything was all right, he could afford to be worried about Dominie again, and he declared himself anxious to get back. He was nowhere near as sure as Doc Fred that his baby was going to wait for him to arrive.

The others would be spending the night, resting their mounts and waiting for daybreak before making their way down the slope, but Jared was accompanied by Dud Owen, who served once again as guide, and Royall's body, tied over the back of his horse. Alex walked with them partway toward the place where the path branched into three separate trails—he had much to thank his cousin for and, being a Barron, had to do it without words—and Maria remained behind to hold and comfort their son.

Mack clung to her for a while childishly, and she sensed he was still frightened and confused. But he recovered quickly. Maria was as amazed at his resilience as she had always been by his seemingly limitless energy. To her relief, he appeared to have accepted their explanation of the shooting, and by the time Alex returned to offer him a ride on his shoulders back to the camp, he was already telling everyone how it was he who had fired the shot that made Royall "jump" so Captain Alex could save his mother.

He seemed quite taken with his own heroism in a swaggering little-boy way, and Maria's heart ached with pride. He was so much more a hero than she hoped he would ever know. He still remained close to her when they first reached the camp, but she noticed that he settled down enough after a while to be drawn into an animated conversation with Rachel, who was snuggled under several blankets with Matthew, trying to keep warm. Minutes later, he allowed himself to be coaxed in between them and promptly fell asleep. The fire was blazing, there was a red glow all around, and his world was secure again.

Maria watched for a while, but that little beloved

face was untroubled in sleep, and she let Alex lead her off into the shadows. She could not forget what had lain so recently under the disturbed earth where the silversword had stood guard. Rachel would take good care of her son, she knew, and she needed time away from the ugliness and the memories.

They stopped briefly to pick up the blanket from behind the saddle on her horse, then made their way to a spot where they would have a view of the crater when the sun came up.

They did not try to speak as they walked. Alex had partially unfolded the blanket and draped it around her, and Maria was aware of the strength and tenderness of his hands on her shoulders. It was hard to believe that it was over. Truly over, and everything was all right at last. She was alive and safe, and they were together. She and this man and the son they shared.

She had had only one awkward moment, when Alex had carried the child over to place him in the blankets with Matthew and Rachel. He had already been drowsy, almost dozing, and his voice had been muffled.

"Are you really my father?" he had said sleepily. "Like Mama says. I heard her, you know."

Alex had looked surprised, but not as surprised as he should have. "Would that be so bad?" he had said quietly. "If it were true?"

Mack had taken a moment to think it over. "No," he had said at last, "I would like that. I would like it most awfully much."

"Then that's the way it will be," Alex had said and deposited him into the waiting arms of Rachel, who had tactfully refrained from making any comment. Mack himself seemed already to have forgotten as he basked in the attention of yet another grown-up who had clearly fallen under the spell of his charm.

Maria knew that Alex had to be remembering that brief conversation, as she was herself. But she also knew that he was being patient and generous enough not to push her until she was ready to talk about it.

The crater was vast and silent as they reached it, an eerie landscape in the moonlight. It might as well have been another world, Maria thought. The great plain that stretched out for miles, broken only by giant cinder cones rising hundreds of feet out of the floor, seemed to have been painted in an iridescent palette of sapphire and cobalt, ebony, and deep, rich violet.

They found a place by a steep, nearly straight-sided outcropping of rock and sat down and leaned back, looking out. The blanket was around both of them now, the heat of one body warming the other, and Maria gave in to exhaustion at last and dared to drift into sleep.

It was almost dawn when she woke. The sky was a paler blue but still clear. Hints of color were just beginning to diffuse the horizon, making it not pink but a luminous lavender. Looking over, she saw that Alex was awake and watching her.

"I never thought you were going to make it in time," she confessed. "I was so sure you were hours behind. I thought I was all alone—and there wasn't anything I could do."

She had started to tremble. Just lightly, for the worst of the horror was gone, but his arm tightened comfortingly around her.

"We were lucky. We were almost to Honuakula when Chang came barreling down the road. Now, *that* was something to see. Remind me to tell you about it sometime, if I can find the words. And Dud was there, so we had someone to show us the way."

"I'm surprised he was able to find it so easily. He's only come a couple of times himself. He's always hated jumping to 'his majesty's' commands. Like some damned trained seal, he says. I would have been afraid he'd get mixed up at that place where the trail forks off."

"He almost did," Alex admitted. "Fortunately, there were enough of us to cover all the possibilities. He was pretty sure it was one turn or another, so I sent Rachel with Matthew straight ahead. I took the direction he thought most likely, and he and Jared went the other way. As it turned out he was right."

"But what made you move so cautiously? I'd have expected you to gallop down the road, hooves thundering, like the cavalry at full attack."

Alex smiled at the image. "I might have at that. But Mack's red glove put me on the alert. Then I saw where you had tethered Kanani, and it occurred to me it might be prudent to do the same and proceed on foot. When I came on Royall's mount a second later, I knew I was right.... And it wasn't the cavalry, love. It was the Indians. Or one lone Indian, sneaking up on the enemy."

Maria began to tremble again, in earnest this time. Not even the solace of his arms could quite assuage her. "There are so many things that could have gone wrong ..."

"I know," he agreed quietly. "I had a bad moment there when I got to the end of that crevice and realized what was going on. I wasn't close enough to hear, but I caught the glint of a gun. The trouble was, you were between me and him. Every time I almost got a bead on him, you moved again and I lost the chance.... I thought about firing a distracting shot to startle him myself. But it was risky ... and I knew damned well what was going to happen if it didn't work."

Maria pulled away, just enough to turn and look at him.

"Mack's shot didn't 'startle' him," she said softly. "I saw the blood myself. It was as if his chest had been blown away. Your shot didn't come until a good second later. From the opposite direction."

"Which I fervently pray he won't remember," Alex replied. "I don't think he will. I don't know when he closed his eyes, but I suspect it was just after he pulled the trigger. It will all be a blur in his mind for a while. Then he'll forget."

"But I won't." Maria looked deep into his eyes in the rising sun. She had never loved him so much. "You didn't have to do that. There are going to be all sorts of questions now. Too many people know how you feel about me. Your motives are bound to come under suspicion. It isn't the same simple matter as if Mack had fired that shot. You freed him from a terrible burden, my dearest . . . but you took it on yourself."

"Did you think I would do any less . . . for my son?"

There it was. Out in the open. But Maria caught a glint of teasing in his tone and sensed he was not angry.

"You knew already, didn't you? I could see by the look on your face when Mack blurted it out."

"Doc Fredericks told me. About the switch in birthdays. It wasn't hard to figure out from there. You might have let me in on the secret, you know."

"I know. I—"

"It's all right. I'm not scolding. I had plenty of time to think about it on the way up here. I didn't make it easy for you, did I? There was a lot of bellowing and blustering about what I would do if Mack were my son, but precious little comment about taking your feelings into consideration. I might, perhaps, have been just a little readier to sit down and discuss the matter."

Maria was silent for a moment. "You forgive so easily," she said at last.

"As you forgave me once. When I sailed off, all arrogance and indignation, without giving you a chance to explain. I was so ready to believe the worst when I should have known your heart was pure. Wounded male pride, it seems, runs deeper than instinct. How hard it was for us to learn to trust each other, love. . . . If I lost nearly eight years with my son, the fault is at least as much mine as yours."

"We were both very foolish," Maria conceded, but she was smiling. It was hard to remember all the pain now that it was over and she could feel him beside her again. "Will he remember in the morning, do you think? That you are his father? How much are we supposed to tell him?"

"Oh, I expect he will. He's quite a sharp little boy. *My* son, of course, would be nothing less. . . . And I think we ought to tell him everything. There've been too many secrets already. But not all at once. In bits and pieces as he gets older and can handle it. In the meantime, it's enough for him to understand that Captain Alex is also father Alex."

He said it so solemnly, Maria almost giggled. "You make yourself sound like a priest," she teased.

"Hardly that," he replied with a playful nuzzle of her neck. "Hardly that, as you should know."

It was not an erotic gesture, not yet, though Maria knew it would be later, when they were safe at home and this was all behind them. For now it was just a reminder that he was there and he loved her. And always would.

"Still," she said, her mind drifting back one last time to her son, "I wonder where he found the courage. It must have been terribly confusing. Even knowing my life was in danger—to act like that! So decisively. It was such an adult decision. And he's just a little boy."

"Ah, but he is a Barron boy, my sweet. Barron males always take care of their women. Haven't you figured that out yet? . . . You're going to have to get used to it. You already have a Barron son. Soon—very soon—you're going to have a Barron husband.''

That, Maria thought contentedly, as she snuggled back in his arms, was something she could get used to very easily. The sun was floating over the horizon now, a great glowing ball, and the deep purple shadows in the volcano had begun to burst into vivid reds and oranges.

An enchanted dawn. The crater almost seemed to catch on fire. The sky above was a brilliant crystalline reflection of its dazzling grandeur. The air felt crisp and clean, the world was glorious, and her heart was at peace.

Chapter 20

It was sunset. The beach was almost empty again. There had been guests all through the day—nearly everyone had come to say good-bye and enjoy the lavish feast that had gone on for hours—but now only the family was left.

It was the last time the Barrons would be together for many years, perhaps forever. New responsibilities beckoned, and their lives were changing. It was the end of an era. The end in a way of their youth, and they were all conscious of it as they gathered with uncharacteristic solemnity for their final farewells.

Matthew and Rachel would be leaving the next day on the *Jasmine Dawn*, bound for Hong Kong. Now that Rachel was sure the *pu'aha-nui* fruit had worked, she wanted to be home in plenty of time to give birth. Jared would be bringing his wife and new baby back to Boston two days after that on the *Jade Dawn*. His last stint as captain, and he was looking forward to it with mixed feelings. He had always loved the sea. It would be good to be in command again, but he was beginning to realize that it was quite as easy to give it up as he had thought.

The baby had not, after all, waited for him to return to Lahaina to be born. Jared had come back to a sound of lusty bellowing and had pounded up the steps to find a little, wrinkly, red-faced, decidedly handsome boy—a typical Barron, he had thought, already bursting with pride—cradled in his mother's arms.

They had named him, as tradition demanded, Gareth. Gareth Denis for the beloved brother Dominie had lost, but they were already calling him by his second name. Pronounced not in the French manner, but "Dennis," because he was, after all, as Dominie had pointed out, going to be an American baby.

Jared had been a little tentative when he had mentioned the name to his cousin. "It should, by rights, go to the oldest boy in his generation," he had admitted. "But I think Mack is going to have enough of an adjustment getting used to a new last name. Perhaps being the first male child officially born into the clan will suffice. But if you feel differently—"

"Not at all," Alex had cut in. "Little Gareth Denis is welcome to the name. I always looked on it myself as a burden. . . . You knew from the start, I suppose, that Mack was mine."

Jared had nodded. "I could hardly have failed to notice. It was like looking into a mirror and seeing the years melt away. That might have been me at that age. . . . As a matter of fact, he had me a little worried for a while. But I couldn't recall any indiscretions that would have accounted for the resemblance."

Alex smiled at the memory. He could just imagine how his cousin had felt the first time he had come face to face with the little boy who looked so much like himself.

Young Gareth Denis, blissfully unaware of the responsibility that went with his name, was dozing in a basket filled with puffy cushions which Dominie had decorated with gaily colored calico ruffles. Mack was leaning over him, an extremely skeptical expression spreading across his face. No doubt trying to decide whether an infant cousin might be as much fun as a turtle—and Alex had the feeling McThuselah was coming out ahead.

In fact, Mack was not having any trouble adjusting to his new last name. He seemed to leave Perralt behind easily, and Alex sensed that, even before that grotesque nightmare in the moonlight, something had happened between them and Mack had already shut Royall out of his life. Perhaps one day he would want to talk about it, but they would not press. He needed laughter now and love, and a home and family he could count on.

They had decided on the simplest course. Maria's marriage to Royall was still legally on record. Now that he was dead, there seemed no reason to contest it in court, and Alex made arrangements to file papers for adoption. Mack had been told a little of the story, as much as he could understand. It hadn't seemed to make any difference to him one way or the other how his name was changed.

He only knew that it was different now, and even though it would be months before it became official, he had already begun calling himself James McClintock Barron. A very important sounding name for a small boy.

His future would be secure. Alex tried not to be too visibly proud as he watched his son tire of trying to figure out the baby cousin and race like a whirlwind across the sand. There had been no investigation, after all. Alex's story had been accepted for the honest account it was. In fact, the governor of the island had been so horrified when he heard of Royall's behavior, he had offered to transfer the remaining years on the plantation lease to his widow in compensation for the abominable treatment she had received.

They had talked it over and decided to accept. Partly for Mack's sake. It would be easier on him if he could remain where he had always lived. But mostly because they had discovered that they really wanted to. The beauty of Honuakula transcended any evil Royall had tried to impose on it. It was the kind of place where they wanted to make a home and raise their children.

They had been married two days after Royall's death, though not without certain difficulties. The missionary who they had approached to perform the service had been horrified. Alex would never understand how the zealously pious mind worked. Royall Perralt had murdered one woman, raped and beaten another, forced her to remain in a bigamous relationship, and then tried to murder her, too—and the good reverend had been shocked that they hadn't wanted to wait a decent interval.

Jared had had to pay a call on him. Jared could be extremely intimidating. There was more than a little of their grandfather in Jared. He had reminded him, quite succinctly, what the Barron name meant in Boston—and how the American Board of Commissioners for Foreign Missions was going to feel if support was withdrawn from certain charitable enterprises because of a mean-spirited action taken by one of their fellows. It was a quiet, tasteful ceremony.

The sun was sinking lower. The soft red glow had deepened, and vermillion streaks were beginning to cut across the sky. Matthew came over with two glasses of champagne, one of which he handed to his cousin.

"I think Jared is about to pontificate. Have you noticed how like old Gareth he's getting? Heaven help Boston with two of them in town."

"Indeed," Alex agreed. "Lucky for me I'm staying here."

"And me halfway around the globe in Hong Kong." Matthew paused with a boyish grin. "I recall saying once that of all of us, you might be the one to do things right way 'round for a change. It seems, after all, you are a true Barron. Love is not to be approached easily—or without considerable risk and grief."

"True," Alex conceded as they strolled across the sand to where the others were waiting. "But it's difficult to regret even the grief when it comes to this in the end."

The western sky had turned bold and dramatic. Torches were already aglow in the sand, but their sparkling flames barely showed against the brilliant colors that dwarfed and made them pale. Clouds billowed over the waves, great masses of amethyst and pinkish lavender, their edges starkly outlined, with a shimmering riot of scarlet and rose and golden orange behind them. A sunset so breathtaking it seemed as if the world had never seen its like before.

Jared, standing a little apart, thought as he watched how appropriate it was. It had been a clear multi-hued dawn that day more than a year ago when they had sailed out of Boston, innocent of what lay ahead. Now the afternoon was ending in a blaze of warmth and beauty. Sunrise to sunset, and they had come safely through the storms.

"A toast," he said, raising his glass. "To the Barron men and their ships and their dreams. To the strength and spirit and will that has brought them this far . . . and to the women who are generous enough to love them in spite of it."

"Here, Jared," his brother protested with a laugh. "You can't toast yourself."

"Can't I?" The sun touched Jared's dark blond hair and turned it almost to flame as he looked down at his wife seated on a blanket on the sand with their baby in a basket beside her. "To Jared and Dominie. A man born with salt water in his veins and a temperament to vie with the winds. A man who has always known what's right and what's wrong—and never let little things like his cousin's feelings and his brother's need to straighten out his own life get in the way. A Yankee, in short, with all his granite pride intact. . . . And the woman who tamed him and taught him that love is more important than righteousness. And hearth and home can be tempting enough to erase all longing for the sea."

Dominie took a very small sip of her champagne and gave him a knowing little smile before turning to the others.

"He seems to be telling me he's ready to settle down and become a gentle and mellow husband, warming his toes by the fire. Do you think I should believe him?"

"Not on your life," Matthew said, getting into the spirit of things as he lifted his own glass. "To Matthew and Rachel. A man, unlike his big brother, of infinite patience and restraint. Not for him those bold, impulsive acts that drive lesser men to ruin and regret. A man of tender sensibilities. . . . And the woman who tried to lead him astray. A wild, wanton creature. She very nearly had her way with him. It would have been a life of the most depraved debauchery. But he held out, steadfast soul, and forced her to make an honest man of him. I hope she never regrets it."

"So do I," Rachel said, touching her glass to her lips and looking mischievously at the third member of the Barron trio. "I think it might be your turn now."

Alex could not resist the infectious warmth of her smile. Mack, he noticed, had come over and was watching the grown-up ritual with a decidedly puzzled look.

"Very well," he said, hoisting his own glass. "I think I can manage. To Alex and Maria—no, to Maria first and Alex very definitely second. I don't deserve her, and I know it. Any more than the two of you deserve the women you have won. . . . But I am still too close to almost losing her to be able to jest with comfort."

He glanced down at his glass. There was just a little champagne left, enough for what he had in mind.

"I would like to propose a different toast. To the new generation of Barron men. To Mack and Denis, and all the strong young lads that will follow them. May they learn to temper their strength and courage with the warmth and common sense of their mothers. May their paths through the wilds of love and youth be easier than ours. . . . And may each find at the end a beautiful young bride with hair the color of flame."

They all laughed as they drained their glasses, drinking with a will to the new generation that was their future and the fulfillment of the best of their dreams. Alex set his glass down to find Mack staring at him dubiously. Clearly this had been too much.

"Why would I want that?" he said bluntly. "I don't like ladies with red hair. Except Mama, of course, and Aunt Rachel. And Aunt Dominie," he added to be on the safe side, though with her dark auburn tresses she didn't really look like a redhead to him. "And I'm not going to get married anyway. It seems an awfully silly thing to do."

Maria smiled as she watched him walk away, shaking his head at the vagaries of grown-ups and the things they said sometimes. The baby was awake again, and he stopped by the cradle, testing with an outstretched finger to see if he could get a reaction. Apparently being mentioned in the same toast, however misguided, was sufficient to prompt at least a second look.

It occurred to her that her toast for her son would not have been quite the same as her husband's. It was not an easier path she would have wished for him. Or a lady with hair of any particular color waiting at the end. Or even that she be young and beautiful. She would wish only that he find the same happiness she felt at that moment.

"It's amazing, isn't it?" she said to Alex, who had come over to stand at her side. "How everything worked out so perfectly. For all of us."

"Hardly amazing." He gave a rakish wink as he slipped his arm around her waist. "We're Barron men. You keep forgetting that, love. . . . And a Barron man always gets what he wants."

bold, impudent caress, was like a brand searing into her skin.

Then the fire was sinking lower. His fingers were following, brazenly and very skillfully, finding the place he had touched her before, manipulating those soft inner lips, preparing her—as if it were necessary—for the final sweet assault they both craved.

Maria twined her arms around him tightly, trying to draw him harder against her. But their bodies were already so firmly enmeshed, not a wisp of air flowed between them. She could almost feel his heart beating in her own chest. Sunlight splashed across them, playing erotic games with the golden tones of her soft skin, the deeper, more vibrant bronze of his.

It was agony waiting. Maria lay beside him, half beneath him, longing desperately for him to initiate the next phase of their lovemaking. He knew she wanted it ... he was making her want it ...

She slid her hand to his hip, inching it tentatively forward. He had never made her wait so long before ... or perhaps she had never needed him so much. If she touched him there, if she let him know she was ready ... if she guided him into her, would he think her unnaturally aggressive?

Then she could bear the waiting no longer. Maria dared to let her fingers coil around the hard shaft of his manhood. An answering convulsion seemed to jolt through his body, and she felt him stiffen.

"I—I'm sorry," she murmured. "I was too bold."

"Ah, love." His voice was thick with unmistakable longing. "You must do whatever you want to me ... and tell me if there is something you want me to do to you. You cannot be too bold. ... I was just afraid I was going to humiliate myself by ending things before they began."

"Then you must hurry," she said huskily, "and come inside where you belong."

He did not make her wait any longer. Even as

her legs were opening, he was sliding between them, entering her.

Maria felt the hardness of him filling and exciting her. It was as if love and passion had merged, and everything they would ever know or have of each other was concentrated in that one perfect moment in time. Each deep, throbbing plunge was the sweetest torture she had ever known, each slow retreat like dying a little, and her hips rose instinctively to force him back again.

Their rhythm flowed easily, naturally, set by him at first, excruciatingly slow and controlled, altering as she let him know with her movements and little panting gasps that she was almost there and needed the long, hard, savage thrusts that would bring her to fulfillment.

He did not try to hold back. He could not have, nor could she. They had wanted each other too long, they loved each other too much, and Maria thrilled to the deep, satisfying shudder that wracked through his body and into hers as they surrendered to the passion that would hold and torment them forever.

Maria laughed softly as she sat at the edge of the pond and dangled her legs in the water. Her whole body was still tingling with the remembered sense of him, the heat and urgency and ultimate tenderness of the passion they had once again shared.

"You're a hard man to *talk* to, Alexander Barron," she said.

"Conversation wasn't exactly the first thing on my mind after eight years of not making love to you," he admitted. He had come over to sit beside her, and their arms were touching lightly, comfortably, as if they had never been separated. "But I'm not averse to talking now, if there's something you still need to say. Although I think we covered everything quite thoroughly before."

"Did we?" Maria smiled as she glanced over at his

profile. That strong, inherently austere jaw had settled into the almost unbearably complacent look of a man who had just satisfied a woman, very completely, and thus knew everything there was to know about her. "And what do you think I was trying to tell you? Before we were, uh, diverted."

Alex squinted distractedly into the sunlight that glittered on the water. He had rather hoped the painful subject of her past would not be opened again. "You were trying to tell me your marriage is an empty shell," he said. "No, that's too coy. You were telling me you don't have an intimate relationship with your husband. It's a marriage of ... I suppose you would say, convenience. Strictly a legal matter. No companionship, no affection ... no trysts between the sheets."

"Ah ..." There was a knowing edge to her tone that caught him off guard. "I thought you weren't listening. I didn't say anything about convenience. Or legalities. There is no marriage. Period. Royall is not my husband because of Claudine."

"Claudine?" Alex frowned, puzzled. This was hardly what he had expected. The name sounded familiar, but he couldn't place it.

"Royall's wife. The one who was supposedly drowned in a storm at sea.... I only found out by accident. I was wandering past the plantation office one afternoon. It was a strange day, very foggy—you could hardly see two feet ahead of you. The door to the office was open. I could just make out a faint yellow glow of lamplight through the haze. Voices seemed to float out of nowhere, and there was this smell of perfume. Cheap and very sultry. Familiar somehow.... I think I knew even before I looked through the doorway. I had seen her sometimes when I was a little girl. She had changed, but not that much."

"You mean, Claudine?" Alex felt slow and dull-witted at the way he was not quite taking it in. "She didn't perish in the storm, then? The reports of her death were mistaken?"

Maria shook her head slowly. "There were no reports. Royall made it all up. I stood in the doorway long enough to catch some of what they were saying. She had been gone for years, you see. He had believed he was safe. I think it was mostly to soothe his injured pride at first. Get her out of his life once and for all . . . but then he decided he wanted to marry me. It was a risk, but a small one. Only Claudine heard about it and came back."

"For what?" Alex asked, leery, though the answer was obvious. She had had no fondness for the man. It was she who had left him.

"For money, of course. They turned around then—or *she* turned around—and saw me on the threshold. I'll never forget the way she looked. She had short brown hair, like a cap around her face. She had had a fever when she was young. I remember hearing that once. All her hair had been cut off, and she had thought it looked winsome and kept it that way. She still looked young, though she could not have been much under forty. Very pretty . . . and there was the most awful, spiteful *pleasure* on her face."

She paused for a moment, reliving the shock and horror of that foggy afternoon. Alex took her hand but remained silent, waiting for her to go on.

"She laughed. I can still hear her. She just laughed and said how funny it was. Only she used the French word, *drôle*, though she had barely a trace of an accent. I just stood there—I couldn't move—and her eyes ran all the way down my body. Taking my measure. It was like having a snake crawl over my skin. Then she looked back at Royall. 'Tell me, *cheri*,' she said, 'Were you a man in *her* bed?'"

"Oh, God." Alex groaned. He loathed the bastard, but even he almost had to feel sorry for him. "What did he do?"

"Nothing. At least not while I was there. He just